# THE CATALYST KILLING

*Also by Hans Olav Lahlum*

THE HUMAN FLIES

SATELLITE PEOPLE

Hans Olav Lahlum

# THE
# CATALYST
# KILLING

*Translated from the Norwegian by*
*Kari Dickson*

MANTLE

First published in the UK 2015 by Mantle
an imprint of Pan Macmillan
20 New Wharf Road, London N1 9RR
Associated companies throughout the world
www.panmacmillan.com

ISBN 978-0-230-76955-7

Originally published in 2012 as *Katalysatormordet* by Cappelen Damm, Oslo

Visit www.panmacmillan.com to read more about all our books
and to buy them. You will also find features, author interviews and
news of any author events, and you can sign up for e-newsletters
so that you're always first to hear about our new releases.

*To Mina –*

*who represents hope for the future*
*and a new generation of politically active*
*idealists . . .*

# DAY ONE

# The woman on the Lijord Line

## I

I saw her for the first time, rather suddenly and unexpectedly, at nine minutes past ten in the evening of Wednesday, 5 August 1970.

Later that evening, I would find out the young woman's name. But over the next seven dramatic days I would continue, in my mind, to call her 'the woman on the Lijord Line'. Had I understood the reason for her behaviour there and then, it might not only have saved her life, but also the lives of several other people.

I had finished my evening shift a few minutes earlier with a fairly routine callout to a hotel by Smestad. If the manager there had been somewhat tense before the Soviet invasion of Czechoslovakia in 1968, he had definitely become a touch paranoid since. He reported a new potential terrorist threat at the hotel roughly every other month. This time he had called about a guest whose behaviour was 'suspiciously secretive', one of the manager's favourite expressions. The guest in question was a man who was

1

possibly no more than thirty, though it was hard to say for certain because of his full beard and apparently suspiciously dark sunglasses. He was well dressed, spoke perfect Norwegian and had been politeness itself when he asked for a room with a balcony on the first floor. He had, however, not reserved a room in advance and did not give a postal address. The guest had said that he was not sure how long he would stay, but paid in cash for the first ten days at least. He did not want his room to be cleaned, and asked for a breakfast tray to be left in the hall outside his room every morning at nine o'clock. As long as the empty tray was put back out in the hall again, one could safely assume he was still there. And this had been the case for the past six days, but no member of staff had seen any other sign of life from the guest.

I dutifully put my ear to the wall in the hallway for a minute or two, without hearing anything suspicious, of course. I ascertained that there was no evidence of criminal activity, and said that there could be many explanations for the guest's undeniably unusual behaviour. Then I promised to check the name he had given – Frank Rekkedal – in the police records, and asked them to contact us should there be any more grounds for concern.

For purely practical reasons – the axle on my police car had broken earlier in the day – I had taken a local train to Smestad. So, at nine minutes past ten, I boarded the train back into the city centre. It was a very quiet summer's evening in Smestad. I had been the only passenger waiting on the platform.

It was just as I sat down that I saw her for the first

time. She emerged very suddenly from the darkness on the road leading up the platform. And she was moving fast, extremely fast.

My first thought was that she must be a top athlete, as I could not remember having seen a woman run so fast before. Then I imagined that I might soon see a man with an axe or a scythe running after her. But there was no sign of any pursuer, even though I could see a good twenty to thirty yards behind her. In fact, there was no one else to be seen out there. And yet the woman ran even faster, despite her extremely tight jeans, hurtling towards the last door of the last carriage. It dawned on me that she might in fact be a madwoman as, despite her speed, she was running in a very odd way. Twice she hopped to the left at full speed, and once to the right.

Despite her tremendous exertion, she did not manage to reach the train in time. The doors slid shut right in front of her. It felt as though the entire carriage shuddered when she ran into them. For a couple of seconds, we stared at each other through the glass windows in the doors. I could see that she had long blonde hair and guessed that she was in her mid-twenties and slightly taller than average. It was, however, her face that struck me. It was a frozen mask of fear. The blue eyes that stared into mine were as wide as could be.

The doors did nothing to stop the young woman's desperation. She hammered on them with her fists in despair and then pointed a trembling finger at me, or at something behind me.

I turned around automatically but could see no one else

in the carriage. It was only once the train had left Smestad station that I realized she had been pointing at the emergency cord on the wall.

I sat and thought about this strange encounter with the woman on the Lijord Line all the way back into town. The trains were still running every twenty minutes, so it could surely not have been such a disaster that she missed it. By the time I got off at Nationaltheatret, I had dismissed the whole incident, having convinced myself that she was obviously a few sandwiches short of a picnic. I did not regret that I had lacked the sense to use the emergency brake, and thought to myself it was just as well as I would probably never see her again.

But I did see her again – that very same evening, in the very same place. At five to eleven, to be precise, only moments after I had jumped out of a police car borrowed from Smestad police station.

In my somewhat feeble defence, I did immediately realize what had happened when I got a telephone call from Holmenkollen at a quarter to eleven to say that the train that left Smestad station at twenty-nine minutes past ten had run over a young woman on the tracks.

When I returned, the woman on the Lijord Line lay immobile and lifeless on the tracks, in sharp contrast to the energy and sheer speed she had displayed in her mad dash to catch the train when I left Smestad only an hour ago. It was without a doubt the same woman. I recognized her jeans and her fair hair.

The driver was understandably beside himself. He repeated over and over that the woman had been lying on the tracks when he ran over her, and it had been impossible to see her in the pitch black until the train was almost on top of her, and by then it was technically impossible to stop. It had all happened so fast and been so terrible that he could not say whether she had been alive or not before he hit her. Fortunately, he seemed to calm down a bit when I assured him for the fourth time that no one suspected him of negligence or any other criminal act.

According to the student ID card she had in her purse along with three ten-kroner notes, a fifty-kroner note, a monthly travel pass and two keys, the woman on the Lijord Line was called Marie Morgenstierne. She studied politics at the University of Oslo and had apparently celebrated her twenty-fifth birthday four weeks earlier. That was all we found that might be of any interest. If she had had a bag with her that evening, it had been lost before her dramatic flight ended on the tracks.

It struck me immediately that I had heard the name Marie Morgenstierne before. But there and then, I could not recall where or under what circumstances.

The train had been coming to a halt when it hit her, but her upper body was so badly injured on impact that it was impossible to establish the cause of death at the scene. Her face, however, was intact. She stared up at me with the same frozen expression of fear that I had seen through the train window scarcely an hour earlier.

Again I wondered whether she might simply be a disturbed woman who had thrown herself in front of the train, or whether there was something else behind this. And then I promised myself that I would not let this case go until I found out. Fortunately I had no idea how many days this would take, or how complex the search for the truth about the death of the woman on the Lijord Line would prove to be.

# II

It was with some trepidation that I dialled the home number of my boss at ten minutes past midnight. I knew that he was a night owl who lived on his own, and he had granted me permission to take advantage of this in the event of 'murder or suspicious circumstances until just after midnight'.

My boss listened carefully to my brief account. Then, to my relief, he immediately said that given my first-hand impressions of both the victim and the scene of the crime, I was obviously best qualified to head the murder investigation.

'Do you know who Marie Morgenstierne was, by the way?' he then asked, with great seriousness.

I had to say no. I still had the uncomfortable feeling that I had heard the name somewhere, but could not remember in what connection.

'Marie Morgenstierne was Falko Reinhardt's fiancée,' my boss said, pensively.

There was silence on the line for a few seconds, before he swiftly added: 'She was one of the small circle around him, one of the anti-Vietnam activists in the revolutionary youth movement. And she was sleeping in the same bed as

Falko Reinhardt on the night that he went missing. She was the first to discover that he had disappeared. A good many people in the police and the public in general, I am sure, would be extremely grateful and impressed if you managed to learn what happened to Falko Reinhardt on that stormy night in Valdres, at the same time as solving the new case. I will have all the papers from summer 1968 sent to your office first thing tomorrow morning.'

I thanked him and put down the receiver.

Then I went to bed, but was unable to sleep. In the course of one and a half hours on what I had assumed would be a quiet Wednesday evening, I had been given responsibility not only for a new murder case, but also the division's strangest and most talked-about missing person case of the past decade.

Only one thing was clear to me when I finally fell asleep on 5 August 1970 after an unexpectedly dramatic day, and that was who I needed to call before doing anything else when I reached the office the next morning. The telephone number for the disabled professor's daughter, Patricia Louise I. E. Borchmann, was still written between the emergency numbers for the fire brigade and Accident and Emergency department on my telephone lists, at home and in the office.

## DAY TWO

# Three parents, four students – and one slightly problematic witness

## I

On the morning of Thursday, 6 August 1970, I woke before seven and realized that I was far too excited to go back to sleep. Following yesterday's encounter with the woman on the Lijord Line, I felt some of the same obsessive thrill that I had experienced in connection with my first two murder cases. The first investigation had been at as good as a standstill for two days before I met Patricia Louise I. E. Borchmann, following a very timely phone call from her father. I waited no longer than necessary to call her, and felt a surge of relief when, at twenty past seven, I heard her clear, confident voice after only three rings.

Patricia, of course, did not know about the discovery of a dead woman on the train tracks at Smestad late the previous evening. She listened with increasing interest to my account, and whistled with appreciation when I mentioned the deceased's name. 'Falko Reinhardt's fiancée,' we both said at the same time. Then we sat in comfortable silence for a few thoughtful moments.

I broke the silence by adding: 'Which can hardly be a coincidence.'

Patricia sniffed so loudly down the telephone that I could just imagine the look of disdain on her face.

'I can most certainly promise you that it is not. You have of course already checked the date on which Falko Reinhardt disappeared?'

I had to come clean and admit that I unfortunately had not, but tried to excuse myself by saying that surely the date was of no importance here.

Patricia's voice held a note of triumph when she replied: 'Perhaps not. But the fact is that Falko Reinhardt, dead or alive, disappeared into the storm in the Valdres mountains on the night of 5 August 1968. And where I come from, that would certainly not be called a coincidence.'

I felt an icy shiver down my spine as my pulse started to race. And I heard myself agree that suddenly the date was of the utmost importance, and that it would not be called a coincidence in my workplace either.

There was nothing to stop Patricia's morning inspiration and she fired away: 'Change is the spice of life, even in murder cases. In the 1960s, we dealt with locked-room mysteries and old men. And now at the start of a new decade, you call me about a young woman and an open-space mystery. I must warn you straight away that this could be more difficult terrain. There were only six flats and a total of seven suspects in 25 Krebs Street. And only eleven people sat down to dine at Magdalon Schelderup's mansion in Gulleråsen. Whereas, in theory, practically anyone could have been at Smestad station last night. Hopefully there will, in practice, be a more limited number of suspects, and I can already give you the names of some of them, having read about Falko Reinhardt's disappearance at the time. But it is important that we find out as much as possible about what happened in the last hours of Marie Morgenstierne's life, and who might have been in the area at the time. Find out what she was doing at Smestad yesterday evening and who she met there, and do not delay in requesting any witnesses who might have seen her walking to the station to come forward. Come here for supper at six o'clock this evening and bring with you anything of interest in connection with Marie Morgenstierne's death and Falko Reinhardt's disappearance. Will that be possible?'

It sounded more like an order than a question. I replied immediately that it would.

'Did Marie Morgenstierne throw herself on the tracks, did she fall, or was she pushed?' I asked.

I should not have done that. Patricia let out a deep sigh, and answered rather pointedly: 'No. She was shot.'

Thus I could confirm with alarmed relief that Patricia was clearly as on the ball as she had been the year before. She waited until I asked for more details, and then replied without hesitation, 'I would be very surprised if Marie Morgenstierne was not shot only seconds after the train you were on pulled away from the station. And I think it is highly unlikely that she was shot with a hunting rifle of this year's model. But hopefully you will know more about that when we meet this evening.'

I replied that I had every hope that I would. Then I put

the phone down and left the flat straight away. My mind was already slightly scrambled, but I did have the clarity to realize that I would not be spending much time at home over the next few days.

# II

At the office I was informed that a routine examination of the scene of the crime and door-to-door enquiries around Smestad had come up with nothing. So I called the national radio station and asked them to make an announcement calling for possible witnesses in Smestad area the evening before. I quickly established that the newspapers had not yet picked up on the death. The headlines were dominated by the new mid-distance running star Arne Kvalheim's victory in a race at the Bislett Games, and the one hundred or so demonstrators who had set up camp in order to prevent the planned development of a power plant in Mardøla in Møre and Romsdal municipality.

Having looked through the papers, I sat for a while deep in thought. There were no files of any sort on Marie Morgenstierne in the police records and the census records only contained a single sheet of paper that was of little help. She was simply recorded as living at an address in Frogner, the most desirable part of Oslo.

It occurred to me that it was rather odd that we had heard nothing from her parents or other relatives. When I looked in the telephone directory, I discovered that a Martin Morgenstierne lived at the same address, and he was listed as bank manager. I dialled the number several times and let it ring for a long time, without getting an answer.

In anticipation of the family getting in touch or of finding any information about Marie Morgenstierne, I threw myself into the rather thick file regarding her fiancé's disappearance in August 1968. It was exciting stuff and, like Patricia, I found it hard to believe there was no connection between Falko Reinhardt's disappearance and Marie's death.

Falko Reinhardt, Marie Morgenstierne and four other young people from radical student circles at the University of Oslo had travelled together to a cabin in Vestre Slidre in Valdres on Saturday, 3 August 1968. The statements were unanimous in that Falko had been the one who initiated the trip, the purpose of which was to have four uninterrupted days to plan the autumn's anti-Vietnam demonstrations and other activities, as well as spend time together. The first two days of the trip had passed without incident.

On Monday, 5 August Falko had left the cabin for a few hours, without saying before or afterwards where he had gone. In the evening a storm had blown up, with driving rain and wind, and the six students had stayed indoors. Some alcohol had been consumed, but as they later remembered it, it was not a lot. The storm had instilled a growing feeling of unease. This had been triggered by an episode earlier in the evening when one of the young women claimed to have seen a face wearing a black eye mask look in at the window. The students had gone out into the storm together, but found no trace of anyone. 'Incident very odd indeed, but statements credible nonetheless' was written across the report from the hearings. I noted this down and continued to read with keen interest.

The real drama in Valdres did not start until two in the morning, when Marie Morgenstierne screamed so loudly that two of the students sleeping in another room woke up.

They came rushing in to find her alone in the bedroom. Falko Reinhardt's side of the bed was empty. His jacket was still hanging in the wardrobe, but the rest of his clothes and shoes were gone. The window was closed, because of the rain outside.

At this point, my reading was interrupted by an irritating, impatient knocking on my office door. It was five past eleven.

# III

I sighed, put down the papers with considerable reluctance and opened the door. The person responsible for this interruption proved to be a very flustered pathologist.

'The woman from the tracks was not only dead before the train hit her, but even before she fell on the rails . . .' he stammered.

With an impatient wave, I indicated that he should continue. 'She was shot. I have already established that!'

The pathologist nodded eagerly and bowed, obviously impressed with the pace of my investigation.

'This is slightly less certain, but I also have reason to believe that she was not shot with an ordinary hunting rifle.'

He nodded even more frantically and bowed even more deeply. 'It is truly incredible what you have been able to work out by yourself without technical assistance. The bullet appears to come from an older, less common 22-calibre gun, possibly a small-bore rifle or some other relatively light weapon, but could also have been a pistol of some sort.'

I asked the pathologist if he had anything else of importance to tell, then sent him out of the office when the answer was no. My thoughts were still in Valdres in the summer of '68, on the stormy night when Falko Reinhardt vanished from a bedroom where the window was closed from the inside.

# IV

How Falko Reinhardt had disappeared from the cabin was a mystery in itself. According to the police statements, one of the female students in the next room had been awake all night with a headache and the door was ajar. She was able to give an accurate account of who had passed the door after midnight. Marie Morgenstierne had gone out to the kitchen for a glass of water, and one of the male students had gone out onto the step for some fresh air. And the other young man had gone to the toilet. But none of them had seen or heard anything of Falko Reinhardt – and yet he was gone.

According to the statements from Marie Morgenstierne and the others, she was beside herself and convinced that her fiancé had been abducted or murdered. They had discussed the situation for an hour in the hope that he would show up again, but the group grew increasingly uneasy when he failed to appear. It was Marie Morgenstierne who had pushed for them to go out into the storm together at around three in the morning. But there was no sign of Falko or anyone else near the cabin. One of the students said that she saw a person in the distance through the storm, but it was too far away and visibility was too poor for any of the others to verify this.

The five students had then retreated back into the cabin. They had stayed awake for the rest of the night, huddled together in the living room, anxious and upset, without any means of contacting the outside world or doing anything at all.

When the storm subsided the following morning, the students went out together again. There were still no footprints to be found. But they did make a very worrying discovery not far from the cabin.

They found Falko Reinhardt's left shoe behind a large stone not far from a sheer drop of around three hundred feet.

This obviously made them fear that he might have fallen, been pushed or jumped off the cliff in the dark, though the latter idea made the students indignant and they dismissed it. The theory that Falko Reinhardt's life had in some way ended on the stones at the base of the cliff was reinforced when his right shoe was found in the scree later in the day.

The only problem was that no one could find Falko

Reinhardt, or any trace of him, even when the area was searched twice by a large contingent from the Home Guard. Dead or alive, the missing man had simply vanished, first from the cabin, and then into thin air.

Falko Reinhardt had taken several language courses at the University of Oslo, but at the time of his disappearance was a good way through writing his thesis for a master's degree in history. He had written about a Nazi network during the war. A few weeks before he disappeared Reinhardt had told his supervisor, the renowned professor Johannes Heftye, that he had made a remarkable discovery that could indicate that parts of the network were still active.

One of the main leads in the investigation after this was an elderly, wealthy farmer called Henry Alfred Lien, a former convicted Nazi, who had been a member of the fascist Nasjonal Samling in Valdres. According to the thesis, he had been active in the network during the war. However, Lien proved to be 'extremely uncommunicative' in his meeting with the police in 1968. He claimed to have been at home on his farm a good few miles away on the night in question, and denied any knowledge of Falko Reinhardt's disappearance.

He also threatened the police with legal action if anything was said to link his name to the case, so of course that never happened. There was no evidence that Falko Reinhardt had been the victim of a criminal act, and even less that Henry Alfred Lien was involved in his disappearance. To be on the safe side, and at his own cost, Lien had travelled to Oslo and taken a lie-detector test, during which he answered only two questions. The first was whether he had participated in the abduction of a student by the name of Falko Reinhardt. The second was whether he had been involved in the death of a student by the name of Falko Reinhardt. According to the attached certificate, the answer from the lie detector to both questions had been a clear no.

No other suspicious activity had been registered in the area on the night of the storm. A slightly sozzled youth on his way home from a birthday party a few miles further down the valley had tried, without success, to hitch a lift from a car that had sailed past him at high speed around four in the morning. He thought there had only been one person in the car, and his description of 'a somewhat overweight man or woman of around forty' was firstly too vague, and secondly bore no resemblance to Falko Reinhardt. As the tipsy young lad could not give a reliable description of either the driver or the car in the dark, his handwritten statement remained a simple appendix in the file.

And with that, the head of the investigation cautiously concluded that 'there is currently no evidence to justify further investigation', and the hunt for the truth regarding Falko Reinhardt's fate came to a halt. The final documents in the file were two short letters from 1969 – a handwritten one from Falko Reinhardt's parents, and a typed one from Marie Morgenstierne – which both complained about the perceived lack of police engagement in the case.

The investigation into the disappearance of Falko Reinhardt had taken place while I was on holiday and had been led by Detective Inspector Vegard Danielsen. He was the youngest detective inspector after me, and was possibly even more ambitious – and he was one of those endlessly irritating people who embody guile, but are also extremely competent.

In short, I did not particularly wish to discuss the Reinhardt case with Detective Inspector Vegard Danielsen, and was even less keen to involve him in any way in my investigation into the murder of Marie Morgenstierne. The idea of solving both cases right under his nose, with secret help from Patricia, was far more appealing. So I put the file to one side, but kept the exemplary list of the telephone numbers and addresses of the witnesses in the Falko Reinhardt case to hand, as it was currently the best starting point for establishing the truth about the murder of Marie Morgenstierne.

# V

According to the file, Falko Reinhardt's parents were Arno Reinhardt, a photographer, and his wife Astrid, who lived at the end of Seilduk Street in Grünerløkka. 'NOTE: NORWEGIAN COMMUNIST PARTY!' had been scribbled in the margin of the filing card in Detective Inspector Danielsen's annoyingly neat handwriting.

I put the card with the two elderly Communist Party members to one side in favour of a list of the names of the four remaining members of the Socialist Youth League who had been with Falko Reinhardt and Marie Morgenstierne at the cabin in the mountains two years ago. It read:

1.  *Trond Ibsen, psychology student, born 1944.*

2.  *Anders Pettersen, art student, born 1945.*

3.  *Miriam Filtvedt Bentsen, literature and language student, born 1947.*

4.  *Kristine Larsen, politics student, born 1945.*

There were addresses and telephone numbers for all of them except the young Miriam Filtvedt Bentsen, whose address was given as a room at Sogn Halls of Residence.

I noticed immediately that Detective Inspector Danielsen, as the entrenched reactionary conservative he was, in addition to all his other unlikeable qualities, had written the students' details down in alphabetical order but had put the men before the women. I was sitting pondering which order to contact them in when the phone on my desk solved my problem.

On the other end I heard one of the switchboard ladies say that there was a man on the line who said that he had potentially crucial information regarding the murder of Marie Morgenstierne. Then I heard a man introduce himself as 'psychologist Trond Ibsen'. His voice was deep, calm and remarkably unrevolutionary. He told me that he had not been at Smestad station with Marie Morgenstierne, but had heard on the radio that a beautiful woman had been shot there, and feared it was her. So he felt he should report that not only was he a close friend of the deceased, but that he had also been with her at a political meeting in Smestad less than an hour before her death.

I thanked him for the information and said that I would like to meet him as soon as possible. He suggested that we should meet at Smestad. He had the keys to the place where the meeting had been held. I agreed and promised to meet him at the specified address at one o'clock.

# VI

Marie Morgenstierne's last political meeting had taken place in a dusty two-room office in Smestad. Five wooden chairs, now empty, were positioned around a small desk. I commented to Trond Ibsen that it obviously had not been a large meeting. He smiled, not without irony, and replied that it was true; there were not many who had realized that the future lay in combining the best elements of Soviet and Chinese communism. It had been Falko's great vision. The small group that had gathered around him was still somewhat scornfully called the 'Falkoists' by other left-wing radicals, and had at various times been ostracized by the Moscow supporters in the Norwegian Communist Party and the pro-China communists in the SYL. The people who had attended yesterday's meeting were the same small flock of visionaries and believers who had been his friends – Marie Morgenstierne, Anders Pettersen, Kristine Larsen and Trond Ibsen himself. The fifth chair had always been Falko Reinhardt's and so was routinely left empty in case of his return.

I looked at Trond Ibsen, bemused. He was a slightly overweight, apparently very easygoing and clean-shaven young man. Apart from a single badge that said 'Victory for FNL!' and some unusually sharp-edged academic spectacles, there was little in his appearance to indicate that he was in any way radical or fanatical. He smiled disarmingly and shrugged.

'The business with the chair was initially for Marie, and for Anders to a certain extent, as he also had a very close relationship with Falko. Then it just became a tradition we all took for granted. It is quite usual after accidents and disappearances for those left behind to continue to wait and hope that their loved one will come back again one day.'

'Even a psychologist?' I remarked.

His nod was slightly sheepish.

'Even a psychologist. Psychologists are also human. We are simply a little better than others at understanding ourselves and other people. One would hope,' he added swiftly, with another charming smile.

Trond Ibsen gave the impression of being a socially gifted man. He was at once suitably serious when I asked if he thought that Falko Reinhardt was alive. Trond Ibsen replied that he had at first, but now doubted it more and more. It was perhaps not so easy for the layman to see, he said, adjusting his glasses, but it had been obvious to him that Falko had been troubled by something in the weeks before he disappeared. Something he knew was weighing on him. It was therefore easy to assume that assassination or abduction were the most likely possibilities. Bearing in mind the topic of Falko's thesis, it was not hard to imagine some kind of Nazi conspiracy – not that he wanted to point a finger at anyone.

I asked immediately if his dark mood in the weeks

before his disappearance might not also support the theory of suicide. Trond Ibsen straightened his glasses again and said that that would generally be a fair assumption. Everyone who had had the pleasure of knowing Falko Reinhardt would, however, dismiss this theory out of hand. He had never met a more charismatic and vibrant person, and what was more, Falko Reinhardt himself believed that he still had so much to do in this life.

Moreover, Trond Ibsen was of the opinion that 'dark mood' was perhaps an imprecise description. It was absolutely clear to him, however, as he had studied psychology, that Falko had had something on his mind. Falko had been very aware of his responsibility as leader in such situations – he preferred to grapple with things alone until he had come to some conclusion, and not to bother others unnecessarily. But given the force of his personality and sharp intellect, he normally found the answer within a few hours, or certainly within a couple of days. This time, it had been hanging over him for several weeks, so it must have been something extremely difficult and important. Trond Ibsen finished with a serious note in his voice.

As far as Marie Morgenstierne was concerned, Trond Ibsen did not like to use the word 'incomprehensible' about anything to do with humanity, but he almost had to here. It was hard to imagine why anyone would want to take the life of such a friendly and kind person. By a process of elimination, one might think that it was the group itself that was the target. But why she would have been killed first was a mystery. As far as he was aware, Marie Morgenstierne had had no personal enemies either within their political movement or otherwise – if she did, it would have to be her capitalist father, with whom she had had strained relations for years now. But it seemed highly unlikely that he would have killed his own daughter. Parents rarely killed their own children, and if they did they were usually alcoholics or people who were seriously mentally ill, the psychologist explained. Marie Morgenstierne's mother had died a few years ago, and she had no siblings. When she had had a glass or two, Marie sometimes complained that it was hard enough to be the child of two reactionary capitalists, let alone the only child. Marie Morgenstierne could be very open with the other members of the group in such situations, but was otherwise quiet and reserved, he added swiftly.

Yesterday's meeting had lasted no more than an hour and nothing of note had happened. The members had first talked about the fact that it was the second anniversary of Falko's disappearance, and had then gone on to discuss the autumn's events and demonstrations and other work. There had been no disagreement worth mentioning. The meeting had finished at ten o'clock and the four participants had left and gone their separate ways. Trond Ibsen was the only one with a car and had, as usual, asked if he could give anyone a lift, but they had all declined. Kristine lived only a few hundred yards away, Anders was on his bike and Marie wanted to take the train. She had set off alone in the direction of the station, and he had seen neither of the others or anyone else go in the same direction. He quickly added that it was some way to walk, so anything could have happened later.

Before we finished, I took the opportunity to ask Trond Ibsen if the addresses of the other members were still correct. He looked quickly at the list and gave a short nod. 'As far as I know,' was his comment when he pointed at Miriam Filtvedt Bentsen's name.

That prompted me to ask why she had not been at the meeting. This triggered a slightly uneasy and irritated expression on Trond Ibsen's face.

'Because she is no longer one of us!' he replied, in a hard voice.

This naturally aroused my curiosity and I asked what had happened.

'When the great schism between the Socialist People's Party and the Socialist Youth League happened last year, all five of us met to decide on our allegiance. We had formally started as a group with the SYL. I had not imagined that any of us would want to follow Finn Gustavsen and the other reactionary, useless SPP members. Anders gave a longish speech about why we should follow the young, true revolutionaries, and added that Falko would without a doubt have wanted us all to follow this path together as a group of independent socialists. We thought that that was that. But then Miriam put up her hand and gave one of her short, incisive arguments, and concluded that we should join the SPP and run their election campaign. There was complete silence after this. I then spoke for some time in support of Anders, and urged everyone to march together on the road that would lead to a better society. Then I asked all who were in agreement to remain seated, and those who were not to stand up and leave.'

It occurred to me that I had never heard Finn Gustavsen described as either a reactionary or useless; and also that the otherwise so relaxed Trond Ibsen now looked both exercised and upset.

'And then?' I asked.

'Well, then the girl got up, said goodbye and left! And that is the last time I spoke to her. I believe the same is true for the others as well, but you will of course have to ask them.'

I assured him that I would, but asked all the same if he happened to know where I might be able to find this Miriam Filtvedt Bentsen.

His smile was both roguish and sarcastic. 'As I said, I have not been in contact with her for the past year, but I would guess that it should be easy enough. If I know Miriam, she will be sitting in the university library between half past eight and five, and will be at the SPP office from a quarter past five until ten. And I believe that between half past ten at night and half past seven in the morning, she will be alone in her bed at Sogn Halls of Residence, but I most certainly have never checked the latter. You won't miss her. She is the one reading a book not only as she walks out of the library, but also when she crosses the road!'

Trond Ibsen laughed charmingly at his own little joke. But I had seen a glimpse of the harder and more fanatical man hidden behind this jovial facade. In addition, I had a strong suspicion that he was holding something back from me. Twice he seemed to be about to add something, and twice he refrained from doing so.

I thanked him for the information he had given me. Without being asked, he said that he would of course be happy to answer any more questions, either at his home in Bestum or his office in Majorstua.

My curiosity regarding Miriam Filtvedt Bentsen had been piqued – the girl who had stood up and left, and who apparently read books as she crossed the street. I had in the meantime concluded that I should speak to all the members of the group as soon as possible, and Kristine Larsen was the one who lived closest.

# VII

I stopped at a phone box on the corner and dialled the number I had been given for Kristine Larsen. She picked up the telephone on the third ring, without much enthusiasm, as far as I could tell. But she was clearly at home and immediately said that she had heard that Marie Morgenstierne was dead. When I said that I was in the neighbourhood and asked if I could come by, she said yes, with a quiet sigh.

Kristine Larsen lived on her own in a one-bedroom flat on the second floor. She came from a small family and had inherited the flat recently from her late grandmother, she added by way of explanation for the rather untidy living room. We sat down instead at a tidier kitchen table, where two coffee cups stood waiting.

Kristine Larsen was around five foot ten, blonde, slim and rather attractive and friendly. She was, however, obviously affected by the situation. She repeated twice that she would of course answer me as best she could, but that she was not used to being questioned by the police, and it had been a shock to learn that Marie Morgenstierne had been killed. Both Trond Ibsen and Anders Pettersen had called her, but she had already heard the news about a young woman who had been found dead at Smestad on the radio and immediately known who it was. As a result, she had remained at home instead of going to her lectures.

I assured her that we had all the time in the world, and she calmed down a bit. I quickly got the impression that behind her cautious manner was a rather strong-willed woman. She also appeared to have a good memory, and to be a reliable witness.

As far as Falko Reinhardt's disappearance was concerned, Kristine Larsen said that it was still a complete mystery to her. She had been staying in the next room with Miriam Filtvedt Bentsen, but had been kept awake by a headache that night. She had left the door out to the hallway ajar because she needed air. She recognized all the others' footsteps and could hear any movement outside her room after she had gone to bed. She had heard Marie Morgenstierne going to the kitchen to get a glass of water, Anders Pettersen going to the toilet and Trond Ibsen going out to get some fresh air for a few minutes. Her roommate Miriam Filtvedt Bentsen had read in bed from ten until midnight, and then gone to sleep. Falko Reinhardt had apparently stayed in his room after he retired just before midnight, and there was no sign of life from him until Marie Morgenstierne raised the alarm that he had disappeared around two in the morning.

As for Marie Morgenstierne, Kristine Larsen had known her since high school. Marie Morgenstierne had met Falko Reinhardt shortly after she started university, and despite their very different social backgrounds, they immediately hit it off. They did seem to fall in love with an unusual passion, Kristine Larsen remarked with a careful little smile. Marie's parents seemed to think that it was Falko who had led their daughter astray politically. She had, however, been moving rapidly towards socialism for about a year already before she met him, and they had in fact met at a meeting for radical students. Marie's political views were her own, as far as Kristine Larsen could tell, but she had been very influenced by her boyfriend up until the time he disappeared. He was also a very dominant figure in the group. However, even though she remained in his shadow, Marie Morgenstierne had a far stronger personality than one might first assume, given her gentle nature.

It was a great tragedy that Marie Morgenstierne's mother had died in the middle of this dramatic period. Marie said that she could not bear to go to her mother's funeral and had, as far as Kristine knew, had very little contact with her father since. Kristine Larsen had been to Marie Morgenstierne's childhood home many times when they were teenagers and had met her parents. They were nice and kind in their own way, but 'terribly reactionary capitalists', and her father in particular appeared to be very strict. Kristine Larsen had known Marie longer and better than she had Falko and as far as she knew, she had never met his parents.

I had noted that possible motives for the murder might be a new lover, or the rejection of a suitor. I took the opportunity to ask Kristine Larsen if she thought that there was perhaps a new man in Marie Morgenstierne's life.

Kristine Larsen answered swiftly that she thought it as good as impossible that there had been anyone else either before Falko disappeared, or immediately after. She did, however, add slightly hesitantly that in recent months she had started to wonder if there might be another man in Marie Morgenstierne's life. The thought had struck her because Marie's moods had swung markedly back and forth over the course of the summer. One moment there was something brooding about her, the next she was unusually happy and carefree.

Kristine Larsen otherwise agreed with Trond Ibsen that Marie Morgenstierne's last political meeting had been very undramatic and could not possibly have had anything to do with her death. Kristine had herself walked home alone to her flat. She had asked Marie if she wanted to come back for some coffee or a beer, but Marie had said that she had to be somewhere else. Kristine had been a bit taken aback and then thought that there might be a new man in the picture, but had not wanted to ask. She deeply regretted that now, she added in a quiet voice.

In answer to my final question about Miriam Filtvedt Bentsen's split with the group, Kristine Larsen said that she had possibly experienced the situation as being less dramatic than the others, but that she had also been taken aback and disappointed when Miriam stood up and left.

She had known Miriam since they were around sixteen years old, and still found it hard to imagine that she would do anyone any harm.

This caught my interest and I asked what harm Miriam might have done, other than leave the group.

Kristine Larsen bit her lip and then started to back-pedal furiously. She made it clear that she herself did not think that Miriam had done anything wrong, and as far as she knew, no one suspected Miriam of having anything whatsoever to do with Marie Morgenstierne's death. But I should of course talk to Anders and Trond as well, she said, when I continued to look at her questioningly.

Then, all of a sudden, Kristine Larsen did not want to say anything more. She sat by the table pale, silent and with tears in her eyes. She had been so helpful until this point that I did not feel like pushing her any further, certainly not at the moment. So I did as she said, and drove in the direction of Anders Pettersen's address.

This group of student activists was starting to interest me more and more. I thought it was more than likely that the group were in some way connected to Marie Morgenstierne's death and Falko Reinhardt's disappearance.

# VIII

Anders Pettersen did not answer his telephone, but did open the door when I rang the doorbell of his flat near Grefsen. He apologized, explaining that he had just come home from a lecture on non-figurative painting at the

Academy of Fine Art, and showed me a timetable that undeniably supported what he said.

This seemed reasonable enough, given that his flat was more or less full of self-signed paintings in a very non-figurative style. I had no idea what any of them were supposed to be, so could not make any comment on their artistic merit.

Anders Pettersen was almost the same height as me, had long dark hair, and was of a more stocky build than Trond Ibsen. It was easy to appreciate that under other circumstances he would appear both charismatic and handsome. Now, however, he seemed very affected by the current situation. He repeated several times that Falko's disappearance in itself was strange, but after all he was someone who provoked powerful emotions in people and it would be easy enough to understand if he had enemies. But it was completely incomprehensible that anyone might think of killing Marie Morgenstierne. He thought it was possible that the intelligence services, or an opposing political group, might want to attack the group. He was increasingly convinced that that was the explanation for Falko Reinhardt's disappearance. But the murder of Marie Morgenstierne was inexplicable. If it was in some way related to Falko's disappearance, why two years later? And if the intent was to strike at the group, why Marie Morgenstierne and not himself or Trond Ibsen?

Anders Pettersen seemed to be an intelligent if some-what unsystematic thinker who had nothing against the sound of his own voice. Given his extremely radical politi-cal views and his agitated state of mind, his line of thought was not entirely unreasonable. But I was more interested in the facts.

Merely saying the name Falko Reinhardt for Anders Pettersen proved to be like pressing a button. He had known Falko since class three at school, and had always regarded him as a kind and wise elder brother. Falko was, for him, Norway's answer to Che Guevara and a possible future leader on a par with Mao. The reason that he had now informally assumed leadership of the group in Falko's absence was precisely because he had known Falko the longest, and could thus best imagine what he would have thought.

As for the disappearance itself, Anders Pettersen had little to add to what the others had already told me. He had initially refused to believe that Falko was dead in the period following his disappearance, but gradually the doubt had crept in. It seemed increasingly odd that Falko had not contacted him or the group if he was still alive. Falko might be in a secret American prison camp and unable to get out, but it seemed more and more likely that he had simply been killed. And Anders could imagine no satisfactory explanation of how any hypothetical kidnappers or murderers had managed to get Falko out of the cabin without being noticed.

In contrast to his impassioned response to questions about Falko Reinhardt and Marie Morgenstierne, Anders Pettersen's reaction to my question about the split between the group and Miriam Filtvedt Bentsen was unexpectedly cool. He shook his head thoughtfully and commented that he had been surprised when she got up and left, but that afterwards it had only served to strengthen a suspicion that he had had for some time.

Anders Pettersen gave me a meaningful and loaded look when he said this. His expression then became mildly patronizing when I asked what he meant by it. It had been clear to him and the other members of the group that they were being watched by the police security service from as early as 1968. However, even though they were on their guard, they had not noticed any direct surveillance. It had also been clear to Anders that there was an informant within the group who was reporting directly to the police – and he had come to believe that Falko shared this suspicion in the months before he disappeared.

Anders Pettersen had spent a lot of time pondering the mole theory after Falko went missing. His suspicion had focused on Miriam, who was also the most critical of the political stance that he and Falko had taken. The night that Falko had disappeared was the only time that Anders Pettersen could remember the otherwise so calm Trond Ibsen losing control; whereas Miriam, who was the youngest, had remained bizarrely unruffled throughout the night. When, at a later date, she stood up and left the group, he had taken that as confirmation that his theory was right.

Having said that, he added slowly and somewhat reluctantly that there was not necessarily any direct link between the supposition that Miriam Filtvedt Bentsen had spied on the group until she left in spring 1969, and Marie Morgenstierne's dramatic death a little more than a year later.

Marie's death seemed more likely to be connected to Falko Reinhardt's disappearance, though Anders was unable to say how. It was Miriam Filtvedt Bentsen who claimed to have seen both the masked face in the window that evening and the shadow of a person out in the storm later that night. He advised me to take both of these incidents with a pinch of salt.

Anders Pettersen added in conclusion that he was pretty sure that the police security service, and therefore, naturally, the CIA, knew a considerable amount – if not everything – about the murder and the disappearance. And if I could get anything out of them, then perhaps something positive might come out of what was otherwise a tragic case. He also agreed with the others who had been present that the meeting the day before had been uneventful. He claimed to have seen Marie Morgenstierne for the last time outside the meeting place. They had waved goodbye to each other as usual as he got on his bike and she set off towards the station.

By the time I left Anders Pettersen, I was even more intrigued by the group and its members. And even more curious about Miriam Filtvedt Bentsen, the only person I had not yet met of the four remaining who had been out in the storm that night in Valdres. I reckoned that it would be easier to find her in her room, or at the SPP office later in the day, than to run around looking in the university libraries. Furthermore, I had some important telephone calls to make. So I drove straight to the main police station from Grefsen and arrived back at around half past two.

# IX

Marie Morgenstierne's family had still not been in touch. And her father Martin Morgenstierne was still not answering the telephone, even though I had now called around ten times. It was starting to be a significant problem that we had not managed to contact the deceased's closest family. The priest had knocked on Martin Morgenstierne's door around midnight the night before and then again at half past seven in the morning, without finding any sign of life.

Given the time of year, it seemed likely that Martin Morgenstierne was either abroad or at a cabin without television, radio or a telephone. His employer was most likely to know where he was. As there were still not so many bank managers in Oslo, I asked one of the secretaries to go through the list and ring all of the banks in the city, if necessary.

In the meantime, I myself called the number provided for Falko Reinhardt's parents in Grünerløkka. Here the telephone was answered on the third ring. An earnest woman's voice announced 'Reinhardt'. I introduced myself and said that if she and her husband were at home today, I would very much like to come and speak to them in connection with the murder of Marie Morgenstierne. She replied equally earnestly that she and her husband had heard about the murder on the radio, but did not know that it was Marie Morgenstierne who had been killed until just now. She added that since their son's disappearance, they were generally always at home.

There was silence for a moment. I asked if it would be suitable to come at either four or five o'clock. She replied, still very serious, that I could come at four, or at five, or whenever I liked. I said that I reckoned it would be sometime between four and five. She said that they would be happy to talk to me, but did not sound as though she meant it. Then she put the phone down before I had a chance to thank her.

The secretary helping me trace Martin Morgenstierne was young and eager, and only a few minutes after I had finished my telephone call, she was standing at my door with the address and telephone number of the bank where Martin Morgenstierne was manager. It was not one of the largest in town, but was well known all the same and had a good reputation.

I rang the bank's switchboard and said that I was from the police and it was urgent. Then I got straight to the point and asked if they knew where Martin Morgenstierne, the manager, was.

There was silence for a moment, then the switchboard operator replied that the bank manager was in his office, as he always was during office hours unless he had important meetings elsewhere.

It was my turn to be lost for words. But eventually I asked if she could put me through to him.

It was a strange and by no means pleasant experience to hear the bank manager's calm voice answer with 'Bank Manager Morgenstierne here.'

I started by saying: 'This is Detective Inspector Kolbjørn

Kristiansen and I am afraid that I have some very bad news for you regarding a personal matter . . .'

The bank manager's voice sounded a touch sharper, but his response was just as measured when he asked if I was alluding to the death of his daughter, in which case his secretary had already informed him. She had been told by a friend of his who was an editor and had called to offer his condolences. He did not think that he would have anything of interest to contribute to the investigation as he had unfortunately only had very sporadic contact with his daughter in recent years. That being said, he would of course answer any questions the police might wish to ask.

There was a brief pause when neither of us said anything. I was at a loss as to what to say to a man I had never spoken to before, who had found out only hours ago from his secretary that his daughter was dead and yet had just carried on with his working day as though nothing had happened.

I offered my condolences all the same and assured him that that the investigation would be given the highest priority, then asked if I could meet him as soon as possible. He replied that he had an important meeting in the bank at half past three, but that he should be back home in Frogner by half past five at the latest. I suggested that I should come there at six and he said that would be fine.

I sat deep in thought, with the receiver in my hand and the tone in my ear, after Martin Morgenstierne had put down the phone. The case seemed to be getting more and more convoluted, the more parties I got to know. The investigation was not yet half a day old and it was already clear that it involved several mysteries and a gallery of fascinating characters. I felt a tremendous sense of relief that I had Patricia behind me. And then I started to wonder who it was knocking on my door.

# X

This time the door-knocker turned out to be Detective Inspector Vegard Danielsen. I had silently hoped that he was on summer holiday in some faraway place, but now remembered that he never went on holiday at any time of year for fear of missing out on a career opportunity.

He had come primarily to 'sympathize' with me about being given sole responsibility for the murder of Marie Morgenstierne, which would no doubt be a very demanding case. Danielsen also wanted to make sure that I knew about the possible connection to Falko Reinhardt's disappearance, as he himself had led that investigation. I was as friendly as could be, thanked him and assured him that I would be in touch should any relevant questions crop up. However, I had already had the pleasure of reading his written report, which was so informative and detailed that I had everything I needed for the present. He smiled and thanked me and told me that the door to his office was always open, should I need any assistance.

He then added, with the falsest smile, that some potentially good news had just come in. A witness had come forward who had been walking behind Marie Morgenstierne on the way to the station the evening before.

I asked jokingly why he had not brought the witness in with him straight away. He replied that unfortunately there were certain practical problems in connection with the witness, and it would therefore perhaps be best if I came out and met her myself.

I smelt a rat, and asked if the witness was under the influence or indisposed for any other reason. Danielsen cheerily shook his head and said that the witness was a sober and undoubtedly reliable person, but was still, to put it politely, 'problematic as an eyewitness'. It would perhaps be best if I went out to the reception area to meet her myself. He could scarcely hide the smile that tugged at the corners of his mouth when he said this.

I understood that something was not right, but did not yet know what. So I followed him out to reception.

The first thing that took me by surprise was the faint sound of a dog whining. But I understood the problem as soon as I saw the dog, and its owner.

She was a rather attractive redhead and she was waiting patiently on a chair, with a white stick in her hands. Her eyes stared blankly at me when she took off her dark glasses.

# XI

I immediately led the witness and her dog into my office. Her name was Aase Johansen, she was twenty-five years old and lived with her parents in her childhood home in Smestad. She had tried to find a course at the university that was suitable for blind students and that interested her, but without any luck. She now therefore spent the greater part of her day listening to the radio and reading. The evening before, she had been on her way to meet a friend with her dog and had been heading in the direction of the station. And even though she had not been able to see what happened, she had heard enough to think she should report to the police, when the request for witnesses to come forward was announced on the radio.

I immediately thanked her for coming and said that it was indeed the right thing to do. I asked her to recall as well as she could what she had heard, and to tell me in as much detail as possible anything she thought might be of interest.

Aase Johansen took this task very seriously. She started by pointing out that she could of course not be one hundred per cent certain, but that she was at least ninety per cent sure that it was Marie Morgenstierne who had been walking in front of her yesterday evening. She knew the road very well, and she was just past the lamppost that was a couple of hundred yards from the station. So the timing fitted, as she had arrived at her friend's flat, which was only a hundred yards or so from there, at around a quarter past ten. Aase Johansen had reacted immediately when a woman who was walking at a steady, relaxed pace about ten yards in front suddenly broke into a run. And they were the fastest steps the blind woman could ever recall having heard on the streets of Oslo. In addition, she had heard someone on the road call out 'Marie!' But the woman who must have been Marie Morgenstierne did not slow down – if anything, she ran faster.

All in all, it had been strange enough for her to feel it was the right thing to come here, my blind witness said in a slightly anxious voice. I nodded reassuringly, then realized that that was not of much help, so put my hand gently on her arm. Then I asked if she had heard any other people on the road.

Aase Johansen nodded eagerly. She had not heard anyone ahead of Marie Morgenstierne on the road, but she had heard two different sets of footsteps between herself and Marie. The first belonged to a man with a walking stick. Our blind witness had automatically assumed that it was an older man, but added that his breathing did not appear to be laboured and he walked at a steady pace. It had sounded as though this man with a stick had carried on walking at the same steady pace even after Marie Morgenstierne had started to run. Behind him, and just in front of the blind woman, were the steps of another younger person, in all likelihood a woman. These steps had at first picked up speed and then stopped completely in the wake of Marie Morgenstierne's sudden flight.

The blind witness said that she could not be certain what happened in this confusion, as the footsteps then became indistinct, but also because she was at this point almost pushed over by a person with a suitcase who tried to get past her from behind. She was fairly certain that the person with the suitcase was a man, given the short and violent outburst when he bumped into her. However, she would not dare to guess his age. It sounded as though the man with the suitcase also picked up speed along with Marie Morgenstierne, but then stopped. At this point, the soundscape was so confused that the witness was not at all sure about the situation. The person who shouted 'Marie!' did sound like a woman, but it was so quick, and there was so much other noise.

Aase Johansen had never regretted being blind as much as she did now, she said. Her whole adult life she had hoped that one day she might do something useful for society, even though she could not see. And now she had unexpectedly been given a chance, but could not be of any real help because she was blind. It was terribly disappointing that she had been present minutes before a serious crime and could perhaps have been able to explain what had happened if she had only been able to see. A couple of tears trickled down beneath her dark glasses when she said this.

I patted her reassuringly on the shoulder and said that she had done more than anyone could expect, and had given information that might prove to be decisive. She beamed and asked if that really was true, then added that I must not hesitate to call her should I have any more questions. However, here and now, she could not think of anything else that might be of importance.

I thought for a moment or two without coming up with any questions, so I asked if she and her dog could wait out in the hall for a few minutes. She nodded happily and replied that she would be willing to wait for a few hours if there was the slightest chance that she could be of any help to me and the investigation.

I guided her out of the room, and closed the door. Then, for the first time in this investigation, I dialled Patricia's number from my office. I had a strong feeling that she would be able to think of some questions that I had failed to ask the witness.

# XII

As I suspected, Patricia was sitting at the ready. She picked up the phone after the first ring and listened with almost devout concentration to my summary of the blind witness's account. Not unexpectedly, her response was quick when I asked if there was anything she would like me to ask the witness.

'I have two simple but very important questions for your ear-witness. First of all, did she hear the sound of the train when Marie Morgenstierne broke into a run? And second, did the person shout Marie's name just before, just after or at exactly the same time as Marie Morgenstierne started to run?'

I jotted the questions down without understanding their significance. I then asked Patricia if we could postpone our planned supper until seven, as I still had to take down several important statements.

'Why not say half past seven, to be on the safe side. You can tell me the answers to my questions then, and anything else that you might think is of interest. And ask for the appeal for witnesses to be broadcast again. It would be both interesting and alarming, to say the least, if none of the other three people who were on the road yesterday evening came forward.'

I agreed, and promised to be there at half past seven. Then I put down the phone and called in the witness again.

Aase Johansen listened intently to my questions and then answered them as quickly and concisely as she could.

She had not heard any noise from the train at the point when Marie Morgenstierne started to run. She had, however, heard it approaching about thirty seconds later, when most of the other confusing sounds had died down.

In answer to the second question, she said that the person had shouted 'Marie' at about the same time that Marie Morgenstierne had suddenly accelerated from a walk to a run. It was possible that she had heard one or two fast steps before the shout, but she registered them at the same time.

I noted down her address and telephone number in the event of any further questions, and then accompanied her and her dog out of the building and paid for a taxi to take them home. She beamed and thanked me for this, and wished me luck with the rest of the investigation. It felt good finally to meet a helpful and obviously truthful person on what had otherwise been a very demanding day so far.

# XIII

It was half past three by the time I stood alone on the pavement and watched the blind witness and her guide dog disappear in a taxi. I still had three important meetings, the first with Falko Reinhardt's parents, the second with Miriam Filtvedt Bentsen, and finally with Marie Morgenstierne's father. If her reputation was anything to go by, the former would still be in the university library, whereas Falko Reinhardt's parents had said they were always at home. So I drove to see them first.

I had found the right address in Seilduk Street by a quarter to four. It was earlier than agreed, but the door was opened promptly all the same when I rang the bell.

Astrid Reinhardt had silver-grey hair, but was still a vigorous woman in her mid-sixties. She said she had seen me from the window. Her husband was not far behind her in the hallway. He greeted me with a noticeable accent, but otherwise in almost perfect Norwegian. One of the advantages of being a Dutchman was that it was easy to learn Norwegian, he commented with a shadow of a smile.

Meeting Falko Reinhardt's parents in the hallway was less of a shock than entering their living room a few seconds later. I had heard that Falko Reinhardt was an only child and that his father was a photographer, but still obviously lacked the imagination to anticipate what was waiting there.

There were a couple of bookshelves, but otherwise, three of the four walls were so full of photographs that it was hard to tell whether the wall behind was painted or papered. Falko Reinhardt was in every single picture that I could see. If you followed the walls from the door, you followed his journey from babe in arms to bearded adult in hundreds of photographs.

The first picture, dated 1 June 1945 in felt tip, was a

simple photo of his parents smiling broadly amongst all the Norwegian flags down at Oslo harbour, holding their oblivious baby in their arms. Arno Reinhardt was younger, darker and happier, but easily recognizable. His left hand was entwined with his wife's, and in his right arm he held their son triumphantly up to the camera.

The Reinhardts looked on with something akin to devotion as I studied the photograph, fascinated. Mrs Reinhardt was the first to speak.

'It was a beautiful, sunny day. We happened to be on the same ship as the prime minister and president of the Storting when they returned from London to the newly liberated Norway. Only three years earlier, Arno and I had thought we would never return to Oslo, let alone come home with a child.'

I noticed that there were no photographs from the time before Falko, and asked when they had met. This time, it was he who answered.

'Rather typically, it was in the trenches, in the fight against fascism. In Madrid on a spring day in 1937. I had travelled from Amsterdam to volunteer as a soldier, and Astrid had come from Oslo to volunteer as a nurse. We met in a trench and stayed together. Then in spring 1938, we and many other volunteers had to leave Spain in order to save our lives. I anticipated that the Netherlands would be occupied by the Nazis within a few years. So I followed my Astrid to Norway. We never for a moment dreamed that Nazism would follow us here.'

The Reinhardts were remarkably well synchronized. His wife nodded as he spoke, and then continued the story.

'But then one day the war came to Norway. Before the war, we had been active in the Norwegian Communist Party and had met Peder Furubotn. So it was perfectly natural for us to support the communists in the resistance movement. We were active even before the Germans attacked the Soviet Union, in case you were wondering. Then everything exploded and we had to escape in all haste. We were with Furubotn when the Germans attacked his camp in Valdres in the autumn of 1942 and miraculously managed to get away and across the border into Sweden. But the authorities there persecuted us for our political beliefs too. So then we went to Great Britain, where we worked in the lower echelons of the government administration for the last two years of the war. And it was there, in autumn 1944, in the midst of all the horrors of war, that we experienced a miracle that we had not dared to hope for.'

I looked over at her husband, who continued: 'We had tried for seven years, and in three countries, to have a baby. In spring 1944, with only a few days between us, we both turned forty. We had definitely given up all hope of there ever being more than two of us in the family. I had lost one of my best friends in an air raid the night before. But I still cried with joy for the first time in my adult life when Astrid came running into my office to tell me. And I cried for the second time in my adult life on 12 November 1944, when I saw my son for the first time. In the midst of all the wounded and dying people, a small miracle was born to us in a half-bombed hospital in London. We feared for his life every day in London. And when the war was over, we took it in turns to watch over him on the journey home, in case the ship should sink. We were both awake for those last twenty-four hours. It was an enormous relief when we could finally go ashore in Oslo, with our little Falko intact.'

The Reinhardts seemed to be so in tune and shared their story equally. Mrs Reinhardt nodded as her husband told his part, then took over when he stopped.

'We wanted so desperately to have a child that we would have gladly welcomed any child. A handicapped child, a blind child – we would still have carried it to the end of the world with us and protected it for the rest of our lives. But it was soon clear that not only had we got a healthy child, but also an unusually intelligent child. Our Falko read out loud for us for the first time when he was three, and could already speak and write Norwegian, Dutch and English before he started school. He got top marks in every subject and was of course the heart and soul of his group of friends. Throughout his childhood he was the sun that lit up our lives. We hope you can understand that, even though you may not understand our politics.'

I looked around the walls, and nodded to show my understanding. Even if one was to take the parental crowing with a pinch of salt, it was impossible not to be fascinated by the collection of photographs that covered three of the living-room walls. There was the three-year-old Falko reading a book, eight-year-old Falko scoring a goal, twelve-year-old Falko speaking from a lectern. Even at that age he stood out from his peers, thanks to his height, his strong face and dark mop of curly hair.

The second-last picture of him was dated 1 May 1968 and showed Falko, again at a lectern, in front of a large gathering of young people.

The last one was dated 29 July 1968, and had been taken here in the living room by the table. The picture showed Falko Reinhardt, Marie Morgenstierne and his parents. They looked at least five years younger in the photograph and were smiling widely.

And there the collection ended abruptly. The fourth wall of the living room, where they had obviously hoped to hang pictures from Falko Reinhardt's adult life, was an empty white wall. I stood between his parents, silent and lost in thought, as I looked at it. I felt their longing for their lost son, and it seemed that they understood that I understood. The atmosphere when we then sat down at the table was moving, despite the deep gravity of the situation.

I expressed my sympathy for their troubles and my hope that he might still come back alive. Mr Reinhardt thanked me and said that they had for a long time hoped and believed that he was still alive. Their son had been so young, so vital and alive, when he disappeared, that it was hard to imagine he was dead. But as days became weeks, months and years, the doubt grew stronger. It seemed incomprehensible that their son would not let them know if he was alive out there, somewhere. They had had many wild ideas as to what might have happened, without ever really finding an explanation they could believe. It now seemed most likely that he had been kidnapped or killed by some powerful enemy, but they couldn't understand how it had happened. His wife nodded in agreement.

I asked who they thought that enemy might be. Without hesitation, he replied the Nazis were a possibility, as the family had always fought against them and his son was, after all, writing his as yet incomplete thesis about them. As far as they had understood, he had made some important discoveries, but he recommended that I contact his supervisor if I wanted to know more about the thesis. Falko had always been a considerate son and had not wanted to involve them in it too much. They had also understood that he needed to live his own life and did not want to put any pressure on him.

They had of course supported his political activities, even though this involved a new left-wing perspective they did not understand. Falko had always shown a great interest in China, even as a child, whereas for them it was a distant, foreign land. They had at first been sceptical of the notion that Moscow communism might benefit from ideas from China, but had eventually been persuaded by their son's long and well-reasoned arguments. They were therefore very happy that he established his own group to embrace the positive aspects of both China and the Soviet.

Anders Pettersen was a childhood friend who had been in and out of the flat since he was ten. They had of course also seen a lot of Marie Morgenstierne in the two years before Falko disappeared. They only knew the others in the group by name, and their son had unfortunately not talked much about them or the group's work. They could not remember having met Trond Ibsen, Kristine Larsen or Miriam Filtvedt Bentsen.

With regard to Marie Morgenstierne, Falko's parents,

like most other people their age, hoped that their son would have his own family and they would become grand-parents. They had been very happy when he came home one day in autumn 1966 and told them that he had a girl-friend. They admitted they had been less positive when they heard about her upper-class background, but were then pleasantly surprised by her character and opinions. They were delighted when Falko and Marie announced their engagement in autumn 1967. They had talked about a wedding in late autumn 1968 or early spring 1969, but no date had been set.

The Reinhardts had never had any direct contact with Marie Morgenstierne's family. They had not made any moves themselves, nor had they felt there was any interest from the other side. Marie Morgenstierne spoke very little about her family, but they had understood that she was an only child and that she had had very little contact with her father since her mother died. Whether the father or other family members might come to the wedding or not was a question that had been discussed at their last meal together, which took place here, on 29 July 1968. Marie Morgen-stierne had shrugged and commented that her father could come if he wanted, as could her uncles and aunts. Falko's parents had thought this was a good answer.

Falko Reinhardt had disappeared a week later. And now, two years on, his fiancée had been shot and killed. It seemed to be as inexplicable to Falko's parents as it was to me. They thought that she had perhaps been murdered by someone who wanted to stop the group, but had nothing to back up this theory.

I thanked them warmly for all they had told me and promised to get in touch immediately should I discover anything that might cast more light on their son's fate. They, in turn, thanked me and promised to contact me if they thought of anything else that might be of interest. It felt as though we had become closer somehow in the course of my visit.

I asked, almost in passing, where they had been the day before. They both nodded in understanding and said that they had been together at home yesterday evening, as they were most evenings. One of them was always at home, in case Falko or anyone else who knew something about what had happened to him got in touch. They were generally to be found here. Arno Reinhardt had sold his photography business shortly before his son's disappearance. They had not been active in politics since they were excluded from the NCP along with other Furubotn followers in 1949. So they seldom went out unless it was to go shopping or some other necessary errand.

It struck me that the Reinhardts fitted perfectly with two of Patricia's concepts from our previous murder investigations. Both parents had orbited Falko like satellites from the day he was born in 1944 until his disappearance in 1968. And since his disappearance they had become human flies who circled round and round what had happened, without being able to move on.

I felt a deep sympathy for them, and was increasingly puzzled by what had happened to their son. And yet my visit had in no way brought me closer to a solution. I still lacked anything that might resemble a theory about either what had happened when Falko Reinhardt disappeared, or what had happened when Marie Morgenstierne was killed.

# XIV

When I left the Reinhardts' museum of photographs in Seilduk Street, there was still an hour left until my meeting with Marie Morgenstierne's father. But there was now a reasonable hope that I might find Miriam Filtvedt Bentsen at the SPP office in Pilestredet.

I would never have dreamed that I would ever want to go there. And my first attempt was a bit of a fiasco. The door was locked and the lights were off, and there was no response to my rather aggressive use of the doorbell.

I was standing outside on the pavement wondering if I should drive to the address I had in Sogn Halls of Residence, when a bus stopped a short way down the street.

Even on this otherwise sad day, I almost burst out laughing when I saw the only passenger who got off. It was the first time I had ever recognized someone because I could not see their face. This was because she was reading an unusually large and thick book as she got off the bus and crossed the road. All that was visible below the book covers was a pair of blue jeans and a multicoloured sweatshirt, and above, some fair hair.

Judging from the front cover, the book was a single-volume work on nineteenth-century English literature. It certainly looked as though it contained most of what could be written about the subject.

When she was only a few feet away, I could not resist saying: 'Miss Filtvedt Bentsen, I presume?'

She came to an abrupt halt, lowered the book and looked at me, more than a little bewildered. The twinkle in her eye rapidly changed to curiosity when I produced my police ID. The first thing I heard her say was a surprise nonetheless.

'How exciting. Am I about to be arrested? In which case, what for?'

She looked up at me with a teasing smile, but was serious again as soon as I said that I unfortunately had to ask her some questions regarding the investigation into the death of Marie Morgenstierne.

'Oh, so it was poor Marie? I heard that a young woman had been murdered at Smestad on the radio while I was eating my lunch today. They didn't give her name, but I was anxious to know whether it could have been her or Kristine Larsen. Then I reasoned that the chances of that were very slim. What a terrible thing to happen, and I will of course answer any questions you might have about the case.'

I stared at her, fascinated, and then shook the hand she held out towards me. Her handshake was firm and her expression somehow both concentrated and relaxed at the same time. I was surprised to notice a necklace with a small cross around her neck. I had heard that there were Christian socialists in the SPP, but had never encountered one before.

It occurred to me that she also disproved the claim that one of my colleagues had made that if there were attractive women in the SPP, he had certainly never seen one. Her fair hair fluttered in the wind. It seemed to me that there was something refreshing and free-spirited about Miriam Filt-vedt Bentsen, something that made me more interested in her than the other three members of the group.

I nodded my agreement as soon as she pulled a key from her jacket pocket and suggested that we should go and sit down in the party office.

The SPP office was even smaller, dustier, more over-flowing with paper and more deserted than I had imagined. There was no danger of us being interrupted as we sat on our chairs by a desk that looked like it was about to collapse.

Miriam Filtvedt Bentsen had now very definitely closed her book and given me all her attention. She leaned across the desk with obvious interest and concentration. I of course could not be seen to be any different. So five minutes after meeting for the first time, we were thus sud-denly sitting in deep and focused conversation, our faces only inches from each other.

Miriam Filtvedt Bentsen quickly proved to have a con-siderably more nuanced view of Falko Reinhardt than the others who had been at the cabin when he disappeared. She agreed that he was an extremely intelligent and charismatic person, and obviously also very well read. He was perhaps one of the best linguists she had ever met. As a socialist, however, he was both too simplistic and too egoistic, and the group had acted too much like a personal fan club and too little like a political work group. The leader of the group was, according to Miriam, 'one of those people who believed that the road was built because he started his car'.

Also, if Falko Reinhardt was a genius, he was a very distracted genius, according to Miriam Filtvedt Bentsen. She commented with a more sadistic than sympathetic tinkle of laughter that he often wrote lists about things, but the problems were rarely solved as he then forgot where he had put the lists.

In addition, Miriam Filtvedt Bentsen thought that when they were at the cabin, and in the weeks leading up to the trip, Falko had been troubled by something, but she did not know whether it was political or personal. She had on one occasion asked him outright, but he had not wanted to answer.

As for Marie Morgenstierne, Miriam Filtvedt Bentsen considered her a sensible and philosophical young woman who, 'like far too many other young women today', had lived in the shadow of her boyfriend. However, she thought that the relationship between Falko and Marie had been good up to the point of his disappearance. Miriam Filtvedt Bentsen had never met Marie Morgenstierne's parents, nor Falko Reinhardt's – or certainly not as far as she knew, she added with a mildly ironic smile. She had had regular contact with Marie herself until the split in spring 1969, after which they had never spoken again.

Marie Morgenstierne was, in Miriam Filtvedt Bentsen's opinion, generally careful and considerate in what she said about others. She had, however, on one occasion after a couple of glasses of wine, intimated that she suspected that one of the other members of the group knew something about Falko's disappearance. But when Miriam tried to follow this up, Marie had swiftly backtracked, and neither of them ever mentioned it again.

All contact was broken after spring 1969. Miriam knew nothing about what Marie had done in the intervening eighteen months, and she therefore feared that she would not be of much help to the murder investigation.

She looked a little sad when she said this; the case had obviously piqued her curiosity. I personally had absolutely no wish to finish our conversation, and so asked how Miriam had interpreted the events leading up to her leaving the group. She looked at me and asked what importance that might have to me or the murder investigation, but then jokingly added that she no doubt remembered things very differently from the rest of the group.

As she remembered it, Anders Pettersen had held one of his 'long, passionate and nebulous' lectures. His argument, in short, was that everything the USA did was wrong and that President Nixon's hands were stained with human blood. China, on the other hand, was the new Soviet and a land of opportunity, and Mao was the greatest leader of our time. The SPP, with its half-hearted support, had proved to be a class traitor both in terms of the working class in Norway and the hundreds of millions of liberated workers in the Soviet and China. Anders' conclusion, therefore – and he believed that Falko would have wanted the same – was that the group should split from the SPP.

As she remembered it, Miriam herself had replied that politics were more about making things right than being right. They should therefore join with the SPP and take part in the election campaign rather than splintering into an unaffiliated group which was not even a party, and which had no realistic chance of winning representation in that year's election. Then she had added that there should be no doubt about the democratic stance of Norwegian socialists, and that if one used one's eyes, it was easy to see that China and the Soviet were one-party systems and that both Mao and Brezhnev also had blood on their hands. She admitted that this was somewhat provocative, but that it was undeniably both true and important. I had no problem in agreeing with her.

Miriam Filtvedt Bentsen gave a crooked smile and assured me that she had not expected to win over the majority of the group. She had nurtured a faint hope that Marie Morgenstierne might come with her, but was not surprised when she left alone. And she had never regretted her decision to leave. She had come into contact with the group through her anti-Vietnam activities, and still agreed with them on that point. But she could not follow the group in their support of dictatorship, and had become increasingly provoked by their simplifications and partiality following the disappearance of Falko Reinhardt.

As far as surveillance was concerned, Miriam Filtvedt Bentsen thought it was overwhelmingly likely that 'the group in general and Falko in particular' were being watched, even though she had no direct evidence of this. In response to my question as to whether she thought there had been a mole in the group, she replied that she found that hard to believe and therefore did not want to speculate who it might have been if that were the case.

The temptation to ask if she was aware that the others suspected her of being the police security service's inform-ant was too great.

I was interested to see whether this might lead to a sudden outburst of emotion. But it would obviously take a lot more than accusations of treachery to knock Miriam Filtvedt Bentsen off balance. She leaned forward a touch and answered that she had not heard anything like that before, but that she should perhaps not be surprised. Then she asked, with noticeable curiosity, who had said that – only to answer her own question by saying that it was no doubt Anders or Trond, and that it really didn't matter anyway. The accusation was, in her own words, absurd. For the sake of formality, she added that she had of course never had any form of contact with the intelligence ser-vices, and would not have answered any questions about the group, or anything else for that matter, had they con-tacted her.

My instinct was to believe her, and in any case, I saw no reason to pursue the idea any further here and now. So I turned instead to the stormy night in Valdres when Falko Reinhardt had disappeared, and asked whether any explanation had ever occurred to her.

Miriam Filtvedt Bentsen answered that she had of course given it much thought, but much to her frustration had not come up with any answers. She had herself also been awake for a long time that night, and had heard nothing. She had gone to sleep around midnight, so trusted her 'roommate' Kristine Larsen's statement that Falko had not been out in the hall at any point.

I asked if she still stood by her statement about having seen a face at the window, as well as a person out in the storm that night. Miriam Filtvedt Bentsen nodded, more serious now. She understood, she said, that her account of a face looking in through the window that night sounded absurd, and the fact that the upper part of the face had been hidden by a mask made it even more far-fetched. But that was exactly what she had seen, and she would never have tried to deceive the police with such an unlikely story.

She looked me straight in the eye when she said this, and I had to agree with Detective Inspector Danielsen's notes from 1968, despite my antipathy towards him. The witness appeared to be reliable, even if her story was rather bizarre.

Miriam Filtvedt Bentsen added that it was a man who had looked in, and that he had a mole on his chin, which she would recognize if she ever saw him again. But otherwise it was not possible to describe him in any more detail, because of the mask and the weather.

She was even more cautious about describing the person she had seen out in the storm, as the visibility was so poor. She had been a short distance away from the others, but was sure enough of what she had seen to shout to them and point at the shadow in the dark. However, it was quite far away and no one else had been able to see it clearly.

Miriam Filtvedt Bentsen looked at me directly again and repeated that she had seen something upright moving through the storm, and that it was too tall, too slim and not the right colour to be an animal. For want of any alternative, she could say with ninety per cent certainty that she had seen a person. She believed that it was a person who was not only walking away from the students, but from the cabin as well. But she added with a disarming and self-deprecatory smile that although her younger brother had inherited the family's sense of direction, she had not, so she could not be sure.

I looked at my watch and discovered to my surprise that it was a quarter to six. I had been sitting here in the SPP office for more than half an hour, in an interview situation, with my face alarmingly close to that of Miriam Filtvedt Bentsen. And at no point had I been anywhere close to catching her off balance. There was perhaps more interest and curiosity in her eyes now than when we first met, but they were still just as calm and confident when they met mine. I was strongly inclined to believe everything she had said, even though I had several times told myself that this appeared to be a case in which no one could be trusted.

Whatever the case, I was now in danger of being late for my important meeting with the victim's father. So I promptly thanked Miriam Filtvedt Bentsen for her answers and asked if I could contact her again should any relevant questions arise. She brightened up and said that she had a busy week ahead, what with her studies and party commitments, but that she would of course make time if it was necessary for the investigation. She unfortunately did not have a telephone in her student room, but for the next few days would be at the university library between nine and five, and at the party office between a quarter past five and ten in the evening.

I managed to swallow my laughter. Instead I commented with a smile that she clearly took her studies very seriously – given that she also obviously read on her way from the university to the party office. Her reply was open-hearted and highly unexpected: 'Before, I even read books in the shower!'

Fortunately, I managed to refrain from blurting out my spontaneous response: 'Now that I would like to see!' At the last moment I realized that it might be misconstrued and insulting. So instead I permitted myself a short burst of friendly laughter. She gave an ironic smile and added that she had stopped when it proved to be impractical. The books were fine as long as you kept them out of the water, but it took so much longer to shower when reading, so it was not rational. Another rather unfortunate consequence was that there was rarely enough warm water left for her parents and little brother.

Miriam Filtvedt Bentsen explained that she believed you had to be a rational idealist to make the world a better place in this day and age. And in order to demonstrate the point, she took out a large pile of papers as she said this and started to sort through them.

I watched the obviously very rational idealist for a few seconds with a mixture of surprise and fascination. She sorted with alarming speed. I thanked her once again for the information and wished her a good evening – and was only too well aware that I would be late for my meeting with the deceased's father.

Miriam Filtvedt Bentsen looked up briefly from her pile of paper, waved and flashed me a crooked smile as I left the office. For want of any other leads, I interpreted it as a good omen for my investigation. I found it reassuring and credible, and not in the least suspect, that she was the only one who had remained calm on the night that Falko Reinhardt had disappeared. And for my own personal record, I noted that the sole dissenter in the group was rather beautiful as she sat there alone, smiling, even if it was by a desk in the SPP office.

# XV

It was ten past six by the time I rang the doorbell of Martin Morgenstierne's house in Frogner.

The house was even larger than I had expected, and the host more correct. He was standing waiting at the door, gave me a firm handshake and immediately accepted my apology that I was a few minutes late owing to other commitments relating to the case.

Martin Morgenstierne was as impeccably dressed as I had imagined, in a black suit and tie. But he was unexpectedly tall and unexpectedly youthful. His hair was still black and his face was free of wrinkles, so he did not look a day over fifty, and his movements were still vigorous and dynamic. He seemed remarkably fit for a bank manager.

Martin Morgenstierne showed me into the drawing room and we sat down opposite each other on very generous sofas. I politely declined his offer of a drink. He poured himself a small glass of cognac from a large drinks cabinet, but left it untouched to begin with. I waited to see if he would say anything first. In the meantime, I glanced swiftly around the room.

The contrast with the Reinhardts' flat in Seilduk Street was striking, and it was not difficult to understand why the meeting of the two families had been such a collision both politically and culturally. The walls here were at least twice as big as the Reinhardts', but with the exception of three impressive bookcases, they were panelled and remarkably empty. There were a couple of plaques honouring Martin Morgenstierne himself, and two pictures of him with an attractive, elegant dark-haired woman, who was obviously his wife. The first was an old black and white wedding photograph, the second a more recent colour photograph from their silver wedding anniversary or some such celebration. Martin Morgenstierne was easily recognizable. However, there was a stark contrast between his broad, apparently genuine smile in the pictures on the wall and his very grave expression now.

The drawing room almost gave the impression that Martin Morgenstierne had had a happy but childless marriage. There was no trace of his daughter, though I suspected that at some point there had been. Below the photographs of himself and his wife were two lighter squares on the wooden panelling, telling of photographs that had been removed.

Martin Morgenstierne was clearly an intelligent man with good social skills. He followed my gaze around the room for the first thirty seconds or so, before breaking the silence.

'You are no doubt somewhat surprised that I do not

have any photographs of my only daughter here, and that I carried on working as usual after I had received the news of her death.'

I nodded my confirmation. He continued, still without a shadow of a smile.

'My family has always had a strong sense of duty and work ethic. I have not missed a single day of work, other than trade holidays, for more than a decade. I have worked extremely hard all my life and my compulsion to work became even stronger after the death of my wife. I realized very quickly that I would go mad if I stayed at home on my own too much. So instead, I worked my way through the greatest sorrow I have ever experienced. And now I will do the same.'

He took a nip from the glass of cognac, and sat for a moment lost in thought. I was relieved to hear that Martin Morgenstierne did feel some grief at his daughter's death, and I hoped that we were getting closer to something.

'There were of course pictures of her on the walls for all the years she lived at home. And I left them there even though she rebelled and turned her back on all the values we held. But in the last few months that my wife was alive, her lack of respect was too much. I phoned Marie one Wednesday in September 1967 to say that her mother was deteriorating rapidly, and that my wife would like to meet her to see if they could be reconciled. Marie replied that it was highly unlikely that a meeting could lead to reconciliation at this stage, and that she in any case had a meeting that evening. She would see if she had the time to come by at the weekend. But by the time the weekend came,

Margrete was dead. So there was a tragic end to a sad chapter in my family story. I hope that you understand and judge my reactions accordingly.'

I nodded. Even though I had only heard one side of the final chapter in the Morgenstierne family history, it was easy to understand that this would have made a deep impression on an old-school family man. The sudden use of her first name reinforced my impression that he had been deeply attached to his wife.

'I continued to treat my daughter with the utmost respect, even though she perhaps did not deserve it. She inherited a quarter of million from her mother, fifty thousand more than was in the estate. But I could no longer bear to see her picture alongside that of her mother. So I put away all the photographs of Marie. I hoped that there would be better times ahead and that we would eventually find our way back to each other. But it seemed, as she said herself, highly unlikely. I sent her a Christmas card and received a card in response for New Year. Other than that, we have had no contact for more than a year now.'

He shook his head sadly and emptied the rest of the glass of cognac.

'In retrospect, I have realized that the situation is in part fate and in part our own fault. Both Margrete and I came from conservative families with strong traditions. I followed in my father's footsteps, serving as an officer in the army in my younger years, then going on to become a successful bank manager. I had great hopes for a large family and a son to carry on the family name. But Marie's birth was difficult, and as a result, my wife could have no more children. So all our hopes and aspirations rested on Marie. It was perhaps too much for her. I have often thought about it in recent years.'

Martin Morgenstierne stood up and poured himself another glass of cognac. He was on a roll now, and carried on without any prompts from me.

'She was the dream daughter throughout most of her childhood. She did everything we asked her to, was kind and polite to everyone, and did well at school. But then suddenly everything changed when she turned eighteen and went to university. I cannot forgive him for leading her astray.'

'By him, you mean Falko Reinhardt?'

He nodded, and an almost aggressive edge sparked in his eye.

'Of course. Though we had noticed some changes before he came on the scene. She was much harder on both me and her mother, and the atmosphere around the table was often not particularly pleasant in the months before she graduated from high school. But it was when she started university and met him that it became unbearable for me to eat supper in my own home. I am fully aware that he is in all likelihood dead, but I have nothing positive to say about him, all the same.'

I asked whether he had ever met Falko Reinhardt in person. He nodded, almost reluctantly.

'We met a couple of times when they first fell in love, and then I met him again at my daughter's request just after they got engaged. He made an admirable attempt to embrace me and even tried to call me father-in-law, instead of his usual sarcastic 'Super Pater', the last time we met. He was intelligent enough not to mention any of the anti-establishment theories he spouted so readily in other social contexts. But we were of course diametrically opposed in terms of politics and status, so any real contact was impossible. I prayed to God on several occasions that my daughter might break off the engagement and had debated vigorously with myself as to whether I would go to the wedding or not. And in the end, I did not have to make that choice.'

He sighed, took a sip from his glass, and then carried on.

'For me, it was a huge relief when my daughter's fiancé disappeared, and I had no desire whatsoever for him to come back. It is understandable that the detective inspector leading the investigation into Reinhardt's disappearance had to ask me where I was on the night that he disappeared. Fortunately, it could be confirmed that I was at an anniversary dinner in Oslo until well past midnight, so it would have been impossible for me to get to my cabin in Vestre Slidre.'

I could not gauge the extent to which this positive reference to Detective Inspector Danielsen was a dig at me or not. I could imagine that the two of them had quickly become chums, but something else that the bank manager said immediately caught my attention.

'So the cabin in Valdres is yours?'

He nodded.

'Paradoxically, yes. I inherited it from my father. I had spent family holidays there since I was a boy, a tradition that Marie had also grown up with and enjoyed. But the cabin had not been used since Margrete died. I could not face going there alone, and Marie knew this. Which is why she took the chance of inviting her friends there without even asking me. I was completely unaware that the group were in my property and at first thought it was a misunderstanding when the police called to say that a person had been reported missing from my cabin.'

'So your daughter had her own key to the cabin, and you still have your own key?'

'Yes, I do still have it, but don't use it any more. I have not been to the cabin since all this happened and definitely have no intention of going there alone now. The police are welcome to borrow the key, if that would be of any help to the investigation.'

I accepted this offer and thanked him, popping the key he gave me into my pocket. It could well be useful to have the key to the cabin where Falko Reinhardt had disappeared.

But right now, I was more interested in the deceased's flat. According to her father, she had lived in a rented two-bedroom flat in Kjelsås for the past three years. He had only been there once and was never offered a key. He could therefore only advise that I contact the owner or caretaker of the building if I wanted to get in. As far as inheritance was concerned, he had no idea whether his daughter had a will or not, or if so, where it might be. If she had not left a will, he would, as her closest living relative, get back all the money she had received following her mother's death. Which was certainly not what he had hoped for, he added hastily.

I viewed Martin Morgenstierne in a more positive light

following this conversation. It now seemed that he had said all that he wanted to for today. He looked at me questioningly over his glass of cognac, with a hint of anticipation.

I still had one unanswered question – which I really did not want to ask, but knew I had to.

'As a matter of procedure, I have to ask where you were at ten o'clock yesterday evening?'

I was prepared for a violent reaction. There was none. Martin Morgenstierne was obviously an impressively controlled man. He emptied what was left of his cognac before answering, but when he did, his voice was measured but not unfriendly.

'I have been a law-abiding man all my life. And I had not given up hope that my daughter would at some point change her views, and that we would be reconciled. In fact, it was my fervent wish for the future. The thought that I might hurt my daughter in any way is absurd. But I fully understand that you have to ask. Fortunately, I can tell you that I was at a colleague's fiftieth birthday celebrations yesterday evening at ten o'clock, and that can be confirmed by about ten reliable witnesses.'

When he said the word 'absurd' it struck me that Martin Morgenstierne the bank manager and Miriam Filtvedt Bentsen the SPP activist, despite all other apparent differences, shared a remarkable sense of rationality. But even though Morgenstierne had risen in my esteem during our conversation, I was in no doubt which of the two I liked best.

I had no more questions to ask then and there. I thanked him for his time and once more gave my condolences, then stood up. Martin Morgenstierne was a very proper host, and he followed me out to the front door.

In the hallway, he said that he would be grateful if he could be informed of any conclusions the investigation might reach concerning his daughter's murder before they appeared in the newspapers. Then he added that he was more than happy to answer any more questions, should that be necessary, but did not think that he had much more to add. He had no idea what his daughter had been up to in the past year. He would guess that the possible motive was to be found in the radical circles she frequented, some of whose members were not averse to the idea of terrorism and illegal activity. But he did not know any of the others involved, and so could not point anyone out as a suspect.

As I was leaving, he suddenly remarked that it would no doubt be some time before his daughter could be buried due to the ongoing investigation, but that when the time came he supposed it would be he who had to do it. I confirmed this assumption: Marie Morgenstierne had at the time of her death been unmarried, and her father was her closest relative. He said he would have to consider the situation, but thought that perhaps she should be buried beside her mother in the family grave.

I pointed out that that had nothing to do with me or the police, but that personally I thought it was a good idea. And in some way in that moment, it felt as though Marie Morgenstierne was one step closer to reconciliation with her parents, albeit after her own and her mother's death. Her father and I shook hands and parted on almost friendly terms.

When I left the house in Frogner at ten past seven, I had still only seen Martin Morgenstierne's smile on old photographs. But little else was to be expected, given what I now knew about the family history. And given the father's alibis it seemed very unlikely that he had anything to do with his daughter's death, or with her fiancé's disappearance.

# XVI

I had plenty of new information to worry about on my short drive to the grand Borchmann residence at 104–8 Erling Skjalgsson's Street. The case was becoming increasingly complex, and a solution was no closer than it had been this morning. However, as I parked the car, it was the thought of how it would be to see Patricia again that bothered me most. My last visit there had been some fifteen months earlier, on the Norwegian national day, and that 17 May had ended dramatically when I more or less fled the house just before midnight.

To my relief, the impressive white building was just as I remembered. To step through the door was still like taking a step back in time to the 1930s. It was Patricia's father, the professor and company director Ragnar Sverre Borchmann, who had contacted me in connection with my first murder investigation two years ago. This time, he was nowhere to be seen. But I was still graciously received. I was, just as before, unable to tell whether the maid was Beate or Benedikte, as they were identical twins. But I assumed that Benedikte would not be back at work yet as she had had a baby the year before, so I guessed it was Beate, and did not ask. She was standing at the ready as soon as I rang the doorbell, and whispered: 'Don't say that I told you, but she's been looking forward to this and waiting impatiently for you all day.'

I gave her a friendly smile and took this as a sign that our complicity from the two previous investigations had been re-established.

The library – where the now twenty-year-old Patricia Louise I. E. Borchmann had spent most of her waking hours since a car accident had killed her mother and left her paralysed from the waist down – was still the same, too. And there she was, surrounded by all her books, sitting back in her wheelchair, apparently relaxed, with a thick notebook and three ballpoint pens at the ready on the large table.

The new decade had heralded few changes in here. The twenty-year-old Patricia I met in summer 1970 looked more or less the same as the nineteen-year-old Patricia I had fled from in spring 1969. I was convinced that she remembered my hasty retreat, but she did nothing to show it if that was the case. The starter to a delicious three-course meal was already on the table.

It did not feel natural for me to shake her hand, or to initiate any form of physical contact, and fortunately she did not appear to feel inclined either. But it did feel absolutely natural that I should come back here to seek her advice, now that I was once again in the middle of a demanding investigation. It had become part of the world order that we both took for granted; I needed her help to solve my murders, and she needed my help to give her life meaning. So we sat down without shaking hands and this time without any small talk either.

'Tell me everything,' she said, the very second that the door closed behind the maid.

Patricia noted down the odd key word as a reminder, but otherwise listened in silence while we consumed the oxtail soup and most of the duck breast. I myself had my work cut out trying to finish both the starter and the first course and still deliver my report of the day's hearings fast enough to prevent any impatient furrows appearing on Patricia's brow. It was half past eight by the time I had gone through all the day's events and reached the end of my visit to the victim's father.

'So, what does the genius have to say about Falko Reinhardt's disappearance and Marie Morgenstierne's murder so far?' I asked, before throwing myself with gusto into what remained of my first course.

Patricia smiled.

'The genius is certainly intelligent enough to see that we still lack too much information to be able to conclude anything about these two rather complicated cases. And at the same time warns that it may take time and energy to solve them. The universes we have dealt with in both our previous cases have been clearly defined, and we have had to separate the truth from lies, and the murderer from the innocent within a limited group of known players. Here we face the curse of public space. Practically the whole of Oslo could in theory have shot Marie Morgenstierne at Smestad yesterday, with the exception of her father and anyone else with a clear alibi. And practically the whole world could, in one way or another, have played a part in Falko Reinhardt's disappearance in Valdres two years ago. However, bearing in mind the dates, it seems likely that there is some kind of connection between these two events. And I think that we can safely say that the person who shot Marie Morgenstierne is someone she already knew.'

I looked at Patricia, impressed, as she slowly and thoughtfully chewed her last mouthful of duck.

'That sounds reasonable enough. But how can you be so sure? And, what's more, how did you know before the pathologist that she had been shot, and with an unusual weapon?'

Patricia was looking at me patronizingly already.

'I thought it was fairly obvious that she had been shot, but the argument does entail further implications that we should bear in mind. As you yourself saw, Marie Morgenstierne was running in fear for her life, even though there was no one behind her. However, she was still cool-headed enough to skip from side to side, clearly to make herself a less easy target for the person with the gun. It had to be a gun, really, as the murderer was obviously quite far behind her. But he or she would obviously be taking quite a chance by walking around Smestad with an ordinary hunting rifle. So it is therefore reasonable to assume that it was a more unusual weapon, one that could in some way remain concealed from other passers-by. In theory it could of course be a powerful revolver or pistol, even though that would require an unusually good shot. So what sort of murder weapon it was, and what it looked like, is a mystery in itself.'

Patricia smiled smugly, finished the water in her glass, and quickly continued before I made any attempt to interrupt her.

'The blind witness can of course not help us with that, but her statement is still very revealing. Something happened to make Marie Morgenstierne break from a steady walk into a mad dash for her life. As the blind lady, with her excellent hearing, could not hear the train, Marie Morgenstierne could presumably not see it either. So she was not running to catch the train – it just suddenly appeared in front of her, and she realized it was her only chance to save her life. We know she panicked, obviously for some justifiable reason, while she was walking happily down the road – but that does not necessarily need to be linked to any of the people walking behind her. She could have seen someone else waiting down a side road, or behind a hedge. But something happened that alerted Marie Morgenstierne to danger, and made her run. And I would dearly love to know what it was. It would seem that it was something that the others there did not understand, but she immediately knew what it meant.'

'Someone she knew, in other words?' I ventured.

Patricia shrugged disarmingly and shook her head at the same time.

'It would certainly seem that it was someone she knew, but not just that. Most of us know one or two people we would rather not meet, but very few of us would suddenly flee in panic at sight of them in a public place. Marie Morgenstierne apparently saw someone she knew, and for one reason or another she immediately knew that he or she was carrying a gun that could be aimed at her at any moment. Who and what was it that Marie Morgenstierne saw yesterday evening? That is now the most pressing question. And it undeniably makes the fact that three of the four people we know were on the street have not come forward in response to the repeated call for witnesses on the radio and television even harder to fathom. Goodness knows what their reasons are. One would think . . .'

Patricia stopped mid-sentence and sat deep in thought for a while. She opened her mouth for a moment, then shut it firmly. I had learned during our last investigation that Patricia hated to make mistakes, and would therefore often keep her arguments to herself until she was absolutely certain they were watertight. So I tried to prompt her by asking a question and airing my own views.

'Surely the shout indicates that at least one person on the street knew who she was?'

Patricia nodded.

'Clearly at least one of them knew who she was, and I suspect others did too. The shout is a mystery in itself, which the blind witness alone cannot help to explain. She heard the shout and Marie breaking into a run almost simultaneously. Was the shout prompted by the fact that Marie suddenly started to run? Or did Marie start to run because she heard the shout? Or did something else happen that only two people on the street understood the significance of, making Marie break into a run and the other person shout her name?'

I ventured to comment that Kristine Larsen was a woman, had been in the vicinity, and knew Marie Morgenstierne. Patricia looked at me sharply.

'That is certainly a possibility to be considered, and I can assure you that I have. But first of all, the blind lady is not entirely sure that the person who shouted was a woman. And secondly, there are many other women in the world who might equally have shouted to Marie. Did you for example ask whether Miriam Filtvedt Bentsen had an alibi for last night?'

I had to admit that I had forgotten to do so. I told myself that I had no reason to believe she had been at the scene of the crime, and what it is more, found it hard to believe that she had anything to do with the murder. But I was wise enough not to mention this to Patricia. Instead, I promised that I would ask her tomorrow.

'Please do,' Patricia said, without any apparent enthusiasm. Then she suddenly continued, 'And ask her two more questions at the same time. One: was the window in the room where Falko Reinhardt and Marie Morgenstierne were sleeping big enough for Falko to have climbed out? Two: ask if she is absolutely sure that she fell asleep that night, and whether she can confirm Kristine Larsen's statement that she did not hear Falko out in the hall from the time they went to bed until they discovered he was missing?'

I looked at Patricia in surprise and with something akin to disapproval.

'Miriam Filtvedt Bentsen said clearly enough that she went to sleep around midnight, and Kristine Larsen, who had a headache, saw her lying there asleep. So surely there is no great mystery there?'

There was a pause while the maid came in to clear the plates after the main course and give us each a dessert plate of ice cream and cake. Even in this new age, Patricia was upper-class enough not to say anything while the servants were in the room. However, she drummed her fingers impatiently on the table to ensure it did not take too long, then eagerly continued her reasoning as soon as the maid had closed the door.

'The boundary that defines sleep is blurred, to say the least. And saying that you have gone to bed is even vaguer. There is, however, a considerable difference between lying in bed with your eyes closed and being asleep, in that you are no longer aware of sounds and movements in the room. I am neither a clairvoyant nor paranoid, but while I am in no doubt that Miriam Filtvedt Bentsen had put down her book and closed her eyes two hours earlier, I do not think she was fast asleep at the point when it was discovered that Falko Reinhardt had disappeared. Nor, for that matter, do I believe that Kristine Larsen was lying awake because of a headache. She seems to have coped very well in the hours after it was discovered, despite the claimed headache and lack of sleep. And leaving the door open to ease a headache is a new one on me, as it increases the risk of noise. Ask Miriam if Kristine had wanted to keep the door ajar on previous nights at the cabin as well, and whether she had noticed any obvious signs of this supposed headache.'

I could not understand what she was driving at, but carefully noted down the questions on a piece of paper.

Experience from earlier investigations had shown that Patricia's apparently bizarre questions and whims could prove to be enormously important.

'What do you make of the coincidence regarding the dates of Falko Reinhardt's disappearance and Marie Morgenstierne's murder?' I asked. For me, this was the greatest mystery, along with how Falko Reinhardt had left the cabin.

Patricia rubbed her hands.

'It is one of the most striking things about the case, and one of the most important questions that needs to be solved. I don't believe in coincidence, and certainly not in supernatural connections. Given the situation, I am fairly sure that there is a direct and man-made link between these two strange events. But what sort of connection remains to be seen. I have too little information to know which of my many possible explanations is right. But I do think that Falko Reinhardt's personality in part holds the key, as do the circumstances surrounding his disappearance.'

'Does that mean that you may have an explanation as to how Falko Reinhardt disappeared from the cabin?' I asked, hopefully.

Patricia gave a scornful snort.

'I already have three possible solutions as to how he left the cabin. But if the answers to the questions you are going to ask are what I expect them to be, then I can possibly eliminate two of them. And in that case, we will be a good deal closer to solving the case. And by the way, all three possible explanations are based on the assumption that Falko Reinhardt disappeared off into the storm that night of his own volition, with or without help from anyone else in the cabin. This of course does not rule out the possibility that something serious happened to him, either outside the cabin or later. He may have gone out to meet someone who it then transpired wanted to kill him. However, I do believe that the chances that Falko Reinhardt is still alive out there somewhere are as great as the danger that he is dead.'

'Well, where do you think he is, then?'

Patricia shook her head.

'I have no idea where in the world Falko Reinhardt might be right now. His disappearance is in itself a locked-room mystery that then spills out into public space. Nor do I have any idea at the moment why he disappeared. But I am not concerned about that. Assuming that we are both still alive in a fortnight, we should have solved both the disappearance of Falko Reinhardt and the murder of his fiancée Marie Morgenstierne.'

This conclusion was immensely comforting, on the basis of previous experience – though I did suspect that Patricia trusted her own ability far more than mine. I did not pursue the matter. Instead, I asked what I should do the next day, apart from asking Miriam Filtvedt Bentsen the questions I had noted down.

The answer came faster than expected.

'Start with that and Marie Morgenstierne's flat. Then check with Falko's parents, and anyone else who might know, whether his passport was left behind and if there is any indication that his money or other possessions have disappeared. Then speak to Falko's supervisor at the university and see what you can find out about the names

mentioned in his thesis. The lead of a possible Nazi network should be followed up. And then, most exciting of all,
but also perhaps most demanding . . .'

I looked at her in anticipation. She swallowed her last
two spoonfuls of ice cream before she continued.

'. . . you should in fact do exactly as Anders Pettersen
suggested, and request to see any information the police
security service might have. My guess is you will not find
the answer as to whether there was a mole in the group or
not; but ask, all the same. And take a note of anything that
they say might be of interest. I have a theory, and if it is
right, it will also be a considerable step forward.'

'Is the theory perhaps, like everyone else's, that Miriam
Filtvedt Bentsen was the mole?' I felt my heart beat a little
harder when I asked this question. To my great relief, Patricia snorted again.

'Not at all. It is incredible how irrational and paranoid
even intellectually gifted people can become in group
situations. I do not trust this Miriam Filtvedt Bentsen for
a second, but "absurd" is in fact a good description of that
claim. There is nothing in the world to say that she had any
sympathies with the police security service, even though
she broke away from the group. The SPP is presumably
watched just as closely. If, by any chance, she had been an
agent with a mission to spy on the group, she would of
course have remained seated, rather than leaving such a
good post. If there was a mole in the group, it would seem
more likely that it was one of the four who remained, not
the one who left.'

I sent Patricia a look that was at once questioning and

firm. She teased me a little, staring into the air thoughtfully without saying a word. I realized that she had a theory about the mole's identity, but was not yet willing to reveal it. So I stood up, made it clear that I was getting ready to go, and remarked that it was going to be a long working day tomorrow.

Patricia stopped me halfway with her hand and one of her short and completely unexpected questions: 'The question for today is, was Marie Morgenstierne wearing a watch when she died?'

I looked at her, taken aback, and wondered secretly if this was some kind of a joke. It was beyond me to understand what significance this detail might have. But Patricia's face remained focused and almost insistent, without a shadow of a smile, so I answered with forced gravity.

'Yes. She was, after all, a woman of means and was wearing a rather expensive watch on her left wrist. And it was still working after she had been run over by a train. But I simply have to ask, in return, what on earth you think the practical significance of that is?'

Now, however, Patricia smiled broadly.

'I thought the practical significance of that would also be obvious. But I am more than happy to explain to you if necessary and you so wish. So far we have, naturally enough, been more interested in why Marie Morgenstierne ran for her life to the train. But what is also interesting is why she was walking so slowly in the first place. Even though she had a watch and knew the time, she was walking at such a leisurely pace towards the train that she would not catch it, and so would have to wait some time for the next one. And she must have known that, as she had taken the train home from meetings many times before. So, one theory that is worth noting is that Marie Morgenstierne wanted to give the impression of heading straight to the train, whereas in reality, she was going to meet someone else or do something else at Smestad yesterday evening.'

I had to admit that this was a theory worth noting. But I felt rather confused. So I excused myself, saying that I was tired after a long day of investigation, and asked with a fleeting smile whether we could meet again and discuss this further tomorrow. By then I would also, hopefully, have some more information to add.

Patricia replied with a bigger smile that she in fact had no other important arrangements tomorrow and that it would suit her very well if I was to drop by sometime after six, for example. Unless the staff had fallen asleep on the job or gone on strike, there was even a hope that I might get a simple meal after my hard day's work. I thanked her and promised to be there before seven o'clock the following evening. Then I followed the maid out, still pensive, but far more optimistic than when I came in.

I had an extraordinary amount to think about when I went to bed, alone, in my flat in Hegdehaugen at around eleven o'clock on Thursday, 6 August 1970. The faces of the various people I had met in the course of the day flashed through my mind. Miriam Filtvedt Bentsen's face stayed longest, even though she was the one I least suspected of being a murderer. But then I could not really imagine any of the people I had met so far as being Marie Morgenstierne's extremely cold-blooded murderer. And if one of them was in fact behind it, I had no idea of who that might be.

And so, just before I fell asleep, I pondered what Patricia had said about the curse of public space, and concluded that the murderer was probably someone else, somewhere else out there in the dark. And I unfortunately had no idea as to how we might find him or her.

# DAY THREE

# More answers, more questions
# – and more suspects

## I

I skimmed the newspapers at the breakfast table on Friday, 7 August 1970 and saw that the Mardøla protests still dominated the headlines, following an attack on the protestors' camp by several hundred reportedly angry Romsdalers the night before. The defence minister had refused to send in troops to remove the activists, but a large group of policemen were on their way to prevent any further scuffles. Otherwise, the debate about Norway's membership of the EEC had intensified after a speech given to Norway's Rural Youth by the Conservative Party and parliamentary leader, Kåre Willoch, where he had highlighted the EEC negotiations as an important national concern that everyone should support.

*Aftenposten* and *Arbeiderbladet* both carried a matter-of-fact report about Marie Morgenstierne's death at Smestad. Both papers had found out that 'the well-known Detective Inspector Kolbjørn Kristiansen' had been given responsibility for the investigation and *Aftenposten* had, 'based on previous experience, every hope that the case would be solved and those responsible arrested within a week'.

I put the papers to one side and set off for Kjelsås to start my working day. I still harboured a small hope that the flat where Marie Morgenstierne had lived might contain something to reveal the identity of her murderer.

Getting in proved to be no problem at all. One of the keys from Marie Morgenstierne's wallet fitted the outside door. The caretaker was at his post and had read about the murder – and about me – in the newspaper, so immediately jumped up when I knocked on the door to his flat on the ground floor. He confirmed that the other key from Marie Morgenstierne's wallet was to her flat. The only real challenge was to stop him coming in with me. In the end I managed to solve this by promising to come and get him if he could be of any help. He stayed outside the door just in case.

Once inside, my greatest problem was finding anything of any relevance in the flat. All my hopes were initially thwarted. Marie Morgenstierne had apparently been a tidy tenant, and there was not much of a personal touch in the flat. There were a couple of rather traditional paintings on the walls and three framed photographs of her and Falko, including an engagement picture, on the chest of drawers. Otherwise it seemed to be an entirely functional flat. Everything one expected to find in a single woman's flat was neatly in place here – and nothing more.

Marie Morgenstierne had a bookshelf full of textbooks on politics and other political literature, including a series of selected works by Marx and Engels. And she had a respectable number of literary works on another bookshelf. She had a fair amount of clothes in the wardrobe in the bedroom, but less make-up in the bathroom than one might expect to find for a young woman of her age. There was no form of contraception anywhere, nor any other indication that she had a new boyfriend or lover in her life. Nor were there any personal letters or diaries that might cast light on the case. In short, there was absolutely nothing to point me in the direction of who it might have been who had shot the woman who lived here two days ago.

I found only one thing of any interest in the late Marie Morgenstierne's flat. And although it was very interesting indeed, it was hard to gauge how important it was.

Under the pillow on Marie Morgenstierne's bed was a small white envelope that had been both franked and postmarked. Her name and address were typed on the front. There was no sender's name or address on the back.

My first thought was that it was perhaps a love letter from a new lover or admirer. However, what was written on the piece of paper inside the envelope was again typed, and was short and to the point:

'Was it you who betrayed Falko? If so, the time has come to confess your sins and tell the truth before 1 August, or else . . .'

The sheet of paper was small and white, and could have been bought in any bookshop. And the typeface was the most usual kind. I did not believe for a moment that the sender had left any fingerprints on the paper, or that there was anything more to be gained from it.

I stood in the late Marie Morgenstierne's bedroom with the letter in my hand and pondered whose hands had danced over the keys when the letter was written. Marie Morgenstierne had been sent a warning not many days before she died. The letter was not dated, but the postmark said 20 July 1970.

Rightfully or not, someone had this summer not only accused Marie Morgenstierne of high treason, but had also issued a threat and given her a deadline, which it would appear had not been met.

To me, the letter was at last evidence of a connection between her death and Falko Reinhardt's disappearance. The problem was that we faced what Patricia had called the curse of public space. In theory, more or less anyone could have written and sent the letter. In practice, I watched the faces of Trond Ibsen, Kristine Larsen, Anders Pettersen, Arno Reinhardt and Astrid Reinhardt flash through my mind in quick succession.

## II

The caretaker was still waiting outside the door in anticipation, but could not be of much help. He had heard about the tenant's extreme political views from a cousin who was in the union, but had not seen evidence of them himself. She had been an exemplary tenant and, to his knowledge, had observed all the house rules. As far as guests were concerned, the caretaker apologized that it was not always easy for him and his wife to know all the comings and goings, as tenants had their own front door keys and could in practice let anyone in as long as they were quiet. Falko Reinhardt's face was familiar to him from the newspapers, and both the caretaker and his wife had seen him there several times before he disappeared. The only other guest they had seen in the past couple of years was a long-legged, young blonde woman whom he might say was rather attractive. I nodded and noted that, reasonably enough, Kristine Larsen had been here.

The caretaker could not remember having seen any other friends. To my relief, he looked slightly bewildered when I asked him if he had at any point seen a young woman who read books as she walked.

There was one thing of interest that the caretaker could tell me about the deceased tenant. And it was of great potential interest. On several occasions that spring, both he and his wife had thought they heard unknown footsteps on the stairs that stopped on the first floor, and Marie Morgenstierne's flat was the only one on that floor that was inhabited. They had both, a couple of times, caught a glimpse of someone they thought was the visitor as he left the building. If it was he, the guest was taller than average, but they could not say much more as he had left in the dark and was wearing a hat and coat. The caretaker was fairly sure that he or his wife, or both of them, had heard the footsteps on three or four occasions – the last time being only a week or so ago.

I remembered Patricia's conclusions from the night before. So I asked if it was possible that this guest might be Falko, as they remembered him.

The caretaker raised his eyebrows, thought about it for a while, and even went in to ask his wife. In the end, however, he reluctantly had to confess that they could not say yes or no to that. There were so many footsteps to remember in the building and it was a long time since they had heard Falko's, he explained, apologetically.

When I asked for a spare key so the flat could be examined, I was given one straight away. I had no real hope of finding any technical evidence, as the flat looked too clean and tidy for that. But I did harbour a small hope that a fingerprint might help to reveal the identity of this mysterious guest – even, perhaps, of the murderer.

# III

There was still a fortnight until the start of the autumn semester, and so it was far easier than I had expected to find my way round the university library. I was told that the section where the literature students usually sat had around forty places. Only one of these was occupied at a quarter past eleven.

Miriam Filtvedt Bentsen, still dressed in blue jeans and a multicoloured sweatshirt, sat in the middle of a deserted landscape of empty chairs like a silent and lonely queen. There was a thick notepad in front of her and around it, an encyclopedia and five French dictionaries.

The sole occupant of the library was reading with such concentration that she did not notice me, even when I was only a few steps away. I stood there for a minute without attracting her attention, before I alerted her to my presence with a half-whispered: 'Do you perhaps know where I might find Miss Miriam Filtvedt Bentsen?'

If I had expected her to start in surprise, I was disappointed. Miriam Filtvedt Bentsen was obviously of a far more balanced nature than I thought, and what is more, she was familiar with the silence rule. It would take more than a whispering policeman in the library to unnerve her. She looked up, nodded with a quick smile, pointed to the exit and stood up. I obediently followed behind her, taking it as a good sign that, after a moment's hesitation, she had left the encyclopedia and all five dictionaries on the desk.

Miriam Filtvedt Bentsen felt that it was too early in the day for a longer break, so turned down the offer of lunch in the refectory. I saw it as positive that she then said yes to a coffee and a piece of cake – especially as she ate incredibly slowly and pensively.

My first question was about the size of the windows in the cabin in Valdres. Miriam Filtvedt Bentsen took her time, chewed on a couple of mouthfuls, and then answered that she unfortunately did not dare say for sure. The windows had been small, and were relatively high, so she doubted that it would be possible for a man of Falko Reinhardt's size to get out that way. But she could not be certain. Whatever the case, the window had been shut from the inside when she went into the bedroom around two o'clock that morning. So if that was how he had escaped, he would have needed Marie's help, she added, with an inquisitive smile.

I did not say anything to the contrary, but asked instead what she herself had been doing at ten o'clock the night before.

I asked with my heart in my throat, and once again anticipated a strong reaction – which did not happen this time either. Miriam Filtvedt Bentsen looked at me with even greater curiosity and asked if I really suspected her of murder? I tried to defuse the situation by saying that I did not, but that I had to ask her as a matter of routine, for the reports.

She replied that good reporting procedures were important in all organizations, and then added on a more serious note that her alibi was unfortunately not perfect. She had been in a meeting with several other people at the party office from six until eight, but had then carried on working alone until ten, when she caught a bus and a train back to her student flat. And at the moment, she was the only one in her corridor who had returned after the holidays.

In theory, there was nothing to have stopped her from being at Smestad around ten. But she had not been there, she said, and suddenly looked very serious indeed.

I thought to myself that Patricia would hardly be impressed by this alibi. And that I personally was relieved that Miriam had not given a boyfriend as an alibi and that there was still no hint of any boyfriend.

I turned the conversation back to their trip to the cabin, and asked whether she or Kristine Larsen had slept closest to the door. She looked at me, somewhat startled, but replied without hesitation that she had been closest to the window, and Kristine closest to the door. She told me in response to my follow-up question that Kristine Larsen had wanted to sleep with the door ajar the night before the disappearance as well.

My next question felt a bit intrusive. But I trusted Patricia, and so I asked if I was correct in thinking that on the night of Falko Reinhardt's disappearance, Miriam Filtvedt Bentsen had also been awake, even though she had had her eyes closed.

Miriam Filtvedt now looked at me with open curiosity and admiration. But her voice was just as calm, and her reply just as measured: she had turned out the light around midnight, but had not been able to sleep, and had thus lain awake. To avoid disturbing her roommate, she had been as still as she could. And given an academic proviso that she might have dropped off or confused people's footsteps, she could therefore confirm Kristine Larsen's claim that Falko Reinhardt's footsteps had not been heard out in the hallway in the hours before he disappeared.

She could not help asking how I, two years later, could know that she had been awake. But then she answered this herself in the same breath, saying that I presumably could not say in light of the ongoing investigation.

I nodded meaningfully, noted down her answers, and reserved the right to contact her again should any more questions arise. She nodded, said that I now knew where to find her if that was the case, and then disappeared back into the library as if to illustrate the point.

Miriam Filtvedt Bentsen left half a cup of coffee and

some cake on the table in her wake. They reinforced the feeling that she had now been given something to think about, even though I could not for the life of me see her as guilty of murder – or any other crime, for that matter.

# IV

After Miriam Filtvedt Bentsen had gone back to the library, I treated myself to another cup of coffee and a couple of rolls for lunch. In the time it took me to eat this, I decided that I would follow up the old Nazi lead before going to the police security service. I was mentally putting it off, and used the excuse that it might be handy to have a clear overview of all the possible threats first.

I therefore went straight from the refectory to the history department. Professor Johannes Heftye was, as luck would have it, alone in his office and said straight away he would be happy to talk to me. He was a grey-haired, grey-bearded and well-dressed man in his sixties, with the Second World War as his speciality. He had also once been a Communist Party politician.

The professor's memory was impressive, as far as I could tell. He immediately remembered not only Falko Reinhardt, but details about his unfinished thesis and the last supervision he had had with him. The thesis was about an NS network from the Second World War, a subject that both the student and supervisor thought was fascinating and important. Falko had called the professor out of the blue one evening during the holidays and asked if he could get guidance as soon as possible about some sensational new findings.

Professor Heftye's curiosity was immediately piqued and they had met here at the university on 2 August – three days before Falko Reinhardt's disappearance. Falko had been unusually excited and said that he had discovered things that might indicate that parts of the network were still active. He had then added in a hushed voice that it looked as though some of them were discussing options for a major offensive of some sort.

His supervisor got the impression that this might be an assassination or sabotage of some kind, but the usually so self-assured Falko Reinhardt was uncharacteristically vague about what kind of plans they might have and when it might happen. When, in addition, Falko Reinhardt did not want to say where he had got the information, his supervisor asked him to think about it and check all the information again, then come back when he had more to report.

Falko had explained that one of the sources made things a bit complicated, but assured the professor that this was something really big. He had seemed uneasy, almost frightened, in a way that his supervisor had never seen before. On his way out, Falko had said in a quiet voice that he now seriously feared for his own safety. The professor had asked if he was talking about the Nazi network. Falko had replied that the right-wing extremists were a possible danger, but with a self-deprecating smile he had added that he no longer felt safe with left-wing radicals either.

And they were the last words he had heard Falko Reinhardt say, the professor remarked gloomily as he puffed on his pipe. He had more or less dismissed the comment about left-wing radicals as a joke. But he regretted not taking the information about the Nazi network more seriously, and still believed that there had to be some kind of connection with Falko Reinhardt's disappearance. He had, without much joy, tried to explain this to the rather unappealing young detective inspector who investigated the disappearance, he added.

I nodded cautiously in agreement. It was easy to believe that Detective Inspector Danielsen had not found the right tone as easily with the radical professor as he had with the reactionary bank manager Martin Morgenstierne.

The first draft of Falko Reinhardt's thesis, around ninety pages long, still stood between two thicker works on Professor Heftye's shelf. He assured me that he had a copy stored away safely at his house, and handed me the thesis as soon as I asked if I could borrow it for the investigation. He added that it was a pleasure to meet a policeman who appreciated the value of history. I was more than welcome to contact him whenever I wished for further information. I thanked him, picked up the thesis and beat a hasty retreat.


# V


I sat in my office from half past eleven until one, reading through Falko Reinhardt's draft thesis. The text was incomplete; a conclusion and several chapters were still missing. However, this did not detract from the impression that the author was intelligent and had a flair for language. Some of

Falko Reinhardt's charisma as a speaker also shone through in what he wrote.

The topic was definitely interesting, not only in terms of the current murder investigation. In the body of the thesis, Falko Reinhardt described the activities of a network of Norwegian Nazis from the upper echelons of society in eastern Norway. He had also started to work on an annex about how parts of the network had remained active throughout the 1950s and 1960s. And it was hinted quite heavily that members of the group had not just met, but had also remained politically active and had discussed possible new actions. However, what this meant in practical terms was not specified in the text and no sources were given in the annex. It was thus unclear what sort of activity they were engaged in or where Falko Reinhardt had found the information.

'The wealthy farmer Henry Alfred Lien, from Vestre Slidre in Valdres' was mentioned as a secondary character and local contact for the network during the war. He did not, however, appear to have played a leading role at that time, nor was he mentioned in connection with activities after the war. According to the draft, 'the Big Four' were the architect Frans Heidenberg, the company director Christian Magnus Eggen, the shipowner Lars Roden and the landowner Marius Kofoed, all from the west end of Oslo. Both their names and professions were decidedly upper-class. I immediately went to find the relevant files in the treason trial archives and police records. They, too, proved to be interesting reading.

Henry Alfred Lien had been an active local leader and

spokesman for the Nasjonal Samling, and had been sentenced to six years' imprisonment after the war. He was released in 1948.

The shipowner Lars Roden had also been a member of the NS, and had furthermore placed his ships at the disposition of the occupying forces. He was sentenced to five years' imprisonment, but released in autumn 1947 due to ill health. He died two years later.

Marius Kofoed, the landowner, appeared to have been the one with most contacts in the NS and the occupying forces. He had, among other things, allowed his property to be used for troop mobilization and celebrations arranged by the NS. He was also deemed to be a personal friend of Quisling. Kofoed could most certainly have expected a stiffer sentence after the war had he not been liquidated by anonymous perpetrators in January 1945. There was a short statement in his papers to say that the murder had in all likelihood been carried out by members of the Home Front, and that further investigation was not advised.

The architect Frans Heidenberg was also a man who had moved in Nazi circles, but his role was harder to pin down, other than being a member of the NS and designing some large buildings for the occupying forces. He had got away with only two years' imprisonment after the war and had been released in autumn 1946.

The company director Christian Magnus Eggen had run his own business trading in jewellery and gold, with extensive dealings in Germany both before and during the war. He had also been a member of the NS, but had not had any formal responsibility. Despite a note to say that he was a friend of Quisling, he had got away with three years' imprisonment and been released after two for lack of any more serious indictments.

In later files from the census rolls, Frans Heidenberg and Christian Magnus Eggen were recorded as having private addresses in Skøyen and Kolsås. And both were listed at the same addresses and with the same titles in the telephone directories for Oslo and Akerhus. According to the files, they were now 72 and 69 years old respectively. I found the lead interesting enough to reach for the phone.

Both Heidenberg and Eggen were at home and answered the telephone themselves. Neither of them sounded particularly pleased that I had called. But both agreed, curtly and correctly, to meet me once I had made it clear that they were not suspected of anything, but that the police would like to ask them some routine questions in connection with an ongoing murder investigation. I promised to do this as quickly as possible and asked that they both stay at home for the next couple of hours.

I then made a short call to the police security service to arrange a meeting with the head of division in connection with the murder investigation, before getting into my car and heading west.

# VI

Frans Heidenberg's house in Skøyen was the largest in the street, and it was not hard to see that it had been designed by an architect. No other houses had seven walls.

My meeting with Frans Heidenberg himself was a positive surprise. He was a slim, suited man with pale hands and greying brown hair, who wore patent leather shoes at home on a weekday. His steps were slow but steady. His handshake was soft and his voice pleasantly relaxed, with perfect grammar and no accent.

Frans Heidenberg explained that his name came from his German father, but that he himself had been born to a Norwegian mother in Norway and had lived here all his life. He had had his own architecture firm in Oslo since completing his studies in 1928, and had been increasingly successful in recent years. A couple of nephews were in the process of taking over the business, but he still had an office and worked there one day a week. Otherwise, he spent most of his time here in his spacious and comfortable home.

Once installed in the living room, I declined the offer of alcohol or coffee, but said yes to a glass of water. I remained seated while I reflected that my host appeared to be the perfect diplomat, and about as far removed from a stereotypical Nazi traitor as I could imagine.

Paintings from Norway and Germany hung on the walls between the monumental bookshelves, as well as some photographs from Frans Heidenberg's childhood and youth in the first decades of the century. I looked around discreetly for signs of other inhabitants in the vast house. My host obviously read my thoughts and shook his head apologetically.

'I am afraid that only I live here, sadly. The house was built towards the end of the 1930s, when my firm had had its first real success. It was built for a larger family that failed to materialize. I never got married. So now I sit here by myself with plenty of space for my books and paintings.'

He took a pensive sip of coffee.

'A woman did live here with me once upon a time, in the final months of the war. We were engaged and planned to get married in July 1945. So the war ended at what was a very inconvenient time for me and under very unfortunate circumstances. I was, as you no doubt know, absent for a year and a half. And when I came back, she and all her things were gone. I was forty-six years old and for reasons that I am sure you understand, I was not particularly active in the city's social life in the years that followed. And there you have it. I gave up any hope of having a family and ceased to be politically active. All my time was given over to saving the firm, which was in a very precarious situation following my absence.'

I stared at him, fascinated. If Frans Heidenberg was still a Nazi, he struck me as being a Nazi with an extremely human face.

'I know what you are thinking: how could I put myself in that situation? It was in part my strong German roots, but more my fear of Bolshevism that had been stoked by tales of horror from the Russian Revolution in my youth. In the 1930s, I thought that the alternative to a strong Germany ruled by the Nazis was a strong USSR ruled by the Bolsheviks. And I saw the latter as a far greater threat. And I might as well admit that I still do.'

He smiled and shrugged disarmingly.

'But all that is now well in the past, and I hope that my life today is of little interest to you. I would of course be more than happy to help you to solve your crimes if I could, but I must say that I do not see how that is possible.'

I asked him whether he had heard of Marie Morgenstierne or Falko Reinhardt. He replied without any hesitation that Marie Morgenstierne was unknown to him, other than what he had read in the papers following her 'unfortunate demise'.

He did, however, to my surprise, admit that the name Falko Reinhardt was familiar to him. He had received a letter from Falko a couple of years before, asking if he would be willing to answer some questions about his role during the Second World War. He had, however, not felt comfortable fraternizing with communists and for his part had no desire to rip open old wounds from the war. He had therefore sent a reply to say that he did not wish to be contacted about the matter. And he had repeated this in a firm and friendly manner when Falko Reinhardt later telephoned him all the same.

He had heard nothing more from the young man. But he did remember the unusual name, and had read about Reinhardt's disappearance in the newspaper only a few months later. Frans Heidenberg had anticipated that the police might contact him, and therefore ensured that he had a written statement from his two nephews and two other employees to say that he had been at a party with them in Oslo on the night that Falko Reinhardt went missing in Valdres. He placed it on the table in front of me and said that rock-climbing had never been one of his strengths

– even less so now than when he was younger, he added with an ironic smile.

When I asked him if he had an alibi for the evening of Marie Morgenstierne's murder two days before, Frans Heidenberg could regrettably only say that he had been home alone. He found it very hard, however, to see why he would be suspected of killing a woman forty-five years younger than himself whom he had never heard of, let alone met.

I assured him that he was in no way a suspect, but that there were still some routine questions that I had to ask. First, I asked him what his reaction was to the fact that Falko Reinhardt had identified him as a member of a Nazi network during the war, in some papers that he had left behind.

Frans Heidenberg remained calm. He shook his head in exasperation and said that he had had a good deal of contact with like-minded people and friends during the war, of both German and Norwegian descent, but that he had never seen it as a network. And this was not indicated in any way in the police investigation after the war. He felt that his sentence had been harsh given that his only sins were being a member of the NS and other symbolic actions, but that he had long since forgiven his countrymen and put the matter behind him.

Frans Heidenberg had known both Marius Kofoed and Lars Roden, and was still on friendly terms with Christian Magnus Eggen. But he had not felt that he was part of any sort of political network during the war, and even less so afterwards. He did not recognize the description of a secret network, and was somewhat dubious that a young communist today would know better than he had at the time. When I mentioned Henry Alfred Lien, he thought about it for a while and then shook his head; no, he could not recall meeting anyone of that name.

In response to my question regarding his political views today, Frans Heidenberg replied that he had been a member of the Farmers' Party for a few years after the war, but had then stopped his membership as he was not happy with the direction that the party was taking. He had not been politically active since the war, and in public he was now a man with no political views. Which party he voted for and any thoughts and opinions he might have on political issues were private matters, were they not?

I had to concede that the eloquent and relaxed Frans Heidenberg was right on this point, and did not ask any more questions. I thanked him for the information and reserved the right to contact him again later, should that be necessary. He continued to play the role of an exemplary host by assuring me that protectors of the law were of course welcome to contact him at any point, but he unfortunately doubted that he could be of any more help.

At the front door, Frans Heidenberg suddenly and unexpectedly asked me if Christian Magnus Eggen was also on my list of people to contact. I saw no reason to deny this, as Eggen had already been told that I was coming. Heidenberg nodded in understanding. He added that he should then warn me that my meeting with him might be rather different. He had been friends with Eggen since they were students, and thought of him as highly intelligent and a good person. But they were very different in both temperament and nature. Eggen undoubtedly felt more strongly that he had been treated unfairly after the war, and could 'quickly become extremely frank and vehement' when he spoke about it, he added.

I thanked him for the warning and wished Frans Heidenberg a good day. He tipped the hat he was not wearing, and opened the door for me. I left him with the feeling that I had indeed met a humane Nazi. I could see no connection between him and Marie Morgenstierne's death. I did, however, note that Frans Heidenberg did not have an alibi for the evening she was murdered. And that there was an elegant walking stick with a silver head just by his front door.

# VII

Christian Magnus Eggen's house was more traditional in style than Frans Heidenberg's, but as good as equal in size. The difference between the two owners, however, could not have been greater.

The white-haired Christian Magnus Eggen was rounder in shape, but from the outset appeared to have much sharper edges. His hand was firm, bony and twitchy, and his voice tense. Judging by his spectacles, the man was very short-sighted, but his eyes felt like gimlets. I was invited into the living room, but not offered anything to drink. And Christian Magnus Eggen was giving his answers before I had asked a single question.

'I am, of course, extremely curious to know what I have done to merit this unexpected visit from a keeper of law and order? Surely it cannot be in connection with the still unsolved murder of my old friend, Marius Kofoed, in which the police showed a remarkable lack of interest following liberation in 1945?'

I started by reassuring him that it was simply a matter of routine questions, and that he was not suspected of having done anything criminal. Christian Magnus Eggen proceeded to answer my questions succinctly, in a curt voice.

When he turned seventy, he had retired as director of his own company, which he had run for thirty-two years without any form of complaint. He now lived very comfortably on his pension and savings. His wife had died following an illness a few years earlier, and as his son had fallen in the fight against the Bolsheviks in Stalingrad, he was now a widower with no heirs. So his life was just fine, thank you very much, but his previous experience of the Norwegian police was not very pleasant and he now simply wanted to be able to live in peace for what time he had left. In short, he was still curious as to why I had now come to disturb a law-abiding and respectable citizen in his own home.

I took the liberty of reminding Christian Magnus Eggen that he had not always been a law-abiding citizen. He snorted in contempt and replied that he had never broken the law of the day – what happened in 1945 was that the law was amended with retrospective effect. He would never have believed that one could be punished in Norway for nothing more than being a member of a political party. And in order to avoid any chance of experiencing something similar again, he had not been politically active since. After all, he remarked snidely, it was impossible to know whether the socialists might suddenly decide tomorrow to ban any of the right-wing parties with retrospective effect.

We had not got off to a good start. And I did not make things any better by allowing myself to be provoked into asking if he denied any knowledge of the persecution of the Jews during the war.

'What persecution of the Jews?' he challenged, looking me straight in the eye.

'The Holocaust – the genocide of six million Jews, organized by Hitler's Germany and supported by Quisling's NS,' I replied, also with a certain antagonism.

He rolled his eyes.

'So even senior civil servants have allowed themselves to be brainwashed by the lies of their parents. What you call the Holocaust is an illusion based on exaggerated lies. A few Jewish criminals were executed, as more criminals and antisocial elements should be. But the Jews themselves are primarily to blame for their persecution in Germany. After all, they chose to stay there rather than give up their businesses, despite all the well-intentioned warnings. It was never a case of industrial genocide. I went there myself and saw the so-called annihilation camps – and they simply did not have the capacity to do anything like that. There are no documents signed by Hitler or members of his government to authorize anything of the sort. Some members of the

German army may, at the height of the war, have over-stepped their orders to tackle antisocial elements, but there was never an organized genocide.'

I stared at the man on the sofa with horrified fascination. His smile was bitter.

'Next you'll be saying that you believe the lie that Norway was occupied by the Germans. There was no German occupation; it was a rescue operation to save Norway from becoming part of the British Empire. There is evidence that the British had already started their invasion and had laid out mines in Norwegian territorial waters when the Germans arrived. And when the government and king decided to leave the country on 7 June 1940 rather than stay here to serve their people, Norway was no longer at war. In 1945, I and many other law-abiding citizens were convicted of being war criminals in a country that had not been at war, because we had used our given right to express our political views while obeying the laws that were current at the time.'

It was not easy to argue with the increasingly passionate Christian Magnus Eggen, partly because he was agitated and talking so fast, but also because I was at a bit of a loss and my knowledge of wartime Norway was obviously inferior to his. So I simply said that his understanding of the war was obviously very different from my own – and that given in Norwegian history books – but that that was not why I had come to see him. He gave an impatient nod, and then calmed down a bit and waited.

When we finally got down to business, Christian Magnus Eggen's story was more or less the same in content as Frans

Heidenberg's, despite their outward differences. Marie Morgenstierne was just a name that he had read in the week's newspapers. But he had first heard of Falko Reinhardt as a prominent young communist. When he then received a letter from him, with some questions about his experiences during the war, he had not wanted to waste 'five minutes and a stamp' on the answers. He had instead said exactly what he thought when Falko Reinhardt subsequently called him. He had thus spoken to Falko Reinhardt on the telephone for a couple of minutes, but had never seen the man.

As it was so long ago, Christian Magnus Eggen could no longer say what he had been doing on the night that Falko Reinhardt disappeared, but he could guarantee that he had not been in Valdres. He had been at home alone on the evening that Marie Morgenstierne was shot.

He did not, however, understand why he had to answer these questions about two people he had never met or had any significant contact with. He had no kind of motive whatsoever, and there was absolutely nothing to link him to the scene of the crime. And in any case, he added with a sarcastic smile, no one knew for certain that one of them had been the victim of a criminal act.

I was starting to feel very angry. I said that some information had come to light that could indicate that he had been a member of a Nazi network during the war.

Christian Magnus Eggen snorted with even more contempt than before. He had done nothing more than be involved with the lawful activities of a political party that was legal at the time, and was engaged in the fight to save

Norway from the threat of communism. He had been a member of the NS and done business with the Germans, but had not played a central role or been part of any network. And in later years he had minded his own business, paid his tax and not been politically active in any way. In addition, his right to vote had been suspended for a decade after the war due to his political affiliations, and he had since chosen not to use it in protest. The Conservatives and Labour were all the same to him. He had, however, continued to have contact with Frans Heidenberg and a few other old friends, which, as far as he was aware, was still not illegal.

To this, I asked if Henry Alfred Lien from Valdres was one of the old friends with whom he had kept in touch.

He shook his head in irritation. He had only met Lien briefly a couple of times during the war, and he had never been in Valdres. And what was more, the government and police should stop wasting taxpayers' money on recording who he kept in touch with or speculating about what he might think about social developments, so long as he paid over fifty thousand kroner a year in tax and did not break the law.

And so I had to stop there for the time being. I had no problem whatsoever imagining Christian Magnus Eggen as a criminal and traitor. He seemed to be the prototype of a bitter old Nazi. Everything he said sounded like self-justification. He was certainly high on the list of people I had met in the course of this investigation who I would be more than happy to arrest. At the top, in fact.

But, unfortunately, he was right: at present, there was nothing whatsoever to link him to Falko Reinhardt's disappearance, and any connection to the murder of Marie Morgenstierne was even more tenuous.

I did, however, take care to note that he did not have an alibi for the evening of the murder, and that he had a walking stick standing out in the hallway.

'Age takes its toll, even for an Aryan,' he remarked bitterly, when he saw me looking at the walking stick.

We parted a few moments later without either of us feeling the need to shake hands.

# VIII

It was half past four when I got back to the office. There was a message lying there to say that the head of the police security service had gone home for the day and would be out on a secret mission the following day. If it was in connection with the murder investigation, however, he could give me fifteen minutes at the end of the day tomorrow, at six o'clock, to be precise.

I immediately confirmed this arrangement and silently hoped that the case would somehow resolve itself one way or another in the meantime. The last thing I wanted was a conflict of interest with the head of the police security service.

My last task for the official working day could be completed with the help of a telephone. It was answered by Astrid Reinhardt, at home in Grünerløkka, after the second ring. She was able to tell me straight away that her son's passport had not been found, but that they did not in fact know where he had kept it before he disappeared. She added pointedly that the family did have a tradition of keeping their passports in secret places.

Her son's post office savings book had been left in his bedroom. There was seven thousand kroner in the account. He had withdrawn a couple of thousand three months before his disappearance, but they had no idea what he had used it for. His parents had at first hoped that the withdrawal was an indication that he was alive somewhere else. But this hope dwindled as time passed, and now they thought that perhaps the withdrawal of the money had absolutely nothing to do with his disappearance. He might have wanted to give the money to a political cause or a friend in need, his mother said. Both would have been typical of him, she added, her voice filled with maternal pride.

I thanked her for her help, and promised to call them immediately should anything new be discovered.

# IX

At five o'clock the calm of my office was disturbed by a knock at the door.

The pathologist was standing outside, once again looking slightly abashed.

'You may perhaps have suspected this already, but I have just discovered something concerning the late Marie

Morgenstierne that I thought you should know immediately,' he said.

I indicated impatiently that he should continue. But his previous visit had obviously made him more cautious.

'First of all I concentrated on the bullet wound in her chest, which was clearly the cause of death. The rest of her body was so badly injured that it was not easy to examine. But I have finished the autopsy now. And there is no doubt that when she died she was . . .'

He looked at me questioningly. I gave an irritated shrug. There was a flash of triumphant relief in his eyes when he carried on.

'Pregnant! Very early stages, possibly no more than the fourth or fifth week. And we can't be sure that she even knew herself, though she may have noticed something. Whatever the case, Marie Morgenstierne was expecting a baby when she died. And I presume that that is of interest to the investigation?'

I nodded, and told him truthfully that I had had no idea and that it was definitely of potential interest to the investigation. He seemed very pleased that he had been able to contribute something, and shook my hand with feeling.

Once the pathologist had closed the door behind him, I sat down to spend the next half an hour writing a report for my boss. It was quick enough to give an account of the day's events, but developments in the case were slower. It was with great relief that I popped the report into my boss's pigeonhole at ten to six, then got into my car to drive to Erling Skjalgsson's Street.

# X

'So, who posted the threatening letter to Marie Morgen-stierne? Trond Ibsen? Kristine Larsen? Anders Pettersen? Or one of Falko Reinhardt's parents?'

Patricia helped herself to a piece of salmon, and smiled briefly.

'Possibly all five of them. But it could in theory have been a lot of other people too. Miriam Filtvedt Bentsen, for example, whom I do not think we should let out of our sight quite yet. Or Falko Reinhardt himself, if he is, as I believe, still sneaking around out there. Or some completely unknown person who, for some reason or another, planned to kill Marie Morgenstierne, and wanted to confuse us by making it look as though Falko Reinhardt's family and closest friends were to blame. The latter is less likely, but still possible. And furthermore, the murderer does not necessarily need to be the person who wrote the letter. Murders in open spaces can be complicated things.'

Patricia did not look as though she was particularly worried and, with a smile, she started to eat her salmon.

'You mean, for example, that the murderer may also be the father of her unborn child?'

Patricia nodded.

'Perhaps, yes. As for who the father might be, it would be natural to assume that it might be one of the others in the group, but it is also possible that she had been sleeping with a fellow student on the quiet, or had a fling with some passer-by who we know nothing about. Whatever the case, we have two alternatives that are both very interesting. Either Marie Morgenstierne had recently been unfaithful to her absent fiancé, or her absent fiancé has been in the area again.'

'What about the Nazi network lead?'

Patricia nodded.

'It could mean everything – or nothing. You should also try to talk to this Henry Alfred Lien, even though it's a slightly longer trip, and even though he does not appear to be very communicative.'

I nodded in agreement.

'Well, it looks like I may not be able to get much done in Oslo tomorrow, so I had wondered about a day trip to Valdres, both to speak to Henry Alfred Lien and to have a look at the cabin. What do you think?'

Patricia helped herself to another piece of salmon.

'I think it might be worthwhile. Then we can perhaps solve the mystery of how Falko Reinhardt managed to leave the cabin. The first theory that has to be checked is the window. If Miriam Filtvedt Bentsen is right and the window was too small for Falko Reinhardt to get out of, then we are left with two alternatives, as far as I can see.'

She fell silent and chewed thoughtfully on a mouthful of salmon.

'And would you perhaps like to share what these two alternatives might be?'

Patricia's smile was sugar-sweet.

'Of course. I apologize, but I thought that would be quite obvious to you too. Falko could have sneaked out down the hall. But given that the door to the next room was ajar, and both the people who were in there were awake, the theory doesn't quite work unless Miriam Filtvedt Bentsen and Kristine Larsen are both lying to cover for him – which is not entirely unfeasible. If they are not, though, that leaves only one possibility, and it is the one that I have always thought to be true.'

Patricia was obviously still more than happy to make fun of me. She demonstratively refrained from saying anything more until I asked.

'So, according to this theory, how did Falko Reinhardt leave the cabin without the other five noticing, if he used neither the window nor the door?'

Her smile was teasing and she was clearly enjoying the situation.

'According to the theory, he didn't!' she said, with her smuggest smile.

I glowered back. Patricia realized she was on dangerous ground and quickly changed her tone.

'That is to say, he did of course leave the cabin at one point or another. But not while the other five were there, or between midnight and two o'clock in the morning. According to this theory, he hid himself away somewhere in the bedroom once his fiancée had fallen asleep and stayed there until the others left the cabin. Then he walked calmly out the door. And in that case, it is highly probable that he was the very person Miriam Filtvedt Bentsen claims to have seen making his way through the storm in the opposite direction shortly after.'

I had not for one moment thought about this possibility, but had to admit that it did not seem completely implausible.

'We are missing a link in the form of a hiding place in the bedroom. It certainly does not sound entirely unreasonable, and is worth investigating as a possibility.'

Patricia nodded vigorously.

'I realize that this may sound a bit odd. But soon it will be the unlikely that is most likely here, as what is most likely has proved to be not possible. It is becoming increasingly clear that a trip to Valdres tomorrow would be very sensible indeed. By coincidence, of course. But it is in fact a good idea.'

I accepted the compliment and nodded quickly in agreement.

'In that case, perhaps I should take a guide with me? I would manage to find the cabin on my own, I'm sure, but would have no idea of who was in which room and what happened where . . .'

Patricia kept a poker face to begin with. After a short pause, she nodded in agreement.

'It could of course be useful. The most obvious person would be Trond Ibsen, or perhaps Kristine Larsen?'

Despite the gravity of the investigation, I relished the situation and smiled a little to myself before carrying on.

'Both are certainly suitable candidates. However, I had thought of asking Miriam Filtvedt Bentsen first. It may be an advantage that she is someone who is no longer in the group, and more importantly, she is the one who claimed to have made these observations that night.'

Patricia had lost, and knew it. There were no good arguments against Miriam Filtvedt Bentsen, as she had already accepted that it would be good to have a witness with me from that stormy night.

Patricia swallowed hard a couple of times, left what remained of the salmon on her plate and drank the water in her glass. Then she accepted with grace and shook her head thoughtfully.

'I would have thought she might not have time for such a long trip, given the amount she studies and works. And it is quite novel to take a guide with you who has no sense of direction. But goodness, it is up to you who you ask.'

She was soon on the offensive again, and leaned across the table in a manner that could be seen as aggressive.

'If Miss Miriam Filtvedt Bentsen accompanies you to Valdres, you might try to tease out of her on the way why Kristine Larsen slept with the door ajar, and why Miriam herself was lying awake but with her eyes closed on the night that Falko disappeared. And in that context, please ask her about a detail I find unusually irritating, as I am very interested to see what she remembers. Kristine Larsen had wanted to leave the door ajar the night before as well; but was the door still open when Miriam Filtvedt Bentsen woke up the next morning?'

I immediately thought that this could only mean one thing. And that I still had no idea what that might be. Patricia had asked me apparently inexplicable questions about tiny details on several occasions previously, and these had always proved to be critical. I looked at Patricia, puzzled, and she for some reason suddenly looked irritated.

'I am allergic to strange details in murder investigations – and the bedroom door is one such detail. And what is more, these days it would be as good as a medical sensation if a group of three young men and three young women managed to survive for several years without any secret liaisons or at least some jealousy. So there may be more than a couple of skeletons under the mattress!'

The latter was not an expression I could remember having heard before. I sent Patricia a sharp look and asked which mattress she was referring to, if that was the case. Patricia gave a disapproving shrug, which I took to be a good sign.

'Well, we should not indulge in pure speculation. But the detail with the door is a tiny mystery within the mystery, which may prove to be of greater significance in solving the case than I imagine at the moment.'

I resisted the temptation to ask Patricia how much significance she thought it might have. Instead I asked her whether she had anything more to tell me about Falko's disappearance. To my astonishment, she nodded.

'The picture is becoming clearer. Regardless of how Falko managed to get out of the cabin, he left of his own will. In fact, there is much to indicate that it had been planned for some time. Add to that his egocentric personality and the suggestions of an imminent attack, and I don't like the outcome.'

I looked at Patricia askance, and she sighed heavily. Her mood seemed to have plummeted even further.

'Hmm, I am going to have to ask Beate for an extra

teaspoon soon. Well, we are talking about a gifted only child who was worshipped and photographed by his parents every day as he grew up. He was naturally the life and soul of any gathering, liked to maximize the attention and seems to have had great faith in his own abilities. He was publicly known, though not as famous and successful outside his circle as he perhaps wanted to be. Imagine for a moment that you were someone like that, and that you had heard rumours about a planned future attack. And you feared that the person or persons planning this might pose a threat to you in the period prior to the attack. What would you do?'

Now I suddenly understood what she meant. I nodded in agreement.

'I might well consider arranging to disappear, thus ensuring my own safety while retaining the ability to gauge the situation regarding the planned attack. And then, when the time was right, come back and save the day.'

Patricia nodded, but there was still no trace of a smile.

'I think there is more and more to indicate that that is what happened. A man who was as resourceful as Falko could of course have secured a cover identity and financial means to live in another part of Norway – or countless other countries. So the fact that he might have gone under cover for two years is in itself not hard to accept. On the other hand . . .'

My eyes were trained on her in anticipation.

'. . . On the other hand, it is something of a mystery why he has remained under cover for so long, and, it would seem, kept his parents in the dark. I see no other explanation than that he expected something major and dramatic to happen.'

My focus sharpened.

'But if your theory is right, and Falko is once again out there on the streets of Oslo somewhere . . .'

Patricia nodded gravely and finished my sentence.

'. . . then we can expect a large explosion of one sort or another soon. And if that is the case, we have no idea where or when things will explode.'

Patricia appeared to be deeply uneasy about the situation. She twitched nervously in her wheelchair while the maid cleared the dinner plates and served ice cream for dessert. In the meantime, I was able to consider the situation in more detail.

'And in that case, it may in some way be connected to the death of Marie Morgenstierne. But whatever the case, we have not come any closer to solving the murder today, have we?'

Patricia responded with a sullen shake of the head. She showed no interest in eating her ice cream.

'No, you could hardly say that. It is both striking and rather unnerving that none of the witnesses who were walking behind her have come forward. I have at least six possible explanations in my head, but lack the information either to confirm or reject any of them. We will just have to wait and see what you get out of the security service tomorrow, and what your trip to Valdres might bring.'

I took the hint and stood up.

'You are of course welcome to come for supper tomorrow evening. But if you take Miriam Filtvedt Bentsen with you to Valdres, remember to drop her off well before you come here.'

I smiled and assured her that I would remember to do that. Patricia's mouth smiled back, but not her eyes.

I quickly thanked her for the evening. It had given us both a lot to think about. The ice cream was left half-eaten in my bowl, and untouched in hers.

# XI

From time to time it still worried me that the professor and company director Ragnar Sverre Borchmann might feel some resentment towards me as a result of the stress and danger that my first murder investigation had entailed for his daughter. It was also possible that he might have heard about my late and hasty retreat at the end of my second murder case, and hold that against me too.

On my way out I therefore remarked to the maid, Beate, that I had not had the pleasure of meeting the man himself this time. I had noticed that the maid simply called him 'the director'. It was no doubt a far grander title to her ear than professor.

She promptly told me that the director was away, and for 'business reasons and the like' it was all very hush-hush where he was, and why he was there.

I gave a complicit nod when she said this. Borchmann's

business empire was so extensive that he could be away on all sorts of business in any number of places both within the country and abroad, and I had more than enough to think about already without speculating on his where-abouts.

I therefore said that I wished the director and his business well, wherever he was in the world and whatever he was doing. Beate replied that they all did, and that he was after all not so very far away. The director telephoned his daughter every evening and had said how glad he was to hear that I had come by.

I heaved a sigh of relief, thanked her and asked her to pass on my best wishes should she have the opportunity. She assured me that she would do her best.

# XII

It was eight o'clock in the evening by the time I got home to my flat in Hegdehaugen. I would never have guessed that I would one day call the SPP party office from my own home. But I did it now with pleasure and excitement.

The telephone in the party office was answered after four rings and to my relief it was Miriam Filtvedt Bentsen herself who answered. After the solemn atmosphere at the end of my visit to Patricia, it was a delight to hear such a happy voice – particularly as it sounded even happier when she heard it was me, and that I was calling about the murder investigation.

She asked if the fact that I was calling meant that there had been new developments in the investigation. I replied that there had been some progress, but that regrettably I could not tell her anything more right now. But I added that I needed a guide for a trip to Valdres in the morning, and that perhaps I could tell her a little more then, if she was willing to volunteer to come with me.

There was silence at the other end of the line for a moment. A breathless silence.

I hastily said that she could of course take a book or two with her, and there would undoubtedly be time to read on the journey. And that it could be of considerable importance to the investigation.

She answered slowly that a murder investigation sounded interesting, and that Valdres was a beautiful place that she knew well. She should be able to take the day off from her studies, given that it was a Saturday and that she still had three months to get through the reading list for her only exam that autumn. As far as the party office was concerned, it might not be so easy, as there were more papers to be sorted than usual.

I immediately promised that she would be back by half past five, and that I would drive her straight to the office on our return from Valdres.

Miriam Filtvedt Bentsen let out a peculiar peal of laughter, and said that it would perhaps be better for her career in the party if she was dropped a couple of blocks away, given that it was a police car – but that she would, on that condition, be able to come. We agreed that I would pick her up outside Sogn Halls of Residence at half past eight the following morning. Then we put the phone down at almost the same time – and, it seemed, in equally good spirits.

# XIII

It was only a few minutes after I had finished the conversation with Miriam Filtvedt Bentsen that it struck me that I should perhaps also check whether the farmer, Henry Alfred Lien, would be there. Directory enquiries were able to give me his number. He answered the telephone when I rang, but was not particularly friendly. His voice was monotone, hard and serious; it sounded as if he had not laughed since 1945.

I explained my errand, assured him that he was not a suspect in any way, but said that I hoped that he would be able to answer a few questions tomorrow in connection with the disappearance of Falko Reinhardt and the death of Marie Morgenstierne.

Henry Alfred Lien was not as negative as I had feared, given the reports of his behaviour in 1968, but it was not a jolly conversation all the same. He had nothing to hide, he said, and was fed up of being accused of things he had not done. He had seen a photograph of the young lady in the paper and thought it was a great shame, but did not understand how he could be of any help in the matter. He had never met the woman and had never been in contact with her.

In the end, however, he agreed to meet me for half an hour around lunch time, on the rather peculiar condition that I did not come in a police car. His reputation in the parish was already bad enough, and gossip could spread like wildfire from farm to farm; he said this without the slightest inkling of humour. He then added that of course he did not want to be associated with the case in the media in any way.

Relieved, I assured him that that would not happen. Henry Alfred Lien gave me some brief instructions as to how to find the farm and repeated that he doubted he had anything of interest to tell – but, he concluded, as I was a policeman and was coming all the way from Oslo, it was only right to meet me.

Towards the end of the third day of the investigation, I felt a growing unease. But I did not think that I could do anything more of value that evening, so in anticipation of my trip the following morning, I called it a day at around ten o'clock.

Two busy days of investigation had taken more of a toll than I had noticed: having watched the news while half asleep on the sofa, I went to bed and was asleep by a quarter to eleven on Friday, 7 August.

But then I woke up with a jolt at two in the morning – as the woman from the Lijord Line was running for her life towards me and the train. When I saw her coming towards me in my dream, I thought at first that it was Miriam Filtvedt Bentsen, but then saw that it was in fact Kristine Larsen who was staring at me in panic through the window.

Luckily, I woke up before she was also shot. But I did lie there for the next thirty minutes or so pondering the meaning of the dream, and what Patricia had said. And suddenly I got the strange and uncomfortable feeling that she might be right: it did feel as though there was a great storm brewing – but I had no idea where it might come from, or who would be hit.

# An interesting trip to the mountains
## – and another running woman

## I

My working day started unusually early on Saturday, 8 August. I got out of bed at a quarter past seven, and twenty minutes later was sitting at the breakfast table. *Dagbladet* expressed disquiet at the situation in South Vietnam and feared that the changes necessary there would not happen as long as the USA continued to support the corrupt regime. *Morgenbladet,* on the other hand, printed a critical commentary on the dictatorship in North Vietnam and was concerned that many more lives would be lost if the USA did not get the support it needed to continue its heroic war effort.

For want of any new developments, the murder of Marie Morgenstierne had fallen out of the headlines – which suited me very well for the moment. I hastily pushed the papers to one side after reading a scathing article in *Aftenposten* about a Swedish policewoman who had fallen head over heels in love with a well-known criminal. He had been arrested following a police raid on the policewoman's flat, and she was now on indeterminate sick leave. The article prompted unfortunate memories in me, but was a useful reminder of just how serious these matters could be.

At a quarter to eight, I was therefore eager to start my working day. It occurred to me that I should at least inform Marie Morgenstierne's father of what had happened so far.

I got hold of Martin Morgenstierne at home at ten to eight. He said that he was on his way to the bank, but asked if there was any news about the murder investigation or if there were any more questions he could answer.

I explained that some unexpected information had cropped up, and asked whether he was certain that he had not heard or seen anything to indicate that there was a new man in his daughter's life in the past couple of years. He repeated that he had had more or less no contact with her during that period, or with anyone else in her immediate circle. He could thus not rule out that there was a new man in her life; but he had not heard or seen anything to indicate this, and if it was the case, he had no idea who it might be.

There was a moment's silence. Then he asked, understandably enough, what sort of unexpected information had led to this rather surprising question.

I could not very well lie to a man who had lost his only child no more than a few days ago. So I told him the truth: that the autopsy had shown that his daughter was pregnant when she was murdered.

His reaction was instant and unexpectedly passionate, given how calm and controlled he had been only hours after hearing of his daughter's death.

'It can't be true! Oh – the shame for the family!' he almost bellowed into the receiver.

We were both silent with shock for a moment. He regained his composure with impressive speed.

'Please excuse my outburst, but this on top of everything else only makes things worse for myself and the rest of the family. As you understand, I have no idea who the child's father is. Are there are any more questions I can help you with? Otherwise, I really should be on my way to the office.'

I said that I had no further questions for the time being and apologized for disturbing him so early on a Saturday morning. He replied that he was grateful to be informed, but that he would be even more grateful if the news could remain strictly confidential. It would only add to the strain on himself and his siblings' families if this got out, particularly if the newspapers started to speculate and ask questions about the case.

I told him that I unfortunately could not promise that I would be able to keep it out of the newspapers forever, but that I would do my utmost to keep it from becoming public knowledge.

Martin Morgenstierne's thanks were polite and succinct. Then we had nothing more to say to each other, and so ended the call.

I was left with my slice of dry toast and cup of lukewarm coffee – and the feeling that it had been a greater shock and blow to the conservative Martin Morgenstierne to learn that his daughter was pregnant than that she had been killed.

# II

Sogn Halls of Residence came into view at twenty-seven minutes past eight. I had driven a little faster than I should have, in order not to be late.

It was a grey morning, the sky above the halls of residence was overcast and there was drizzle in the air. The students who had stayed there over summer had presumably gone home to their parents for the weekend, or were sleeping off the festivities of Friday night.

Much to my relief, Miriam Filtvedt Bentsen had done neither. She was standing there alone in the cool morning air, wearing a blue raincoat with no hood and holding a small string bag in one hand. I took it as a good sign that she was there early, and was not looking around for somewhere she could read.

She looked momentarily confused when I pulled up, but her face lit up when she recognized me.

As she got in, Miriam Filtvedt Bentsen remarked that she had been expecting a police car. I told her that I had taken a civilian car so I could drop her off at the office door that afternoon, and added that I was disappointed to see that she had not been reading while she waited.

She laughed her peculiar laugh and retorted that it would be unwise to let the books be damaged by the rain, and as they were borrowed from the university library, it would also show a lack of solidarity. She was almost triumphant when she produced a huge tome about English literature in the nineteenth century from her string bag, but, much to my relief, made no attempt to open it. Then we sped away from the Oslo drizzle, towards the mountains of Valdres and the two-year-old riddle of a disappearance.

# III

I thought it safest to wait with any critical questions until we were well out of Oslo. So I started by asking my passenger to tell me a bit about herself. This proved to be the right approach. The next hour or so was filled with pleasant chat about her parents and brother in Lillehammer, more details about her life at the university and predictions of how the SPP might do in the coming election. The weather brightened as we started to climb the narrow road up towards Valdres.

The mood in the car was very jolly. But then, on a rather desolate stretch of road, I finally 'thought' of a little question that I had in fact been dreading asking for the past two hours. I asked as kindly as I could about a tiny and possibly irrelevant detail – that is, was the door to the bedroom where Kristine Larsen and Miriam Filtvedt Bentsen had slept still ajar in the morning, the day before Falko disappeared?

There was a resounding silence. For about thirty seconds, the only sound to be heard was the steady purring of the engine. The atmosphere felt all the more intense as we were passing through a desolate landscape. It suddenly felt as though we were the only two people in the world. Her voice was somewhat tense, though still controlled, when she finally broke the pregnant silence.

'No. The door that had been ajar the night before was closed in the morning, even though I woke up before Kristine. I'm afraid it is possibly not a completely irrelevant detail.'

I gave her a meaningful nod, but was still not quite sure where this was leading. She was fortunately now on a roll, and carried on without prompting.

'I really didn't mean to hide anything from you. But it's quite a step to talk to the police about a friend's private life. Especially as I am still not sure whether I saw what I thought I saw, or whether I dreamed it.'

This time my nod was encouraging and I assured her that I did not blame her in any way. But I added that it could be very important, and that I was certain that she had seen what she thought she had seen.

She nodded.

'Unfortunately, I also think I did. In fact I am increasingly certain that what I saw that night was real and not a nightmare.'

Then she stopped again and looked at me expectantly. I gave her the little push she needed.

'And that was . . .'

She met me, but still only halfway.

'Well, it was in fact me rather than Kristine who had a headache. I normally sleep very heavily, and Kristine knew that. But I had a headache and it woke me up sometime in the middle of the night. I still don't know when it was, but that doesn't really matter. It was dark outside, so I guess it was the middle of the night.'

We were still beating about the bush. And my patience was wearing thin.

'So, despite the fact it was dark, you still saw something that you did not expect to see, something so unexpected that you were not sure if you had dreamed it or not the next day. But you had seen it. And to stop me from putting words in your mouth, what you saw was . . .'

She cooperated, fortunately, as I was still unsure about what she was going to tell me.

'Despite the dark, and with the proviso that I may have dreamed it, I saw Falko Reinhardt. In our room, in the bed – on top of Kristine.'

I should have realized. But the news was still a small shock, especially as it came from Miriam Filtvedt Bentsen's delightful little mouth.

'And Kristine certainly did not seem to be unhappy about the situation. It's not surprising that the whole thing seemed rather unreal to me, and that I still struggle to believe that it was true.'

Miriam Filtvedt Bentsen's hand touched the cross she wore around her neck, consciously or unconsciously. Her voice was apologetic when she continued.

'I have been so unsure as to whether I should tell you or not. It was bad enough to have to tell the police about a friend's private life, but on top of that I really wasn't sure if it was the truth or a dream.'

Again, I nodded. Then she did too.

We nodded in rhythm and drove in silence for a short while before I said that I fully understood her dilemma. On the other hand, the police was in fact me, and the context was an investigation into the murder of another friend of hers. In other words, she should tell me immediately if there was anything else of possible importance she had not mentioned.

Miriam Filtvedt Bentsen quickly replied that she could not think of anything else, but that she would tell me if she thought of something later.

So I followed up by saying that her explanation as to why she had not slept the following night was now clear enough, but that she could explain it for me again all the same.

I had expected a blush, or some other form of visible reaction. But there was nothing. Miriam Filtvedt Bentsen answered without any awkwardness that she was quite curious by nature, and had found being so unsure very perplexing. So she had stayed awake in the hope of confirmation the following night.

'But it didn't happen. I can guarantee that Falko was not in our room the night he disappeared. And as far as I could hear, he was not out in the hall, either,' she added hastily.

I asked how certain she was today that what she had seen that night was real and not a dream. She gave it some thought and then answered in a steady voice: 'At least ninety per cent. There was a long dark hair on the sheet the following day, which could not be explained in any other way. And Kristine, who was otherwise normally so calm, seemed to be in more of a state than Marie in the hours after Falko had vanished. I was interested to see if she would say anything to me later. But she never said a word, and I didn't want to ask.'

I nodded and said that I thought she had handled a difficult situation well. She thanked me warmly and gave me an almost mischievous little smile.

For the final short stretch up to Vestre Slidre, we drove in comfortable if pensive silence. It felt as though we were thinking the same thing. In short, Kristine Larsen might suddenly have had a strong motive for killing Marie Morgenstierne, especially if Falko Reinhardt was still out there somewhere.

A few minutes later we stopped outside the cabin where he had so mysteriously disappeared exactly two years and two days ago.

# IV

My expectations regarding the standard of Martin Morgenstierne's cabin were considerable, but it surpassed them. It was more like a large family home with its four bedrooms, kitchen, living room and bathroom, complete with toilet and shower. But it would appear that it had been standing unused for two years now. According to Miriam Filtvedt Bentsen, the bed linen belonged to the cabin and was the same as had been on the beds that fateful night. She still remembered the night in impressive detail, and promptly pointed out the living-room window where she had seen the masked man peer in earlier on in the evening.

We carried on to the bedrooms. Trond Ibsen and Anders Pettersen had each a room to themselves by the front door. Then there was the double room where Kristine

Larsen and Miriam Filtvedt Bentsen had slept, and the double room where Falko Reinhardt and Marie Morgenstierne had shared their last nights together.

I made an attempt to sneak past the door without any shoes on, but the floorboards creaked loudly under my feet and Miriam heard me straight away from the bed in the room where she had slept. It seemed unlikely that anyone could have sneaked out that way.

Miriam had been right about the window, much to her relief. It was high up on the wall and no more than twelve inches wide. I had to stand on a chair to reach it, and even then could barely stick my head out through the opening. It would not have been possible for Falko Reinhardt to squeeze his body out through the frame.

In short, two of three possible ways in which Falko Reinhardt could have left the cabin were swiftly eliminated. Miriam looked at me with great curiosity when I said that I had another theory to test. Then she sent me a pleading look when I asked to be left on my own in the room for a few minutes. She was, however, very disciplined and obedient by nature, and took her book out of her bag without protest when I shrugged apologetically and pointed to the living room.

I spent the next quarter of an hour making a crude investigation of the room's walls, ceiling and floor. Everything looked pretty normal, and I was sceptical of Patricia's theory to begin with. And my scepticism in no way diminished when I had tapped my way across all four walls, including the cupboard, and across the few feet of open floor.

However, my pulse started to race when I discovered first one and then two more loose nails in a floorboard under the bed where Falko and Marie had slept.

My excitement increased when it turned out that the double bed was not attached to the floor in any way.

I pulled it to one side and took out the four loose nails in the floorboard, and could then confirm that a space just wide enough and deep enough to hide a person had been dug out below. And none of the nails in the floorboard in question, nor the one beside it, had been hammered in properly.

I stood there looking down at the secret chamber. It was easy enough to picture it now. Falko Reinhardt had either discovered or dug out this space himself beforehand, and on the night of the storm, he had loosened the floorboards and slipped down there. I stood for some time and pondered why he might have done this.

I then went to get Miriam, told her about the cavity under the bed and asked her if she had ever seen or heard about it before. She looked at me, impressed, and with naked curiosity peered down into the secret hollow. She shook her head firmly and assured me that it was not something she had heard about – or even imagined existed.

When I asked if it could have been Falko Reinhardt she saw going in the other direction that stormy night, Miriam Filtvedt Bentsen nodded eagerly. The thought had crossed her mind and was certainly not entirely implausible.

'In which case, he then obviously left the cabin of his own accord, having first planned his escape,' she remarked in a matter-of-fact voice. I nodded my cautious agreement and said that there was much to indicate that.

There was nothing more to be found indoors. So I asked Miriam Filtvedt Bentsen to show me the way to the cliff where Falko's shoe had been discovered the morning after he disappeared.

We found it on the third attempt. The distance to the cliff was about a quarter of a mile. When we got there, I saw the stone beside which Falko Reinhardt's shoe had been found. It was a large white stone, almost three feet tall, and had sheltered the shoe from the wind.

The view from the cliff was spectacular. The drop was about three hundred feet down onto scree, and Falko Reinhardt could hardly have survived if he had fallen over the edge in the storm. Both Miriam Filtvedt Bentsen and I allowed ourselves to be captivated by the view for a few moments. But, as was to be expected, we found no new traces of the missing cabin guest and no new clues as to what might have happened to him.

With Patricia's help, I had solved the riddle as to how Falko Reinhardt had left the cabin in the raging storm. But the more crucial questions as to why he had left and where he then went remained unanswered.


# V


At a quarter to one, we locked the door to the cabin, got into the car and drove on to Henry Alfred Lien's farm. The journey only lasted a matter of minutes. Miriam gave an understanding nod when I said that I could not take her in with me, and as soon as I parked the car on the driveway up to the farm, she pulled out her book.

The weather had improved and the sun was shining now. As I got out of the car, it struck me that the farm with the mountains in the background would have been a perfect motif for one of the NS propaganda posters of the 1930s.

The farmer himself, paradoxically, would not have fitted in. He was far too old, too grey and a little too fat. Henry Alfred Lien turned out to be a stocky man of around seventy. His gait was confident yet slow as he progressed across the farmyard. His face was serious and stern, as though carved in granite. And his handshake was firm when he invited me, in a not unfriendly manner, to come into the living room in the main house.

I liked Henry Alfred Lien better than expected, even though he was as taciturn as I had imagined he would be. At close quarters, his voice reminded me of a tractor; it was loud, slow and monotone, and made steady, solid progress. He seemed to be a reasonably well-read and cultured man, and switched promptly from his Valdres dialect to a more standard pronunciation.

Stepping into Henry Alfred Lien's house was like stepping back into the interwar period. The furniture was wooden and dated from around the time of the First World War. The most recent family photograph on the wall was a black and white picture of a far younger Henry Alfred Lien, together with a very serious wife, a son and two daughters. The photograph was dated 1937. It was hanging below an old cuckoo clock that sang out when the clock struck one, just as we were sitting down at the table.

The table was set for coffee and cake for two, and I could see no sign of any other inhabitants. My host almost immediately disappeared into the kitchen and I used the time to have a quick look around his living room. It gave the impression that the elderly farmer had little social engagement and no political views of any sort. There was nothing on the walls or the tables to indicate his fascist past. I noted with some interest that he did not appear to be a hunter. There were no trophies or weapons to be seen.

Henry Alfred Lien returned with some sugar, poured the coffee and then sat down and looked at me in anticipation.

The interview was problematic from the outset. Henry Alfred Lien had already answered negatively to the routine questions on the telephone. With a poker face and booming voice, he still denied any knowledge of or contact with either Marie Morgenstierne or Falko Reinhardt. He only knew their names from the newspapers. He had been at home on the night that Falko Reinhardt had disappeared, and, unfortunately, he had been alone. The farmer's wife had died many years ago and the seasonal workers on the farm had been given the weekend off. It had been a very unpleasant echo from the past to be unfairly suspected of being in some way involved with his death or abduction.

Henry Alfred Lien was obviously prepared for my visit. From his pocket, he produced a lie detector certificate and repeated once again that he was innocent. He was extremely grateful that his name had been kept out of the papers at the time, and would take dramatic action if anything about the case was now to appear in print. Gossip travelled quickly in these parts, and he had felt ostracized in the months following Reinhardt's disappearance.

As far as Marie Morgenstierne was concerned, Henry Alfred Lien claimed to have been at home on the evening she was shot, but once again he had no witnesses to confirm this. A couple of the workers would be able to confirm that he was here when they went home at six o'clock, and again when they returned at eight o'clock the following morning. However, in addition to a small tractor, he owned a large old Volvo and could have driven to and from Oslo within that space of time. So the opportunity was there, but as yet, no motive.

Henry Alfred Lien paused for thought when I asked if he, as a local, had any idea of what might have caused Falko Reinhardt's disappearance. He emptied his coffee cup and finished a biscuit before his tractor voice rolled calmly on.

'The mountain has taken lives in mysterious ways before, certainly if one is to believe an old story . . . So I should imagine that perhaps something similar happened here, even though it is hard to understand how. But I'm not sure that you, a young man from Oslo, would be interested in tales?'

He sat still and looked at me askance, then rattled on once I had said that I was interested in anything that might cast light on the mystery. This time he trundled on for some time without stopping,

'Once long ago, sometime in the last century, there was a boy called Karl. He was the son of a poor farmer, but was said to have a good head all the same. And then, a few years after his confirmation, he turned into a megalomaniac. One day he claimed to be the son of King Karl Johan, the next he talked about flying to the stars and on the third day he suddenly disappeared from work. He had been working on one of the neighbouring farms with some other lads. They didn't see him again until they were on their way home for the night. Then there he was, standing at the edge of the cliff.'

I looked at Henry Alfred Lien with keen interest. He was encouraged and picked up pace.

'My grandfather was one of the young lads who saw Karl standing there at the top of the cliff. And according to what my father told me when he was an old man, they heard him screaming as he fell. They saw him plummet head first down onto the scree. But when they got to where he had fallen, he was nowhere to be found. They gathered folk from the neighbouring farms and scoured the area on foot without ever finding a trace.'

Having released the story, Henry Alfred Lien's mouth slammed shut like an iron gate. We sat looking at each other across the table for a few seconds before I attempted to encourage him to continue.

'A remarkable story. Was the mystery of this lad Karl ever solved?'

Henry Alfred Lien shrugged.

'His remains were found a few weeks later. His body was discovered one morning in the middle of the scree where they had searched so many times before, his head crushed. So it's possible that the fall did kill him, but how it had happened remained a mystery. As long as there was some-one alive who remembered Karl, people speculated about murder and gods and devils.'

'And what do you think happened?'

For a moment, Henry Alfred Lien seemed to be glad that I had asked his opinion. Not that there was a hint of a smile on his face, but he straightened his body when he answered.

'As you ask, I am a down-to-earth old farmer who does not believe in murder, gods or devils. I think that the lad jumped to his death and someone in his family or a close friend ran to the body and covered it up for a few days in order to avoid the shame of suicide. And it would not sur-prise me if something similar happened to this Falko chap a couple of years ago. According to what was said in the papers, he was also a young man with some wild ideas.'

I asked Henry Alfred Lien if he knew exactly when the mysterious death of Karl had taken place. He nodded and his face became even graver.

'I don't remember if my grandfather ever told me the exact date, but I do remember the year as clearly as if I had been told yesterday. The lad Karl met his mysterious end in the mountains in the summer of 1868. And that is a strange coincidence. I thought that perhaps this Falko had heard the story of Karl's death and that had somehow tipped him over the edge himself.'

I nodded pensively. My discovery at the cabin did not substantiate the notion of a suicide, but nor did it disprove it. And I had to admit that it certainly was a remarkable coincidence.

But I did not pursue it any further, and instead probed a bit more into my host's history with the NS.

Henry Alfred Lien sank a little into his chair again as soon this topic was raised. He hunched up his shoulders and replied that it was a phase in his life that he had hoped was now behind him. He had received an unexpectedly harsh sentence after the war, but had taken his punishment and had not had any contact with members of the NS since. Of the names I mentioned, he could only remember having met Frans Heidenberg briefly during the war.

We sat in silence after this. I did not have any more questions and he did not say more than he needed to. So I improvised and asked why he had ended up joining the NS in the first place.

The question seemed to open a tiny crack in his otherwise stony defence. Henry Alfred Lien took a minute to drink some more coffee before he answered. Then suddenly his voice rumbled on a fair distance.

'There are evidently a great many who say they can't explain why today. But I can. I have never been a Nazi for ideological reasons, or a man of ideology in any way really. In my youth, I flirted with the Liberal Party, but was not really politically active. In 1940, I believed it was set in stone that Germany would win the war and did what I could to ensure that my farm, community and country would suffer as little damage as possible. I entirely misjudged the situation and ended up as a NS section leader and spokesman, and could then not withdraw later without risking my life. In the last year of the war, I realized that we were hurtling towards an abyss and that it was too late to jump ship. I didn't dare jump before the war was over, for fear of the Germans – and only hours after they capitulated, the Home Front was at my door. Believe me or not, the choice is yours. But that is the truth.'

I believed him instantly. Rarely did the people I questioned so openly declare themselves to be opportunists and cowards, without those words being mentioned, to be fair.

We sat in silence again. It felt as though we had touched on something interesting and I tried to push a little more. I pointed to the photographs on the wall and asked if the children were doing well. This proved to be another bull's eye. Henry Alfred Lien sank even further into his chair before answering.

'My daughters are both doing well, though I don't see them as often as I would like to. But unfortunately I know very little about my son. Apparently he's a lawyer and politician for the Labour Party in Trondheim now, and is said to be doing very well. And I have two grandsons, twins, who are nearly old enough to be confirmed. But I've never met them and their grandfather from Valdres will certainly not be invited to their confirmation.'

We were definitely onto something now. The stony crevices of his face were shifting. He stopped talking, but I could see that he wanted to continue. He lit his pipe, his hand still steady, and sat smoking in silence. His gaze drifted out of the window towards the mountains on the horizon.

'The children, that's the saddest part of it all. Had I not had a family, I would never have joined the NS. I wanted to secure the children's future. I hoped that one day they would thank me for it. But it was quite the opposite. First of all, my choice created problems for them, and they never forgave me for that. It was hard enough to serve my sentence after the war, worried as I was about the family, but it was even worse to get out afterwards. For the first three years, my wife and I lived here together on the farm like strangers. We did the work together that we had to, exchanging only short messages where necessary. We slept in separate rooms and made our own food. When the children rang, it was to speak to her, and they hung up if I answered the telephone.'

Henry Alfred Lien stopped abruptly, but then continued after a short pause, when I nodded encouragingly.

'Then my wife fell ill in 1953. It was terribly sad, but in a strange way it also marked a transition to something better. We started to talk again and I was able to show how much I loved her in those final years. She finally forgave me some months before she died, and, as was her wish, so did our daughters. The three of us sat together at her funeral. Even though it will never be the same, they do come to visit me now. And they have started to call me father again.'

'Your son, on the other hand . . .'

He sighed and leaned his great arms on the table, which sagged slightly under their weight.

'It's hopeless. He sat on his own in the church at his mother's funeral and has never set foot here again since. His sisters were nearly grown up when the war started and left home as soon as it was over, so perhaps it was easier for them. But my son was only eleven when the war came, and was still a youth when it was over. It wasn't easy to be the son of a Nazi at high school in those days. And my son is like me: stubborn as an ox and slow to change. So I still hope for a miracle every time the telephone rings and every day when the postman comes, but I have stopped believing that he will forgive me.'

He suddenly pointed at the floor, his great, coarse hand trembling dangerously in the air.

'I remember in the autumn of 1940, before my son turned twelve, he stood in the middle of the room and screamed at me, Father, you can't do this to us or yourself. Hitler is a dictator, Nasjonal Samling are traitors and Germany will lose the war. What you are doing will only bring trouble. And he was right, of course.'

Henry Alfred Lien sat there and stared at the floor for a while, as though his son was still standing there. His eyes were fixed as his voice continued. The tractor was making very unsteady progress now.

'I have sent him letter after letter, begging for forgiveness, without ever getting an answer. He put the phone down every time I tried to call, even after his mother's death. Then one day in autumn 1960, I drove to Trondheim, found his house and waited at the gate with a present until he came home from work. But even then he did not want to talk to me. He said that Nazi scum would always be Nazi scum, no matter what age, and that he no longer believed a word I said. I stood there like a dog at the gate and stared at my son's closed door for over an hour. Then I drove all the way home again without having resolved anything. Every time I drove over a bridge I thought that it would perhaps be just as well if I drove off it. And since then the years have passed with no change, and I have no idea what might make him change his mind.'

Henry Alfred Lien's eyes turned reluctantly up from the floor. He looked me in the eye again when he carried on.

'So that is the story of the greatest mistake of my life. I'm not a Nazi, never have been, and every day I regret that I pretended that I was during the war. I did it for my son's sake and he will never forgive me. So I hope you can understand why I want to leave it all behind me now, and that under no circumstances do I ever want to be associated with the Nazis again. If my son saw any mention of that in the newspaper, all hope would be lost.'

I nodded with understanding. It was about half past one when I finally stood up to leave. It was a powerful story and I really wanted to believe that Henry Alfred Lien deeply repented his sins. And what was more, there was no stick of any sort to be seen. I did jot down, all the same, that he admitted that he had been in contact with other Nazis during the war. And that he did not have an alibi for the night when Falko Reinhardt disappeared, or the evening when Marie Morgenstierne was killed.


# VI


Miriam Filtvedt Bentsen was obviously an impressively fast reader. When I got back into the car, she suddenly had only fifty pages left to read of the thick book on nineteenth-century English literature. She continued to read these at the same time as having a rather interesting conversation with me while we drove back down the valley.

Then for the rest of the journey, we spoke uninterrupted. She reassured me that nothing I told her about the case would ever get out, but hastened to add that she fully understood if I was not able to tell her anything about it, as was probably the case.

Instead we talked about Valdres and hiking in the mountains, which proved to be a shared tradition in both our families. To my relief she only read book number two, on French grammar and linguistic theory, for about five minutes while I filled the tank at a petrol station outside Hønefoss.

Miriam Filtvedt Bentsen was easily persuaded to stop for a bite to eat at a cafeteria shortly after, once it had been established that we would only be half an hour and would still easily be able to reach the party office on time.

It was while we sat there in Hønefoss with our plates of meatballs that I suddenly thought of another question I could ask her – whether she could remember ever hearing, during any of her childhood trips to Valdres, the almost mythical story of the young lad, Karl, who had also vanished in the mountains up there.

Her reaction was so unexpected that I almost jumped. Miriam Filtvedt Bentsen pointed at me across the table in a manner that was almost accusing.

'Yes, in fact, I read it in a parish yearbook from Valdres when I was twelve. It's an incredible story. But where did you hear it? And does it have any bearing on Falko's disappearance?'

I told her honestly that I had no idea yet. But I had heard the story now and thought that the similarity was remarkable, especially given that it had apparently happened in 1868.

Miriam Filtvedt Bentsen nodded eagerly and pointed at me again, then leaned forward across the table.

'The year is one thing, certainly, but if I remember correctly, it was in fact on the night of 5 August 1868 that Karl vanished into thin air on his way down the mountain in Valdres. I may be wrong – after all, it is ten years since I read the article. But I am pretty sure it was, and could easily find the book and check again as soon as the libraries open on Monday. And if I'm right about the date, then it really is a remarkable coincidence, isn't it? How exciting!'

I felt my pulse rising, but was not quite sure whether this was due to the incredible coincidence of dates or the sudden outburst of the otherwise so calm Miriam. So I asked her to check the date at the library on Monday, and to contact me as soon as she had. I told her I agreed that if she had indeed remembered the date correctly, it was a very interesting and exciting find. She nodded eagerly again, an unexpected glow in her eyes.

So the mood in the car was very jolly once again for the last two hours as we headed into Oslo. I ventured to ask a bit more about the others who had been at the cabin. She took the hint and spoke only of them for the rest of the trip. However, there was not much new to be gleaned, compared with what she had told me before.

Kristine Larsen was an only child. Both her parents were teachers at Hegdehaugen, but we quickly established that I had not been taught by either of them in my final years.

Anders Pettersen was, in Miriam Filtvedt Bentsen's words, 'the prototype artist and communist. Quite possibly talented, but very definitely self-absorbed and ambitious.'

In Miriam Filtvedt Bentsen's opinion, Trond Ibsen was a far more gifted man, socially, even though he often pushed his psychological reasoning too far.

She had seen Anders Pettersen as Falko's loyal younger brother, whereas Trond Ibsen had a far more independent role. Anders Pettersen and Trond Ibsen generally shared the same political views, but there had been some rivalry between them since Falko's disappearance, as they vied for the role of leader. There was a degree of jealousy on Anders' part, as he could not compete with Trond when it came to family traditions and wealth. The legendary playwright, Henrik Ibsen, was a distant relative, and a number of well-known names from cultural and philosophical circles were in Trond's immediate family, including, for example, the famous communist and historian Johannes Heftye, who was an uncle on his mother's side.

She threw me a questioning glance when she said this, and I said that it could well be an important link. It crossed my mind that it was rather odd that neither Trond Ibsen nor Johannes Heftye had said anything about this to me. And that it was a blessing that Miriam Filtvedt was so open with me, and showed no apparent sign of any kind of sympathy for either of the men in the group.

When we drove past Grefsen, I said that I would quite possibly have to contact her again in the course of the investigation. It was fine by me if she wanted to tell her parents that she had been questioned by the police, but I asked her not to mention this trip or any of the details we had spoken about to anyone, not even those closest to her. I then waited with a pounding heart to see if she used the opportunity to mention a boyfriend – which, to my huge relief, she didn't. She smiled, remarked that it was important keep one's family life and private life separate, and assured me that she would keep everything that she had seen and heard today strictly to herself.

When I dropped her off outside the party office, I said that her company had been refreshing in the midst of the murder investigation. She replied that it had been 'extremely interesting' to follow a murder investigation for a few hours. I would have preferred it had she said 'extremely pleasant', but was happy enough with that for the moment. Especially when she added with a little smile that I was welcome to contact her again should I have any more questions that she might possibly help me with. Then we waved happily to each other through the car window.

My fascination with this calm and knowledgeable young lady was growing in the midst of this grisly business. As I drove back to what would no doubt be a far less engaging meeting with the powerful head of the police security service, I could unfortunately not think of any new questions to contact her about at the moment, but very much hoped that some would soon crop up.

# VII

It was with a degree of awe, as well as some dread, that I knocked on the door to Asle Bryne's office in Victoria Terrace at exactly six o'clock. I had never spoken to the revered head of police security before, but had heard his voice on the radio and seen his face in the papers. He had, whether it was justified or not, acquired a reputation for being alternately temperamental and uncommunicative.

My first impression was that he was relatively calm. His jet-black eyebrows were even bushier than I had imagined, and his face was unexpectedly controlled for the moment. He nodded briskly at a chair in front of his desk and when I held out my hand, gave it a firm, equally brisk shake. He had a pipe in the corner of his mouth and his eyes followed my every movement as I sat down.

I started by introducing myself and the case in brief. He nodded and replied curtly that he was of course familiar with it. I did not venture to ask him how. Instead I got straight to the point and asked if he could tell me about Marie Morgenstierne and the rest of the circle around Falko Reinhardt.

The head of the police security service was, as expected, well prepared. His answer was brief: that they would of course be happy to help with the murder investigation, but that the security service had to follow strict procedures when it came to divulging information. Then he said nothing more.

In answer to my initial question as to whether the police

security service had the group under surveillance, he answered, 'yes, of course.' When I asked if this was the case both before and after Falko Reinhardt had disappeared, he replied, 'yes, of course.'

Bryne exhaled some smoke from his pipe following these two succinct replies and paused for thought. Then he added, with a bit more vigour: 'The greatest threat to our country is still from the supporters of Moscow communism. The second greatest threat is probably the Peking communists. We would therefore clearly be neglecting our duty to our country and its people if we did not keep our eye on a group that was trying to worship both Moscow and Peking at the same time.'

When I asked whether the police security service had at any point received information from members of the group, Asle Bryne replied brusquely that he could under no circumstances comment on that. He added that the security service was dependent on getting information from a range of different sources, and that it could have disastrous consequences if these sources were identified and at risk of being made public.

I permitted myself to remind him that this was after all a murder inquiry and for the present would only involve one policeman and some confidential information.

No more was needed for Asle Bryne's temperament to make an appearance. He suddenly leaned forward in his chair and launched into a lengthy tirade about the security service's responsibilities, the essence of which was that they were the country's only hope in the fight against communist infiltration and Soviet occupation, and that they therefore needed room for manoeuvre without any interference from either politicians or the other police organs.

I waited until he started to calm down. Then I asked if they had found anything to indicate that this small group of students had contacts abroad, or constituted a threat to the status quo in Norway. This unleashed another almost equally violent eruption behind the cloud of smoke. The fact that they did not always uncover something in the short term should not fool anyone into relaxing their focus on potentially violent terrorist groups. Furthermore, it was better that ten innocent groups were kept under surveillance than that they did not watch the one group that might prove to be a real threat to society.

I took this as a 'no', and quickly carried on when he paused for breath a couple of minutes later. I told him that I fully understood that the security service could not reveal their contacts and that I could see why they had kept the group under surveillance – which could in fact be of great benefit to the investigation. I therefore would dearly like to know what the security service knew about Falko Reinhardt's disappearance and the murder of Marie Morgenstierne.

Asle Bryne took a couple of deep breaths, nodded – and made an attempt to answer my request. He assured me that as long as one respected the security service's situation and work methods, they would of course be more than happy to do what they could to help solve any crimes that were under investigation by other police divisions.

As far as the disappearance of Falko Reinhardt was concerned, however, the police security service knew nothing about it and had no information that might be of any help.

Again, when it came to the murder of Marie Morgenstierne, no one from the police security service had been in the vicinity. They had, however, successfully bugged the group's meeting place in Smestad, and could thus provide a recording of the last meeting that Marie Morgenstierne attended. The meeting had been short, and the security service had not picked up anything of interest from the recording. But if it could be of any help to the murder investigation, they would be able to lend it to the head of investigation for a day or two, in the strictest confidence, and on the condition that the tape was returned within forty-eight hours and that no reference was made to it in public.

He then made a great show of taking the tape out of the desk drawer and placing it on the table between us.

To humour him, I thanked him for his help and assured him that the conditions would be upheld. I then reached for the tape and pulled it over to my side. To my relief, he did not protest.

I casually added that the investigation had brought me into contact with old Nazi circles, and I asked if the security service was familiar with them. Bryne peered out at me from under his great bushy eyebrows, obviously taken aback, and shook his head almost before he had heard the names.

Another long tirade followed, about how he himself had fought against the Nazis during the war, and that 'now it is the Cold War that is important, my young man, and not the Second World War.'

These old Nazi circles only involved 'a bunch of random, bitter' individuals who hardly constituted a threat to anyone but themselves. The security service was of the definite opinion that the focus should now be on left-wing rather than right-wing extremists. In that sense, he added, both the government and the opposition were in agreement with the security service.

I made a blunder just before I stood up, when I remarked briefly that there was perhaps no reason to believe that military intelligence might know any more. Asle Bryne leaned even further forward across the desk and boomed that there was absolutely no reason to believe that military intelligence might know more than the security service about anything. In fact, military intelligence with its incompetent management was perhaps the second greatest threat to the security of the Norwegian people after communism. It was incomprehensible that neither the government nor the Storting had taken the matter in hand and transferred all surveillance to the police security service.

Asle Bryne was struggling to control himself, and I realized that a far more serious outburst was now imminent. I was genuinely concerned that he might have a heart attack in front of my very eyes. When he eventually stopped for breath again, I gave a disarming shrug and assured him that I was extremely happy with the help the police security service had given so far and did not really think that military intelligence would know any more about the matter. He sat in silence after this, and we then shook hands briefly before I left.

I suspected that the security service knew more than they were willing to tell me. But I was curious to see what the recording from Marie Morgenstierne's last meeting might reveal, and relieved to be able to take it with me when I left the room.

# VIII

Patricia listened intently to my report of the Valdres trip and my meeting with the head of the police security service. When I finished by telling her about the tape, she nodded with cautious appreciation and pointed at the stereo player. I personally was very keen to know what might be on the tape, so quickly put it on.

The recording lasted no more than half an hour. It was very odd to hear the late Marie Morgenstierne's voice in amongst the other three now-familiar voices. In the short sequences where she spoke, her voice was quiet and soft, but firm and clear at the same time. It also sounded young and vital. I identified the various voices for Patricia the first time they spoke, then we listened to the rest of the tape in silence.

*Anders: Well, it's time then to start our first meeting after the holidays. We will discuss our planned demonstration against the imperialistic war in Vietnam and other plans for the autumn. But first, do any of you comrades have any other points you would like to raise?*

*Kristine: No other points. But we should perhaps start by marking the second anniversary of Falko's puzzling disappearance, and renew our hope that he will soon come back.*

*[Applause]*

*Anders: Unanimously agreed. We hope and believe that our comrade has not fallen victim to some plot by imperialists, capitalists or class traitors, that he is alive, and that he will soon return to continue his work in the fight to liberate his country's oppressed people. Does anyone have anything else to say on the matter?*

*Trond: In cases like this it is often the person who is closest who is the first to notice a change. There are many examples, even among non-religious groups, where the person who was left behind felt something before the missing person returned. So it would be particularly interesting to know what you, comrade Marie, think about the situation?*

*Marie: I still hope, but no longer know if I dare believe. Falko has been gone for so long now and there has been no sign of any change. So, like you, I can only hope that he will suddenly reappear one day and take up his role again in the class struggle.*

*Anders: We all share that hope, and once again express our sympathy to you, as you have suffered the greatest loss in his absence. And now we must move on to discuss our planned demonstration and prepare our activities as best we can without Falko. To begin with, we need to plan our participation in the big anti-Vietnam rally on the last Saturday in August. I hope that everyone is able to take part?*

*Kristine: Yes, of course.*

*Trond:* Yes, I have taken time off from work on Friday afternoon and Saturday morning.

*Marie:* Yes, I'll be there.

*Anders:* Excellent. We will announce it through the normal channels and hope for strong support from the anti-Vietnam movement and others on the far left. It has not yet been decided whether to demonstrate outside the American Embassy, the Ministry of Foreign Affairs or the Storting. I personally think we should take imperialism by the horns and demonstrate outside the American Embassy.

*Trond:* I agree with you in principle, but I think that psychologically the Storting is better. A mass mobilization there would put pressure on the politicians who are warming to the idea of demanding a change in the Vietnam policy. A good many Labour Party politicians are pushing in that direction and pressure on the government is mounting. No one in the American Embassy is up for election, and no one there is sympathetic to our calls.

*Kristine:* I see advantages in both, but Falko always said that the American Embassy was the root of all evil in both the Ministry of Foreign Affairs and the Storting. So I think that the first demonstration after the second anniversary of his disappearance should be there.

*Marie:* I support Anders.

*Trond:* Then I accept. Should we send invitations to the Labour Party and SPP youth leagues, or just to the Vietnam Committee and other contacts left of SPP? Don't get me wrong, I am sceptical of any flirtations with the Labour Party, and even more sceptical of any pandering to the SPP. But I do think we should send invitations to both as I think that would make the situation harder for them both, tactically.

*Anders:* Well-meaning members of the Labour Party and SPP

are welcome to join us, but we will not invite them. It's important to show the Americans how strong the far-left radicals in Norway really are. Clear slogans and committed participation are more important than numbers here.

Marie: I agree with that.

Kristine: I also agree. Reminds me of what Falko used to say: that few can become many if they are just patient and stand united.

Trond: Well, I will back down then. It is easy to compromise on the choice of method as long as the goal is fixed. And what about our other plans for the autumn? I have to look after my practice and my duty to my patients, who have all suffered in some way under the heavy yoke of capitalism. But I have a flexible timetable and will keep patient numbers at a level that allows time for meetings and agitation.

Anders: I have cleared my timetable and work schedule for a very activist autumn. A few daytime lectures are obligatory, but I'll get a sick note if the good cause so requires.

Kristine: Same here, a few obligatory lectures that I can skip if necessary. But it would be good if I knew about important activities a few weeks in advance.

Marie: Concurred. I don't quite know what's happening with my course this winter yet, but I have to get on with my masters. What-ever the case, it shouldn't be a problem for the first part of the autumn, and I'll be there for whatever we decide to take part in.

Trond: Excellent. Then our conscience is still clear, in terms of both Falko and society's repressed masses.

Anders: Agreed. We should also note the good news from China, where new advances in Mao's Cultural Revolution have been reported. The progress continues, and in sharp contrast to the situation in the USA, it is of benefit to the entire population.

*A united nation celebrates in the streets in Mao's China, whereas there are more and more demonstrations against the war in Richard Nixon's USA. There is no doubt which country and which ideology is on the offensive. We still have the present against us here in Norway, but the future is behind us. In just the same way that the heroes of the Resistance are now honoured for their stand against Hitler's Nazism in the Second World War, we and other likeminded people will be honoured in the next century by future generations in a new and fairer Norway. The great awakening will reach the sleeping masses in our country within the next few years.*

*[Applause]*

*Marie: Thank you for your uplifting words. When shall we meet again to continue our struggle?*

*Trond: What about the Tuesday before the anti-Vietnam demonstration? There may be a need for more preparations by then, and it's free in my diary at the moment.*

*Anders: Suits me very well. I can, if everyone is happy, volunteer to open with a few minutes on communism's development in China and neighbouring countries. There is exciting news that communism is now advancing fast in Cambodia under the charismatic leadership of the young general secretary Pol Pot, and it would seem that the USA's lackeys there are on the verge of collapse.*

*Marie: That sounds like a very interesting theme. And Tuesday is good for me too.*

*Kristine: And for me. So let's close then by reiterating our hope that Falko will be back by then to take his seat and place at the rally outside the American Embassy.*

*[Applause]*

*Trond: So that concludes the meeting. I've got my new car outside. Does anyone need a lift somewhere?*

*Anders: No thanks, I am becoming more and more environmentally aware and prefer to cycle.*

*Kristine: I'll be home by the time you've got in the car, but thank you.*

*Marie: And I'm on the train, as usual.*

*Trond: Have you got enough time before the next train? Otherwise, I'm happy to give you a lift.*

*Marie: There's plenty of time. Thank you for a good meeting and see you soon. No doubt we'll have a lot to talk about this autumn.*

It was a poignant conclusion to the meeting and the recording, to hear Marie Morgenstierne say that she looked forward to seeing more of the others during the autumn. Her voice was just as calm and even as it had been at the start of the meeting.

But a few minutes later, I had seen her running for her life in sheer panic. As I stopped the tape, I wondered more than ever what had happened on the way from the meeting to the station. Patricia had now finished her main course, and was staring at me across the table with an expression that was unusually sharp and concentrated.

# IX

'Well, did you get anything out of that?'

Patricia nodded and rubbed her hands.

'Yes, absolutely. Lots of interesting things. What did you think was most important?'

This question put me in an awkward position, as I had not immediately recognized that the tape contained anything important to the murder investigation. There was nothing in the recording to indicate that there was any conflict between Marie Morgenstierne and the others, or that her life was in danger. So I mumbled that the ending was quite interesting, but it gave no reason to believe that she had any idea of the danger that waited outside. If that had been the case, she would obviously have accepted the offer of a lift to the station. It was strange to think now how different the story might have been, had she accepted.

Patricia nodded impatiently.

'But it was hardly accidental, and it is also odd that Marie Morgenstierne lied about having plenty of time to catch the train. And then proceeded to walk slowly, even though she should really have got a move on if she was going to catch it. It is clear that she did not want to go with Trond Ibsen – without us yet being able to say anything as to why. Otherwise, the others in the group appear to have given a pretty truthful account of the meeting. And even though there does not appear to be any open conflict, one can detect an obvious tension between Anders Pettersen's principled, sectarian line and Trond Ibsen's more pragmatic approach. Marie Morgenstierne consistently supports Anders and goes against Trond, as does Kristine Larsen. So there may be some opposition, even suspicion, levelled at Trond Ibsen. But there are many other interesting things here as well. There is something that Kristine Larsen does that Marie Morgenstierne does not, even though they always seem to concur.'

I thought furiously, but looked at Patricia in desperation. She let out a heavy sigh.

'Dear detective inspector . . . it is perfectly possible to hear that right from the start it is Kristine who constantly talks about Falko, and expresses her hope and belief that he will come back. Given that Marie is Falko's fiancée, she is remarkably defensive and almost sceptical.'

We were interrupted by the maid, who cautiously knocked on the door and popped her head round to ask if we wanted dessert. Patricia replied 'yes, please', but drummed her fingers so impatiently on the table that the maid served our apple cake and ice cream in great haste before almost running out of the room with the dinner plates.

Patricia mumbled something about the maid moving slower and slower while time was passing faster and faster. When the door had closed, she immediately turned back to the case.

'It could of course be a psychological mechanism, in which case Trond Ibsen would no doubt be able to tell us more. But based on what we have just heard, it is reasonable to believe that Kristine Larsen's desire for Falko to come back was stronger than Marie Morgenstierne's.'

I had now had the time I needed to link the two things together, and nodded in agreement. 'And that would tie in very well with what Miriam Filtvedt Bentsen told me earlier today.'

Patricia's acknowledgement was serious.

'Yes, young Miriam Filtvedt Bentsen was already sharing gossip about a friend with the police before she claimed to have qualms about sharing gossip about friends with the police. But what she said was reasonable enough and certainly fits. Falko Reinhardt clearly had unlimited confidence in his own magnificence and was enjoying himself with Kristine Larsen only hours before his planned disappearance. She was obviously in love with him. And the recording from the meeting reinforces the idea that she still is. Thus here there are signs of a possible conflict between the two. Given the picture that is emerging, I think you should confront Kristine Larsen with this as soon as possible, and see if she wants to change her statement.'

I gave a quick nod.

'So it seems increasingly likely that my guess is correct – that the woman behind Marie Morgenstierne who called out to her was Kristine Larsen?'

Patricia shook her head, looking pensive and rather disapproving.

'Yes, that would seem to be a reasonable assumption. But: one, we still do not know for sure. And two, even if Kristine Larsen was the woman behind Marie Morgenstierne on the road to Smestad station, that does not prove in any way that it was she who shot Marie Morgenstierne. And there is nothing here to rule out that any of the others is the murderer. Trond Ibsen could easy have driven around in his car and been waiting on one of the side roads. Anders Pettersen could have done the same on his bike. Miriam Filtvedt Bentsen, who clearly knew about Falko's infidelity, could, for all we know, have been anywhere around there. And the same is true of Falko himself.'

Patricia continued.

'Now that we can confirm that Falko's disappearance from the cabin was voluntary and well planned, there is much to indicate that he is still out there somewhere. But unfortunately I lack the information to say any more.'

I voiced my understanding and concluded that my next visit should be to Kristine Larsen.

Patricia nodded, as she pointed at the stereo player.

'By all means, but the security police question should also be followed up. I do not trust them at all, and I am curious as to how they got such a good recording from the meeting so fast. I have a theory about how it might all link up. But there is a danger that Asle Bryne will not answer if you ask how he got the tape.'

I could only too well imagine that Asle Bryne would not answer that, and said so.

Patricia let out a heavy sigh.

'My theory is therefore far too weak to be used as the basis for any confrontation. So we will have to test the security police procedures and send the tape to be finger-printed. And otherwise hope that new information will crop up that can help to explain this side of the case.'

I looked at Patricia. Her eyes met mine without turning away – or blinking.

'I do not leave any stone unturned in the hunt for a mur-derer. And you should not either. I think that one of the four who were at the meeting made the recording at some point. And I would dearly like to know which one of them it was. It could be of crucial importance to the motives in this case.'

I concurred, and promised to have the tape checked.

Then, in conclusion, I asked about the strange story from Valdres. Patricia grew pensive and sighed again.

'Let's wait and see what young Miriam Filtvedt Bentsen finds out about the date. But if she is right, it is too incredible to be a coincidence. Henry Alfred Lien also said several very interesting things that are starting to make me think there is a link with Falko Reinhardt's disappearance. But I can't be sure yet, and any connection to the murder of Marie Morgenstierne is still unclear. Send the tape to be checked for fingerprints, and in the meantime, pay Kristine Larsen another visit; and then talk, if necessary, to the rest of the group. Contact me immediately when you have anything new to tell, whether late this evening or early tomorrow morning. I will in the meantime ruminate on both things and any possible connections between the two.'

I noted with some surprise that Patricia was happy to talk about possible links between Falko Reinhardt's disappearance and the murder of his fiancée. Then I retired in order to continue the investigation.

# X

I made a pit stop at the police station and sent the tape off for a forensic check. I reminded the laboratory of the strict confidentiality clause and that they should report directly to me. There was fortunately no kind of marking on the tape that might link it to the police security service.

It was half past eight by the time I got back into the car. But I was increasingly keen to get on with the case, so having started in the direction of Hegdehaugen, I then turned off and headed towards Smestad.

The theory that the relationship between Marie Morgenstierne and Kristine Larsen was tainted by jealousy was of increasing interest, especially now that there was more to indicate that Falko was still alive. It was not hard to imagine that Kristine Larsen might have been behind both the written threat and the murder, particularly if she had been the woman following behind Marie Morgenstierne. Whatever the case, I wanted to hear what possible explanation Kristine Larsen would give of her relationship with Falko Reinhardt as soon as possible.

I arrived at Smestad at just the right moment, at five to nine. There was no response when I rang on Kristine Larsen's doorbell. But when I turned my head I saw her on the other side of the road, apparently ambling along.

'Kristine!' I called over to her.

I immediately thought that I should perhaps not have shouted. But her reaction made me forget everything else.

Kristine Larsen froze.

For a brief moment she stood like a statue on the pavement.

Then she turned on her heel and ran off in the opposite direction, at ridiculous speed. It crossed my mind that she was running in the same direction that Marie Morgenstierne had run. She was running towards the station.

I also stood paralysed for a few seconds before I pulled myself together and started to run after her. To my surprise I did not seem to be able to catch up at first. Kristine Larsen had a good start on me, and her long legs carried her remarkably fast.

Kristine Larsen did not look back once. She just ran and ran and ran. She hurtled down the road at terrific speed, without even slowing down when she reached the crossroads. Fortunately the drivers were able to stop in time and stayed there, astounded, until I was well clear myself.

It was only when I was halfway over the crossing that I realized that Kristine Larsen was now running in blind panic.

For the rest of the chase, I did not doubt for a moment that I was pursuing a murderer. The prospect of solving the case and my hunting instinct helped me to pick up pace. And even though I was now close to my limit, I still had not closed the distance before reaching the crossroads. But then a couple of hundred yards later, Kristine Larsen seemed suddenly to collapse. At the next crossroad, she was barely across before I charged out onto the road. A few seconds later I was close enough to get my arms round her.

At which point she screamed.

A terrible, piercing female scream, so full of anguish and pain that it hurt my ears. She was shaking uncontrollably, and still struggling. I locked my arms hard around her and eventually managed to stop her, thanks to my greater body weight.

I spun her round to face me and got another shock. The face of the running woman was just as I remembered the face of the woman on the Lijord Line: distorted and rigid with fear. Only this woman's face was even closer to mine, and there was no window between us.

'Oh . . . is it *you*?' Kristine Larsen whispered, her voice cracking.

Then she fainted in my arms.

# XI

It was a strange Saturday night. The clock on the wall behind me struck half past ten. I was sitting alone with Kristine Larsen in an interview room at the police station. When she had come to after fainting, she agreed to give a statement without a lawyer present.

She had asked for permission to smoke, and this had been granted.

Then she had admitted that she had been Falko Reinhardt's lover in the weeks before he disappeared, and still hoped that he would choose her should he return. As she could not talk to anyone, it had been hard for her to live with the pain of Falko's disappearance and the nagging of her conscience with regard to his fiancée. Kristine Larsen's guilt had, however, gradually given way to a growing jealousy, and a suspicion that Marie Morgenstierne might have had something to do with Falko's disappearance.

So, driven by loneliness and despair, she had in the end sent Marie Morgenstierne the threatening letter, in the hope that it would in some way resolve the situation. Which it had not. On the evening in question, she had started to walk towards her flat after the meeting, but had then turned around and tried to catch up with Marie Morgenstierne so she could talk to her face to face. And she had shouted 'Marie!' spontaneously in surprise when Marie Morgenstierne bolted.

The chain-smoking Kristine Larsen had, in short, managed to confess an impressive amount in the course of the fifteen-minute interview.

The problem was not only that she denied, in horror, any knowledge of Falko Reinhardt's whereabouts, but also denied, even more horrified, any knowledge of how Marie Morgenstierne had died.

According to her statement, Kristine Larsen had stopped running and watched Marie Morgenstierne disappear in wild flight. Furthermore, Kristine Larsen did not have any weapons on her at the time, and had never owned a gun. She had no idea who the murderer was, but had lived in fear of him or her since she heard that Marie Morgenstierne had been killed.

So when she heard someone shout her name, she thought that the murderer had come to shoot her and had therefore run for her life without looking back. If she had known it was me, she would have stopped straight away. She repeated this three times within a minute.

Kristine Larsen smoked and cried until ten to eleven. She looked as though she was on the verge of a nervous and physical breakdown. But she stuck to her statement with forceful despair and declared her innocence with open arms.

After five unsuccessful attempts, I realized that I was not going to get any further and so instead asked her to describe in detail what had happened when Marie Morgenstierne started to run.

Kristine Larsen told me that there was an old man with a stick walking in front of her and that he stepped to one side to let her pass. There had been a blind woman with a guide dog behind her, and a man farther back behind the blind woman, but she only caught a glimpse of him.

She had spontaneously shouted 'Marie' when she saw her take off. Marie had first glanced back and then looked all around. Kristine Larsen had assumed that it was the sight of her that made Marie Morgenstierne bolt.

'But then, as I shouted, I also looked around. And that was when I saw something that made me stop in my tracks.'

I gave her a sharp look. She lit another cigarette with shaking hands and took a deep drag.

'That was when I saw him. He was standing there by the corner of a house on one of the side roads, looking at us.'

She said nothing more, and looked at me with an odd mixture of confusion and joy in her eyes.

'And the man who was standing there was . . . ?'

She nodded gravely. Then she whispered the name I had guessed before she said it, and which made the room spin.

'Falko.'

I stared hard at Kristine Larsen. Her eyes were wet with tears, but she did not look away for a moment.

'He was just as tall, just as dark and just as irresistibly handsome as when I last saw him. I would have recognized him anywhere in the world. He stood by the corner of the house for a few moments without moving, then disappeared from sight again between the houses. I don't know whether he was waiting for Marie or me. And I don't know if she saw him. But I did. It was my Falko standing there in the road – I am as sure about that as I am that I'm sitting here on this chair.'

At first I did not really know what to say to this highly unexpected turn of events. So I kept quiet for a few seconds. Behind me, I heard the clock on the wall strike eleven. And then I heard myself say to Kristine Larsen that she was under arrest and would be held on remand, on suspicion of murdering Marie Morgenstierne.

# XII

It was by now half past eleven. I sat on my own in my office and thought about the situation.

Kristine Larsen had accepted being taken into custody with unexpected dignity, saying that at least in prison she no longer need fear the faceless murderer as she had every second since the news of Marie Morgenstierne's death. But she continued to maintain that she was innocent, and that the murderer was still out there somewhere.

She begged me in earnest to continue with the investigation. And with even more urgency, she asked that Falko Reinhardt be informed of where she was, if he was found. She had to see him as soon as he turned up. He would no doubt then be able to corroborate her version of what had happened the evening that Marie Morgenstierne died.

At twenty-five past eleven, I rang Patricia. She picked up the telephone on the second ring. It sounded as though she was stifling a yawn, but she soon perked up when I started by saying: 'Following some dramatic developments this evening I have now arrested the person I believe to be Marie Morgenstierne's murderer!'

I waited for some sign of delight, but it never came.

'Gracious, do tell!' Patricia said, instead.

Then she listened silently to my brief account of my meeting with Kristine Larsen and her ensuing statement.

'Very interesting indeed. But who have you arrested as a result?' she asked, when I had finished.

'Kristine Larsen, of course,' I replied.

There was not a sound to be heard on the line for a moment or two. Not a sound.

'Oh, for goodness' sake, what have you done now?' Patricia exclaimed in disbelief.

Something, I realized, was terribly wrong. But the indications that Kristine Larsen was guilty were so clear to me that I was not going to give up without a fight.

'The case is of course not solved yet, in terms of all the details. But even so, you cannot deny that Kristine Larsen had both the motive and the opportunity to shoot Marie Morgenstierne.'

This gave about two seconds' respite. Then Patricia's voice slammed back into my ear like the recoil from a gun.

'Absolutely. Kristine Larsen could have shot Marie Morgenstierne. But why on earth would the sight of Kristine Larsen have caused Marie Morgenstierne suddenly to panic and run for her life? Have you thought about that?'

I had not given that side of the matter any thought at all. And now that I was forced to think about it, I found no good answer.

The memory of the terrified Marie Morgenstierne hammering on the train doors in desperation popped up in my mind. Kristine Larsen's harmless appearance could not possibly have made Marie Morgenstierne run for her life. Particularly not when she had in fact left the meeting with Kristine Larsen, had turned down the offer of a lift, and then walked slowly and calmly towards the station.

Either something inexplicable had happened in the meantime that alerted Marie Morgenstierne to the fact that Kristine Larsen was now going to shoot her – or it was, quite simply, not Kristine Larsen from whom Marie Morgenstierne was fleeing.

The floor was heaving beneath my feet when I asked Patricia if she had any plans for Sunday. She replied that she had no plans that could not be changed, and that I was very welcome to come for lunch around midday if that suited. Then she added that I should bring with me any fingerprints that had been found, and anything else of interest that I might discover in the meantime.

I promised to do so. Then I put down the receiver and sank back into my chair.

Kristine Larsen remained on remand. There were still reasonable grounds to suspect her, but it was with a heavy heart that I went out into the dark just before midnight.

I kept my eyes peeled as I walked the short distance to my car – and thus realized that I obviously still assumed that the person who had shot Marie Morgenstierne three days ago was out there somewhere, in the dark. And that I still had no idea who it was.

I continued to ponder who it was who had shot Marie

Morgenstierne as I drove home and got ready for bed, and until I eventually fell asleep. In the minutes immediately before I slept, I was able to relax a little when I recalled Miriam Filtvedt Bentsen's calm face and mischievous smile. But after all the evening's drama, it was still Kristine Larsen's terrified eyes that stared at me and followed me into my dreams.

## DAY FIVE

# A running man and a torn photograph

## I

Sunday, 9 August 1970 was certainly not one of the quiet-est Sundays of my life. The dramatic events of the previous day continued to rattle around my head as I slept. I was out of bed before eight, and in the office by a quarter to nine.

My long run in pursuit of Kristine Larsen at Smestad the evening before had been, not unexpectedly, registered and reported. Three newspapers and nine private individuals from Smestad had already called the switchboard at the main police station to ask if it was true that a young woman from Smestad had been arrested in the case.

I, for my part, had already started to regret my action, and wanted it to receive as little attention as possible. So I issued instructions to say that a person had been taken in for questioning the evening before, but that no formal charge had as yet been made and that it was not possible to give any more details in light of the ongoing investigation.

The arrestee proved to be remarkably calm and com-posed despite a restless night's sleep. Kristine Larsen had nothing to add or withdraw from the statement she had given the night before. In her dreams she had three times fled from the faceless murderer, she told me. She still insisted that she had done nothing wrong. But given how unsafe life now felt outside the prison walls, she would be quite happy to stay here for a few days more.

With an apologetic smile, she repeated her hope that I would soon find out who had murdered Marie Morgenstierne and that I would tell Falko of her whereabouts as soon as I found him. I promised to do this. The conversation ended on almost a friendly note. When I said that it might be necessary to do a house search, she pointed out the front door key on her confiscated key ring without hesitation. Kristine Larsen did not want a lawyer, but did ask if she could telephone her mother to explain the situation. Her parents would no doubt be worried if they had heard about her panicked reaction yesterday, she remarked, especially if they been unable to get hold of her today.

As she sat there in front of me, it struck me that Kristine Larsen was a very considerate and unthreatening person. But I still felt far from sure that she was not the murderer. I recalled her much harder voice in the recording from Marie Morgenstierne's last meeting, and the incredible will and energy she had demonstrated in her flight the day before. The motive was obvious, and the fact that she had sent a written threat to the victim still remained.

Following a brief summary of developments over the telephone, my boss agreed that there were still reasonable grounds for suspicion and remand, but that we should perhaps wait to issue a charge. He would talk to the public prosecutor's office straight away. We no doubt thought the same thing as we put down the receiver. In other words, that holding a young woman on remand, whether she was guilty or not, would increase the pressure to solve the case.

# II

Kristine Larsen had for one reason or another tidied her living room since my first visit. Her flat in Smestad reminded me of the late Marie Morgenstierne's flat. This was also the home of a neat young woman who lived alone, and who lived a relatively well-regulated life and seldom had parties or overnight guests of any sort. The bed was made and the draining board was clear. The flat was smaller than Marie Morgenstierne's flat, as were the bookshelves. A faint smell of smoke clung to the walls, which had not been evident in Marie Morgenstierne's home. But otherwise, it occurred to me that in terms of their homes, Falko Reinhardt's two women were almost interchangeable.

The only evidence of Falko himself was one single, rather unremarkable photograph of the group under an anti-Vietnam slogan. And the only other things on the walls were a black and white picture of an older couple who I presumed were Kristine Larsen's parents, and a new colour photograph of a woman with a small child. Given the similarity in the shape of the face and stature, I guessed it must be her sister.

I only found one thing of possible interest to the

investigation in Kristine Larsen's home. But then, it was of considerable interest.

Under a pile of underwear on a shelf in the wardrobe was a brown envelope with two photographs in it. One was a picture of Kristine Larsen and Falko Reinhardt in light summer clothes, possibly taken with a self-timer at a cafe somewhere. She had her hand affectionately on his shoulder. She was looking at him adoringly and he was looking straight at the camera, full of confidence. But his hand was visible around her bare waist.

This picture confirmed what Miriam Filtvedt Bentsen and Kristine Larsen had told me: in other words, that Falko Reinhardt had embarked on a relationship with Kristine Larsen, who was now being held on remand. Her situation was no worse and no better as a result.

However, the other picture that I found hidden in her wardrobe made Kristine Larsen's position far more vulnerable. It had obviously also been taken with a self-timer, but this time all the Falkoists were in the picture. It had clearly been taken on the trip to Valdres when Falko disappeared. The furniture in the Morgenstiernes' cabin was easily recognizable.

I registered with slight relief that Miriam Filtvedt Bentsen was sitting on her own in a chair to the far right of the picture. Typically enough, Anders Pettersen was leaning forward over the table whereas Trond Ibsen was leaning back in his chair on the left-hand side. And even more typically, Falko was sitting in the middle of the sofa, between Marie Morgenstierne and Kristine Larsen. There was no physical contact between any of them. Kristine Larsen was sitting close to Falko, but looked calm and collected. So far, so good.

Kristine Larsen's problem was, however, that an attempt had been made to eradicate Marie Morgenstierne from the picture with the aggressive use of a black felt pen.

I took both photographs with me when I locked the door and left Kristine Larsen's flat. It looked very empty and lonely without her. But my belief that it would be some time before she returned had been reinforced by the discovery of the photograph.

# III

Once I was back in the office I decided to telephone Falko Reinhardt's supervisor, who, according to Miriam Filtvedt Bentsen, was also Trond Ibsen's uncle. I took a gamble that Professor Johannes Heftye was not a regular churchgoer, and this proved to be true. He answered the telephone on the second ring, and without any hesitation said that he would be happy to answer a couple of quick questions in connection with the investigation.

There were a few moments of silence when I cut straight to the chase and asked if it was correct that he was Trond Ibsen's uncle, and if so, whether they had at any point discussed Falko Reinhardt's thesis.

The professor firstly confirmed that he was Trond Ibsen's uncle. Then there were a few more moments of silence, before he confirmed that he had 'once, and only for a few moments' discussed Falko Reinhardt's thesis with his nephew.

No names or other details from the research were discussed and he hastened to add that he could guarantee that the conversation was of no importance whatsoever to the investigation. The two had met at a 'purely family do' and had talked about mutual acquaintances, including Falko Reinhardt. Professor Heftye had taken it as given that Trond, who was in almost daily contact with Falko and shared his political vision, was familiar with the thesis. However, this proved not to be the case. Trond Ibsen had looked very bewildered when his uncle said that it would be interesting to see if there was anything to the theory that the old Nazi network from the war was still active.

Professor Heftye could only apologize for this 'small indiscretion', but added that he 'had immediately closed the conversation'.

I told him honestly that it was very unfortunate all the same, in the light of later developments.

I could practically hear the professor squirming on the line as he assured me that it could not possibly have anything to do with the case, as his nephew was far too intelligent to get involved with anything criminal or to pass on something that should not be passed on. He hoped that it would not be necessary for the institute to hear about it, as he had some powerful and reactionary enemies from the Labour Party there who would be sure to use it against him.

I replied that there was certainly no reason to inform

the university at the moment, but that the professor had to lay his cards on the table immediately if there was anything else he had forgotten to tell me.

He assured me that there was nothing more and that he had not tried to hide anything from me on purpose. He had deemed it a minor indiscretion that was of no particular relevance, and so had not wanted to waste my time by mentioning it.

Finally, I asked if the professor could remember the date on which this brief but rather unfortunate conversation with his nephew had taken place. He was quiet for a moment before he replied that it must have been in connection with his sixty-fifth birthday, on 28 July 1968.

I pointed out to him that it was then only a week before Falko Reinhardt disappeared. He sighed and said tersely that he realized this, and was extremely sorry. We both hung up at the same time without saying goodbye. And just then, there was a knock at the door.

# IV

Outside my door stood a constable, who said that a man had asked to speak to me immediately. This proved to be Trond Ibsen, who had once again turned up without being asked. I waved the constable off straight away and showed Ibsen into my office. Behind his placid exterior, I caught an inkling of the fervour I remembered from the end of our first meeting. His voice was controlled, but he started to speak before he even sat down.

'An acquaintance of a friend called to say that a young woman from Smestad has been arrested in connection with the murder case. It can only be Kristine Larsen. And in that case I felt it was my duty to drive here immediately to point out there must have been a terrible mistake, which can only damage the police investigation in the long run.'

I looked at him and waited. He took a deep breath and continued, at an even faster pace, 'Anyone with a basic knowledge of psychology would tell you that Kristine Larsen is about the least likely murderer you could find on the streets of Oslo. She is a vegetarian, a pacifist and opposed to any form of violence. We voted against her to kill an unusually irritating wasp on the windowsill in the cabin on the day that Falko disappeared. It is absolutely unthinkable that Kristine would have anything to do with Falko's disappearance or Marie's death. A court case against her would only end with her walking free, and would constitute a further blow to police credibility and a weakening of public trust.'

Having said this, he blanched a little. I humoured him, pretended to take notes, and assured him that this information would be taken into consideration before any decision was made regarding charges. I asked then if he knew if there had ever been any romantic liaisons in the group other than the well-known relationship between Falko and Marie.

At first, Trond Ibsen shook his head emphatically, and then looked very serious and pensive. I asked him to tell me what he was thinking. He hesitated, but then launched forth when I started to look increasingly agitated.

'On my oath, I don't know whether there have been any other romantic liaisons. Certainly not as far as I am concerned, and I think you can forget Miriam Filtvedt Bentsen in that context . . .'

He fell silent again and glanced around the room, as if he were looking for an emergency exit.

'But . . .' I prompted.

He nodded, and his response was then fast and intense.

'*But*, now that you ask, it is easy to see that the apparently confident Anders suffers from a little brother complex. To an extent in relation to me, but mostly in relation to Falko, of course. Anders is the youngest in his family, he struggles financially, he did not get top marks at university and has only had modest success as an artist. He has without much joy tried to take over Falko's role as leader in the group. The idea that he might also try to take over Falko's fiancée in his attempt to achieve this has crossed my mind. I thought that Anders, who otherwise does not have much empathy, showed her a surprising amount of sympathy for a while. But I cannot imagine that it got him anywhere. He was three years below Falko, and she has immense self-control and comes from a better background, and is no doubt very particular about who she lets into bed. It would of course have been very controversial within the group, especially so long as Falko's fate remained unknown. But for Anders it would certainly be the ultimate self-assertion, in terms of how he saw himself and how others saw him.'

I nodded and this time really did take notes.

'But nothing in terms of Kristine, at any point?'

Trond Ibsen thought for a moment, but then shook his head again.

'I have never seen Kristine with a boyfriend, or heard her say that she had one. It's rather odd, really, as she is such a beautiful and kind girl. But she has dedicated herself to our cause and her studies. And as I have discovered myself, that doesn't leave much time to find someone and have a relationship. Of course, Kristine admired Falko more than anything in the world, as we all did, but he was taken and I don't think she was open to anyone else. At one point, I wondered if Anders might not be interested in her, but that was long before Falko disappeared, and I reckon he was given the cold shoulder.'

He laughed a little. I noted that there was clearly a rivalry between the two remaining men in the group. I swiftly changed the subject by remarking that he had not told me that Johannes Heftye was his uncle, or that he had spoken to him about developments in Falko's thesis.

Trond Ibsen was definitely an intelligent and balanced man. He looked suitably confused for a moment, but then nodded and continued.

'You mean on his sixty-fifth birthday? Yes, my uncle and I did have a brief conversation about it. Falko had been very secretive and evasive about his work for a few months, so naturally I was curious. I had thought of asking Falko face to face when no one else was around, but never found the opportunity before he disappeared.'

'And you can rule out that it had anything to do with his disappearance?'

Trond Ibsen furrowed his brow and looked at me.

189

'It is of course not possible to rule out completely that developments in Falko's thesis had anything to do with his disappearance. But I would guess the opposite to be true. And the fact that I knew about these developments definitely had nothing to do with it. I had nothing to do with his disappearance whatsoever, and did not tell anyone about the thesis in the meantime.'

I did not have any more questions, and Trond Ibsen did not have any more answers to the ones I had already asked. We sat and looked at each other in charged silence.

He asked with a wisp of worry in his voice whether he was suspected of having done something criminal. I chose to answer 'not at present', but asked him to remain available for possible further questioning. He nodded, and enquired if there was anything more I would like to ask. When I said no, he stood up and rapidly left the office.

I now had a greater understanding of how the case was gnawing at the remaining members of the group, now that one was dead, one was missing and one was in custody. But I still did not feel that I could trust any of them.

Just after half past eleven, the telephone on my desk rang. The call was from a rather flustered technician who felt it was his duty to tell me about a finding that was potentially of great interest. The cassette had been wiped, but not very well. On the edge of the tape was an incomplete, but still recognizable, fingerprint. It belonged to one of the five members of the group around Falko, who had all provided fingerprints after his disappearance in 1968.

When I heard who had left the fingerprint, I sat deep

in thought for a few minutes with the telephone receiver in my hand. Then I dialled Patricia's number and asked if it would be possible to have a quick lunch meeting, as there had been a sensational new development in the case.

# V

'So, whose fingerprints do you think we found on the police security service's recording of Marie Morgenstierne's last meeting?' I asked, and reached out to help myself to a piece of cake.

Patricia's eyes were steady and confident when they met mine. She answered before I had reached the cake.

'Almost certainly Marie Morgenstierne's own finger-prints. I have for several days now suspected that it was she herself who was in contact with the security service. But to have this confirmed is still a very important step forward, so congratulations.'

I thanked her for the rare compliment and hurried on without waiting for any possible jibes.

'So the others were right that there was a mole in the group, but they were wrong about who it was. It was Marie Morgenstierne, not Miriam Filtvedt Bentsen, who was the informer. And if any of them had discovered this, they could all have a possible motive for murder.'

Patricia nodded, and chewed thoughtfully on a piece of cake before she answered.

'Betrayal is always a possible motive for murder, par-ticularly in sect-like political and religious groups such as this one. And it would now appear that Marie Morgenstierne was an informer. But that does not mean that she was one before Falko Reinhardt disappeared. You should put pressure on the head of the security service and demand to know when she became their informant. You are in a far better position to force him to tell you the truth now. Particularly if you then add that a representative of the security police was obviously at the scene of the crime.'

I looked in astonishment at Patricia, who sighed heavily.

'Dear detective inspector, the situation should be fairly clear by now. Given that Marie Morgenstierne took the recording with her when she left the meeting, she must have passed it on to someone before she started to run. It is no coincidence that there was a man with a suitcase walking behind her, and that he still has not come forward. He is of course the person she gave the tape to. And therefore a very interesting witness. Ask to speak to him as soon as possible!'

I nodded, fascinated, wondering desperately how I should present this to the head of the police security service without setting myself up for a fall if Patricia's reasoning proved for once to be wrong.

'But today's finding also makes it far more likely that Kristine Larsen is the murderer after all. She had a clear motive if she saw the tape changing hands, and in that case, Marie Morgenstierne also had reason to fear her reaction. And what do you say to this? I found it in her wardrobe.'

I laid the photograph, in which Marie Morgenstierne had been blacked out with a felt pen, on the table. Patricia looked at it and gave a pensive nod.

'Not very nice. And not very smart either, if after shooting Marie Morgenstierne, Kristine Larsen left this in a place where it obviously would be found in the event of a house search. She is definitely guilty of being vehemently jealous of Marie Morgenstierne, but still highly likely not to be guilty of her murder.'

I noted the formulation 'highly likely not' and commented that it was still a possibility that could not be ruled out.

Patricia squirmed restlessly in her wheelchair, but granted me a reluctant nod.

'In this case, we should both be aware that nothing can be ruled out. And one should never trust pacifism either, in the case of a jealous woman in love. But I still cannot get it to tally with the overwhelming fear that seized Marie Morgenstierne on the street. The man from the police security service was a fair way behind her, and the blind woman was between them. So the tape must have been handed over a good deal earlier. If Marie Morgenstierne realized that Kristine Larsen had seen the handover and understood the significance of it, why did she then only start to run a few hundred yards later? Could the sight of Kristine Larsen have been so terrifying, even if Marie Morgenstierne did not know that she had seen the handover? Or . . .'

Patricia fell silent – into deep thought. She had definitely forgotten about her slice of cake now, even though it was only half eaten. I could see her mind processing the new information at top speed, running through the various possibilities.

'Or . . .' I prompted.

'Or it was the far more surprising sight of Falko Rein-hardt waiting in one of the side streets that frightened her. Or someone else in another side street or behind a hedge, whom neither the blind woman nor Kristine Larsen could see. There are still a number of possibilities. But either Kristine Larsen is lying so much that her nose will soon start to grow, or Falko Reinhardt is at large somewhere out there. And if that is the case, the mystery is greater than ever. Why has he not contacted the police, given that he was then an eyewitness to his fiancée's murder, or now that his lover has been arrested?'

'The most likely explanation in the latter case would simply be that he was not there, because the whole story about him being there was made up by Kristine Larsen to deflect any suspicion from herself,' I said, cautiously.

Patricia seemed both to nod and shake her head.

'That is possible, of course. But it strikes me as being equally likely that Kristine Larsen did in fact see Falko, and that he is out there, but he is waiting for something to happen before making contact. This Falko chap seems to be a rather self-centred person with a sense of melodrama. But what on earth could he be waiting for? It must be something major if he first hides away for two years, and then continues to do so even after a murder.'

Patricia looked almost frightened. I jumped when, out of the blue, she slapped her hand down on the table.

'Pass! There are too many unresolved questions here, and I will make no headway unless some of them are answered. If it does transpire that Kristine Larsen either had a gun in her hand that was clearly visible, or she saw the handover of the tape, then I will start to take your theory that she is the murderer more seriously. In the meantime, however, I will concentrate on other possible solutions while you try to find someone who can give you more relevant information. The security service would seem to be the best lead now, but put increasing pressure on both Kristine Larsen and the other remaining Falkoists through the course of the afternoon.'

This was a very clear hint. I stood up to leave, but Patricia stopped me halfway with her hand.

'Come back for supper at seven, if you can. And in the meantime, call me immediately if anything new crops up.'

I realized that Patricia's voice was trembling – as was her hand. She noticed the surprise in my eyes and continued without prompting: 'It could be my general fear of things I do not understand. It does have something to do with who or what scared Marie Morgenstierne so much, but more with the question as to why Falko disappeared and why he is not making himself known now. It seems to me that we are running against time to prevent an even greater catastrophe.'

This whisper of fear in Patricia made a strong impression on me. I followed the maid out of the room with unusual alacrity, and overtook her just before the front door.

# VI

Once back in the office, I made the phone call I had been dreading most of all: to the head of the police security service, Asle Bryne. I called him at home. I feared that he might not appreciate being called at home early on a Sunday afternoon, particularly when it concerned a difficult case, and had made up my mind to put down the phone if he had not answered after five rings. But he picked up the receiver on the fourth ring. The situation was not made any easier by the fact that instead of saying who he was, he opened the conversation with a curt 'Who is it?'

His voice, however, banished any doubts I may have had that I had got the wrong number. I resisted the temptation to slam down the receiver, and instead launched myself out into deep waters.

'This is Detective Inspector Kolbjørn Kristiansen. I met with you at your office yesterday. I apologize profusely for having to disturb you at home on a Sunday, but we have some new information in the murder case I am investigating, which could put the security service in a rather unfortunate light, should it become known. I thought I should discuss the matter with you immediately and try to minimize the negative consequences it could have for both our organizations.'

For a moment, there was silence on the other end of the telephone. I braced myself for a furious outburst that never came.

'I see,' Asle Bryne said, eventually. And then said no more.

After a few seconds I realized that he was waiting for me to continue in order to ascertain how much I knew. It felt as though I was teetering on the edge of the cliff in Valdres when I spoke: 'The current investigation has first of all discovered that the murdered Marie Morgenstierne herself acted as a security service informant for a while. And secondly, and more importantly, a member of the security service appears to have been present at the scene of the crime when she was killed.'

Again, there was silence. Absolute silence. Delightful, liberating silence. And the silence lasted for a long time.

'I see,' Asle Bryne said, once more. And then was silent again.

I obviously had to launch myself into a new attack, and did so.

'It is still my hope that we can keep this from the press and politicians. But then I need any information that may help to solve the case quickly, now.'

'I see,' Asle Bryne's voice repeated. 'What do you need, then?' he added hastily.

'I need to know the details of your contact with Marie Morgenstierne. But first and foremost, I have to speak to the man who was at the scene of the crime about what he might have seen and heard.'

'I see,' Asle Bryne said yet again, still sounding remarkably cool and collected.

'Come to my office at six o'clock this evening, and I will give you all the help I can,' he continued swiftly.

Then he put down the phone without waiting for confirmation.

I heaved a sigh of relief and looked at the time. It was
still only half past two. I still had time for a couple of
meetings with the group around Falko Reinhardt before
the end of the working day. The one I wanted to speak to
most was without a doubt Miriam Filtvedt Bentsen, but
I had more crucial questions to ask Anders Pettersen. So in
the end I dialled his number, and when I had established
that he was at home, I headed over there.


# VII


Anders Pettersen sat leaning forward in a chair beside his
untidy coffee table and stared at me in disbelief. It was
not a pleasant situation, and became even less so when he
started to speak.

'That is completely absurd. No one could honestly
believe that Kristine would kill anyone, let alone a member
of our group. If you believe that, you have either been
duped by a conspiracy or are part of one yourself. Kristine
is the most consistent, helpless pacifist I have ever met, and
I have met quite a few. We all knew that she would not be
up to much in the great struggle when world revolution
reached Norway. She had been in touch with another revolutionary group before, but was told that they had no use
for pacifists.'

The man was politically provoking and personally
unbearable, but I chose to ignore both aspects for the

moment. There was a considerable risk that he was right about Kristine Larsen and my chances of getting anything out of him about the rest of the group would not increase with confrontation. I therefore replied that the question as to whether Kristine Larsen would be charged or not was still open, but that there was much to indicate that jealousy and rivalry within the group had played a part. He looked at me with a little more interest when I said this.

So I then asked Anders Pettersen the same question that I had asked Trond Ibsen earlier in the day: if he had ever noticed any signs of romantic relationships within the group other than that between Marie Morgenstierne and Falko Reinhardt.

His reaction was more or less the same. He rolled his eyes and looked as though he was about to dismiss the whole question, but then paused for thought and frowned for a moment.

'I never thought I would mention this to anyone outside the group, and certainly not to a policeman. But this is an extremely serious situation as one of us has been murdered, and I should do everything I can to disprove the clearly mistaken view that Kristine is the prime suspect.'

I nodded in agreement, said that he should absolutely do that, and assured him that for the time being it would be an unofficial statement and would not be written down or shared with the other members of the group. This prompted a sudden sense of confidentiality between us. Anders Pettersen leaned even further forward over the table and lowered his voice when he spoke.

'I have never heard or seen anything to indicate that

Kristine had any kind of romantic ties, if that is what you mean. Not with anyone, either in or out of the group. But there is a romantic secret in the group that you should perhaps know about, as it might be of some importance here . . .'

He looked at me, his eyes almost twinkling, and continued to talk even faster and more intensely, but in a whisper.

'Our psychologist has a complex, and it is called women. Trond comes from a very good family, has plenty of money and a good education and all that. And, as far as others are concerned, he is without a doubt an extremely good psychologist. And as you have perhaps noticed, he appears to get on relatively well with other men. But his relationships with women have been less happy in all the years I've known him. As far as we know, he has never had a lover of any kind, through no lack of interest on his part. Trond is either too laid-back and distant, or too eager and intense in his dealings with women. In recent years, he seems to have focused more on his psychology and has been outvoted by the group more and more often. Since Falko's disappearance, I've had a growing sense that he is part of the group not so much out of political interest, but rather romantic interest.'

'So what you are saying is that . . . he may have been romantically attached to the late Marie Morgenstierne?'

Anders Pettersen nodded and gave a derisive smile.

'He definitely had a romantic interest in Marie Morgenstierne; or perhaps a crush on her is a better way of putting it. And on Kristine Larsen. And his later contemptuous talk of Miriam Filtvedt Bentsen was perhaps also an attempt to hide the fact that he had tried it on with her too, without any success. I know him and his complex so well that I could see it, without even having a basic degree in psychology.'

This was said with an undertone of triumph. Once again I felt the tension and rivalry between the two remaining male members of the group, even when only one of them was present.

It seemed that we were getting close to something now in a case that really needed a boost and to pick up pace. So I threw down the trump card that I had had up my sleeve for several days now, and asked whether, if Marie Morgenstierne had been pregnant when she was killed, Trond Ibsen might be the father.

The reaction was unexpectedly instant and marked. His head sank down towards the table.

He asked if it was really true, and if so, how far gone she was.

I told him the truth, that she was pregnant, but probably only in the fifth or sixth week.

Anders Pettersen looked even more confused at this. He replied that he thought that Trond Ibsen was in love with Marie Morgenstierne, but that he had not thought he had a chance. Then he suddenly took this back and said that one could never rule out anything in such situations, and that this was becoming ever more mysterious. If Marie Morgenstierne had been pregnant when she died, he could not rule out the possibility that Trond Ibsen was not only the father but also potentially the murderer, though both things seemed highly unlikely to begin with. The first explanation that came to mind with regard to her pregnancy was that Falko had come back. He shook his head firmly when I asked if he had seen any indication of this, and added that it would be very odd if that were the case and Falko had not been in touch.

Anders Pettersen seemed to change completely in the course of the thirty minutes or so that I spoke to him. When I left, he stayed sitting by the table, totally confused, and it was easy to feel sorry for him. I understood him only too well: the case was equally confusing for me. But I still did not trust him.

# VIII

I thought I could see people in the windows of both the neighbouring buildings when I parked my police car and knocked on the door of the SPP party office. I did not feel entirely comfortable with the situation.

There was no problem this time either, fortunately. The door was open. It was almost impossible to get into the office, as there were large piles of envelopes all over the floor. But the people who were stuffing the envelopes had obviously taken the weekend off. Three of the four desks were empty. At the fourth sat Miriam Filtvedt Bentsen, eagerly working her way through a pile of papers in just a T-shirt, with her strange multicoloured sweatshirt thrown over the back of the chair. She was engrossed in the papers, with an impish look on her face, and had obviously not noticed me.

The sight of her gave me a rush of joy on an otherwise serious day. I realized I had come more because I wanted to see her than because I needed answers from her. But it never occurred to me to turn around.

She suddenly became aware of me, but was not startled at all. Her equanimity was impressive. I was hugely encouraged by the fact that her face lit up with an even bigger smile, and that she pushed the pile of papers to one side at the same time.

'Hi. Anything new to report?' she asked.

It was not the most gushing personal greeting I could imagine, but still a promising start.

So I replied that there was something new that I should perhaps tell her about, and in connection with that, I also had a few questions that I would like to ask her as soon as possible. And then hastily added that I really should get something to eat after what had been an incredibly demanding Sunday, and that perhaps she deserved a break and something to eat too.

This proved to be a good move. Five minutes later the SPP office was locked and the two of us were installed at a discreet corner table in a cafe a hundred yards down the street. Again, I vaguely noticed that there were people in the windows of both neighbouring buildings as we left the party office. I was not sure whether Miriam Filtvedt Bentsen had noticed it or not. But I comforted myself with the thought that if she had, she certainly did not seem to be worried about being seen with me.

'So, what's happening?' she asked, and looked at me

expectantly. She continued to eat the *plat du jour* with laudable efficiency while she waited for an answer.

It occurred to me that I had in fact put myself in a very vulnerable position. I had talked so much to her on the trip to Valdres that I now did not have many questions I could ask without giving away more than I should about the case.

I asked again whether she had ever noticed any sign of romantic ties or interests within the group, other than Falko's now known relationships with Marie Morgenstierne and Kristine Larsen.

She dutifully thought about it for a few seconds, then shook her head – and, naturally enough, asked if there was any reason why I was asking again.

This question only served to highlight my dilemma. I took a deep breath and launched in, told her that in order to move forward in the case, I had to tell her some more about it, but only on the condition that nothing of what I said would be passed on to anyone under any circumstances.

She nodded vehemently, crossed her heart and promised that she would not tell another living soul anything that I said, and then leaned impatiently over the table to hear more.

I started with some caution and told her that Marie Morgenstierne had been pregnant when she was killed, and asked Miriam if she had any idea of who the father could be. She fiddled with her pendant for a moment, and remarked with a sigh that it must obviously have happened after she had broken from the group. If one of the three men was the father of the child, she reckoned Falko to be the most likely candidate and Trond Ibsen to be the least likely. But that was something she thought rather than knew.

I then told her about yesterday's dramatic events and the arrest of Kristine Larsen. She had clearly not heard about this, and looked genuinely surprised. Then she said what I expected and feared, in a controlled and firm voice: that she could not see Kristine Larsen as a murderer, and certainly not of a friend like Marie Morgenstierne.

I showed her the defaced photograph from Kristine Larsen's flat. She took it in, and then offered the same opinion as Patricia – that it proved a deep jealousy, but that the leap from there to murder was enormous. Particularly for a young woman who, as far as one could see, had never handled a gun before.

I caught myself nodding in agreement. My belief that Kristine Larsen was the murderer was ebbing.

So far, I was on relatively safe ground with regard to what I had told her. The arrest of Kristine Larsen was in the process of becoming semi-official, as was Marie Morgenstierne's pregnancy.

Towards the end of the conversation, however, I crossed a new threshold with Miriam Filtvedt Bentsen. And this happened when I lowered my voice and said that the investigation was very demanding because there was reason to believe that a major attack of some kind or other was being planned.

Miriam Filtvedt Bentsen now completely forgot her food and looked me directly in the eye. I hurried to say that it was still very uncertain what this involved, and that I could not say anything more about it at present. She nodded in understanding, and asked whether I knew which of the groups involved had initiated it.

I shook my head lightly.

She stared straight ahead, deep in thought, showing little interest in the food, and remarked that it must be hard to say anything about it.

'From what you have told me, there seem to be three groups involved that all comprise a small cluster of people who believe that they have an almost God-given mission, and that the means are justified by the ends in each case. That is always a very dangerous situation,' she concluded, pensively.

'The Nazis, the communists – and who else were you thinking of?' I asked.

'Surely you have been in touch with the police security service by now!' was her wry remark. She smiled mischievously and met my eyes again.

I could not help smiling, and even laughed for a moment. There was a lot of magic in the glance of this odd and charming young SPP member.

But the magic passed; she looked away, and then resumed eating. It did, however, still feel as though we were now a little closer. Enough for a quick hug and a longer 'good luck with the next stage of the investigation' when we parted outside the cafe around five.

Miriam Filtvedt Bentsen had obviously been given food for thought as well. I noted with a small chuckle that she walked past the party office on the way back. As I drove on,

I speculated on whether she was thinking about me, or the case. I hoped it was the former, but guessed it was the latter.

Whatever the case, I felt remarkably calm having spoken so openly with her. I felt much the same way as I did about Patricia, though different at the same time: that Miriam would not betray my trust. I had to admit, thinking of my previous murder case, I had misjudged a couple of young women in the past, but I felt almost a hundred per cent certain that I had not done so this time.

# IX

I arrived at Victoria Terrace at five to six, and was shown into Asle Bryne's office without delay. He was waiting there in his swivel chair, his smoking pipe and bushy eyebrows in place. To my disappointment, he was alone in the room.

Patricia had obviously guessed correctly that the man with the suitcase was a member of the security service, but that was not enough to coax him out into daylight.

We did not shake hands; Asle Bryne nodded curtly at the chair in front of the desk, and I sat down in the spirit of cooperation. We looked at each other across the desk for quite some time. This time, it was he who broke the silence.

'You are to be praised for your work and for the discreet manner in which you have handled this new information so far. There are no doubt others, both at the main police station and in the military intelligence, who would instead have tried to use the case to blacken the name of both myself and the police security service.'

I nodded to show my continued cooperation. He puffed on his pipe and his voice was a touch sharper when he continued.

'I have decided, all the same, to have this meeting with you alone. I alone am the head of the security service. It is my responsibility and I cannot under any circumstances put the life of an employee who has simply done his duty for his country and organization on the line, as is the risk here.'

I tightened my lips and was about to say something, without having any idea of exactly what, but Asle Bryne stopped me and quickly carried on talking himself.

'Since we spoke this morning, I have, however, been in touch with the employee in question and taken a written statement from him. This is for strictly confidential use only and you may read it here and now, when only we are present. If you have any further questions once you have read it, we will then have to see if I can answer them on behalf of the security service. Are the conditions clear?'

Without waiting for an answer he opened the desk drawer, took out two typewritten pages, and placed them, text down, on the desk between us.

This was less than I had hoped for, but definitely more than I had feared. And even though I now had some pretty good cards up my sleeve, I still wanted to avoid a confrontation with the head of the security service, if at all possible. So I nodded and turned the pages over.

The statement was quick to read. The undersigned, 'XY', confirmed that he was the man with the suitcase at the scene of the crime on the evening of 5 August and that he had received a tape from Marie Morgenstierne only min-utes earlier. The handover took place as she walked past him on the road. At the time of the handover, there was no one to be seen behind them, and in front they could only see a woman with a guide dog.

As was usual, XY had then continued to walk down the road once he had received the tape, but at a slower pace than Marie Morgenstierne. A man with a walking stick and wearing a long coat had come between them at the cross-roads. The man had been too far away for XY to see any detail. He had assumed, given the stick, that the man was either old or had trouble walking, and had not identified him as a risk.

A tall, fair-haired woman had then passed him from behind. He recognized her as Kristine Larsen from earlier observations. She passed him at great speed, and was as good as running after Marie Morgenstierne. Both Kristine Larsen's hands were visible and she was not carrying a weapon of any description, and looked so harmless that she had not introduced any drama into the situation.

XY had heard Kristine Larsen shout 'Marie' at more or less the same moment that Marie Morgenstierne sud-denly broke into a run. He had instinctively started to run himself, only to bump into the blind woman. XY had then stopped running, as he saw that Kristine Larsen had also stopped. Following his instructions to avoid all possi-ble attention, he had held back with the tape while Marie Morgenstierne ran on, apparently with no one in pursuit.

The people that XY had seen at the scene of the crime were listed at the end of the report. In addition to Marie

Morgenstierne, this included Kristine Larsen, who had stopped running; the man with the long coat and stick, who carried on walking unperturbed at a steady pace; and the blind woman, who also stopped and seemed very bewildered. There were also two men down two opposite side roads.

The latter two were both too far away for XY to say anything as to their identity, other than that they were both young, dark-haired men who were above average height. He was, however, slightly taken aback by the fact that they were both standing waiting, rather than walking. As far as he could tell, neither of them made any attempt to follow Marie Morgenstierne. XY thought that she had seen the train and was running to catch it, and had, despite some confusion, not deemed the situation to be dramatic.

I read through the report twice, with interest and frustration. It confirmed a lot of what I already knew, without adding much else. Any suspicions against Kristine Larsen now foundered on the fact that she could apparently not have seen the tape being handed over and clearly did not have a gun in her hand. It was difficult then to understand why the sight of her might have provoked such a sudden and terrible fear in Marie Morgenstierne. There were also purely technical issues that undermined the theory that Kristine Larsen was the murderer, including the fact that she came to a standstill when Marie Morgenstierne started to run.

I had to admit to myself that XY's report supported not only Kristine Larsen's statement, but also Patricia's theory regarding Falko Reinhardt. It was tempting to believe that he was one of the two men who, according to XY's report, had been standing in one of the side streets. The only remaining question of any importance was: who was the other man, whom I had not heard about before? I concluded, in brief, that the rather sketchy description did not rule out either Trond Ibsen or Anders Pettersen, but could equally fit ten thousand other men in the Oslo area. I understood now what Patricia had meant by the curse of public space.

Asle Bryne showed unexpected patience as he waited in silence while I read the report through twice. He was enveloped in a thick cloud of smoke when I looked up.

I said in all honesty that the report was very informative with regards to events at the scene of the crime, but that I needed more information about Marie Morgenstierne's earlier contact with the security service.

Asle Bryne filled his pipe again and puffed pensively a couple of times. Then he replied that it would be dangerous and potentially damaging to recruitment if the police security service were to give out information about their contact with informants.

I retorted that as one of his informants had now been shot, it would certainly not be positive in any way should it get out that a member of the security police had been present at the scene of the crime. It would be even less positive if it got out that they then did not do everything they could to help solve the crime.

Bryne gave a curt nod, let out a heavy sigh and put his pipe down on the desk. Suddenly he seemed like a tired old man, a grandfather havering as to which family secrets he should divulge to younger generations. He looked at me in anticipation before drawing breath and speaking.

'You may well be right about that. We never recruited Marie Morgenstierne – she volunteered herself. Exactly where she was later shot, and to the same person that she met there on this occasion. According to our man's report of 12 September 1968, it was a few weeks after her fiancé disappeared. Our man had followed her after a political meeting. Just by the station at Smestad, she stopped, waited for him to catch up, then said: 'You're from the police security service, aren't you, so maybe we can help each other? I think Falko is dead or has been abducted, and I suspect that one of the others in the group is behind it!' Then she offered to help us with information that might help to solve the mystery.'

We were both silent for a moment. Asle Bryne lit his pipe again and continued to puff pensively on it.

I asked, with a rising pulse, whether Marie Morgenstierne had at any point indicated whom she suspected. Asle Bryne shook his head glumly.

'She did not want to tell us whom she suspected, nor why she had her suspicions. It was our job to find out if there was anything to it, she said. So that is how the partnership started. She discreetly handed over recordings of their meetings. She never asked for a penny in return, and was never offered it either. I never met her myself. Her only contact was the person she gave the recordings to. We did not like her and never trusted her, and the feeling was no doubt mutual. She was, as far as we can understand, a fervent communist to the end. But we needed the tapes and she seemed to be obsessed with finding out what had happened to her fiancé and who was responsible.'

'And she never got an answer?'

'Not as far as we know, and certainly not from any of us. The information she gave us never provided an answer as to what had happened to her fiancé and we never managed to establish which of the others might be responsible. The security service is none the wiser about what might have happened to him and has mainly focused on the potential threat to society that the activities of the remaining members of the group might pose.'

'Have you otherwise found any evidence that this group constitutes a threat to Norwegian society?'

Asle Bryne livened up again, thumped his pipe down on the table and leaned forward.

'Of course they constitute a threat to society. One never knows what a group of fanatical, revolutionary communist sympathizers like that might decide to do. They are at worst traitors to their country, and at best useful idiots for other traitors. It is alarming enough in itself that the group is interested in international issues relating to Vietnam and other countries in Asia, as well as the Soviet Union. We have not yet found anything to confirm that the group or members of the group are planning any definite action. But we have every reason to fear that they might, and as such it is our duty to our country and people to keep an eye on them!'

I was about to answer, but bit my tongue at the last moment. I remembered Patricia's remarks that a major action might be in the planning, but that it was difficult to say by whom or against what. I had some new, important information: Marie Morgenstierne had definitely been an informant for the security police, but only after her fiancé had disappeared. And most important of all, she had later suspected one of the other four of being responsible for her fiancé's death or abduction. The faces of Trond Ibsen, Anders Pettersen, Miriam Filtvedt Bentsen and Kristine Larsen flashed through my mind.

For a brief moment I regretted having been so open with Miriam Filtvedt Bentsen earlier in the afternoon; nevertheless, my suspicions were still focused largely on the other three. I wondered whether Trond Ibsen or Anders Pettersen might be the other mystery man down the side road at the scene of the crime, and changed my mind yet again about Kristine Larsen being a potential murderer. I thanked the head of the police security service for the information and left Victoria Terrace, deep in thought.

# X

'The cook has not outdone herself today, to be fair, but you are still eating suspiciously little,' Patricia remarked halfway through the main course.

I dutifully took another couple of mouthfuls of the delicious venison, and thoughtlessly excused myself, saying that I had had to eat a little something earlier in the afternoon in connection with the investigation.

Patricia looked at me with raised eyebrows, but fortunately did not ask any questions.

I gave her a simplified account of the afternoon's developments, without saying that I had asked Miriam Filtvedt Bentsen out for something to eat. It was not something I wanted to tell Patricia, nor did it feel like something she would want to know. We eagerly talked about the case over the rest of the meal.

'The case is of course complicated, and enough to make you lose your appetite,' I said.

She nodded vigorously.

'I absolutely agree. The picture is now somewhat clearer regarding the police security service, but they are still holding so much back that one could be forgiven for wondering if they are hiding something serious. Let us hope that this can finally be cleared up when you talk to the man with the suitcase tomorrow.'

I stared at Patricia, astounded.

'And how exactly do you think I am going to do that? The head of the security service seemed very unwilling to cooperate on that point.'

Patricia let out a great sigh.

'Have you really not considered the reason why the head of the security service seems so unwilling to cooperate and would not let you meet the man with the suitcase? You tell the good Mr Bryne tomorrow that you know that this man has a large mole on his face and remind him of the potential scandal that might ensue should it ever get out that he was also at the cabin in Valdres on the night that Falko Reinhardt went missing. My guess is that you will be able to talk to him pretty quickly after that. I am less certain, however, about how much help it will be.'

215

I felt as though I had been punched in the stomach. It struck me that if Patricia's intelligence had increased from the time she was eighteen until she was twenty, so had her arrogance. Fortunately, she continued in a softer tone.

'The picture is becoming more detailed, but also more complex and confusing. The same is true of the picture at the scene of the crime on the evening that Marie Morgenstierne was shot.'

I nodded in agreement.

'Just when we have now identified one of those present, we have discovered a new shadow in the wings. Do you have any ideas about who this other man in the side road might be?'

Patricia's smile was secretive.

'I nearly always have my theories, but these are at present so uncertain that I cannot share them with anyone else yet – particularly as there is a considerable chance that it was just a random passer-by who happened to be standing there. I am currently more interested in the man who it is becoming ever clearer was there, and who is perhaps out there somewhere with the solution: in other words, Falko Reinhardt himself. But based on the information given, I unfortunately have no way of knowing where he might be. Once again, the curse of public space.'

I commented that the information from the police security service also allowed for the possibility that Marie Morgenstierne might have suspected Kristine Larsen of being responsible for Falko's disappearance.

Patricia replied that it was of course a possibility that

Marie Morgenstierne's suspicions were of considerable importance, even though it would seem that they were unfounded: Falko was alive, and had disappeared of his own free will. But it was first of all highly unlikely that the person Marie Morgenstierne suspected was also the person who killed her. And, furthermore, there were other people whom Marie Morgenstierne had reason to suspect just as much as Kristine Larsen.

I asked Patricia outright if she was now alluding to Miriam Filtvedt Bentsen. She looked at me, slightly surprised, and to my relief, shook her head.

'No, it was not primarily her I was thinking of. On the contrary, she is perhaps the least likely of the four. If that was where Marie Morgenstierne's suspicions lay, it seems unlikely that she would continue to act as an informer for the police security service for a year after Miriam Filtvedt Bentsen had left the group.'

I had not thought of that, but apparently was too enthusiastic in my nodding. Patricia sighed heavily again and continued.

'Marie Morgenstierne may of course have started to act as an informant because she was suspicious of Miriam Filtvedt Bentsen, and then continued for other reasons. But no matter what this Miriam Filtvedt Bentsen may or may not have on her conscience, or what she believed, there is nothing at all to indicate that she had anything to do with Falko's disappearance. It is, however, not impossible that she might have something to do with Marie Morgenstierne's death. But I have to say it seems unlikely.'

We left it at that. For a moment, Patricia suddenly seemed to be deflated. She sat in silence with her dessert, before pushing it aside after only a few mouthfuls of ice cream.

'I am allergic to something there is far too much of in this case, and that is coincidences. The strangest of all is that you yourself were there on the train when Marie Morgenstierne came running for her life. You have never actually told me what you were doing at Smestad that evening.'

I chortled briefly and told her in five sentences the story of the overwrought hotel manager and his suspicious guest.

Never before had I experienced such a rapid and dramatic change in Patricia's mood. Within two seconds she went from sitting in her wheelchair, disheartened and almost resigned and passive, to leaning forward over the table, breathless and on the verge of angry.

'And in the five days that you have come here, you have not thought once to tell me this remarkable story?'

'But – the hotel manager is completely paranoid and rings about things like this every three months or so,' I stammered.

Patricia was not pacified by this. She hit the table, making the dessert bowls jump.

'As a great many people in both the United States and the Soviet Union can confirm, being paranoid does not prove in any way that one is not being persecuted! Did this bizarre guest give a name, by the way?'

'Frank Rekkedal,' I said, and at that moment realized my blunder.

Patricia became so agitated and spoke so fast that I almost feared she might leap out of her wheelchair and over the table to get at me.

'If it had been illegal not to see the simplest of connections, you would have to arrest yourself right now! Frank Rekkedal, hardly – the guest's name is Falko Reinhardt and he is even more confident and theatrical than I thought! Go to the hotel immediately and let's hope he is still there. And if he is, it may be decisive in solving the murder, and in preventing something even more dramatic that is being planned by someone out there right now.'

I was shocked, both by my own oversight and by Patricia's extreme reaction. But her conclusion, as she now presented it, was very convincing. The possibility of being able to close the case soon was suddenly within reach. So I jumped up, and more or less ran through the corridors and down the long stairs of the Borchmann home.

I vaguely registered that Patricia shouted something to me as I ran out of the room. The two sentences continued to rattle around my brain as I bounded down the stairs, and it was only when I was out in the driveway that they fell into place.

'If you find Falko, please ask him if he recognized anyone other than Marie at the scene of the crime. But first, ask him if he knows what they are planning and when it is going to happen!'

# XI

The hotel manager had gone away for the weekend, and would not be back until Monday morning. It was a shame, the young, dark-haired receptionist commented with a jaunty little smile, because he was her uncle and would no doubt have set great store in being here right now. She soon became serious again and added that the mysterious guest in Room 27 was still here, as far as she knew. He had paid until tomorrow and had put his empty breakfast tray back out again this morning. I asked if she had a spare key to the room. She nodded gravely.

I said that there was not likely to be any drama, and that the guest was at present not suspected of anything criminal. It might, however, be advantageous if a representative from the hotel was there as a witness when I knocked on the door of Room 27. She nodded and put her hand to her mouth in a moment of anticipated adventure. 'Almost like a James Bond film,' was her quiet remark. Then she was once again the same rational receptionist who was responsible for her uncle's hotel. She found a key that was marked 'Spare 27', put out a sign that said 'back shortly', and pointed me in the direction of the room.

We mounted the stairs in concentrated silence and walked down the corridor past rooms 1–10. She pointed out Room 27 for me with a slightly trembling finger as soon as we passed Room 23. It was clearly a quiet summer weekend in the hotel: there was no one to be seen, and not a sound to be heard in the corridor.

The atmosphere was somewhat uncanny as we stood there outside Room 27. My companion made her way discreetly to the end of the corridor and pressed a light switch. This certainly helped. The whole corridor was lit up by three large ceiling chandeliers. But nothing more of any interest was to be seen in the corridor as a result. And it still felt slightly unreal to be standing outside Room 27. The door was a very ordinary brown hotel door. It could be hiding either an empty hotel room, or the solution to both the murder and missing-person mysteries.

As we stood there for a few moments more, I considered whether I should do something I had thought about on the way over: that is, to call out a stronger police presence before knocking on the hotel door. But the situation did not feel dramatic or in any way threatening. There was much to indicate that the bird might have flown the nest already – if, indeed, it had ever been here. If the hotel room was empty, or we found a poor, nervous tourist in there, a stronger police presence would be an overreaction that Danielsen and other envious colleagues might use to poke fun at me. And if Falko Reinhardt really was behind the locked door, he was contained. It seemed rather unlikely that he would attack a policeman in such a situation, even if he was armed.

There was still not a sound to be heard from inside the room. The receptionist's hand was shaking a little, her eyes darting between me and the door. A strange understanding had developed between two people who had never met before. It struck me I did not even know the young receptionist's name – and that she might in fact be in danger if she followed me into the room. I did think, however, that the risk was microscopic. And I was extremely curious as to who or what was hiding in the hotel room. She was now visibly trembling, but pulled herself together and gave me an encouraging smile. I took a deep breath and hesitated one more time. Then I changed my focus and knocked on the door.

The knocking produced no reaction. All remained quiet in Room 27.

My voice sounded like a peal of thunder in the tense silence.

'We know that you are there, Falko Reinhardt. Open the door immediately. This is Detective Inspector Kolbjørn Kristiansen, and I need to speak to you about the planned attack!'

The receptionist let out a small gasp and looked up at me with large blue eyes, as if I really were James Bond in a film. But the situation was real enough. And all was still quiet in Room 27.

The idea that I had arrived a few hours too late and that the room was now empty was increasingly convincing. However, the tension ratcheted up a further notch when I tried the door handle. The door was locked. And it was not possible to see anything through the keyhole, because the key had been inserted from the inside.

I waved my hand for the spare key. It was with some relief that she put it between my fingers. I pushed it into the lock and heard the key on the inside fall out. At the same time, I also heard more noises from inside the room.

The receptionist instinctively gripped my arm, but nothing dramatic happened. The sounds from inside the room were not easy to identify. It could have been drawers and wardrobes being opened and closed again. I was suddenly seized by a fear that the receptionist might get injured when the door opened. So I as good as lifted her to one side and out of sight of the door. Then I turned the key.

The light in Room 27 had been switched off. But it was easy enough to look around the room, which was a good hundred square feet, in the light from the corridor. And the room was empty. There were no personal belongings to be seen on the bed, chairs or desk by the window, and there was no trace of Falko Reinhardt or any other person.

My eyes turned instinctively to the bathroom door. I pulled it open. But there was no trace of anyone either on the floor or in the bathtub. The only sign that a guest had been there was a red toothbrush and a half-used tube of toothpaste. A forgotten electric shaver indicated that it was a man who had left the room in such a hurry. But the man himself was nowhere to be seen.

When I went back out into the room I almost collided with another person, but quickly regained my composure when it proved to be the receptionist. She pointed at the balcony door with a trembling hand.

I was so annoyed with myself at having overlooked this possible escape route that I almost swore out loud. The balcony door was ajar. I rushed over and looked out. The drop down to the lawn below was barely nine feet. I leaped over the railing and ran across the lawn down to the street.

I caught a glimpse of the fleeing hotel guest from Room 27 on the road outside the hotel. He was just turning into a side street about fifty yards away, and he was running fast. But he turned to look back for a moment, and I recognized him straight away. He was a tall, dark and muscular man, with long, curly hair that made him easy to recognize.

I ran after him down to the side road, but quickly had to face up to the fact that pursuing him any further was hopeless. Falko Reinhardt had a head start of at least fifty yards, and was not to be seen anywhere. He could have run in any direction.

I carried on running, but now heading back to the car to alert police patrols in the area via the radio. I quickly made contact and could give them a description, but had to accept that the chances were slim. There were only four patrols out on a Sunday evening, and I had a strong suspicion that Falko Reinhardt had planned his escape route. Whether he was in any way responsible for his fiancée's death or not was still unclear, but what was clear was that he had been ready to escape from his hotel room at short notice if necessary.

I went back into the hotel by the main entrance and found the receptionist still standing, bewildered, in the middle of the room. She heaved a sigh of relief when she saw me and put a trembling arm round me. I was touched by her care in the midst of all the chaos. I took time to explain the situation and added that it would appear that the guest had not been armed, so there had been no immediate danger to her or myself. On hearing this, she calmed down impressively quickly and asked for permission to go back to the reception desk. There might be someone waiting there, and if not, she would try to contact the manager by phone. I thanked her for her help, asked her to send my greetings to the manager, and then turned my attention back to the hotel room.

Falko Reinhardt had either had very few belongings in the room, or had been very good at taking them with him. There was nothing to be found in the wardrobe or the two desk drawers. But under the pillow of his unmade bed, I found two things that immediately piqued my interest.

The first was a handwritten note with the following cryptic text:

*1008: KK. Warn of attack and that SP is the murderer!*

The tiny note gave me an enormous shock. I stood there looking at it for several minutes. I remembered what Miriam Filtvedt Bentsen had said about Falko's to-do lists, and could confirm it to be true. He had written a to-do list in order to remember something important, and had forgotten where he had put it in the rush.

I could not get the initials SP to tally with any known suspect; but they could of course refer to someone unknown to me. And if not, it was alarmingly obvious to think of Miriam Filtvedt Bentsen herself, as the only person in the case who was a member of the SPP. It made me even more anxious to note that it did not say 'the hitman', simply 'the murderer'. That meant that the person in question might also be a woman.

The other object that lay hidden under the pillow in Room 27 provided a degree of relief, but also a new mystery. It was a black and white photograph, dated '07.06.1970', and there was no trace of Miriam Filtvedt Bentsen in the picture. It showed what was clearly a meeting, with four people round a table at one of Oslo's finer restaurants. But only three faces were visible, and all three were known to me.

As soon as I saw the photograph, I felt a strange sympathy for a man I had never met or spoken to – and that was Henry Alfred Lien's son in Trondheim. His father had obviously not only cooperated with the occupying forces during the war, but had also told me barefaced lies only two days ago about his contact with other Nazis after the war. In the photograph, Henry Alfred Lien was sitting squarely, with a wary smile on his face, between Frans Heidenberg and Christian Magnus Eggen.

Another person in a grey suit was sitting beside Eggen, to the far left of the photograph. Judging by appearances, the fourth person was also a man. But his bare hand, without any rings or markings of any sort, gave no indication as to his identity. His face was not in the picture. The corner had been torn off, so the fourth man remained faceless.

I stood and studied the picture for a few minutes.

Then I took both it and Falko's forgotten to-do list, and wandered deep in thought back down the hotel corridor.

The receptionist stopped me to say that she had spoken to the hotel manager, who looked forward to hearing more details about the day's drama and its significance for the country when he returned home. She then thanked me for the 'day's action film' and added in a quiet voice that she would be delighted to talk more to me once the case was solved and closed.

The proposition was not at all unattractive. Her body was slim and her breasts looked firm in her uniform jacket, and her otherwise pretty face became mysteriously alluring when she now gave me a small, mischievous smile. But I had too much to think about and too many people to worry about to consider the possibility at any greater length. The receptionist vanished from my mind as soon as she vanished from my sight. On my way to the car, my thoughts ping-ponged between Miriam Filtvedt Bentsen and Patricia Louise I. E. Borchmann. And in the end, I drove back to the latter, with the to-do list and photograph on the seat beside me.

# XII

'Hmmhh,' was Patricia's surprisingly protracted response. It was now half past nine on what had turned into a long and hectic Sunday.

Patricia had drunk two cups of coffee while she listened in tense silence to my report from the hotel. Then she drank another half cup while she studied the photograph and to-do list that I had found there.

The coffee in my own cup was still warm and sweet, but Patricia now seemed cold and bitter. For a moment, she reminded me of a grumpy Norwegian teacher when she looked at Falko's list one last time, then let it fall to the table.

'Well, any schoolchild could understand the first bit. 1008 is the tenth of August, which is tomorrow. And KK is Kolbjørn Kristiansen, which is you.'

I nodded in agreement and pretended to have understood this all along. Patricia looked at me, somewhat taken aback, but was quick to continue.

'So, Falko was planning to contact you tomorrow. That much is clear, and good news. But the rest is not so clear or such good news.'

'So you have no idea either who this SP might be – or what is being planned?'

Patricia gave an almost annoyed shake of the head.

'There is not much to go on here. It seems most likely that SP is someone's initials, in which case we don't know whose. There are presumably thousands of people in Oslo alone whose initials are SP, so it is like looking for a needle in a haystack. It could be that SP is the fourth person in the picture, but then we still do not have much to go on. And there might not be any connection between the photograph and the note, even though it is natural to assume that there is. By the way . . .'

Patricia stopped speaking and stared intensely at the faceless fourth person in the photograph, as if she was trying to scare the truth out of it.

'By the way . . .' I prompted tentatively.

'By the way, I was wondering who might have taken the photograph and who has torn off the corner. Was the photograph already like that when Falko got hold of it, or was it he who tore off the corner? And if so, why did he do it? You must ask him if and when you speak to him. But for goodness' sake, start by asking about this attack that someone is planning against someone else, somewhere out in the real world.'

The latter was said with resignation in her voice. Patricia had ventured beyond the safety of her home's four walls, out into the world for what proved to be the very dramatic conclusion of our first investigation. The case had been solved, but only after a terrifying moment which I could only assume had plagued her for many nights since. We never talked about it. It was simply understood that Patricia's place was here indoors. She had withdrawn from what she herself on occasion called the real world.

I did not want to talk about it now either. And as she had not mentioned the possibility that SP could stand for Miriam Filtvedt Bentsen, as a member of the SPP, I for some unknown reason had no wish to point it out. So I thanked her for her help and stood up to leave.

Patricia raised her hand hastily and I immediately sat down again in the chair opposite her like an obedient child.

'One more thing it might be worth thinking about . . . I am constantly struck by how different this case is from our last ones. But there are still human flies and satellite people involved. Magdalon Schelderup, who was the first to be murdered in the last case, was a rich and powerful old patriarch, who had a great many people spinning round him like satellites. Marie Morgenstierne, on the other hand, was a young woman without a family or social status. There was no one spinning around her, and she was not a star. But her murder may have been a *catalyst killing*, and in that case, it may have even more dramatic consequences for others than the murder of Magdalon Schelderup.'

I looked at her, slightly confused. Her smile was utterly disarming.

'I am sorry for using a concept that I made up myself, without thinking. I've used it so much that I forget it is not a given for everyone else. A catalyst murder is a murder that, intentionally or unintentionally, sparks or accelerates other dangerous processes. A catalyst murder can involve both very famous and completely unknown people. A prime example from world history is the murder of the Austrian crown prince, Franz Ferdinand, in 1914. It set in motion processes that only a few weeks later, with almost chemical predictability, sparked a world war that would cost millions of lives – without that ever having been the murderer's intention. In much the same way, it feels as though the death of Marie Morgenstierne may have accelerated dangerous processes in several of the circles she moved in, either directly or indirectly, and the risk of an explosion will continue to increase by the hour until we find the murderer.'

I nodded and used the opportunity to impress her with some borrowed reason.

'I perfectly understand what you mean. And the risk of an explosion is also mounting because Marie Morgenstierne moved in a grey zone between three circles that are all relatively small and driven by a perilously fervent belief in their cause.'

Patricia furrowed her brow and looked at me with something that resembled suspicion.

'Did you come up with that by yourself? It is a valid point, and I have given it considerable thought myself. If you mean the old Nazis, young communists and police security service, we are talking about three extreme sectarian groups, each in their own way, where one or more individuals could easily get it into their head that the end justifies the means.'

I nodded again to show my agreement, without answering the question. It crossed my mind that Patricia and Miriam were in fact more similar than I had previously thought, despite being so different on the outside. And I definitely had no thought of mentioning that to either of them.

Patricia had finished her cup of coffee, but was still not finished for the evening.

'It is difficult to say whether it was the intention of the person who shot Marie Morgenstierne or not. But something very dangerous is brewing in one or more circles out there. I have no doubt that we will find poor Marie Morgenstierne's murderer within the next few days. But I am very worried that we may lose the fight against time with regard to preventing a greater catastrophe. We will get no further at the moment, but contact me as soon as you find any new information that I might be able to wrestle something more from.'

I took the hint, and stood up to leave just as the clock on the wall struck ten.

Despite our very different backgrounds, Patricia and I had started to understand each other rather well by now. As she talked, I had understood that she had a very definite theory about who had shot Marie Morgenstierne, but that she was not ready to air it yet. And after the day's events, I shared her fear that the countdown to a major explosion might have started.

As I drove home alone through the dark, my thoughts continued to circle round the day's events and tomorrow's possibilities. It could prove to be a very interesting, if not very pleasant, Monday. I clearly had to speak to the two old Nazis again and put more pressure on the head of the police security service.

# XIII

I locked the door to my flat in Hegdehaugen at twenty past ten. At twenty-five past ten, I got an unusually late telephone call.

The voice at the other end, which I had heard before, asked if this was 'Detective Inspector Kolbjørn Kristiansen'. But the voice sounded different on the telephone and the man who was calling was far more confused than when I first spoke to him. I knew who he was before he even said his name.

'Please forgive me for phoning at this time, but it is because I have something that might help you with the investigation and could be very important. My wife and I have discussed it and neither of us felt it was right not to call you, even though it is late. This is Arno Reinhardt. And something absolutely incredible has just happened!'

He stammered and swallowed. I gave him the time he needed. Then suddenly everything tumbled out.

'Falko came back to see us this evening! He's alive and unharmed. At around nine o'clock, there he was standing at the door, out of the blue. He looked exactly the same as before, it was as if he had not been gone a day. My wife and I both thought it was a dream. But we hugged him and even took a picture of him before he disappeared again!'

It was easy to imagine the scene. And it was very moving, in the middle of a murder investigation.

I told him how pleased I was, and said that it must be an enormous relief for him and his wife. His voice sounded happy when he continued, but it also sounded bewildered and anxious.

'Yes, thank you, it was the greatest moment of our lives, after taking him home with us in 1945, of course. But now he's vanished again, and the mystery of who might have shot his fiancée remains . . . So we're overjoyed, but worried about him all the same. We thought that we should tell you immediately, and ask you to let us know if there is anything we can do to help solve the case.'

I threw myself at this opportunity straight away and asked if Falko had said anything about where he had been or where he was going. However, it transpired that his parents, in a state of shock, surprise and joy, had not grasped much other than that their son was alive. He had told them in brief that he had first gone to the Soviet Union and from there on to China, as Norway was under great threat, and that he had come back now, despite this danger, because he had an important task to fulfil. The future of the nation might depend on it, he had said.

Falko Reinhardt had promised to come back again in a few days, and had asked to borrow the keys to his father's car in the meantime, which they of course gave him. He had let them take one single picture and then, despite his parents' protests, disappeared into the night as suddenly as he had come. He had assured them that everything was under control, but in their flustered state, they did not know if they dared to believe that. They had begged him to contact me and he had told them that he planned to do that, without giving any more details.

We finished the call at a quarter to eleven, with a mutual agreement to let one another know immediately if anything important happened.

I felt as confused as Arno Reinhardt sounded in those late evening hours. Things were hotting up on the trail of Falko Reinhardt in Oslo. But not only was it still unclear where he was hiding, but also whom it was he feared, and what he was waiting for before contacting me.

# XIV

At eleven o'clock I decided that there was not much more I could do on the case that Sunday evening, and that the best thing would be to go to bed so that I was well rested for what would no doubt be a demanding Monday. I was in bed by ten past eleven, but was still lying wide awake at a quarter to twelve. The ongoing investigation was in danger of becoming an obsession.

And at ten to twelve, the telephone rang again. I jumped out of bed and raced into the sitting room to get it.

I reached the telephone after the sixth ring. The first thing I heard was some pips that told me that the call was being made from a telephone box. The second thing I heard was a voice that I had never heard before, but immediately recognized. It was just as I had imagined: educated and confident, with only a hint of an accent, but otherwise grammatically perfect Norwegian.

'My apologies for calling so late, but as I am sure you understand, I have had a rather hectic day. My name is Falko Reinhardt, and I have reason to believe that you would still like to talk to me?'

I very quickly assured him of this and asked where he was now. The answer was accompanied by quiet laughter.

'The answer to that is obviously that I am in a telephone box right now, and I don't have any more change than the two krone coins that I've already put in. But we should definitely meet tomorrow. And for reasons that will become apparent, we should meet in Valdres. Can you meet me at the bottom of the cliff there at six o'clock tomorrow evening?'

I croaked out a yes.

'Great stuff. See you tomorrow, then. I will definitely be there, and will tell you everything. But there are a couple of things I need to confirm first. I also have to apologize for my rather hasty departure from the hotel room earlier on today, but I feared for my life and didn't dare to trust that it was really the police. If I had walked into a trap today, there is so much that could have gone wrong, for the country as well as me.'

I told him to take good care of himself tomorrow as well, and asked whether he was certain that there would be no action before we met. To my relief, his voice was just as calm and confident when he continued.

'I have of course considered the possibility. An attack is planned that will shake Norway, but it will not happen until the day after tomorrow at the earliest. Just come to Valdres tomorrow at six, and we will be national heroes, you and I, by the end of the week.'

There was no denying it sounded like an attractive opportunity, and Falko's calm confidence certainly worked its magic – even on me, and even on the telephone at close to midnight. Just then, however, it was interrupted when the telephone pips were drowned out by the single tone that warned that your time was soon up.

I realized that he did not want to say any more tonight about the planned attack, so instead asked in a flash whether he had seen another man he knew when his fiancée was shot.

'I saw a man I knew in another side road. In fact, I saw several people I knew at the scene. There are two possibilities as to who shot Marie, and both are very tr . . .'

The line went dead.

I sat there with a warm receiver in my hand and a cold dialling tone in my ear. And even more unanswered questions. Despite the potential drama involved in the planned attack, my thoughts drifted back to my encounter with the woman on the Lijord Line four days earlier.

What was it that Falko had tried to say about two possible answers to who shot Marie Morgenstierne? That both were troubled? Both were tragic? Both were now threats? Whatever the case, it felt natural to believe that Falko Reinhardt had, from where he was standing, recognized the man in the side road and had inferred that he might have murdered Marie. But it was also possible that he had seen and recognized Kristine Larsen, and that meant it could also have been her.

I decided that it was too late to ring Patricia that evening, but I needed to talk to someone, as I was in no state to sleep following my dramatic conversation with Falko Reinhardt. So at two minutes to midnight, I used the permission I had to telephone my boss if the situation so required.

My boss was awake, and after listening to a brief summary of the most important events of the day, he thanked me for the update, much to my relief. I suggested that indications of an imminent attack were now so concrete that we should perhaps inform the government. Then I hesitated slightly before saying exactly what I thought: that we should above all else try to prevent an attack that would shake up the whole country, and that we could put ourselves in a very vulnerable position if there was a catastrophe and it got out that we had not heeded the warnings. Again, to my relief, my boss agreed.

'I will contact Asle Bryne first thing tomorrow morning. And if he is in agreement, we will then contact the prime minister and opposition leader – and the royal family,' was his conclusion at ten past midnight. It was only then that it dawned on me just how serious this case was. It was half past twelve before I got into bed again, and a quarter to two before I finally fell asleep on the morning after Sunday, 9 August 1970.

## DAY SIX

# By the cliff – and near boiling point

## I

To my surprise, I was able to eat breakfast without being interrupted by any telephone calls on Monday, 10 August 1970. The newspapers had nothing new or alarming to report. The main focus was once again on international politics. The prospects of a so-called SALT agreement on nuclear disarmament were suddenly so good that the German chancellor Willy Brandt had had to cut short his holiday in Norway to travel to Moscow for further negotiations. The broadsheet *Aftenposten* had managed to snap him just before he left from the military airbase at Gardermoen. Otherwise, yesterday had been a dramatic day in the Norwegian Football Cup, with Gjøvik-Lyn beating Rosenborg as the greatest surprise.

The feeling that this was the calm before the storm intensified when I got to the station at half past eight. My boss was sitting waiting in my office, together with a besuited and very serious man I had never seen before.

'Bryne agrees that there is every reason to be cautious.

We have set up an appointment with Prime Minister Peder Borgen in his office at eleven o'clock, and then with the leader of the Labour Party, Trond Bratten, at Young's Square at midday,' my boss told me in an unusually formal manner.

'But first of all, please tell the Head of Royal Security what he needs to know about our information, and what we have grounds to fear might happen within the next few days,' he added promptly.

If the man sitting opposite me was a policeman, I had certainly never met him before. His posture hinted at a more military background. I guessed that he must be around fifty, and his face was devoid of any expression. His handshake was firm, but he did not introduce himself and I saw no reason to ask him any questions. Instead, I quickly told him the parts of the story that involved the risk of a future attack.

My boss and I both looked at our guest in anticipation when I had finished talking. His face was just as expressionless and grave.

'The threat remains somewhat diffuse, but the situation is definitely to be taken seriously. Thank you for keeping us informed,' he said, following a short pause. His voice was just as expressionless as his face, but was slightly more animated when he continued.

'The crown prince is on a sailing holiday and has no official duties this week. We will, however, ensure extra cover for the coastal guard over the coming days. His Majesty the King only has two official engagements this week. He is due to open a new swimming pool in Asker at six o'clock this evening, and at the same time tomorrow evening will be the guest of honour at an event hosted by the Military Association of Oslo. Both events have been in the calendar for a long time. They can of course be cancelled on the grounds of illness or suchlike, but that might easily result in unfortunate rumours and speculation. With your knowledge of the case, do you have any thoughts as to whether His Majesty should cancel his appearance at one or both of the events, or not?'

I had not expected the question, and the whole situation suddenly felt rather absurd. The thought that the king might be subject to an attack was so dramatic that I nearly advised them to cancel everything. But then, the thought of being held responsible for disappointing the crowds of people who had turned up to see the king, with no good grounds, was not very appealing either.

In the end, I said that I would advise that the day's event should go ahead as planned with reinforced security, and to wait and see how the situation developed before making any decision about the event tomorrow. I realized that I was now simply pushing the problem ahead to the next day, but also that I trusted Falko Reinhardt's judgement that the possibility of an attack today was unthinkable.

To my relief, the man with the stony face nodded his approval.

'I will monitor the situation over the course of the day, but I think I agree with your opinion as long as there is no direct threat to the royal family. Please make sure that I am informed immediately of any new information that might give grounds for concern.'

Without waiting for a reply, he stood up and left the office, accompanied by my boss.

I was left sitting in the office on my own, with an ever greater sense of responsibility for the case and its potential for catastrophe.

Two minutes after my boss had left the office, I checked my pulse just to make sure, and it was still racing at 150. And that was even before I started to dial the number of the head of the police security service, Asle Bryne, at Victoria Terrace.

# II

Asle Bryne gave a stifled sigh when he heard my voice on the telephone. It was just the encouragement I needed to complete my offensive.

'I am sorry that I have to disturb you again, but you really have put both me and the investigation in a very difficult situation.'

'I see,' he said. His voice sounded somewhat resigned, but also guarded in anticipation of how much I knew.

'I have every reason to believe that the security service agent was not only present on the evening that Marie Morgenstierne was shot, but also on the evening when Falko Reinhardt went missing. The agent is easy to identify physically, even though it seems he was running around in Valdres wearing a mask. One can only imagine what the press will make of it should the story get out.'

For the last time, I expected an outburst that never

happened. There was an embarrassing silence on the line. I smiled at the phone and mentally chalked up Patricia's win over the security service, 3–0. Asle Bryne gave what could only be described as a heavy sigh before he continued.

'It is unfortunately true that one of our agents has overstepped his authority and made some mistakes in this case. But he is an excellent agent who for many years has contributed to the security of our land and its people. And you can take my word for it that he has nothing whatsoever to do with either the murder of Marie Morgenstierne or the disappearance of Falko Reinhardt!'

I heard myself say that I of course did not doubt his word, but that, given the developments in the case, I now had to meet this man in confidence to hear what information he could give me.

Then I heard Asle Bryne reply in a very faint voice that he totally understood that, and that the most important thing now was to make sure that the press and politicians did not get wind of it, and that I could of course meet the man in private if I came to Victoria Terrace at midday. To which I replied that I unfortunately already had a meeting at midday that was of crucial significance to the country and its people, but that one o'clock should be fine.

Asle Bryne's reply was even curter than usual: 'Fine,' he said, and put down the telephone.

I sat with the receiver in my hand and laughed out loud. But it was not long before I was serious again. It was now past nine o'clock, and on my list of people to speak to before my meeting at eleven with the prime minister were two former Nazis and an elderly couple.

# III

By five past nine, I had decided to drive over to Falko's parents in Grünerløkka first, and then, if time permitted, to Frans Heidenberg and Christian Magnus Eggen.

But just as I stood up, the telephone on my desk started to ring. I registered that the mounting pressure in the case now resulted in a quickening of my pulse every time the telephone rang.

The first thing I heard was the pips from a telephone box. I waited for a moment, expecting to hear either Falko Reinhardt's voice from the evening before, or an unknown, threatening man's voice. But it was in fact Miriam Filtvedt Bentsen's pleasant, measured voice that spoke: 'Hi. I'm sure you are very busy today, so I won't keep you long. But the library has just opened and I checked in the book, as I promised I would. And it really was on 5 August 1868 that Karl jumped, fell or was pushed over the cliff in Vestre Slidre. Source: Local history yearbook for Valdres, 1955, page 14.'

As Miriam Filtvedt Bentsen spoke, several things oc-curred to me in rapid and rather messy succession. First of all, she had obviously recognized my voice and taken it for granted that I would recognize hers. And secondly, her matter-of-fact voice had a calming effect on me in the midst of all the chaos. Thirdly, she must have been standing ready at the entrance when the library opened in order to have got this information by five past nine. And fourthly, I was going to Valdres again that day and wanted to ask her to come with me.

I opened my mouth to ask if she could come. But she beat me to it.

'And is there anything new to tell? Or anything else that I can help you with today?'

The questions were asked in the same level, helpful and prosaic manner. And yet they felt like two cold showers in succession. The letters 'SP' began to echo in my mind. I sat there for a few seconds and wondered if this was just another manifestation of her desire for knowledge, or if it was a cynical attempt to get information about any developments in the case.

The fear of misjudging, and of a possible police scandal, got the better of me. Against my own will, I did not ask Miriam Filtvedt Bentsen if she would like to come to Valdres again. Instead I thanked her briefly for her help with the yearbook and said that there had been a number of developments, but that I was not able to talk about them on the telephone. I promised to contact her if and when I could tell her more.

Miriam Filtvedt Bentsen said that she perfectly understood, but her voice sounded less happy when she said it. And at that moment, the long pips told us that the line would be cut in a matter of seconds. She wished me good luck with the day's work, said that she had to get back to the library and then put the receiver down before I had time to say goodbye.

I sat for a minute or two and wondered if I had done the right thing, or just made an enormous mistake. I obviously continued to ponder this subconsciously in the car, because after driving for three minutes I discovered that

I was heading west towards the university instead of east towards the photograph gallery in Grünerløkka. I stuck resolutely to my decision, turned around at the first opportunity and went east.

# IV

Falko Reinhardt's parents were waiting, and opened the door as soon as I arrived. The red rims round their eyes told of a sleepless night, and it seemed they were both still in the grip of very mixed emotions. It crossed my mind that I had never before seen such a well-harmonized and close couple. As if to illustrate this, they were holding between them a large, newly developed black and white photograph.

Falko was embracing his mother in the picture, but still looking at the camera squarely, evidently self-aware. He was still very much himself even after two years' absence. The man in the photograph was tall, muscular and dark, with curly hair, and looked as though he was firmly convinced that he could fulfil a difficult and important task. I was not sure whether I would actually like Falko Reinhardt or not, when we finally met. But I certainly hoped that his confidence in this case was well founded. Despite Patricia's accurate conclusions, the outcome of the investigation was entirely dependent on what Falko Reinhardt could and wanted to tell me.

I told them that Falko had called me just before midnight and that we had arranged to meet in Valdres that evening. They thanked me sincerely for letting them know and said that they were happy that he had been in touch. But they had no idea why we should meet that evening, or in Valdres. This new small puzzle within the greater puzzle seemed to make them more anxious about the situation.

Otherwise, they did not have much news to tell. Their son had suddenly turned up at their door without warning the night before, giving them the best shock of their lives. Then he had disappeared out the door with the key to his parents' blue Peugeot half an hour later. They had asked where he was going to spend the night, but he had replied that it was safest and best for them if they did not know. He had promised to take good care of himself and asked them to be careful about who they let in. They had asked him to contact the police as soon as possible, which he had promised to do. On his way out, he had added that he had something big and important to do for the country, but that everything would be sorted within forty-eight hours.

I asked whether he had had anything more to say about his fiancée's dramatic death. They both looked down and with something akin to humiliation said that he had not mentioned it, and that they in their confusion had not asked. Their astonishment and joy at seeing their only son again had been so great that they had had no thought for anything else until he had gone. Later, when they talked through the night, they concluded that Marie Morgen-stierne's death was now even more inexplicable than before. They were utterly convinced, though, that Falko had nothing to do with it, and tended to think now that his fiancée must have been murdered for other reasons that had nothing to do with him. Their initial theory that some political enemies were intent on liquidating the whole group had foundered, as Falko himself was alive.

The conversation then dried up, with a few repetitions. I declined the offer of coffee, saying I had a long and busy day ahead. Still in perfect harmony, they nodded together with understanding.

'Given our story, we hope you understand why we have never trusted the police. For the past couple of decades, the police in Norway, as in so many other countries west of the Iron Curtain, have only been there to repress people like us, and have never been there for us when we needed help. But we do have confidence in you. We trust that you will come back with our son alive and close the case so that any danger that threatens him disappears. Only then can we relax and enjoy life.'

Astrid Reinhardt smiled gently as she said this. Her husband was silent in his consent. It felt like a very personal and significant vote of confidence, but I also felt that the pressure on me was mounting. I rushed out to the car.

# V

I deliberately started my second round of visits to the former Nazis with the architect Frans Heidenberg in Skøyen. I reckoned that there was more chance of getting something out of him than his far more temperamental friend, Christian Magnus Eggen.

The house was just as impressive as it had been the first time, and the lawn was newly cut. Frans Heidenberg opened the door with same friendly smile, then showed me into the same grand living room. But it was never likely to be such a pleasant and relaxed visit as the first time round, and that certainly proved to be the case.

I did not have much time, so I got straight to the point and reminded my host that when I last came to see him he had told me that he had not met the Valdres farmer, Henry Alfred Lien, since the war. He nodded, and then pointed out that that was of course as far as he could remember. He had spoken to so many people at social occasions in the past twenty-five years that it was impossible to remember everyone, given his ageing memory.

I put the photograph that had been left behind by Falko Reinhardt in Room 27 down on the table in front of us. With a slight edge to my voice, I expressed my hope that his memory was at least good enough to be able to confirm whom he had eaten with at a restaurant this summer.

I caught a glimpse of a different and far less friendly Frans Heidenberg as soon as I put down the picture. For a few seconds, his mouth was drawn and his eyes got flinty. But he kept up appearances and controlled his voice extremely well when he spoke after a short pause for thought.

Frans Heidenberg's explanation of the picture was that he and Christian Magnus Eggen had gone to the Grand Café for a good dinner, and had started chatting to two other gentlemen in the bar who were friendly and made a good impression. So they had chatted for a while, but he had no reason to pay attention to their names and certainly could not remember them now. He 'remembered vaguely' that one of them did have a Valdres dialect, and would in no way protest if I said that he was Henry Alfred Lien. But when he had answered the question the last time I was there, he had done so in good faith.

I pretended to believe Frans Heidenberg and asked with forced camaraderie if he knew anything about the fourth person in the picture. He gave me his friendliest smile back and shook his head apologetically. The fourth person at the table had apparently been an older man in a suit, who he thought came from Oslo. It wasn't easy to guess his age and the man had said very little about himself. And it was difficult for him to give me a more detailed physical description. He talked rather vaguely about a dark-haired man, somewhere between sixty and seventy, but there were so few details that it could hardly be called a description. Unfortunately his eyes were not what they used to be, and he did not like to be impolite and stare too much at people.

We got stuck in this rather stilted, mutually guarded mode of communication. I understood that Frans Heidenberg was either lying outright or, at the very least, failing to divulge some important information. But I also realized that, for the moment, I had no way to prove it. And he knew this, too. So we continued for a few minutes, locked in a war of wills; in the pleasantest of voices, I asked for more details, and he apologized that he could not remember or had not noticed anything else. Sadly, his sight, hearing and memory were no longer what they used to be.

My final question was whether Christian Magnus Eggen

appeared to know the other two men from before, and if so, to what extent. Frans Heidenberg again gave an apologetic shrug and said that he had no idea. If it was important, I could of course pay Eggen a visit and ask him myself. I saw the hint of a mocking smile playing both on his lips and in his eyes when he said this, but yet again, it was something that could not be pinned down.

I took Heidenberg at his word and said that I would do just that, and asked him to keep our conversation confidential. The conversation ended fittingly enough with him promising to do this, when we both knew perfectly well that he would break that promise as soon as I left the house.

Frans Heidenberg accompanied me to the door like the perfect host, held out his hand and wished me good luck with the investigation and a good day. After a moment's hesitation, I took it. Shaking his hand now felt like biting into a sour apple. As I walked down the driveway, I suddenly disliked Frans Heidenberg even more than Christian Magnus Eggen. But this did not mean that I looked forward to meeting the latter.

# VI

It was half past ten when I rang Christian Magnus Eggen's doorbell in Kolsås. I did not have much time left before my appointment at the prime minister's office. However, I did not anticipate that this would be a long conversation. And in that sense, I was not disappointed.

Christian Magnus Eggen opened the door and leaned on his stick. He made no sign of inviting me in, and I had no desire whatsoever to go in.

He set the tone by asking if I had anything new to tell him about the murder of his old friend, Marius Kofoed, in spring 1945 – in which case, he would be happy to talk to me.

I replied with measured calm that the case was not my responsibility, and furthermore was now time-barred, so he could perhaps, happily or unhappily, talk to me about more recent murder cases. Christian Magnus Eggen rolled his eyes, denied any knowledge of any more recent murder cases and said he was curious to know if I had any proof linking him to such cases.

I held the photograph up in front of him and asked how this fitted with his previous statement that he had not seen Henry Alfred Lien since the war.

I had thought that Christian Magnus Eggen would have coordinated his explanation with that of Frans Heidenberg. But instead he chose another strategy.

'This very personal photograph, which you have some-how or other managed to get hold of, simply shows that I have gone to a restaurant with other people. And as far as I know, that is still legal, even here in Norway. I have not registered any new exemption laws that forbid people from eating in restaurants, and they would no doubt have been reported in *Morgenbladet* and *Aftenposten*. I do not see any connection between this picture and any criminal activities that have gone on either this summer or before. If you are investigating the murder of that young communist woman,

252

it is hard to see how a photograph of four elderly men in a restaurant could possibly be of any relevance. Or perhaps you can explain it to me?'

I replied that it was I who was there to ask questions and that it would not be in his favour if he refused to answer these in an ongoing investigation. This did not humour him in any way.

'In that case you will have to present it before a judge and see if there is strong enough evidence for you to summon me as a witness. In the meantime, I have no desire to give any information to you, the police or anyone else about which friends I see and when.'

I made a final attempt and asked if he could give me a more detailed description of the person who was unidentifiable in the picture. It could well be of even more interest to check him out of the case than Eggen himself.

'I could, but I do not want to. And what is more, I do not want to prolong this conversation with you any more.'

Christian Magnus Eggen's eyes shone with an almost childlike defiance when he said this. I understood then and there that his hatred for society that had been building over the years had now found an outlet, and was directed at me.

I ventured to remind him that when a young person was murdered, the parents and other close friends and relatives were left bereft.

He seemed taken aback by this. He leaned heavily on his stick for a few moments, then sank down into a chair in the hallway. His voice was suddenly grave and sad when he spoke again. But it had not lost any of its intensity or speed.

'I know absolutely nothing about the murder you are

investigating and have nothing to say that might help those left behind. But I have to say that my sympathy for the parents of murdered communists is somewhat limited. Which might perhaps have something to do with the fact that my only son was shot by the communists in the war.'

Christian Magnus Eggen now seemed to be both upset and tired at once. He gasped for air a couple of times and then continued.

'And as you mentioned those left behind, parents and children, let me tell you about another old murder . . . My friend Frans may well have already told you that his fiancée had disappeared when he got out of prison after the war. But he is such a considerate person that he perhaps did not mention the child?'

I shook my head and sent him a piercing look. He took a deep breath and carried on.

'Frans's perfidious fiancée was pregnant when he was arrested – in the fourth month, no less. According to the law of the day, killing a foetus was a crime, even in Norway. But that did not prevent the death of Frans's only child while he was being held on remand, with the help of both the police and the health service. Frans and I have paid our taxes for decades and have had to take care to uphold all kinds of strange laws, but have never had any rights ourselves, not even to our children's lives. So you might perhaps try to understand why, today, we are not particularly cooperative with the police and do not feel much sympathy for those left behind by communists. And now it may well be best for us both if you just leave me in peace!'

I gave a short nod to this as I turned on my heel and walked away. It was now twenty to eleven, and I would soon be very short of time to make my meeting with the prime minister. But I had got an interesting glimpse of the bitter person behind Christian Magnus Eggen's mask, and I did feel a smattering of understanding for both him and Frans Heidenberg. I had also lost all my illusions of what these bitter and lonely old men might be capable of doing in relation to a society they felt had let them down, and that they hated with a vengeance.

I was becoming increasingly curious and worried about the mysterious fourth man. I left the photograph lying on the passenger seat where I could see it, and studied it at every traffic light. There was still not much to be had. Both Frans Heidenberg and Christian Magnus Eggen had indicated that he was an older man, around their age. But the photograph did not prove or disprove this. The only lead was a right hand with no wedding ring or any other form of visible distinction. It could, in theory, as easily belong to a twenty-year-old as to a seventy-year-old.

It did feel as though I had touched on something significant that morning. But what exactly it was, I still could not say.

# VII

I had to use my blue light for the last part of the journey in order to get to the meeting on time. At one minute to eleven, I stood for the first time at the door of the prime minister's office.

The office was smaller than I had imagined. A very correct secretary asked me to go straight into the prime minister's personal office. And when I went in, the prime minister was sitting alone at his simple desk.

Even though I, as a city lad, had never considered voting for the Farmers' Party, or the Centre Party as they were now called, I had considerable sympathy for the down-to-earth farmer, Peder Borgen. This was in no way diminished by meeting him. In sharp contrast to the representative for the royal family's security service, Norway's prime minister stood up and shook my hand heartily.

I knew only too well that the prime minister was facing a very demanding autumn and winter. It was widely acknowledged that growing disagreement between parties in the coalition government would soon come to a head in the debate about Norway's position regarding the Common Market. My father, who had a good nose for politics, and also good contacts in several parties, had expressed several times this summer his belief and hope that the government would fall apart in good time before Christmas. And any avid newspaper reader could see that following their good results in the autumn elections, the Labour Party was now putting on the pressure in the Storting and preparing to take over the reins very soon. Given all this, the prime minister seemed to be remarkably relaxed and calm.

I began by remarking that I would not take up more of his time than strictly necessary. He replied, however, that he had nothing special that had to be done today, and that he would like to hear what I had to tell about the case.

My plans for a brief ten-minute orientation soon went out the window, but through no fault of my own. The prime minister interrupted me repeatedly with the strangest detailed questions about the facts of the case and my thoughts on them. It took a full forty minutes before we were finished. The prime minister remained calm when I spoke of the danger of an attack or sabotage and explained that it might, in the worst-case scenario, involve him or other members of the government.

When I asked about his public engagements over the next few days, he conferred briefly with his secretary and then said it was quieter in summer and he had no official engagements today, whereas the next day he was giving a talk at a Norwegian Farmers' Union seminar and then was doing the honours at the official opening of a small national park at six.

I noted down the times and said that he would have to decide for himself whether he thought it was sensible to participate in the planned events or not. This triggered a sudden and unexpected change in the prime minister's mood. Suddenly he looked anxious and almost upset. He said that the decision to cancel two such arrangements that he had promised to attend was very serious indeed, and that it should be discussed and looked at in more detail.

I had some problems in keeping a straight face, but told the prime minister that he would have to make a decision before the next day's events. This seemed to heighten his anxiety even more. He said that might well be the case, but it was therefore all the more important to think things through and discuss the matter thoroughly before making a decision. I said, taking professional confidentiality into account, he could discuss it with his family and other members of the government, the party leadership and the prime minister's office. Peder Borgen thanked me and promised to do that. He then asked if I would be available for further discussion if necessary.

I replied that I was honoured and would of course talk more about the case to him if he so wished, but that it might be difficult to reach me on my telephone due to the ongoing investigation. He said he understood and jotted down my telephone numbers right away. I was rather surprised then to receive a handwritten note with the prime minister's own numbers on it, clearly marked 'home' and 'work'.

I was even more astonished to hear him say that I could call whenever it suited, whether it was about the case or other issues that might interest me. In the end it was decided that I should try to call him around two the following day, and in the meantime make sure that he was informed immediately if there was any more news in relation to possible attacks and demonstrations. At the door, he shook my hand heartily again and thanked me for 'a very interesting hour in good company'.

It was only then that it struck me that it was now two minutes to midday, and that I would be late for my next important appointment, even though Young's Square lay relatively close by. I left the prime minister's office with a favourable impression of the man himself, but also wondering if Norway's leader was perhaps a little too dialogue-oriented and patient.

# VIII

I arrived at the People's Theatre building on Young's Square at three minutes past twelve, and was immediately ushered into the office of the Labour Party leader, Trond Bratten. I almost ran in and apologized for being late, due to an overrun at the prime minister's office.

The party leader himself was sitting at his desk behind great piles of paper, looking very relaxed about the whole thing. He remained seated and just nodded almost imperceptibly at the chair on the other side of the desk. I hesitated for a moment, then went over to the desk, held out my hand and introduced myself. His handshake was brief and limp, accompanied by a careful, almost shy smile.

'Trond Bratten,' he said in a quiet voice, as though it was something to be ashamed of.

The loud reaction came instead from the third person in the room whom I suddenly realized was there – his wife, Ragna Bratten. She leaped up from her chair by the wall, pumped my hand and commented that it was rather unfortunate that the country's future prime minister had to wait.

Despite being in the middle of an increasingly hectic investigation, my fascination at meeting the leader of the Labour Party was even greater than my delight at meeting Peder Borgen. I had voted for Trond Bratten's party at every election in the 1960s. I had always had a strong liking for him, both politically and personally. It was a joy to hear his arguments in speeches and debates. And what I knew about his life, from his childhood in relative poverty in

Vestfold and the years as a prisoner of war in Germany to his position as chairman of the party and many years in office as minister of finance, engendered my deep respect. For as long as I could remember, Trond Bratten had been a member of the Labour Party leadership and one of Norway's leading politicians. It felt like a great honour to meet such a living legend from Norway's political life.

I mustered my courage and said this to him. The response was very positive. Trond Bratten himself smiled, slightly abashed, and his wife patted me enthusiastically on the shoulder.

My planned orientation was done in ten minutes here. The party chairman closely followed everything I said, and nodded pensively a couple of times. But he sat and listened without asking any questions or making any comments.

When I had finished my orientation, I looked at him questioningly, without getting a response. Trond Bratten sat without saying a word, almost without moving, even when I asked him if he had any public engagements in the coming days. Again, it was his wife who broke the silence.

'My husband has only one public engagement over the next few days, but it is an extremely important one that must not be cancelled under any circumstances.'

Trond Bratten gave the tiniest of nods, but still said nothing.

I turned and looked askance at his wife, who then continued.

'You may perhaps have read that my husband was seriously ill in the Easter holidays and then had to take several months off work. Well, the political situation has fortunately been rather quiet so far this year. It looks as though autumn and winter, however, might be more dramatic, as the Europe question is once again high on the agenda and the coalition government is falling apart at the seams. On top of this, my husband's sick leave has led to malicious rumours that his health is now permanently impaired, so the deputy leader and other ambitious men have started to position themselves to take over. The former party leader and several older rivals who envy my husband's unique abilities and position are also jostling in the wings. My husband is due to give his first major speech since his illness at Frogner Square tomorrow at five o'clock and it has been a long time in the planning. It is an attempt to appeal to new workers' organizations in the west end, but will also be a large-scale mobilization of the labour movement. The unions in several workplaces have put on transport for employees to get there after work to hear my husband's speech, which he has spent several hours preparing. No matter what reason was given, it would be a catastrophe if it did not go ahead as planned, which could have untold negative consequences for both the party and the nation.'

This tumbled out at speed and with passion. I looked at Trond Bratten, who at first simply nodded.

'Norwegian democracy must never again allow itself to be intimidated into silence. And the leader of the Norwegian Labour Party is responsible for ensuring that democracy is not intimidated into silence!' he said suddenly, with great conviction.

For a second, I recognized the Trond Bratten of his best

and most pointed debates on the radio and television. His wife clapped with delight and I found myself almost doing the same. I stopped myself just in time, and instead asked if he had any other commitments in the next few days.

His wife answered swiftly, 'No. He will have to rest well after tomorrow's speech.'

Trond Bratten nodded and smiled at her. For a moment, he seemed to forget that I was present in the room.

I noted down the time and place of the next day's engagement and said, as was the case, that we so far had no indication of any targeted action against Trond Bratten or anyone else from the Labour Party. I promised to let them know if we got any new information. And I was bold enough to advise Mrs Bratten that until the situation was fully established, she should be especially mindful of her husband.

This hit the mark. She smiled back and assured me that she always kept an eye on him, but that she would keep an even closer eye in the days ahead. She would, as usual, drive him to and from the rally tomorrow herself, and would personally ensure that her husband's good friends in the labour movement were watched like hawks.

We parted on a positive note at half past twelve. She followed me to the door, and he waved a couple of fingers gently from his place behind his desk. I had lost none of my respect or fascination for Trond Bratten when I descended the steps. The contrast with the prime minister was strik-ing. But I found it easy to like them both. And I thought to myself that I had just seen a rare and fine example of a couple who worked well together despite a considerable difference in age and temperament. For several reasons, it had been an enjoyable break from the investigation.

# IX

I barely had time to grab two dry buns from a baker's shop for lunch before arriving at Victoria Terrace as agreed.

This time, Asle Bryne was not sitting alone in his office. Beside him sat a far younger man, with a prominent mole on his chin. I was relieved to discover that Miriam Filtvedt Bentsen was observant and still to be trusted.

I held out my hand to the new man, but was stopped by Asle Bryne's authoritative hand.

'Please wait a moment before you start talking: we first have to clarify the terms. The fact that I am allowing an employee to be at such a meeting is exceptional. But then, the situation is exceptional, and I understand your need to resolve it. I would like to state, however, that this man has done nothing criminal, but on the contrary has made a considerable and important contribution to our country and its people. I expect him to be treated with respect, and this conversation to remain strictly confidential. Are the terms clear?'

I gave a quick nod. Asle Bryne then made a great fuss of lighting his pipe, and disappeared behind a cloud of smoke. The man beside him held out his hand. His handshake was firm and strong, though I detected a slight tremor.

I sat down and asked first of all if he was the 'XY' who

had written the report. He nodded. I proceeded to say that I now needed to know his name, in the strictest confidence. He turned and looked at Bryne, waiting for a response. Somewhere inside the grey cloud of smoke, Bryne's great black eyebrows rose and fell.

'My name is Pedersen. Stein Pedersen. But I would be extremely grateful if no one else heard it, as that would make my continued work in preventing a communist take-over very difficult.'

Both Bryne and I gave a nod, though mine was more reserved than his. I was surprised at how well I was managing to play my role. The opening was a small sensation. Were the initials SP just a coincidence, or was I now sitting opposite the man who planned to carry out an attack against someone or other, at some place, within the next few days? Was it really possible that such an attack would come from inside the police security service?

I focused my concentration and asked him first to tell me about his impressions from the evening that Marie Morgenstierne was shot. Stein Pedersen nodded, and repeated in a monotone voice the main points of his written report. He did not give any new details about the two men on the side roads, or about any of the other people who were on the road.

When I asked if anyone might have seen the cassette being handed over, he was 'at least ninety-nine per cent' certain that they could not have done so. It was done in passing, and he had not seen anyone ahead or behind them on the road either before or after it happened. Kristine

Larsen had only appeared behind him several minutes later, and had then overtaken him quickly, with determined steps.

As for his earlier contact with Marie Morgenstierne, Stein Pedersen did not have anything of importance to add. She had contacted him a few weeks after Falko Reinhardt had disappeared, and had later routinely provided him with tapes, but it had been a very perfunctory contact with little extra information. He had been given her telephone number and had rung her on a few occasions, but claimed never to have been to her home. And he denied, somewhat horrified and indignant, that he had ever had any kind of romantic or physical relationship with her.

'First of all, my work for my country does not leave me any time for women. And what is more, were that not the case, young communist women would certainly not be my preference!' he objected.

It looked as though Asle Bryne's eyebrows approved of this, but the smoke around him was now so dense that I could not have said for certain.

I swiftly changed the subject to talk about the circumstances surrounding Falko Reinhardt's disappearance. Pedersen immediately sank a little into his chair. Asle Bryne, on the other hand, perked up. Between two long puffs on his pipe, he said: 'Procedures have unfortunately been broken, albeit with the best intentions and without any harm being done. Just tell the truth!'

Pedersen nodded gratefully, and immediately continued.

'My behaviour was unprofessional in the extreme. But I had for months spent a lot of time on the group and was convinced they were going to plan something serious while they were at the cabin – perhaps, in the worst-case scenario, meet some foreign agents. I felt that my most important duty and responsibility was to protect society against them. Our budgets and work schedules did not allow surveillance of the group in Valdres, but I was off work that week and, following a struggle with my conscience, decided to go up there on my own initiative. Hence the mask, which was in clear breach of normal procedures. I did this partly so that they would not recognize me if they saw me, and partly to prevent any suspicion that the police security service was involved.'

I attempted to give an understanding nod.

'And what was the outcome of your trip? Were there any indications of foreign contacts or that any of them were planning something serious?'

He shook his head.

'The whole thing was, technically, a fiasco. I am still convinced that they went there to talk about something that they wanted to keep under wraps. But the cabin was far less accessible than I had thought, and the weather was terrible. I was not able to hide any microphones in the cabin, and I barely managed to get within sight of it. My first attempt to spy through the window ended with me being spotted by Miriam Filtvedt Bentsen. So I beat a hasty retreat and drove back down to Oslo again. I only heard that Falko Reinhardt had gone missing on the radio the following day.'

'A large car was seen driving down the valley in the middle of the night, after Falko had disappeared. Was that your car?'

He shook his head again.

'I was driving my own car, which was a small Ford, and by the time that happened, I was already back in Oslo. I know nothing about the car you mentioned, or who might have been driving it. I do know, however, where Falko went when he left the others for a couple of hours earlier in the day, and whom he met there.'

He sent me a meaningful look. I tried to stay collected, and waved him on impatiently.

'I watched him from a distance, with the help of ordinary binoculars, from my stakeout in the forest. He was walking fast and passed only twenty yards or so from me. Then he carried on out of the forest and across the fields of the neighbouring farm. There he met the farmer himself, who appeared a few minutes later with a mowing machine as a cover. It looked as though the meeting had been planned, and that they did not want anyone to see!'

He said this in almost a whisper. I gave a short nod of acknowledgement.

'And was the farmer a well-built, older man?'

He nodded quickly.

'His name is Henry Alfred Lien, and he is a convicted former member of the NS. I checked his name when I got back home. But, as far as we know, there is nothing to link him to any countries in the Eastern bloc or to radical, left-wing groups in Norway. So it is not at all clear what the meeting might have been about, and is hardly likely to be relevant.'

My nod was less approving, and I asked if he observed anything else of interest – for example, any romantic liaisons between members of the group.

For the first time, his otherwise earnest face broke into a small smile.

'Such internal liaisons are very usual in groups like that, but seldom of relevance to us. I may have observed something of the kind, but it depends on who you are alluding to.'

I took a deep breath and started the list.

'Trond Ibsen.'

He promptly shook his head.

'Anders Pettersen?'

Again, he shook his head immediately. I noticed that my heart started to race when I mentioned the next name.

'Miriam Filtvedt Bentsen?'

Another shake of the head, and this time he made a dismissive gesture with his hands to reinforce it.

'She was definitely not the type to get involved in that kind of thing. I cannot understand what she was doing with the group in the first place.'

I keenly nodded my approval and suddenly liked him a little more. The situation was demanding and my dislike of surveillance considerable, but I had to admit that Stein Pedersen certainly seemed to have talents in the field.

'Marie Morgenstierne?'

'Only with her fiancé, and then it was far less public

than is normal. But she came from a good family, after all, and was therefore very well behaved.'

I nodded. That was as I had imagined.

'But, on the other hand, Kristine Larsen, and Falko . . .'

He chuckled, but very soon was serious again, in fact, almost angry.

'Bingo. One almost has to admire his self-confidence, but morally it was rather repugnant. He had come back from a short afternoon walk hand-in-hand with his fiancée. Then two minutes after she had gone into the cabin, there he was in the shadows outside with his hand down Kristine Larsen's trousers. She was so very in love that it was a wonder that no one else noticed it. But in a strange way, they all circuited him in awe. With the exception of Miriam Filtvedt Bentsen, who was in her own world with her books.'

Again, I nodded my approval. And then spoke the truth. Pedersen's behaviour had been very unprofessional and as such unfortunate, but he had also been very observant and I had to thank him for some potentially useful information. The matter would henceforth be treated with absolute confidentiality, and would not be included in any formal minutes or reports, or brought to the attention of any officials. Unless, of course, he had anything more serious to hide.

Stein Pedersen brightened. He assured me earnestly that he had nothing to hide, and that he had committed no crime. I said that we could then see the matter as closed, but reserved the right to get in touch with him to ask more questions, should this prove necessary in connection with the murder investigation.

Asle Bryne put down his pipe, nodded curtly and held out his hand. Like an echo, Stein Pedersen did the same. He wrote down two telephone numbers on a piece of paper and handed it to me.

I left Victoria Terrace with plenty to think about. I had been given a few more details and also a new and very interesting insight into the police security service. Having heard Stein Pedersen talk about his mission, it was even harder to imagine him as a killer. I was very relieved to discover that his account did not contradict any of the others on any point. But it had taken a suspiciously long time to get that statement from him, and I still did not trust that he had told me everything. And the strange coincidence between the initials of his name and those on Falko Reinhardt's to-do list hounded me all the way back to the main police station.

# X

It was a quarter past two by the time I got back to my office. So there was still an hour left before I had to drive to Valdres. And it was, to my relief, unexpectedly quiet in the station.

As soon as I could I popped in to see Kristine Larsen in her cell, to update her on the latest developments concerning Falko. She perked up, the colour returned to her cheeks, and she asked me to give Falko her greetings as soon as I saw him.

I hinted that we could now arrange for her release on bail. She thanked me, but added that as she was safe here, she would rather stay where she was until the case had been solved and Falko had returned. Her parents had been informed of the situation and were extremely worried that she too might be shot.

'Just think how tragic it would be if, after two years of waiting, I was released only to be murdered hours before Falko came back to me,' she added, with an almost playful smile.

Her argument suited me well. I preferred not to have to explain her release either internally or externally, until I had a new suspect to arrest. I had by now almost dismissed the theory that Kristine Larsen was the murderer, having heard a third version from the security service agent. Despite her jealousy and betrayal of the late Marie Morgenstierne, it was almost impossible not to feel sympathy for this clearly besotted young woman, who had been waiting for two years for her beloved to return. I hoped in my heart that Falko would be with her again within the next twenty-four hours, and that he would prove worthy of her love.

On my way back to the office, I bumped into Detective Inspector Vegard Danielsen in the corridor, apparently by accident. With one of his most ingratiating smiles, he said he hoped that the investigation was progressing well. He had heard that someone had been held on remand for a couple of days now, and hoped that this meant that the person in question would be charged shortly and the case could be closed.

I assured him that we were keeping the arrestee on remand, rather than pressing formal charges, with good reason. With a bitter taste in my mouth, I added that I hoped that his door was still open should I need any advice. He promised me that he would be there whenever needed, 'with an open door and an empty desk'.

In a way, our parting in the corridor felt just as false as my parting from Frans Heidenberg at his house. Detective Inspector Vegard Danielsen knew that I would never ask him for help if I could avoid it, and I knew that he knew.

I hurried on to my boss's office and gave him a report on the day's developments. He approved of my methods and plans, both with regard to the trip to Valdres and to keeping Kristine Larsen on remand until the case was solved. Otherwise, like me, he was concerned about the danger of a major attack of some kind or another. The risk of an assassination that the police could not prevent hung like a dark and threatening cloud over both of us. This had to be balanced against the possibility of sparking unfounded fears among the royals, top politicians and the population at large.

My boss agreed with the advice that I had given to the prime minister and opposition leader, but asked that he be informed as soon as possible after I had spoken to Falko Reinhardt. I could ring at any time in this evening, no matter how late, if there was anything new to report. We shook hands on that. My boss's confidence in me was certainly a great support in the midst of so much uncertainty.

After the visit to my boss, I telephoned Patricia from my office and gave her the most important new information. She was once again very interested in the police security service's work. The teenage gossip in Patricia reared her head again: she chortled down the line when I told her the story of Falko and Kristine at the cabin.

Then all of a sudden she was serious and grown up again.

'I have only one question regarding the security service and Marie Morgenstierne, but it is important. Did the security service representative at any later point tell Marie Morgenstierne what he knew about Falko and Kristine? And if so, when? Ask him as soon as you have the opportunity, if the meeting with Falko has not cleared everything up in the meantime.'

I jotted down her question and promised to follow it up the next day. Then I asked if she could give me any advice for the Valdres meeting. She replied without any pause for thought.

'Just one thing, but again, it is important. If you have time, go to see Henry Alfred Lien before you meet Falko, or otherwise, drive there immediately afterwards. Ask him first and foremost about the former Nazis and the mystery man in the photograph. But also ask him if he is willing to take a lie detector test stating that he did not drive Falko down the mountain the night he disappeared. And if possible, check his bookshelves to see if you can find the local history yearbook for Valdres, 1955!'

I replied that it was not likely that I would manage to drive up the mountain and question Henry Alfred Lien before six o'clock, but I promised to drive directly to his farm if Falko did not pitch up at the bottom of the cliff and explain everything.

'Good,' was Patricia's response. Then she said no more.

There was something unsaid on the line between us. It felt as though she wanted to say more, only I was not sure what.

'Well, then all that remains is to wish you a good trip to the mountains. Are you going alone this time, or together with someone else?' she asked, finally.

I replied, perhaps somewhat curtly, that I was driving on my own this time and that I should probably be on my way very soon.

It sounded as though Patricia let out a sigh of relief before hastily wishing me good luck and then hanging up. I felt that we had drifted away from one another again.

With a stab of irritation at Patricia's new jealousy, I wondered again if I should perhaps swing by the university library on my way to Valdres. But instead, I set off on my own at three o'clock as planned.

# XI

The drive to Valdres felt far less inspiring than the previous trip. Long before I passed the Tyri Fjord, I regretted not having asked Miriam Filtvedt Bentsen to join me.

The weather, however, was clement and the traffic minimal, so the journey was smooth once I left Oslo. And following a hectic day with many mood swings, it was good to be able to think about the case in silence. When I reached Vestre Slidre around half past five, I still did not have any clear theory as to who had shot Marie Morgenstierne.

I was now leaning towards the idea that the mysterious other man who was either Trond Ibsen or Anders Pettersen was also the murderer, but more for want of a better theory. And as for the possible assassination plan, I now feared that it involved the former Nazis more than the young communists and the police security service, but still without any idea of what was going to happen and when.

The closer I got to the foot of the mountains, the greater I felt my potential fall could be. When I parked the car at the end of the dirt track at a quarter to six, I held a deep wish that Falko Reinhardt would give me the whole explanation, or at least enough for me to piece together the rest of the puzzle with Patricia's help. It dawned on me that an alarming amount was now dependent on what he could, and wanted to tell us; and that a short and somewhat frantic late-night telephone conversation was my only guarantee that he would actually meet me here.

The first touches of autumn colour were in evidence, but it was still a magnificent late-summer evening in Valdres. I scoured the landscape, unable to enjoy it, for the city boy Falko Reinhardt, and wondered why he had insisted on meeting me here. His calm, convincing voice the evening before had made an impression: I trusted that he was in control of the situation and would come.

However, it was now five to six and there was no sign of him or anyone else. I wandered around in a small circle and looked in every direction to make sure I had not missed him. The countdown ran from five to three minutes, and then from two to one, without anything happening.

I stood and watched the second hand progress steadily through the last seconds to six o'clock. I felt both a little disappointed and a little anxious when I could still see no sign of Falko anywhere. I hoped that, for one reason or another, he was simply delayed, but as the minutes ticked by I soon began to doubt this.

At five past six, I asked myself just how long I should stand there waiting for a man who might have no intention of coming. And I also suddenly felt worried about my own safety. Something I had not considered before occurred to me: that I myself might be subject to a sniper attack out here in this open terrain. I comforted myself with the thought that if I had been lured into a trap, they would have got me straight away. This did not make the idea of standing here much longer any more tempting.

At seven minutes past six, I decided that I would wait until ten past. If Falko Reinhardt had not shown up by then, I would drive up to Henry Alfred Lien's farm in the hope that I could salvage something useful from this trip to Valdres. Then I would have to decide whether it made sense to come back again and see if Falko was here.

At nine minutes past six, I looked around in every direction. There was still no sign of Falko or anyone else. I raised my eyes to the top of the cliff, in the direction of Henry Alfred Lien's farm and the Morgenstiernes' cabin. Neither was visible from here. But at just over three hundred feet, the cliff was an impressive and frightening sight in the evening sun.

For a moment, my thoughts returned to Henry Alfred Lien and the story of his grandfather, who had stood down here just over a hundred years ago and watched the lad Karl jump, fall or be pushed over the edge.

I looked at my watch and saw that it was now ten past six.

It was when I looked up again that I saw the human body falling over the edge and down towards the rocks in front of me.

I could not tell whether it was a man or a woman. It was just a small dark shadow falling fast, feet first. I could not later be certain whether I had actually heard a scream or not. But that was what I thought, with the story of Henry Alfred Lien's grandfather fresh in my mind.

I stood there as though paralysed and watched the person fall to a certain death on the rocks below, and heard a scream that certainly echoed in my ears. It felt like an eternity, although I later understood that the fall could not have taken much more than five seconds.

I recognized a man I had never seen alive before only as he hit the ground. His curly black hair was buffeted by the wind for the final seconds of the fall.

I stood there like a pillar as he fell.

A tiny movement on the periphery of my vision woke me up. I looked up to the top of the cliff and saw a small dark smudge of a person standing looking over the edge.

It was too high up for me to be able to see without

binoculars whether it was a man or a woman, let alone make out any details. I was not sure if the person up there could see me, but I was absolutely sure that I could see a person standing up there at the edge of the cliff, staring down in my direction. It was a very strange feeling to see a murderer with my naked eye, without being able to recognize the person or make an arrest.

It did not last long. The smudge of a person soon moved back from the edge and out of my sight. And at the same time I heard a loud, painful moan. I realized that it must be Falko Reinhardt, who was lying where he had fallen without being able to move. I felt a stirring of hope and rushed over to him.

Any hope of survival soon vanished. His body and legs had been mangled in the fall, and he was bleeding from the chest and neck. But the hope that he might be able to tell me the little I needed to know still lived as I bent down over him. Blood was dribbling from his mouth, but his eyes were still alive.

Falko Reinhardt whispered a word as soon as I reached him. His voice gave way at the end of the word, but I heard it loud and clear all the same.

'The window.'

We stared into each other's eyes for an intense moment. I gripped his shoulders without it making things any better. His shoulder had obviously been broken or dislocated. His body was heavy, burning hot, and limp.

'What about the window? Which window?' I almost shouted at him.

I thought for a moment that he could no longer hear me. His eyes slid closed as I spoke and a terrible shudder ran through his body.

'Look out for the window!' Falko Reinhardt whispered in a barely audible voice, his eyes shut.

Then he died.

# XII

It was a miracle that Falko Reinhardt had managed to stay alive as long as he did. Not only was he injured from the fall, he also had two bullet wounds: one in the foot and the other in his chest. He was wearing jeans, a shirt and boots, but no jacket.

I found only one thing in his pockets, but it was all the more sensational for that. In his right trouser pocket was a Walther pistol with three bullets missing from the magazine. It was an unexpected find which left me even more baffled and anxious about the situation.

I had no choice other than to leave the body where it was on the scree. I ran to the car and drove to a telephone box just over a mile back down the road. From there I alerted the local police and hospital, having first got their numbers from the operator.

I then called Patricia. To my relief, she was obviously ready and waiting, and answered the phone on the second ring. I told her quick as a flash what had happened.

I had expected a pensive silence, but instead I got a swift and hard command.

'You cannot do anything more for Falko now. Leave him where he is and drive to the top of the cliff straight away. But drive via Henry Alfred Lien's farm – and drive fast. I think you may get there too late to talk to him, but there is still a slight chance. If Henry Alfred Lien can and wants to tell you what he knows, we may be able to solve this tonight. If not, we still have absolutely no idea what tomorrow might bring!'

As Patricia talked, I realized that this was the only sensible thing to do. By the time she stopped, I was almost frightened by the gravity and alarm in her voice. So I drove back up the mountain at well over the speed limit.


# XIII


I vaguely registered that it was ten past seven when I swung into the drive up to Henry Alfred Lien's farm. I hoped that no one had ever driven so fast up to the house. But in the last few minutes I had started to get the same feeling that Patricia had had. Even if Henry Alfred Lien was the person I had seen at the top of the cliff, I would still get there too late to meet him. I had a strong feeling that he had vanished, without knowing where he had gone or why.

As soon as I got to the farm, I saw the first warning that something was amiss: a car that had not been there the last time I visited. It was a blue Peugeot which looked like it had more years behind it than it had to come. It was a direct link to the now dead Falko Reinhardt, and made it even more unlikely that Henry Alfred Lien was still there.

Henry Alfred Lien was not out in the yard waiting to greet me, as he had been the last time. In fact, there was no one to be seen or heard on the farm.

With Falko Reinhardt's final words etched in my mind, I quickly surveyed all the windows before going up to the front door. There was no sign of any danger. All the windows were closed, with the curtains drawn.

I rang the old-fashioned doorbell and waited for a minute or two without any response. This only served to heighten the feeling that the bird had flown the nest. I rang the bell again and rapped hard on the door, without expecting an answer. There was still no reaction from inside.

That was when I noticed the second warning: the door was not locked.

The lights were on in the hallway and living room. This reinforced the impression that Henry Alfred Lien had left his home in a hurry. I nodded when I went into the living room and saw that the table where I had sat a couple of days ago was again set for coffee and cake for two. Either the expected guest had not come, or the person in question had shared such dramatic news that the party was over before it began. The cups, the plates and the cakes were all untouched.

It was only when I popped my head round the door into the kitchen as a matter of routine that I understood I had totally misinterpreted and underestimated the situation.

Henry Alfred Lien had not left his home in a hurry. He was still there.

There was no mistaking his broad body, even though he was lying face down. I put my fingers to his neck and could quickly confirm that there was no pulse, and that all life had left his body. It was already getting cold. I did not need to look long for the cause. When I turned him over, the bullet hole in his forehead resembled an accusing third eye.

I let go of the second victim of the evening and hid my face in my hands for a moment. The whole situation felt like a surreal nightmare, and I sincerely hoped it was. But I did not wake up. So once I had established that there were no weapons or other people on the ground floor, I went over to the late Henry Alfred Lien's living-room table to use his phone.

# XIV

As expected, the sheriff was out on a call, but his wife answered the phone and promised to give him the message about a second suspicious death as soon as possible. She almost burst into tears when I told her where he should come and who it involved. Even though Henry Alfred Lien's story during the war was well known, and even though he had kept a low profile as a widower in recent years, he had been a highly respected man and no one in the local community had a bad word to say about him. He had been a good man who had done some unfortunate things during the war, but it was hard to imagine who would want to kill him now.

I replied that it was in truth a very odd and tragic case, and that I had to get on with the investigation. She thanked me. When I put down the telephone, I felt even more uncertain about who Henry Alfred Lien actually was and what had happened to him.

My conversation with the hospital was less friendly. The operator recognized my voice, and suspected that I was a morbid prankster when I called to tell them about a second murder in the space of an hour. Fortunately, I managed to convince him, and he finally agreed to send the ambulance over as soon as it returned from the last callout.

And then, once again, I called Patricia. This time she answered after one ring, with an impatient: 'Well, what is going on?'

I told her that I had found Henry Alfred Lien and that I was now sitting alone in his house. Patricia let out a deep sigh.

'That's just as I thought – and feared. The number of murders is rising, and the danger that it might continue to rise over the next few days is high. Come here as soon as you get back to Oslo, and I will have dinner waiting for you, no matter how late it is. In the meantime, check to see if Henry Alfred Lien has the local history yearbook for Valdres, 1955 in his bookshelf. But more importantly, search for a diary, a note or any other document that might tell us a bit more about what happened – and about what might happen!'

There was a moment's silence as I contemplated what this meant. Patricia took a deep breath and continued.

'The identity of the fourth person in that photograph is now perhaps the most pressing question in Norway.

Christian Magnus Eggen and Frans Heidenberg know, but I doubt that anyone could get it out of them in time. Judging by what has happened, Falko Reinhardt and Henry Alfred Lien also knew, but were killed before they had a chance to tell you. I have no idea who this is or where he or she is; it could be almost anyone out there. But I am increasingly fearful of the consequences if we do not soon find out. And these two murders can leave no one in any doubt that this is something major!'

On hearing Patricia's words, I felt fear tugging at me, not least because it was more audible in her voice towards the end than I had ever heard it before. So I thanked her, put down the receiver and set about investigating the scene of the crime.

# XV

Patricia had of course been right. In the largest bookshelf, Henry Alfred Lien had a series of local history yearbooks for Valdres. The 1955 edition was also there. And even though a rubber had been used in the margins of the article in question about Karl and his dramatic death in the mountains, it was impossible to hide the fact there had once been notes there and parts of the text had been underlined.

Finding any diaries or other notes proved to be a bit harder. Henry Alfred Lien was not a writer by nature. He did not appear to own a typewriter. Other than a shopping list on the kitchen counter, I found no handwritten notes in the living room or kitchen.

He had, however, made himself a simple office on the first floor, and in the desk drawer I found several books filled with his elegant, old-fashioned handwriting. They mostly involved bookkeeping and taxes, but also production figures for the farm, and they showed that he had been doing well even in the last year. According to his post office savings book, Henry Alfred Lien had over three hundred thousand kroner in his bank account when he died. But I found no photographs or notes that might shed light on his dramatic death.

In the bottom drawer was a notebook with handwritten diary entries from 1967 to the present day. Henry Alfred Lien's entries were short, often just keywords, and he seldom wrote more than four or five pages a year. I quickly read through what he had written in previous years, but found nothing of interest. In connection with the disappearance of Falko Reinhardt in summer 1968, Henry Alfred Lien had noted that he had been questioned and taken a lie detector test in Oslo, but there was no new information.

By far the most interesting thing in Henry Alfred Lien's diary was a page that was not there.

The diary ended suddenly in April 1970, and the next page had been torn out.

I stood pondering for a long time when it might have been torn out and by whom. It could of course have been torn out and destroyed by Henry Alfred Lien himself. But it was also possible that it had been removed earlier in the day by the person who had shot him. In which case, I sorely wanted to know where the missing page was now, and what secrets it might reveal.

# XVI

The sheriff arrived with the ambulance at ten past eight. He was a sombre older man who gave an impression of solidity, and seemed more than willing to cooperate with a detective inspector from Oslo. We called for a forensics team from Lillehammer, but were told that we should not expect them until tomorrow morning.

I left the sheriff in charge of the farm and then walked the few hundred yards to the top of the cliff to see if I could find anything there. Rain was forecast overnight, and I had no illusions as to what the technicians would then be able to find in the morning.

The Morgenstiernes' cabin was locked. I opened it with my key, but found nothing to indicate that Falko or anyone else had been inside.

It was a very strange feeling to stand alone afterwards at the top of the cliff in the evening breeze. There had obviously been a violent struggle up here earlier in the day that had ended with Falko Reinhardt's fall and death. It would appear that Falko Reinhardt had first parked his car at Henry Alfred Lien's farm and then, for some unknown reason, either run or walked here to the edge of the cliff.

I found a couple of footprints on the path that went past the cabin and on to the edge of the cliff, which were very similar to Falko Reinhardt's in size and shape. And I found some other footprints which were also of men's shoes, but slightly smaller than Falko's. I found more of these footprints in the moss a couple of yards away from the cliff. But there were no clear prints from Falko's large feet there.

It seemed reasonable to assume that the other prints belonged to the person I had seen standing at the edge of the cliff after Falko Reinhardt's fall. But there was no way of being certain, and even if it was the case, it gave no pointer as to that person's identity.

I wandered around at the top of the cliff, without really knowing what I was looking for. In an otherwise clean landscape devoid of human traces, the small piece of paper fluttering in the breeze behind a boulder immediately caught my eye.

My mind naturally jumped to the missing page from Henry Alfred Lien's diary. However, it transpired that this piece of paper was smaller and of a different type. It was a plain white sheet, of the sort I had found in the late Falko Reinhardt's hotel room. And the writing was his too, and once again was extremely brief, written in keywords that were a mixture of numbers and letters:

*1108*

*Heftye 66*

Professor Johannes Heftye's face immediately popped up in my mind. Given the rare surname and the fact that the number 66 coincided with his age, it was hard to avoid the conclusion that Falko Reinhardt was alluding to his supervisor here. And 1108, according to Falko's usual shorthand for dates, was then 11 August – which was tomorrow. But the link between the date, the supervisor and the note were still a mystery to me.

As I walked around on my own up there by the edge of the cliff, it started to drizzle. This quickly developed into proper rain, and I was soaked to the skin by the time I got back down to the car and Henry Alfred Lien's farm. This did not help to lift my spirits. I drove back to Oslo in wet clothes and a grim mood.

As I drove, the theory that Falko Reinhardt had shot Henry Alfred Lien developed in, and occupied, my mind. He had parked his car there, and the pistol in his pocket had been three bullets short when he fell down the cliff a few hundred yards away. The three fired shots would be two to Falko Reinhardt's own body, and one to Henry Alfred Lien's head. But somehow the idea of suicide did not seem right. Falko Reinhardt had certainly not struck me as a suicide candidate when I had spoken to him the evening before. On the contrary, he had seemed to be bursting with a powerful will to carry out an important mission for his nation and then reap the honour. It seemed highly unlikely that he would ask me to come to Valdres only to take his own life by jumping over a cliff; and it was also very impractical to shoot yourself in the foot before such a jump. In any case, the presence of the person I had seen standing there more or less ruled out the possibility of suicide.

So the most likely scenario remained that Falko had first intended to meet Henry Alfred Lien, and then me. He had, for unknown reasons, ended up killing Henry Alfred Lien. But who had then shot Falko Reinhardt? And why had Falko Reinhardt gone with that person to the edge of the cliff? What secret was so great that both Henry Alfred Lien and Falko Reinhardt had to be murdered today, in order to keep it from getting out?

The questions about what had happened, and why, were starting to mount up. And on top of them came the question of what I should do now. I stopped at a telephone box in Hønefoss and managed to get hold of a priest in Grünerløkka via the operator. I told him what had happened, and asked if he could break the tragic news to Falko Reinhardt's parents. However, he turned out to be the conservative and categorical type, and he firmly refused to have anything to do with the case. The whole Reinhardt family had left the state church, and the priest himself had had a serious argument with the parents when they refused to let their son be confirmed. They had asked him to leave and made it very clear that they would not open the door should he knock on it again. Before he left, he had warned them that their son might go straight to hell as a result, so it would be impossible to lie and say anything else to them now. And certainly not so late at night. I ended the call, and drove on.

For the rest of the trip, I dreaded being the messenger of death – to Falko's parents as well as to Kristine Larsen. The world would quite possibly collapse for all three of them.

The fact that it was so late was my excuse: it was past eleven o'clock when I finally drove into town. I would have to tell them in the morning, and use the rest of the evening on the investigation. I drove straight to 104–108 Erling Skjalgsson's Street.

# XVII

Patricia had kept her word, and was waiting patiently. The maid Beate opened the door immediately when I rang the bell, and assured me that she would serve dinner as soon as it had been heated. It was only then I realized that I had not eaten for nearly ten hours. And then, on top of all my other worries, I was suddenly beset with anxiety about how Patricia's father might view my late visit. Professor Director Ragnar Sverre Borchmann was still someone I would not care to provoke or get on the wrong side of.

I cautiously asked the maid if the professor had already gone to bed. She replied that the professor was away, then added with a shrewd little smile that the director would certainly not object to my visit, however late it was, had he been here. This was a token of encouragement and recognition from a childhood hero that I still held in high esteem. I asked Beate to pass on my greetings the next time he rang home. With another smile, she promised to do this.

The dinner that later appeared on the table was a superb roast pork. But this time, it was only for me. Patricia had obviously eaten already. She took careful sips from a cup of black coffee, but otherwise remained motionless in her wheelchair. I could not remember having seen her so serious before. Her concentration was intense.

'There is much to indicate that Falko Reinhardt killed Henry Alfred Lien. But who then killed Falko afterwards? It could hardly be suicide?' I said, eventually.

Patricia choked on her coffee and only made things worse by trying to speak before she had properly cleared her throat. It seemed to me that her nerves were on edge. Her voice, however, was just as sharp and confident as usual when she managed to use it.

'Falko Reinhardt definitely did not kill himself. And nor did he kill Henry Alfred Lien. The situation now is very frustrating, as I can tell you more or less what happened, but not the most important thing, which is who shot Henry Alfred Lien and Falko Reinhardt. And this double murderer might be at large out there. It is most likely to be a person we have not met and do not know the name of. And now that both Falko Reinhardt and Henry Alfred Lien are dead, I have no idea how we might find out. This person is clearly both driven and dangerous, and everything seems to indicate that he is planning to do something terrible in the next few days. One obvious danger is that we are talking about a hired assassin of some sort.'

'You mean the man who has been removed from the photograph?' I asked.

Patricia nodded.

'Of course, we cannot be certain, but it does seem highly likely. The former Nazis were probably right when they said they were not responsible for Marie Morgenstierne's death. But they have obviously survived as a network, and have for many years played with ideas and plans about how to take their sweet revenge on society. Marie Morgenstierne's death and the attention it has been given has in some way accelerated the process, and things could explode at any moment now. The key to the two deaths today and the planned attack are buried somewhere in all this.'

She let out a measured breath, and then carried on.

'It was obviously not the king's engagement in Asker this evening. They reported on the radio that the opening of the swimming pool had been a great success. So Falko was right when he said that there was no danger of an attack today. But now that Falko himself is dead – anything might happen from tomorrow on.'

I dared to venture that the initials SP in Falko's first note fitted with Stein Pedersen, whom the police security service had wanted to protect for so long. Patricia gave a thoughtful nod.

'Yes, it is an odd coincidence, and one should be wary of ruling things out in such circumstances. But all the same, the idea of an assassin being employed by the police security service does seem a bit unlikely. And how did Falko then get the person's name? And why did he not just tell us?'

I had to admit that I had no answers. Instead, I asked her about the other note that referred to Heftye, which could hardly mean anyone other than Falko Reinhardt's supervisor, given the number 66? There were not many other Heftyes left in Oslo, I dared to add.

Patricia pulled out the telephone directory for Oslo and Akerhus from the shelf behind her, and looked it up.

'Eleven, including the professor. That is not many. But the number sixty-six is only nearly right – if the professor celebrated his sixty-fifth birthday a few days before Falko disappeared in 1968, then he must have turned sixty-seven a couple of weeks ago. A somewhat distracted Falko could of course have thought that he was still sixty-six. Do check with the professor where he was today, and what his plans are for tomorrow. But what on earth would he have to do with an attack? If I were to imagine an old radical left-wing history professor being involved in a terrorist attack, it would certainly not be in cooperation with old Nazis. And I do not understand why Falko would use the abbreviation 'SP' for Professor Johannes Heftye. Nor, for that matter, why he would then write out the name when he otherwise appears to use abbreviations for people in his notes.'

And neither did I. The new note was more and more mysterious.

'What happened in Valdres, then?' I asked.

For a moment, Patricia looked confused, but then she straightened up and leaned across the table.

'Sorry, I thought that was fairly obvious. All the pieces fit here. We have discussed at length who was the security service's mole in Falko Reinhardt's group – but not who was Falko Reinhardt's mole in the Nazi network. But it was obviously Henry Alfred Lien, who saw this as his chance to be forgiven by his anti-Nazi son. It is possible that this was the main reason for him taking up again with his friends from the war years. He and Falko Reinhardt were both useful to each other. Falko Reinhardt was tipped off by Henry Alfred Lien in 1968 that the Nazi network was considering some form of action. Relations within the group may also have contributed to Falko Reinhardt's decision to disappear. After discussing this with Henry Alfred Lien – and possibly with some practical assistance – he escaped from the cabin in the most ingenious way, and disappeared down the mountain and out of the country. The incident in the local history yearbook certainly corroborates the theory of cooperation. Henry Alfred Lien knew the old story and Falko, with his sense of drama, got an idea that he could not resist. Falko dreamed about coming back as a national hero; Henry Alfred Lien hoped he would be forgiven by his son. They kept in touch, and Falko returned when he heard earlier this summer that an attack by the former Nazis was imminent. Are you following so far?'

I nodded, and waited with bated breath for the continuation.

'Today, Falko was due to have a final meeting with Henry Alfred Lien before his meeting with you, when he would tell you what he knew about the planned attack. The plot is so big that he expected to be some kind of national hero if he single-handedly uncovered it. But Henry Alfred Lien's role as double agent had been discovered, possibly because Christian Magnus Eggen and Frans Heidenberg found out about the photograph. Henry Alfred Lien had set the table for his meeting with Falko when he suddenly stood face to face with someone completely different altogether: someone who had come to kill him, and did so. Falko arrived just after this, and was unarmed and suddenly facing an armed murderer. They both immediately understood the context and gravity of the situation. Falko must have run out of the house in a blind panic, and was pursued and shot, first in the foot and then in the chest. In the meantime, he managed to lose the note that you found. The murderer then, in cold blood, dragged the wounded Falko the last few yards to the cliff, stuffed the gun into his pocket and pushed him over the edge. It was an impressively quick-witted attempt to make it look as though Falko Reinhardt had shot Henry Alfred Lien and then taken his own life, or at least to cover his own tracks. Both bodies could have lain there for days, until it was all over, if you had not been there.'

She had convinced me. I could, having been there myself, imagine the scene, but I still could not see the murderer's face.

'And no one else would have been able to see the connection, if you had not been here!'

Patricia nodded, but her smile was reluctant.

'Thank you, but it remains to be seen how far it will get us. We still do not have the most important information, and I cannot squeeze much more out of what we already know.'

'What about the missing page from the diary?'

Patricia's nod was keener this time.

'Presumably it says all that we need to know and is one of the things we can hope to find now. If the murderer took it, we are likely never to see it again. But if the diary contained something important about the plans, it is far more likely that Falko knew about the diary rather than the murderer. Imagine for a moment that Falko found Henry Alfred Lien dead, but thought that the murderer had gone and that he was alone in the house. He would then find the diary to safeguard it. He met the murderer on the way out. There is every reason to hope that this might have happened.'

'But then what happened to the diary page? Falko did not have it when he died, in which case it is possible that the murderer took it from him.'

Patricia nodded, with a grim expression on her face.

'It is not only possible, it is highly likely. But is it really the case that Falko only had the pistol in his pocket when you found him?'

It was my turn to nod.

'He was not wearing a jacket and the pistol was the only thing I found in his trouser pockets.'

Patricia gave a crooked smile.

'Then we have another mystery, which could either be irrelevant or our saving grace. Where on earth is Falko's jacket?'

I looked at her astonished. She continued quickly.

'Falko had a car, but no car keys. And he had pockets, but no wallet. He must have had a jacket with him, and both the wallet and the keys must still be in the jacket. And probably also the page from the diary – if, as we hope, he had it. Where is the jacket? Did the murderer take it? Or did he leave it in the house, or did he lose it somewhere on the way to the cliff? It is perhaps clutching at straws, but it might work. Could you check with the sheriff in Vestre Slidre?'

I nodded. Patricia pushed the telephone across the table towards me.

I got hold of the sheriff just as he was going to bed. The deceased's jacket had not been found, but he agreed that its absence was strange, and said that he would personally organize a search for it as soon as he went back to the scene of the crime in the morning. They had found nothing of note, but he promised to phone immediately if they did.

I thanked him, and put the receiver down. Patricia and I then sat in oppressive silence for a while. It was close to midnight and the situation was electric, but neither of us had anything more to say about it.

I thought that the possibility of the jacket was brilliant, but it was a very thin straw indeed. And otherwise, we had no clues about the murderer, and were not likely to find any here tonight.

I realized, without either of us saying anything, that Patricia was thinking the same. We were getting to know each other rather well by now.

So I thanked her for her help and said that I had to call my boss and get a few hours' sleep, but that I would telephone her as soon as anything of importance cropped up. She said that she would be sitting waiting by the phone from half past seven, and that we could only hope that we would get some new information in time to identify the murderer and prevent a catastrophe. Otherwise we were facing a hopeless fight against time and evil, she remarked with a sigh.

'One could cancel all public engagements for the king, the prime minister and the opposition leader for the next two days. But one cannot lock them and all other potential targets up for the whole summer and autumn. Norway is an open country, full of important people who are constantly expected to make public appearances. If the attacker wants to take innocent lives, he could attack any holiday village or scout camp. And there are windows everywhere, so Falko's final words are not of much use to us either.'

We had to accept that there were an alarming number of possibilities for a person who was well prepared and wanted to carry out an attack, and that we would not get any further that evening. I promised to ring her as soon as there was any news in the morning, and said that I still hoped and believed that we could solve the case without any further deaths. My voice sounded more confident than I was. The car felt unusually lonely and the dark unusually threatening as I drove home that night.

# XVIII

It was well past midnight by the time I got home, but I still had one more telephone call to make – to my boss.

My boss was also obviously affected by the frustration of this potentially dangerous situation in which we knew that something was being planned, but had no idea about who was going to attack, or where and when. He answered the telephone as soon as it rang, and asked me to update him on the latest developments. He had only heard a brief announcement on the radio, in the last news of the day, that there had been a couple of deaths in Valdres.

I told him what had happened, and expanded on Patricia's theory about possible connections – without mentioning her name, or being as cocksure.

My boss was impressed, much to my relief, in particular

that I had thought about the missing jacket and the possible significance of this.

'You have obviously thought of most things and done a good job. No one could have done better. But all the same . . .'

I felt my throat tightening. I knew what was coming and hated it intensely.

'. . . All the same, we now have three unsolved murders and the danger of further action. There will be a tidal wave of questions tomorrow from our own people and the press. And I cannot justify letting you continue with the investigation without reinforcements.'

I was about to protest, but realized it was pointless. My boss had given me his trust for many days now, with no results. And it would seem odd if the investigation was not stepped up and prioritized following two more murders. So I said that I perfectly understood, but hoped that I would still be allowed to lead the investigation. He replied straight away.

'Of course. I have absolute confidence in you and ask that you continue to report to me. You will be our contact with the local police in Vestre Slidre, and you can decide how many people you need here in Oslo. But from tomorrow, Detective Inspector Danielsen will be your deputy in the investigation. You can decide yourself how best to use him, but he will be part of the team.'

This made my blood boil, but I managed to control myself enough to thank my boss for allowing me to continue leading the investigation, and to say that I was sure I could find useful things for Danielsen to do. In a flash of inspiration, I said that the two Nazis should be called in for questioning again the next day, and that perhaps Danielsen could do that. My boss agreed and then wished me good night.

I could not help but chortle when I thought of Danielsen's new task, but my good humour did not last long. I fell asleep around two o'clock in the morning of Tuesday, 11 August 1970. It was six and a half hours until I would greet what had the potential to be a very demanding day at work, with a still entirely unpredictable outcome.

# The countdown and the explosion

# I

At a quarter to eight on Tuesday, 11 August 1970, I was once again on my way to the office, having wolfed down my breakfast. I had woken half an hour before the alarm clock, and immediately decided that I wanted to be in control of the agenda by being in the office before Danielsen.

There were no messages of any interest waiting for me on my desk. The morning papers only carried short notices about 'two highly suspicious deaths in Valdres', without mentioning any connection to me or to Marie Morgenstierne's murder. Professor Arne Næss was on his way to show his support for the demonstrators in Mardøla, and the Institute for Nuclear Energy had suggested that building a nuclear power station in Porsgrunn could solve the country's energy problems. And in Sweden, the debate regarding a ban on motorsport events had flared up again following a dramatic fatal accident during a rallycross race in Karlskoga. The fact that one of the five dead was a Norwegian guaranteed a front-page report in *Dagbladet*.

In short, there was no spectacle in the morning papers. The operator, however, reported a rise in the number of calls from journalists, even before eight o'clock.

I formulated a brief press release to confirm that two as yet unnamed people had been shot in Valdres, and that the police had linked these two deaths with that of Marie Morgenstierne in Oslo five days earlier. It was not possible to release any further details in light of the ongoing investigation. The investigation team had, however, been reinforced following the two latest murders, and the police believed there was a good chance that the case would be solved before the end of the week.

My hand trembled slightly as I wrote the final sentence. I was aware that this might buy me a couple of days, but that the pressure would quickly mount if there was still no good news by the time the weekend came round. Part of me trusted Patricia's reassurances that the murder of Marie Morgenstierne would be solved in a matter of days now. And part of me would be happy if we managed to get through the next couple of days without a major catastrophe, given the situation.

I had secretly hoped that Detective Inspector Vegard Danielsen might be ill or have taken an unexpected holiday, but was of course disappointed. That only happened once every leap year, if that. Danielsen was already sitting in our boss's office when I knocked on the door at a quarter past eight to get the press release approved. Luckily, my boss had no comments to make, and Danielsen limited himself to pointing out two possible comma errors.

My boss then confirmed that the investigation had been

expanded to include Danielsen. To Danielsen, he pointed out that I was still leading the investigation. We both nodded quickly, and shook hands with forced friendliness.

For the next fifteen minutes I told Danielsen what I thought he needed to know about the case so far. I then repeated that it would be natural to call Frans Heidenberg and Christian Magnus Eggen in for questioning again, and asked if he could take on this important part of the investigation at such short notice. He nodded eagerly, and then left the office once he had the addresses and a copy of the photograph from Falko Reinhardt's hotel room. I myself ran more than walked back to my office to carry on with the investigation, having first agreed with my boss that he would get an update during the lunch break at midday.

# II

I had thought of giving the sad news to Kristine Larsen first, and then hearing if she had anything more to add. She had not heard about her lover's dramatic death the evening before, and was still sleeping with a smile on her lips, according to the female prison warden. I thought it was going to be difficult enough to tell Kristine Larsen the news without having to wake her from a pleasant dream as well. So I left the quiet unit without having been in her cell, but instructed the warden that no one should talk to her until I returned.

I was no less apprehensive about telling Falko's parents of the death of their only child. But it was easier than I had anticipated. They seemed to support each other in an impressive way through what must have been the most terrible hour of their lives. They were standing side by side and hand in hand in the hallway when I arrived, and looked at me with serious eyes.

'Falko has gone forever this time, hasn't he?' the father asked, in a quiet voice.

I nodded, and braced myself for a dramatic outburst or breakdown that never came. I saw tears in Falko's mother's eyes, and deep, deep despair in his father's. But they stood there, their thin hands locked together.

I told them that it had been midnight before I came back to Oslo, following my hunt for their son's murderer, and I had been unable to find a priest who could come in my place.

They nodded and said that was understandable, and that it was better to get the news from me than from a priest. Given a choice, they would rather it was me, Arno Reinhardt said, and pursed his lips.

They had expected the worst after hearing about the suspicious deaths in Valdres on the news the evening before, and had sat up all night waiting to hear more, on the radio, on the telephone or at the door.

Astrid Reinhardt asked me to tell them what had happened. They both listened without asking any questions or criticizing anything that I told them, which was really only a brief outline. Falko had been wearing a summer jacket when he went out of the door here, they said, and had his wallet and the car keys in the pocket.

Otherwise, they had little to add that might be of any benefit to the investigation. The note with 'Heftye 66' meant nothing to them, other than that it was his supervisor's name. They knew him superficially from his time in the communist party and found it hard to believe that he might have anything to do with their son's death. But they found any of it hard to understand.

'In a way, we have always thought it would end like this,' Falko's mother remarked, with a heavy sigh. I looked at her questioningly. It was his father who answered. After decades of marriage, they seemed to have reached the stage where each knew exactly what the other was thinking.

'We said to each other when we saw him for the first time that we never believed we would experience such joy, and that we didn't know what we had done to deserve it. Our Falko was the most beautiful child in the world, brighter and stronger than all the others. We worshipped him, but we clearly never really understood him. We were not wise or clever enough to do that. And now our only son is dead, and we can't even help you catch the murderer. We didn't manage to win our son's trust enough for him to confide in us the danger he was in, so we couldn't protect him. We will have to live on our memories from all the happy years we had with him.'

Arno Reinhardt's voice was shaking terribly, but did not break. His wife nodded in agreement and lovingly put her arm around him. 'Despite all our failings, we did have many more happy years with him than those who have never had a child,' she said.

The silence was tense, and yet resigned.

Finally I said that I would do my utmost to hold the murderer to account, and added that it appeared that Falko had been trying to warn me of some imminent catastrophe when he was killed. And I hoped that this catastrophe could be prevented, on the basis of what I now knew, so that their son's contribution would be recognized even in death.

They nodded simultaneously.

'We are not even able to feel hate for the murderer. Our son has gone forever. All his life, he was distrusted by many, just as we ourselves have been, because of his political views and visions of a better world. It would be an enormous relief if you could highlight that and give us some answers about what actually happened. And until you return, we will sit here with our questions,' his mother said, and looked me straight in the eye.

The air in the flat felt more and more oppressive. I said that I would do my best and that I would telephone them immediately if there was anything more they could help me with, but for now, I had to leave and get on with my work and, if possible, prevent any more deaths.

They nodded together again.

I stood up, took them both by the hands and gave my condolences once more on their great loss.

They were remarkably composed again when I left. On my way out I passed the last photograph of Falko, which had now been added to the collection but hung at the end, by itself. His eyes challenged me, and their eyes pleaded with me as I walked out of the flat.

# III

Kristine Larsen was awake in her cell by the time I got back to the station at around half past nine. The prison warden told me with a sigh that she still appeared to be in a good mood. I asked the warden to let her know I would be there in five minutes, but I waited seven, and stopped twice in the corridor before I went in.

Kristine Larsen was dressed and sitting smiling on the bed when I came in. She gave me a cheerful wave. It is possible she noticed immediately how serious I was. Her smile certainly vanished and her voice was tense when she asked if there was any news of Falko.

I did not trust that she would be able to answer any questions after she had heard the truth, so I started by saying that the investigation had entered a new and even more dramatic phase, and that I first had to ask her a couple of questions. She looked at me intensely with a knitted brow.

I started by telling her that Marie Morgenstierne had been two months pregnant when she died, and asked who she thought might be the father, if we assumed that it was not Falko.

She nodded gratefully and said that it was somewhat unexpected, but that she did not think it could be Falko who was the father. As he had not contacted her, it was hard to believe that he had been there for anything more than a few days.

She found it hard to imagine that Trond Ibsen or Anders

Pettersen might be Marie Morgenstierne's lover, but guessed that it must be one of them all the same. She said this because she had never seen or heard that Marie Morgenstierne mixed with any other men. She was known as the 'lone wolf' by her fellow students at university.

Kristine Larsen took longer to answer my question as to whether Marie Morgenstierne might have suspected that she was having a relationship with Falko before she died. She finally answered that she had thought a lot about this in prison, and reached the conclusion that Marie Morgenstierne had become more distant with her during the spring and early summer. She had wondered if her friend had realized, and had feared a confrontation. But nothing more had happened. If Marie Morgenstierne had a new lover herself, that would be a good explanation, Kristine Larsen added hopefully.

'But please don't keep me in suspense any longer. Do you have any news of my darling Falko?' she asked, when I could not think of any more questions. There was a tense, almost frightened undertow to her voice when she asked this.

It would be hard to hide the truth any longer, and I did not think it would be any better if I tried to drag it out.

So I told her the truth – that I was now trying to prevent some kind of national catastrophe that Falko had wanted to warn me about, but that he had unfortunately been killed before he could do that.

For the first few seconds, things were better than I had anticipated. The colour drained from Kristine Larsen, and she hid her face in her hands and mumbled that she had feared that might happen and that she of course had never expected to be able to keep him.

But then suddenly her slim frame teetered on the edge of the bed, and she fainted.

Kristine Larsen slipped towards the floor before I could stop her. I lifted her gently back up onto the bed, without her showing any sign of regaining consciousness. I stood there, looking at her, for a few seconds.

Then I more or less crept out of the cell, and whispered to the prison warden that she should call a nurse to be on the safe side. When she came to again Kristine Larsen could be released, if she was in a fit state. But it was possible that she might have to be admitted to hospital, and it was equally possible that she might feel safest if she stayed here for a few hours more.

The warden looked somewhat surprised, but nodded and touched her hat in an uncertain salute. I felt a bit of a coward when I left without looking back. But in truth there was little more I could do for Kristine Larsen here, and I still had three murders and a planned attack to solve.


# IV


My desk was just as empty when I got back to the office. No messages. It suddenly dawned on me that I should perhaps let someone else know about the most recent developments, and that was Marie Morgenstierne's father, the bank manager Martin Morgenstierne. I assumed that he would not want a long report, but realized it would be formally correct to give him a brief update if he wanted it.

I rang the bank first, but was told by the switchboard operator that the bank manager was not well and had taken both yesterday and today off. It was the first time he had taken sick leave for more than ten years, the switchboard lady said in a quiet voice. His daughter's death had no doubt affected him more than he liked to show, she now almost whispered. I asked her to let him know that I had called if he was in the office again tomorrow.

After some hesitation, I tried to call Martin Morgenstierne at home, but put the telephone down when it had not been answered after five rings. I actually had nothing new to tell him about the murder of his daughter. And it seemed very unlikely to me that he would be able to tell me anything that might help me in the hunt for the person or people out there who were now planning an attack.

A few minutes later, I got a far more interesting telephone call. On the other end was the sheriff in Valdres. He sounded very flustered today.

'We have examined both the crime scenes and found something that could be of great interest. I have already sent it with my son in a car to Oslo, but I thought that I should call and let you know as well.'

I said that was kind, and asked what they had found.

'I really am impressed by . . . just as you said, we found a jacket that clearly belongs to Falko Reinhardt. It had been blown about, but then was stopped by a boulder some yards away from the cliff. The jacket was wet from the rain, so you can forget the idea of any fingerprints. But the pockets were zipped, and what was inside is intact. And if you can guess which three things we found in the pockets, I am your humble servant.'

I felt the pressure, but in my mind I thanked Patricia with all my heart as I replied: 'I think that you found a wallet and a key ring that included the car key, and I hope that you also found a page from a notebook with some strange handwritten notes.'

There was a small gasp at the other end, and then an even more impressed voice.

'I have no idea how things are done in Oslo, but you certainly have managed to impress a mere country sheriff. That is precisely what we found. They told me nothing, but I am sure it will mean something to you. I examined them quickly and then sent them with my son to the main police station in Oslo. The wallet contained a driver's licence and some banknotes in several currencies, as well as some boat tickets that would indicate that he sailed from the Soviet Union to Germany, and arrived in Oslo a couple of weeks ago. But there was not much more in there. The page with the handwritten notes did not name any people or places, so you mustn't expect to get a great deal out of it.'

I asked if the page looked as though it had been torn from a diary and if the sheriff had transcribed the text. There was a moment's silence at the other end, before he hesitantly continued.

'Yes, it could well have been a diary, the edge was torn and the page had several dates on it. But I am afraid that I did not write down the text. I should of course have done so. I just thought that as there was nothing obvious there, it would be best to send the jacket to you immediately.'

I felt enormously irritated with the sheriff, but could only forgive him when he carried on hastily: 'It was a mistake, I realize that now. And I apologize deeply. But you will have the jacket and its contents soon enough now. My son drove directly from the scene of the crime, and he left about an hour ago now, and was told that it was urgent. So he should be there in no more than two.'

The sheriff sounded disheartened and he really had done his best to help me. So I thanked him sincerely, and promised to contact him as soon as there were any new developments in the case. He was almost touched by this and repeated that I should have the jacket and the diary page by around half past one. I told him that the fact that it had been found was a huge breakthrough in the investigation.

We finished the call on a good note, though I was silently annoyed at not knowing what it said on the missing diary page.

I telephoned Patricia and gave her a brief report about what had happened so far. She sounded very stern, but whistled appreciatively on hearing about the jacket. She asked me to come over with it as soon as possible, and she would ensure that a late lunch was waiting.

We would have plenty of time to look at the diary page before the opposition leader's speech at half past four, but not before the prime minister's speech at three, I said.

Patricia sighed into the receiver and said that it was hard to justify the sudden cancellation of such an important event without a definite threat. But she added that I should come as soon as I could if the missing page proved to contain anything of interest.

# V

There was a spread of open sandwiches on the table in my boss's office when I got there at two minutes to midday. And Danielsen was already sitting comfortably in the chair closest to our boss.

I told them that Falko's jacket had been found, and that it might well contain something of interest, without giving any more details; but that other than that, I had no news of any significance. Both nodded, but did not show much interest in the jacket.

I asked Danielsen, not without some *schadenfreude*, if he had made any progress in his meetings with the two former Nazis. He took his time.

'Well, it would be untrue to say that. They were very uncooperative to begin with, and even though things did improve, there is little that is new. They either do not remember, or do not want to remember, anything about the fourth person in the photograph. And as for alibis for yesterday, they both have one. They had a meal together at the Grand Café between four and six, and I have confirmed this with the head waiter there. I asked, just in case, if the staff could remember having seen them there with others, but they couldn't. It is of course difficult to remember months back, when the place is so popular. And by the way,

Mr Eggen commented that we only had to ask the officers watching his house if we wanted to know when he went out.'

We all smiled slightly sheepishly. I said that I knew nothing about his house being under surveillance.

'Generally, the two of them have very little confidence in society, the police in particular. They obviously feel they are being persecuted for their political views. And given their background, it is easy to have some sympathy, no matter what one might believe and think about their politics.'

My boss and I both looked at Danielsen with slightly raised eyebrows. He quickly changed tack.

'Neither of them is particularly nice, though one of them is more polite than the other. Having said that, their criminal offences are now well in the past, and I am not convinced in any way that they have much to hide now.'

I stared at him, my eyes wide, but noticed with some concern that my boss seemed to show more interest. Danielsen obviously noticed this too, and straightened up in his chair before continuing with his argument.

'Both have been law-abiding citizens for twenty-five years, both have an alibi for yesterday, and it could well be no more than a form of protest that they refuse to tell us about the person they had dinner with all that time ago. Strictly speaking, the photograph really only proves that they had a meal with a man who is now dead. I have another theory that might fit just as well.'

Danielsen now had our full attention. Ingeniously, he waited until both my boss and I had asked him to tell us his alternative theory before carrying on.

'I think it is more likely that we will find the murderer among the young communists than these relatively frail old ex-Nazis. I accept your theory that Henry Alfred Lien passed on information to Falko Reinhardt. But there is nothing to disprove that Reinhardt might have killed both Lien and his fiancée, Marie Morgenstierne. The pieces all fall into place if he himself was then killed by one of the other communists. Arresting Kristine Larsen was obviously a mistake, and she should be released immediately. After all, she was in prison in Oslo when Reinhardt and Lien were shot. Trond Ibsen and Anders Pettersen do not seem to be very trustworthy and, unless otherwise proved, they could well have killed Falko Reinhardt. If one of them had inherited Marie Morgenstierne and was the father of her unborn child, then jealousy or revenge could be a motive.'

I asked Danielsen if this meant that he thought there was no danger of an imminent attack. Again, he was annoyingly prompt with his answer.

'Well, there are two possibilities, if my theory is right. This Reinhardt fellow seems to have been so self-centred that he may have made up the whole story of an attack just to get attention. But it is also possible that he knew that one of the others in his group was planning an attack, and that is why he was killed. So my answer is that I do not believe in the idea of a Nazi plot, but that I am open to the idea that an attack of some sort is being planned. And in that case, we need a breakthrough in the investigation, as time is of the essence.'

He was very pleased with himself as he looked from the boss to me, and then back to the boss. I heard myself say that it seemed pretty improbable to me. But I immediately felt very uncertain, and I was extremely worried that Danielsen might present a theory, only a few hours into the investigation, that proved to be true.

Danielsen gave a serene smile.

'The case is obviously complex, so of course I cannot guarantee that my first theory is right. But in complicated cases like this, it is often wise to keep different options open. So, unless you have anything up your sleeve that disproves my theory, allow me to suggest that we each continue to work on our respective theories this afternoon. You can continue working with the so-called Nazi network, while I have another round with the communists. It would in any case be beneficial to learn whether they have alibis for yesterday.'

My boss sent me a questioning look. I swallowed quickly, and replied that while I was not convinced by this alternative theory, I of course did not object to splitting the work this way. Danielsen smiled broadly before carrying on.

'Splendid. Just one thing more: any conflicts and conspiracies in the communist group may well go back to the time before Falko disappeared, so with your permission, I would like to have a serious talk with Miriam Filtvedt Bentsen as well.'

For a moment I started to wonder if I would be suspected of anything next. And I hoped fiercely that Danielsen would then not suspect me of being a little bit in love with

Miriam Filtvedt Bentsen, because in that case, I would find it very difficult to disprove.

I was as relaxed as I could be in my reply. I said that I had questioned her on several occasions without discovering anything of interest, and that I would be very surprised if he found anything, but that he was of course free to look for her at either the university library or the SPP office. He thanked me with forced friendliness, and noted down the addresses for Trond Ibsen and Anders Pettersen.

'I should manage to do this rather quickly, if I am efficient, and the risk of an attack means that the case should be prioritized . . . Shall we say we'll have another meeting at a quarter to three?' he said. He then stood up without waiting for an answer.

I nodded without thinking. He had already left the room before I realized that this would delay my meeting with Patricia.

I had to admit that Danielsen was a man of considerable capacity when it came to work and the ability to think independently. But that did not stop him from being an even greater thorn in my side than I had expected.

I rang Patricia, quickly explained the situation to her and said that it was not likely that I could be there much before half past three. She accepted this and again asked me to telephone straight away if anything happened that might give us a breakthrough. Patricia added that I must use my time as well as I could, and try to find the answer to her question about the police security service. I promised to do that. If the truth be told, there was not much else I could follow up on by myself.

# VI

I got through to the police security service agent on the number he had given on my second attempt, at one o'clock. Understandably, he did not say his name when he answered the telephone, but I immediately recognized his voice. It was clear that he recognized mine too. I heard a stifled sigh and an almost harassed 'well, well' on the other end when I explained that he still was not suspected of anything, but that there was a question I had to ask, following the two most recent murders.

His sigh reinforced my suspicion that there might be something lurking here. This feeling was strengthened even more when I asked him if he could guarantee that he had never at any point told Marie Morgenstierne what he knew about the relationship between her fiancée and Kristine Larsen.

Pedersen let out another heavy sigh and asked, unexpectedly, if we could meet rather than talk about this on the phone. I said that it was urgent, but that I could come down to Victoria Terrace straight away. Stein Pedersen seemed to think this was an even worse idea than talking about it on the telephone. He suggested instead that we could meet for a cup of coffee at a quarter past one at a cafe on Young's Square. I promptly agreed to this. I was becoming increasingly curious as to what the police security service had not told me in their three statements so far.

Pedersen ambled in, discreetly disguised with upturned collar and sunglasses, at exactly a quarter past one. He seemed more relaxed and nicer once we were comfortably seated at a corner table with a coffee each, and no one within thirty feet of us. But he still spoke very quietly from the start.

'I appreciate your discretion and goodwill. I know that this cafe is not bugged, which is more than I can promise of Victoria Terrace and my telephone there,' he said, by way of introduction.

I looked at him, somewhat baffled, but saw no reason to pursue the subject of working practices in Victoria Terrace here and now. But he clearly did, if indirectly, when he leaned over the table and whispered: 'I want to be honest with you and to help the investigation if I can. Can I take it that for the moment this is a conversation between you and me, and that he will not hear it from you?'

I nodded reassuringly. Pedersen lowered his voice even more, all the same.

'In that case, between you and me, I can say that Marie Morgenstierne had known about the relationship between her missing fiancé and Kristine Larsen for several months. I told her in early May this year. But I would like to point out that it was not my idea to tell her.'

I looked at him, a little bewildered. His voice was even quieter when he spoke again.

'When she was handing over the recording she suddenly asked me straight out if I had noticed any signs before he disappeared that he was having a relationship with someone else. It was an unexpected dilemma. At first I thought it was best not to answer. But then she was an informant who was doing us a service, and based on what I had seen, I had very little sympathy for him . . . So it was perhaps not standard practice, but understandable all the same?'

I nodded in agreement. He looked at me with something akin to gratitude.

'The way he behaved was so morally shocking and provocative. And it did not help that she had obviously remained loyal to her fiancé, and suspected that one of the others had betrayed him. So I felt sorry for her, and had wondered on a couple of occasions whether I should tell her or not. I had not until then, but could not say no when she asked me directly.'

It was my turn to lean across the table and say in an equally quiet voice: 'And I take it as given that communist women are not your personal preference, even if they are informants and have been badly treated by their fiancés. Certainly not officially, and when your boss is present.'

I feared an angry explosion, but to my relief he simply nodded slowly.

'Well observed. Based on what I knew and what I saw, I became fond of her. But nothing ever happened, and it was never discussed. The leap was too great for both of us.'

I nodded. That sounded reasonable enough.

'But as I am being honest with you . . . Well, I once asked her a question that might be of interest to you . . .'

I told him that all questions relating to Marie Morgenstierne were of interest to me now, and that nothing that he told me would be passed on to anyone else, unless strictly necessary. He nodded gratefully and continued in a whisper.

'I saw that pompous psychologist, Trond Ibsen, hanging around her on several occasions. I wondered if it was him she was afraid of. So on one occasion I used the opportunity to ask if he was perhaps getting a bit close for comfort. She smiled and said that maybe he was, but that there was no danger that he would get any closer. He was bothersome, but definitely not dangerous, she said.'

'So he was not the one she suspected of having something to do with Falko's disappearance?'

He shook his head.

'No, that certainly did not seem to be the case. What I said was true, she never actually told me who she thought it was. I don't know for sure. But if you were to ask me, unofficially, who I thought she suspected . . .'

He looked at me expectantly, with an almost teasing smile. I immediately asked him who he thought it was that she suspected, but underlined that this was in no way official.

'. . . then I would say that it was Kristine Larsen. Marie certainly said: "That's what I thought. Thank you!" She did not appear to be angry or concerned, more relieved, in a way. I think it was something she had mulled over for a long time.'

I pondered these words. When I looked up again, Stein Pedersen was gone. I took it in good faith. I had, after all, got answers to my questions. And I could not be certain whether he had said goodbye or not.

# VII

The jacket had still not arrived when I got back to my office at five to two. At two o'clock on the dot, I rang Prime Minister Peder Borgen, as arranged. He greeted me in a jolly voice, but then became thoughtful when I said that we would soon have to make a final decision regarding his talks. His relief was tangible when I said that we had not received any threats in connection with his engagement today.

We concluded that he would give his talk to the Norwegian Farmers' Union, and that I would ring straight away should there be any reason to cancel the evening's event. He was very pleased about this, and said that I could ring at any time. He repeated that other than these two events, he had practically nothing else in his diary this week.

At a quarter past two, a younger, slimmer version of the calm sheriff from Valdres came to my door with a sealed bag and gave a breathless apology, explaining that he had had a puncture near Hønefoss. I thanked him for his efforts and asked him to give my greetings to his father, then wished him a safe journey home. He once again apologized for the delay and then gingerly asked for my permission to go and see Karl Johans Gate, the main street in Oslo, before driving back.

The bag contained a light-coloured sports jacket, and the contents of its pockets were just as the sheriff had said. In the right-hand pocket was a key ring with two car keys. In the left-hand pocket was a wallet containing three hundred and fifty kroner in Norwegian banknotes, some Russian rubles and around ten German marks. I also found a Norwegian driver's licence, issued in 1967, and a boat ticket that showed that Falko had arrived in Oslo on 26 July, following a ten-day voyage from Moscow via Kiel. This fitted well with the picture we had drawn so far, but got me no further.

It was the diary page that grabbed my attention. The writing was unmistakably that of Henry Alfred Lien, and the style characteristically brief. In 1970, he had only made three notes:

> *17 May 1970: Met A, B, and D. A and D strongly in favour of implementation, B hesitant.*

> *7 June 1970: Another meeting with A, B and D. A and D almost aggressive in applying pressure. B still sceptical, but in agreement – feared consequences for families.*

> *8 August 1970: Telephone call from A. Had talked to D and B, and reported that B was now ready for action!*

I noted that the date of the middle entry in Henry Alfred Lien's diary coincided with the date on Falko Reinhardt's photograph – and given that they were both dead, this could not be down to chance. But other than that, I had to admit that the sheriff had been right. There really was not much here that would help us to identify the people mentioned. And there was certainly no lead on what it was they were planning, or when it would be implemented.

The page reminded me of Falko's note with the mysterious reference to 'Heftye 66'. I rang Professor Johannes

Heftye and confronted him with this. The professor sounded genuinely bewildered, but confirmed that he had been sixty-six until only a few weeks ago. He had, however, turned sixty-seven now and he had no idea why his former student should have this handwritten note. He had not had any form of contact with Falko since he disappeared, and had certainly not made any arrangements to meet him during the next few days.

When I asked him about the previous day, Professor Heftye told me that he had been working at home. He lived alone and, other than a couple of telephone calls in the early afternoon, he had not spoken to anyone, so unfortunately he did not have an alibi from two o'clock for the rest of the day. He hastily added that he did not have a car, and could not drive any more, even if he had had one – and so, in short, could not have been to Valdres.

I assured him that he was not suspected of anything at all, but that we had to check these things as a matter of procedure following the last two deaths. He said he understood, though his voice was a touch sceptical. As for today, the professor said that he had been in his office all day so far, and reckoned that he would stay there until late this evening. He added somewhat brusquely that he had never in his life owned a firearm of any sort, and certainly had never been suspected of using one.

It felt as though the relationship between Professor Heftye and myself had taken an unfortunate turn after a more promising start. I found it hard to imagine, however, that he was a criminal, and even harder to imagine him as a murderer running around in the mountains of Valdres. Falko's note remained a mystery.

It was nearly a quarter past three by now, and there was still little progress to report on my part. Despite my growing anxiety about an imminent attack, I quietly hoped that Danielsen had not made much progress either.

# VIII

I took it as a good sign that I was in the boss's office before Danielsen this time. He arrived, however, two minutes late and at great speed, with an unnerving grin on his face. I felt my heart pounding when I asked if there was any news from his side.

'Well, as far as Miriam Filtvedt Bentsen is concerned, I can only say that I agree with your evaluation. She was so unconcerned about the questions to begin with that it aroused my suspicions. She gave me the telephone numbers of two people who had been in the SPP office with her in the evening, and they immediately confirmed that she had been there. But as we are investigating a radical left-wing group, I am not sure that two SPP members are an entirely convincing alibi. However, two staff at the university library could confirm that she had left at five, and as such would not have had time to get up to Valdres by six o'clock without the use of a fighter plane. Otherwise, I have to say she made an unexpectedly favourable impression, and broke with the group a long time ago.'

My heart stopped thumping quite as hard after this

account. I nodded in agreement, but was impatient to hear more. It followed swiftly.

'Anders Pettersen, on the other hand, gave the impression of being an extremely political and temperamental man. I think he could be capable of most things. In this case, however, his alibi was solid: he had been at a well-attended art exhibition between six and eight, and had met several friends and acquaintances there.'

He said no more, but the corners of his mouth twitched in that irritating way he had.

'On the other hand . . . ' I prompted, in the end.

'Yes. I am almost convinced that the somewhat suspect psychologist, Trond Ibsen, is, if not a psychopath, very possibly a murderer. He looked at me with distrust from the moment I entered his office, and was clearly very unsettled by both me and my questions. As far as an alibi is concerned, the books showed that he left the office unusually early yesterday at around half past two. He drove off in his new car, which could easily have got him to Valdres within three hours. He said to both his secretary and me that he had gone home. But the secretary whispered to me that she had seen him drive towards the city centre, which was the opposite direction from his home. And most striking of all, he would not say what he had done for the rest of the day, other than denying that he had been in Valdres or knew anything about the murders there. He might consider answering you, but categorically refused to answer me.'

Danielsen made a dramatic pause and visibly enjoyed the attention we both gave him when he continued.

'I thought about arresting him on the spot, but decided

instead to get a constable to keep him and his car under surveillance for the rest of the day. Ibsen also informed me that he would be working late today, until at least seven o'clock, perhaps even later. So in the event that the attack is in any way related to him, today's events should be under control.'

He hesitated, but then continued with a little smile.

'And by the way, Anders Pettersen also said that he would rather deal with you in the future. So you seem to be far more popular and easy to get on with than me, certainly as far as younger male left-wing radicals are concerned.'

My first instinct was to answer that one could only hope the same was true of female left-wing radicals. And then I wanted to say that he, on the other hand, seemed to be more popular with the older male Nazis. But I did not allow myself to get rattled. So instead I replied that given their history, it was to an extent easy to understand their scepticism, no matter what one might believe or think of their political opinions. I added swiftly that none of them had entirely convinced me either, and that one should in principle keep that lead open.

Then I put my only trump card on the table: the page from the diary that had been found in Falko Reinhardt's jacket. I said that new information had, however, been found that reinforced the theory that the Nazis were involved.

My boss and Danielsen quickly looked over the page. Danielsen pulled a face and had to admit that the entry regarding the meeting on 7th June did fit extremely well with the date on the photograph. However, he felt that 'the content of the document was otherwise so vague that it could hardly provide the basis for anything more than a general suspicion.'

At twenty past three, we concluded that we should meet again at nine o'clock the following day. In the meantime, I would continue with the Nazis as the main focus of my investigation, but I also promised to interview Trond Ibsen again.

As for the advice we would give to top politicians regarding any public engagements over the next few days, our boss said that it was up to me to assess the situation regularly, but it was after all a very drastic step to cancel a major event without there being a definite threat. Danielsen nodded, and added that he for his part still believed that the danger of an attack was minimal, as long as Trond Ibsen was under surveillance.

We said our goodbyes. There was no direct animosity, but the atmosphere was tense due a certain amount of rivalry. I got the feeling that behind the jovial facade, the other two thought the same as me. The danger of an attack seemed to be mounting by the hour, without us getting any closer to knowing when, where or who.

# IX

I left the police station just after half past three. The drive to Patricia's was unexpectedly slow. For the last few blocks, the stream of cars, bicycles and pedestrians was unusually heavy. I finally realized why when I passed two groups of young Labour supporters only yards apart on their way to Frogner Square. The hordes of people on their way to the rally where Trond Bratten was going to speak were a reminder of the gravity of the situation.

I turned on the police radio and to my relief discovered that all was quiet. There was nothing to indicate that anything dramatic had happened in connection with the prime minister's speech at the Norwegian Farmers' Union. But I knew that Borgen, Bratten and other well-known people had public engagements over the next few days, and I did not look forward to living with the constant fear of what might happen.

Just before I parked the car in the parking space closest to 104–8 Erling Skjalgsson's Street, the police radio suddenly went dead. This was not due to sabotage, but rather a defective wire that could be changed as soon as I returned to the station. But it did not feel like a good sign. I was not in the best of moods when I rang the doorbell at ten to four.

Patricia did not appear to be any more cheerful. She gave me a grim and silent nod as I came in, and the door had barely closed behind the maid when she fired her first question.

'Well, has the missing page from the diary shown up? I hoped that you would take the time to call me as soon as it did!'

I replied that the messenger had had a puncture on the way to town and that otherwise, there was not much to be gleaned from it. She nodded, and held out her hand with impatience. I gave her the slightly crumpled page. She did not say thank you, but instead asked to have Falko's note and the photograph as well.

I then told her about the day's developments over the meal, but I was unfortunately unable to savour the taste of the superb loin steak. As far as I could see, Patricia only ate a few mouthfuls. She listened intently to what I had to say, but barely looked at me. Her eyes were fixed on the page from the diary, and only occasionally looked over at Falko's note and the photograph.

'As far as Marie Morgenstierne is concerned, the picture is getting clearer. If you get the answers I expect from Trond Ibsen and Anders Pettersen, we may even have this solved by this evening. And I can assure you that this Danielsen is very definitely on the wrong track, if not also the wrong planet,' she said, when I had finished giving my account at around twenty past four.

That was of course music to my ears. However, it appeared that Patricia had no intention of saying any more about the matter. She sat there staring at the page from the diary.

'But the matter of the attack is more urgent, and it really is not possible to get much more out of this mysterious document. The answer must be there staring us in the face right now, but very annoyingly, I can't see it. The dates are interesting enough in themselves.'

I nodded and said that the middle one was the same as on the photograph. She nodded impatiently.

'Yes, obviously, any child could see that. But that's not all that is of interest; 17 May has been our national day since 1814, and on 7 June we mark our independence from Sweden in 1905. These Nazis have certainly chosen to meet on symbolic days. But 8 August means nothing to me, other than that it is only a matter of days ago, and was after Falko Reinhardt had come back and Marie Morgenstierne had been murdered.'

'The document says nothing really about any of the people,' I said.

Patricia sighed and gave me a curt nod.

'It seems reasonable to assume that A and D, who wanted to take action, are Messieurs Eggen and Heidenberg, and that they have tried to persuade the fourth man in the picture to join them. But what more do we know about him? That he is probably slightly younger and more physically fit than they are. That he is not wearing a wedding ring on his hand, but does have a family of some kind. That could still be any one of tens of thousands, if not hundreds of thousands, of men in eastern Norway. And Falko has for some reason used the abbreviation SP for this person.'

'And the letters on the page do not refer to any known names. It seems to me rather that he has just used the first four letters of the alphabet?'

Patricia shook her head in irritation.

'Yes and no. Henry Alfred Lien talks about A, B and D. Where is C then?'

'Maybe he is C himself?' I suggested.

Patricia was not convinced by this either.

'Possibly, but if he was referring to himself you would have thought he would use A or D. It seems strange to use

C about yourself, particularly if you never otherwise use the letter . . .'

Patricia's focus switched intently between the pages and the photograph.

'Wait a minute! Their professions. Of course: A is for architect or Heidenberg, D is for director Eggen . . . What do you think B stands for, then?'

Suddenly it all fell into place within three seconds.

First, I saw sparks in Patricia's eyes.

Then she screamed.

And then she asked me in a terrified whisper: 'What time is it?'

I looked at Patricia, and wondered if the pressure of the past few days had resulted in some kind of nervous breakdown. Patricia was wearing a gold watch on her left arm, but she did not check it; she sat as if paralysed from the neck down. Only her eyes were alive, her eyes and her voice.

'What is the time?'

When she repeated the question, the whisper was even quieter and the fear even more tangible.

I looked at my watch and told her that it was twenty-five past four.

That was evidently all that was needed for Patricia to come back to life. She suddenly leaned forward across the table in an almost aggressive manner.

'Then run for your life and country! You have only five minutes before he shoots Trond Bratten!'

I was the one who was now paralysed for a few seconds. Patricia leaned forward and was even more forceful.

'Run! I would run with you if I could. The address is 66 Thomas Heftye's Street by Frogner Square. He'll fire from a window. Look up and see if you can see an open window. But for God's sake, man, run now!'

I ran. As I leaped to my feet, I asked who was going to shoot from the window.

Patricia almost screamed the answer – and pointed wildly at the door.

The pieces all fell into place in my head within a couple of seconds. Then I ran as fast as I could ever remember having run. I ran out of the house, down the road towards Frogner Square.

# X

*The murderer stood by the window of 66 Thomas Heftye's Street with a gun in his hand, and looked down over the mass of people below.*

*He glanced at his watch. It was twenty-five past four.*

*Only five minutes to go until the man in the window would shoot the Labour Party leader on the stage down there in Frogner Square. He felt remarkably calm, all the same.*

*B had never met Trond Bratten, but had still hated and scorned the man ever since the war. It rankled with him endlessly that a country bumpkin and small farmer's son who did not have even basic school exams could become minister of finance, and then promptly fail to take the advice of the entire banking sector. And what was even more pathetic was that the small, thin man had to hide behind his wife in any given situation because he lacked any great oratory skills, but still insisted that he should be prime minister, rather than any of the better-qualified men in the country. To the murderer, Bratten was the symbol of a new era where ambitious upstarts and speculators were succeeding in taking power over the country, without either the education or the cultural heritage and wisdom that coming from a good family gave.*

*Ever since he was a child, the man at the window had felt immense contempt for people who did not recognize and accept their place in society. And he had hated Trond Bratten as good as all his adult life – both for his disproportionate ambition, and for every word he uttered as a politician. It all sounded like polished Marxism.*

*But this was not just a matter of personal contempt and political hate. Trond Bratten's death was now necessary in order to secure the future of the country. The murderer had thought a lot about it over the years, and then more recently discussed it at length with his late father's friends, Christian Magnus Eggen and Frans Heidenberg. All three had hated and scorned Trond Bratten for many years, but they were now starting to fear him. They all agreed that the government's days were numbered. If Trond Bratten was allowed to live, he would become Norway's prime minister within the next couple of years.*

*This was in itself a terrible thought, but also a tragedy because of the consequences it would have for the nation. A split between the right-wing parties and the Labour Party's ascent to power could herald a new and long period in government for the party: at the very least, as long as the last one. The financial cost of the party's taxes and charges would be catastrophic for business. But what was worse was that Trond Bratten, with his ridiculous hero status from the war, could now become the prime minister who would abandon the country's independence and guide it into a new union. In a matter of decades, this would leave the country open to mass immigration from other countries all over the world. And it would be a national catastrophe. The murderer had himself been in the USA and seen the results of the increasing numbers of black and yellow faces on the streets. Criminality had mushroomed, and no white man could feel safe on the streets of any American city. The murderer did not want Oslo to look like that when he was an old man.*

*Fortunately there was only one man who stood in the way. Trond Bratten reigned supreme within his own ranks. His deputy was young and inexperienced. If Bratten fell, the Labour Party would no longer have a leader to unite them and would perhaps even be thrown into a bitter leadership struggle. The best that one could hope for was that this, combined with the debate on the union, would spell the beginning of the end for the party.*

*The man in the window had in his youth been fully prepared to kill people. He had been a sniper and an extremely diligent soldier. Already in his late teens, he had pushed his mental boundary and abandoned any blocks to taking human life. During the Second World War he had never been in combat, and the next great war that he had anticipated, with a mixture of fear and glee, had never happened. So he ended his military career. But he had continued to carry with him an immense curiosity as to how it would feel to kill a man. For many years, it had seemed unlikely that this would ever happen. But he had always carried it within himself. If he was not born to be a murderer, then he certainly had been trained and prepared to become one from his youth.*

*B had not killed anyone until the evening before. And then he had killed two people within minutes. He had been curious to* know how it felt. But when he did kill his first victim, it was entirely according to plan and without drama. He had felt no sympathy for either of the men he had killed. After the murders, he had thought, just as he had before, that a fat country farmer and a long-haired student were not very important people, no more than a couple of small pawns that had to be sacrificed for the great cause.

The uninvited guest had left a murderer, and it had involved very little drama. He had seen Henry Alfred Lien as a traitor to the cause and decided in cold blood that the farmer had to die. He had not had anything against killing Lien, but he had not felt any great hatred for him either.

A measure of hatred had come later – when he suddenly stood face to face with Falko Reinhardt in the living room. Reinhardt had recognized him, seen the gun and run. The murderer had felt his hatred and contempt for the long-haired young man flare up. And he had known that the man now must die so he could not blow the whistle. The situation had instilled a different tension.

The murderer had pursued his victim, relishing the fact that he could keep pace with a younger man, and had first shot him in the foot. He had meant to kill him with the bullet to his chest, but had hit him a little too low. Reinhardt lay there, paralysed and helpless, only yards from the cliff. That was when the murderer had had the idea to cover all his tracks by pushing the victim over the edge. He was very pleased with himself and his quick thinking. He had got rid of the gun along with the victim when he heaved Reinhardt over the cliff. There was every reason to hope that Reinhardt would not be found until after Trond Bratten had been assassinated. And if he was found before this, the pistol in his pocket would support theories of murder and suicide.

It had been quite a shock for him to look over the edge and see someone else down there on the scree, close to where Reinhardt had landed. The murderer had immediately run to his car and taken off with a pulse well over 150. The fear of being caught and stopped before the planned attack had nearly driven him to despair in the first few minutes. But then he reasoned that Reinhardt had to be dead, and that the person down there could not possibly have recognized him from that distance. B had after all exceptional vision himself, and had only been able to see that there was a person down there, without being able to recognize him or her. His pulse had gradually slowed as he drove away from Valdres without any more drama, and without seeing any police cars.

He did not go home in the event that the police might have in some way tracked him down, and instead stayed overnight in a hotel near Hønefoss, under a false name. The atmosphere among the few guests at dinner was relaxed. None of the guests or staff appeared to recognize B in any way, and there were no policemen to be seen. B had fallen asleep without difficulty when he went to bed, and had slept long and well after the day's excitement. After checking out, he had eaten an excellent lunch at the hotel without being disturbed. Then he had driven back into town two hours before the planned attack.

Everything had gone as hoped and planned. It was an office building that was under renovation, and the workmen were still on holiday.

The murderer had an escape route that would take no more than a minute, out the door and down the back stairs. All being well, he would be able to use it and then slip out and vanish into the mass of people below. A middle-aged man in a suit would hardly be the first to be suspected.

*The man by the window did not think that he could get away with such a heroic deed, but the possibility of succeeding was very real. It was a seductive thought, that he might be able to walk home calmly after the assassination and go in to work as normal in the morning, while the whole of Norway and half of Europe talked about the murder of the leader of the Labour Party and speculated about what sort of cunning, daring man might do such a thing.*

*No matter what happened, he was standing here now, by an open window on the third floor, ready to raise the gun as soon as Trond Bratten went up onto the stage. If Bratten did this as planned, everything else would be simple. The angle was perfect, and the lectern stood there like the bull's eye at a shooting range. He could see the leader of the Labour Party standing with his wife just below the stage, papers under his arms. It was so typical that he could not even do the simplest thing without a manuscript and hours of preparation.*

*The man in the window looked impatiently at his watch and saw that it was still only twenty-eight minutes past four.*

*It was when he looked up again that he noticed a worryingly fast movement on the periphery of his vision, down on Frogner Square.*

# XI

I later remembered remarkably little from my wild dash towards Frogner Square. When I got out onto the street, I remembered in a flash that the car was too far away and that the car radio was not working anyway.

So I carried on running down the street. I heard the soles of my shoes hitting the asphalt, without feeling that they were part of my body. I ran past people on the pavement, without ever thinking that they were people and that I might bump into them. When I then saw Frogner Square, I accelerated.

People continued to slip away in front of me until one of them, on the edge of the crowd in Frogner Square, did not see me in time. I vaguely noticed that she was holding something in her hands, and that she was just standing there without moving. And then we collided.

For a moment I stared straight into a pair of familiar eyes. I first saw confusion, then a spark of happiness, and then visible disappointment as I ran on. And somehow I still did not register that it was Miriam Filtvedt Bentsen I had bumped into.

Following the collision, I stopped and looked around but saw none of the four constables that I knew had been assigned to the rally. To make my way through the throng of people was never an option I considered. The sea of people in front of me looked impenetrable, and I had no idea where Trond Bratten might be. I was entirely focused on 66 Thomas Heftye's Street, a four-storey brick building that faced onto Frogner Square. I saw two open windows, one to the right on the second floor and the other to the right on the third floor. Not a person was to be seen in either of them.

As I forced open the front door, I ran past a wall clock. It was one minute and forty seconds to half past four. I set my aim for the second floor and, still without feeling my feet, bounded up the steps two at a time.

# XII

The murderer recognized the running man as soon as he saw him, and once again felt the adrenalin surge through his body.

It was Detective Inspector Kolbjørn Kristiansen, who had come to his house to talk to him only a few days ago. The one that the newspapers, with their renowned lack of style, called 'K2'. Kristiansen had seemed pretty stupid to him, but the murderer had later suspected that he might be smarter than he first appeared. The murderer had said more than he intended in the course of their conversation.

Christian Magnus Eggen had told him on the telephone yesterday that Kristiansen was on the right track, but they did not think he would manage to piece it all together in time. So his presence now was something of a shock, especially as he was heading at full speed towards the building. There was an odd little interruption when the detective inspector bumped into a young woman in the crowd who was standing there reading a book. But Kristiansen almost immediately carried on running towards the building.

The man by the window paradoxically felt some relief when he saw Kristiansen carry on. His greatest fear was that someone would warn Trond Bratten and stop him from getting up onto the stage. When Kristiansen appeared, the murderer instinctively feared that he would plough through the crowd and do just that. He heaved a sigh and relaxed when the detective inspector then carried on running towards the building, and he noted that there were no uniformed police to be seen in the sea of bodies.

The door to the room was locked from the inside and was solid. Even if the detective inspector found the right door in time, he would take an age trying to get it open.

B would in practice have no hope of escaping via the back stairs after the murder. But that was a sacrifice that he now, as a widower with no children, was prepared to make for the great cause. If his peers and countrymen wanted to condemn and punish him, he was certain that he was doing the country a service that he would later be thanked for. He would leave behind no descendants, but his name would be remembered and praised by many for generations to come.

The murderer hurried over to the door to make sure it was locked.

When B got back to the window, he saw the woman with the book. And instantly cursed her.

Following the collision with the detective inspector, the woman had first simply picked up her book and watched him run on, bewildered. But now she was making her way through the crowd towards the stage, where Bratten was still waiting.

The compère was a well-known union man, a big fat idiot who had no doubt lived on taxpayers' money for years. He was standing ready by the stage, but made no sign of moving. It was one minute to half past four.

The man by the window stood there with the gun in his hand for the next thirty seconds. Down on Frogner Square, the compère had still not gone up onto the stage to introduce the party leader. Bratten was standing between his wife and some others in the shadows below the stage. The woman with the book was snaking her way through the crowd with unexpected force.

On the positive side, there was still no noise from the corridor. Kristiansen still had a long way to go before he got into the room.

And finally, the compère now went out onto the stage to undeservedly rapturous applause down on Frogner Square.

# XIII

Without knowing whether the murderer was on the second or the third floor, I instinctively headed for the right-hand door on the second floor. The door was locked, but I could hear sounds from inside.

I rapped on the door and shouted: 'Open up, this is the police! We know you are in there! Open the door immediately!'

Suddenly all was quiet inside. I heard heavy steps across the floor. But I could not tell whether they were moving towards the window or the door, nor did I know if it was the right floor. My desperation rocketed when I then looked at my watch just as the second hand passed half past four. Then, without saying any more, I threw my entire body weight against the door. It shuddered, but remained locked. It was a wooden door with a new frame, which looked like it could take a thump or two.

After this, however, I heard a frightened man's voice shout from inside: 'Don't knock down the door, I'll be there as soon as I can unlock it.'

There were a few seconds of fumbling by the door before it opened. In the opening stood a thin, obviously frightened man in overalls, with a small paintbrush in his hand. He calmed down a bit when he saw my police ID, but his voice and body were still trembling. The man mumbled that he was a joiner and janitor for the building, and he was only trying to varnish the new window frames while the workmen were on holiday.

I pushed him briskly to one side and ran into the room.

It was an unfinished office of around two hundred square feet. And there was no one else, nor any weapons, to be seen.

Just then, we heard thunderous applause from outside.

I ran over to the window. My arms were stiff with fear, but my legs were still working. My legs and my eyes. In a trance, I saw that the applause was fortunately only for the compère, a large and stocky union representative who was standing by the lectern to introduce the party leader's speech. I could only just see Bratten standing by the stage with his wife, and some papers under his arm.

I vaguely registered a woman with a book in her hand who at that moment broke through the last rows of the audience and stopped right in front of the party leader. And all of a sudden I realized that it was Miriam Filtvedt Bentsen.

Then I heard more applause, which woke me from my trance. I spun round, once more thrust the even more bewildered janitor aside and ran up the stairs to the third floor.


# XIV

*The murderer stood at his post by the window with the gun in his hand. There was still no noise to be heard on the third floor. But he had heard sounds from the floor below, which clearly indicated that Kristiansen was working his way up the building, with or without reinforcements.*

The compère had fortunately not prolonged the embarrassment down on Frogner Square. The applause soon turned into a rhythmic clapping and stamping of feet when he introduced the party leader. But the woman with the book had just managed to get through. She was now engaged in an apparently animated conversation with the leader's wife – the party leader himself a reticent onlooker.

Bratten's wife did not seem particularly keen to stop him from going onstage. Nor did the audience around them. Several of them shook their fists at the girl with the book, and the applause and calls for the party leader increased in volume. But the party leader hesitated. And the girl with the book did not give up. She threw up her hands and twice pointed quite clearly at the building.

The murderer pushed himself up against the window frame and swiftly hunkered down. His mind was in overdrive trying to deal with the unexpected situation. His pulse rose even more when he heard footsteps running down the corridor, following by a pounding on the door.

Trond Bratten had to die before Detective Inspector Kristiansen broke into the room. But the woman with book and intense body language did not give in, and Bratten was still hesitating.

'This is the police. We know you are in there! Open the door and come out, or we'll break down the door!'

Kristiansen's voice was powerful and determined. It carried easily through the door.

For a second, the man by the window considered opening the door and shooting Detective Inspector Kristiansen. He would then have the time he needed until Bratten got up onto the stage. But the murderer had no idea whether Kristiansen was armed or not, or whether he had more policemen with him. And a shot being fired up here in the building would probably be heard down on Frogner Square. And in that case, the party leader would dive for cover.

The man by the window rejected the idea. Instead, he weighed up the possibility of aiming the gun right now.

It would be far harder to shoot Bratten standing where he was beside the stage than by the lectern. But it should be possible to hit the pathetic coward there, too. The party leader's wife was standing side on to him, covering half his body. But to the right of her, he could aim straight at Bratten's head and chest, past the woman with the book.

Bratten said something or other to the woman with the book. But he made no sign of going up onto the stage. It was so contemptible and typical of him, not to be able to make up his own mind but to let the women do it for him.

There was another thud from the door. Someone had thrown their shoulder, or some heavy object, against it. The door held, but another thump put increasing pressure on the hinges.

With a deft move, the man raised the gun and aimed the barrel out of the window at Trond Bratten's head. The murderer was taken aback to realize that his hand was shaking and cursed this sign of weakness. The seconds ticked as he tried to get a clear aim at his target. He cocked the gun so that he could fire immediately if anyone burst into the room.

Trond Bratten had to, and would, die, but he could only fire one shot. The party leader's wife and the woman with the book made it hard to get a clear aim. The woman with the book suddenly reminded the murderer of his own dead daughter.

It struck B that he would not be sitting here if he had not first lost his wife and then his daughter. He had always held back out *of consideration to his family. It was the person who had shot his daughter who had triggered all of this. But now there was no going back for a man with no family and no means of retreat. He had nothing to lose.*

*Memories of his daughter burned behind his eyes. The murderer now had a clear aim at Bratten's forehead. But his hand was shaking more than ever before.*

# XV

In desperation, I threw myself against the door for the third time. It shuddered, but the hinges held.

It was only when I was about to hurl myself against it for the fourth time that I realized there was someone else in the corridor. A small, terrified janitor, with a large bundle of keys in his hand.

I almost screamed at him: 'The key to this door, quick! There's a man in there who is going to kill Trond Bratten!'

The janitor was so shocked that he dropped the keys on the floor. It took a couple of seconds before he picked them up and then a couple more before he found the right key. I expected to hear a shot at any moment, but the gun was not fired.

Finally the janitor found the right key. I snatched it from him. My hand was shaking so much that I could hardly get it into the lock, but when I did, it turned easily.

I opened the door and stormed into the room.

Martin Morgenstierne was sitting alone by the open window, with a gun in his hands. He turned his head and glanced back when I charged in.

For a moment, I feared that he would turn the gun on me.

But he looked back out of the window to Frogner Square, took his final aim and curled his finger round the trigger.

I leaped forward and grabbed hold of him just as he fired the gun. I was horrified to hear the shot and the sound of the screams that followed from outside. But I did not have time to think about it. The gun was gone, and I was lying on the floor on top of an unarmed Martin Morgenstierne.

The fight that followed was fortunately brief. He was a generation older than me and had obviously been entirely focused on firing. He had also landed in an awkward position underneath me. I felt a surge of fury and hate for him, and with zero sympathy, wrenched his arm up behind his back in the hope of breaking it.

'I give myself up,' he said, and it struck me that he was frighteningly calm and controlled, given that he had just shot the opposition leader.

Whereas I was shaking so much that I fumbled in frustration for a few moments before I managed to get the handcuffs on him. Meanwhile, we heard the sounds of running feet and screams from outside.

When I eventually stood up, he remarked: 'It would seem that I got him.' He was still alarmingly calm, and a small smile tugged at the corners of his mouth.

I feared that I had come a second too late to prevent the death of the party leader, but still did not know what had happened outside the window. So I hauled him up without answering.

We stood side by side in silence and looked out of the window.

What we saw was not what either of us had expected, and it grieved us both.

After the gunshot, the crowd had obviously panicked and scattered from the stage. There were only three people in the cleared space.

Trond Bratten had dropped the manuscript for his speech, but he was still standing, leaning against the stage, very much alive.

The party leader's wife was standing in front of him with outstretched arms, like a human shield in the event of more gunshots.

A large book lay open on the ground in front of her. And Miriam Filtvedt Bentsen was lying on the ground beside the book.

Her fair hair fluttered in the wind, but she herself was not moving, lying on her stomach, as a dark stream of blood poured from her head onto her sweatshirt.

It was a terrible sight, and everything inside me froze instantly. Which was perhaps a good thing. I remembered later a wild urge to throw Martin Morgenstierne out of the window, and then to jump out myself. All I remembered from those unreal seconds was that feeling. And Martin Morgenstierne saying, in an almost apologetic voice, 'She looks like my daughter. I deeply regret that. He was the only one who was supposed to die.'

# XVI

The wall clock at the main police station showed half past six as I made my way to my boss's office. He beamed and offered me his hand. The story of how I had saved the life of the opposition leader Trond Bratten, and at the same time solved both of yesterday's murders, had already been broadcast on the radio and TV. Congratulatory telegrams were streaming in. Unless the nascent rumours that the crown princess was pregnant were confirmed, it would headline the evening news, and be on the front page of all the major newspapers tomorrow. But no matter what, I had been right all along and was a role model for the country's police force.

Normally my boss's effusive congratulations would have had me in seventh heaven. But this time I remained downcast, almost depressed. I thanked him and told him the truth: that the fate of the badly wounded young woman hung heavily on my conscience.

He nodded appreciatively and said that I not only was I an exceptionally good policeman, I was also an exceptionally good person. I thanked him once again, but certainly did not feel like one.

My boss asked in an irritatingly casual manner if there was any news about the 'wounded party'. I replied that she had still been alive on arrival at hospital, but that it was touch and go whether she would survive or not.

We sat in silence for a while after this.

As we sat there, I ran through the two terrifying moments I had experienced with Miriam Filtvedt Bentsen.

The first was when I looked out of the window at 66 Thomas Heftye's Street and saw her lying on the asphalt below, covered in blood and not moving. It suddenly felt as though it was my fault and I was entirely responsible if she died. I was the one who had bumped into her, and what I had told her had prompted her to push her way forward to stop Trond Bratten from getting onto the stage. And I was the one who had pushed the assassin to one side so that the bullet hit her. I thought I would never smile again if she died. I had never met her parents, or her little brother. But all the same, I could feel how painful it would be to have to tell them of her death.

The second horrifying moment was at Ullevål Hospital, when I got there just after the ambulance. After waiting for fifteen minutes, I was able to speak to the surgeon and senior doctor for a couple of minutes while preparations were being made for the operation. It was an unnerving experience.

The surgeon, Bernt Berg, was in his fifties, and his measured movements instilled confidence and trust. He had a very grave face, and only replied in short sentences when asked a question. He reminded me a little of Martin Morgenstierne, which made the situation feel even more alarming and unreal.

I said that Miriam Filtvedt Bentsen had been shot while

trying to save Trond Bratten from being assassinated, and that her survival was also extremely important for my ongoing investigation. Given this, I asked him to call me at the station as soon as there was any news following the operation.

His face was devoid of expression and emotion when he replied 'yes' to this.

I then asked what he thought the chances were that she would survive.

With equal equanimity, he said: 'About fifty-fifty, if we are able to remove the bullet.'

So I asked him what the chances were of that.

His voice still sounded unmoved when he told me: 'There is an imminent danger that she will die soon if we cannot remove it. The bullet is lodged just beside her main artery.'

I thanked him, once again asked him to call me as soon as there was any news, and wished him luck with the operation. He nodded briskly and left without saying any more.

The surgeon inspired both fear and confidence at the same time. I thought he seemed like a man who knew what he was doing, someone who was not likely to lose control or tremble, no matter what happened.

I caught a brief glimpse of Miriam Filtvedt Bentsen as she was wheeled into the operating theatre. This vaguely reassured me. The bleeding had stopped. I could see she was still breathing. And even though she was in a coma, her face still seemed to emanate strong will. Otherwise, she lay completely still, with bandages around her neck and shoulders.

I felt totally impotent and feared that I might faint if she should suddenly die there in front of me. So I turned and walked away as quickly as I dared down the corridor.

I was suddenly roused from my thoughts when the telephone on my boss's desk started to ring. And I jumped when he then immediately said: 'Yes, he is right here. I'll pass on your message immediately.'

He saw the fear in my eyes and hastily carried on: 'The Labour Party and the Confederation of Trade Unions send their thanks and congratulations. Flowers are on the way!'

I needed to think about something else and said that we should perhaps discuss the murder of Marie Morgenstierne again. My boss nodded.

'Even after all this upheaval, you still think about your duties. I have called Danielsen, who was unfortunately unable to come at such short notice.'

I saw the hint of a smile on my boss's face when he said this. We both knew that Danielsen lived alone, and never went anywhere other than work.

'He asked me to congratulate you on solving the case, but added that the mystery of Marie Morgenstierne's death remained unsolved. I take it there is still nothing to indicate that her father had anything to do with it?'

I shook my head.

'Martin Morgenstierne confessed his part in yesterday's two murders in the car on the way here, but fiercely maintains that he had nothing to do with his daughter's death. It was, on the contrary, the loss of his daughter that removed the final hurdles that prevented him from carrying out the planned assassination. He had been under considerable pressure from Christian Magnus Eggen and Frans Heidenberg for some time. They have expressed their disappointment that the assassination was unsuccessful, but still maintain that it was justified and necessary. And this all corroborates what Henry Alfred Lien wrote in his diary.'

My boss nodded.

'How did you work it out? Danielsen and I thought it seemed almost impossible to get anything out of the diary entries.'

I remembered what Patricia had shouted at me just as I left, 'B is for bank manager, and SP is for Super Pater, that's to say, Martin Morgenstierne!' and quickly stitched together an official explanation that fitted.

'Lien used abbreviations based on occupations. A was for architect and D was for director. So B could then well be bank manager. It also seemed to fit that SP in Falko Reinhardt's note might stand for "Super Pater", which was his nickname for Martin Morgenstierne. Luckily I realized this in the nick of time when I was only a few hundred yards away.'

My boss whistled and looked at me wide-eyed.

I was afraid that he would ask me for more details about where exactly I had been, so I hastily continued: 'But yes, the murder of Marie Morgenstierne remains unsolved, even though her father has now been arrested for two other murders.'

My boss was back on track.

'Yes, that's where we were. Danielsen mentioned that he thought it was one of the other communists, that is to say Anders Pettersen or Trond Ibsen, who was behind it. And if you would like a day off after today's drama, I could of course get him to follow this up tomorrow . . .'

I shook my head and assured him that I had every hope that we could clear up the remaining murder as well in the course of the week, given today's developments. My boss smiled his approval.

'Excellent. Then you will of course continue to be head of the investigation, and can use Danielsen wherever needed tomorrow.'

I nodded eagerly. When I got up to leave, the atmosphere was almost buoyant. So I jumped all the more when the phone rang again.

My boss picked up the receiver and immediately looked very grave. He answered: 'Yes, he's here. One moment, please.'

He passed the phone over to me.

'From the hospital,' he said.

The voice at the other end was just as I remembered it.

'This is Bernt Berg, the head surgeon from Ullevål Hospital. You asked me to phone as soon as there was any news on the operation.'

'Yes,' I said, and held my breath.

'The operation was successful and the bullet has been removed.'

'Thank you so much for letting me know. But are the chances still fifty-fifty, as you said before the operation?' I asked, forcing myself to breathe.

'Yes. The next few hours are critical, but if there are no complications, this will improve,' the monotone voice at the other end of the line told me.

I thanked him as politely as I could and asked once again if he could ring me if and when there were any changes.

'Yes,' he replied.

Then we both put the phone down.

I felt both relief and a whisper of optimism. But I knew all the same that there was still a danger that she might die in the course of the evening or overnight, and that it would now be even harder to accept.

I told my boss that there had been an improvement, but that the patient's condition was still critical. Then I asked if I could take the rest of the day off, and continue with the investigation tomorrow. My boss immediately agreed to this and congratulated me again on the day's extraordinary outcome.

It was undoubtedly well meant. But it occurred to me that poor, sweet Miriam Filtvedt Bentsen's fate was of far less consequence to everyone else than the fact that an important man had escaped an attempted assassination unharmed.

# XVII

I was eventually able to call Patricia at five to eight. She was once again in control of her mood, but seemed unexpectedly muted. I told her that I had got there just in time to prevent Trond Bratten from being shot. She replied, slightly sarcastically, that she had now heard that twice on the radio and again on the evening news on television.

I apologized for not having rung her sooner, but explained that the situation had been a bit chaotic, what with the arrest of a double murderer and a critically wounded onlooker.

Patricia's voice softened a little when she said that the onlooker had been mentioned on the television, but no details had been given.

I told her that it was Miriam Filtvedt Bentsen, and that she had been shot while warning Trond Bratten not to go on stage.

'Oh,' Patricia stuttered, obviously taken aback, but still not sounding particularly concerned. Only after a short pause did she ask which hospital she was at, and how she was.

I told her that Miriam Filtvedt Bentsen was at Ullevål Hospital and that the first operation had been a success, but that there was still a risk that she might not live through the night.

Patricia pulled herself together. She said brusquely that it was of course perfectly understandable that I had not been able to call before, and that one could only hope that the patient would get better.

I came to her aid, thanked her once again for her invaluable contribution and asked if we should perhaps meet this evening or tomorrow to discuss the continued hunt for Marie Morgenstierne's murderer.

Her reply was unexpectedly swift.

'As soon as possible this evening, if you can. I have every hope then that we can solve the mystery by midnight. But first you must drive over to see Trond Ibsen and ask him what he was doing yesterday, and see what else he has to add.'

I felt my head was still spinning, but looked at the clock and suggested that we should try to meet at half past nine. She said that would be fine, but that she would be there all the same if I could get there any earlier.

To my surprise, Trond Ibsen was still in his office at a quarter past eight, and picked up the telephone. I said that it had been a long and dramatic day, as he might have heard, but that I was now following a lead on Marie Morgenstierne's murder and had to talk to him as soon as possible.

I added that I would be happy to send Detective Inspector Danielsen, but had understood that he would prefer to give a statement to me. Trond Ibsen sighed, then replied that he would most definitely prefer to give his statement to me, and that he was currently alone in his office if I could come there.

# XVIII

Trond Ibsen was sitting in a large armchair behind his desk when I came in, and immediately put aside the patient journal he was reading. I stayed well away from the sofa, but felt rather inferior all the same when I sat down on a far smaller chair in front of the desk.

But this time, the psychologist did not seem particularly arrogant. For a change, he seemed rather nervous. His hand trembled as he congratulated me on the day's breakthrough, which he had also heard on the radio. He had not been aware that the person who had been critically wounded was Miriam Filtvedt Bentsen, and this news seemed only to increase his unease. He repeated twice that he sincerely hoped that she would survive, and also that he himself still knew nothing about any of the murders.

I replied that yesterday's murders had now been solved, but that where he had been himself the day before remained a mystery. He let out a deep sigh.

'I hoped that would be of less interest now that the murderer had been caught. So, well, I was absolutely not in the Valdres area. I was in fact indoors with a woman here in Oslo, and for personal reasons I had hoped that I would not need to tell the police or anyone else about her.'

His eyes begged me.

A thought fluttered through my mind. Kristine Larsen was still being held on remand yesterday, and there were not many other young women involved in the case. A terrible thought was forming.

'Are you saying that you were with . . . a former female member of the group yesterday?'

He shook his head and sank even deeper into the chair.

'No, if only that had been the case, I would gladly have told you. I did try my luck once upon a time, but there was never any interest from her side. But she was more gracious in her rejection that either Marie Morgenstierne or Kristine Larsen were. I really do hope that she pulls through.'

My nodding agreement was perhaps a little too enthusiastic, so I peered at him sternly.

'In that case, I have no idea who it might be and why it might be so troublesome. If the woman concerned is married, we must surely be able to check your alibi without her husband knowing about it?'

Trond Ibsen drew an even heavier sigh and sank still further into the chair.

'Strictly speaking, I cannot rule out that the woman I spent yesterday evening with was not married, though I would be very surprised. The problem is that I in fact don't know her name and she would hardly be a reliable witness if the police were to find her. But I couldn't claim that I had been at home alone, because if that had then come out in the papers, she could accuse me of making false statements.'

He sent me a pleading look, then buried his face in his hands. It was only then that I understood the situation.

'So what you are telling me is that you spent yesterday evening with a woman you had paid to keep you company?'

His head and hands nodded for a couple of seconds. Then suddenly, everything poured out.

'Tactfully put, yes. It would be extremely embarrassing and potentially a disaster for my practice if it were to get out. My relationship with women is hopeless. I have never been caressed by a woman other than those I have paid. And believe it or not, this was the first time I had actually done it. It was my first ever physical encounter with a woman, and I have regretted it ever since. But this murder investigation has just made everything even more unbearable, and reminded me of my last and greatest humiliation.'

My mind started to put the pieces together.

'Of course, when Marie Morgenstierne finally got over Falko, she chose Anders Pettersen and not you?'

He nodded. This was followed by another furious outpouring. The psychologist was obviously letting all his pent-up frustrations out now.

'That was the final and hardest straw. The fact that Kristine Larsen preferred the missing Falko was less of a blow. Anders is politically simple, generally lazy, constantly broke and not particularly talented as an artist. And he gloated in the most disgusting, arrogant way. I don't understand what she saw in him, and it felt like the greatest and most demeaning of all my failures with women!'

This was said with great indignation. I feared he was going to explode, and allowed him some time to settle down again before I continued.

'So what you are saying now is that Anders Pettersen had managed to do what you wanted most in the world, that is, to go to bed with Marie Morgenstierne. And that it is very likely that he is the father of her unborn child?'

His nod was instant and, it seemed to me, a little spiteful.

'Yes. That fits with the timescale. It was at the start of June. I saw it in his smile first. And then he told me straight out: by the way, I have now been where you have always wanted to go. A delightful, undulating landscape. I might just settle there for good. I understood immediately what he meant, and hated him more than ever.'

Trond Ibsen had now hit rock bottom, only to bounce back. When he carried on speaking, he suddenly became the psychologist, with only the hint of an undertone in his voice.

'Bedding her was possibly Anders' greatest physical achievement. He felt that he was Falko's successor in both political and personal terms. He no doubt wanted their relationship to be public, but I don't for a moment imagine that he wanted to become a father. He often said that having children was a form of egotism that could not be combined with revolutionary work, and should therefore be left until after the revolution. So it could well be that you now have the motive and the murderer you are looking for.'

I nodded.

'It will be followed up. But you do understand that this does not exonerate you? Based on what you have just said, jealousy could be your motive, and that clearly does not rule out the possibility that you killed Marie Morgenstierne.'

Trond Ibsen gave yet another deep sigh, but looked me squarely in the eye when he replied.

'Formally, you are of course right. But then I would definitely have killed him, and not her. And, given my history with her and others, I obviously wouldn't want any kind of investigation that involved us. I have always feared that it would end like this, with me being acquitted of murder, but exposed to ridicule. As far as women are concerned, I'm useless and I know it. But I have honestly never killed any of the women who have rejected me, even though there are quite a few now, and some of them have been very cruel.'

This was said with great emotion. Trond Ibsen's mask was definitely crumbling in front of my eyes. The man who emerged was complex, and held secrets that no one would have expected. But even when I saw Trond Ibsen unmasked, I still did not see a murderer.

So I said that I would do my utmost to prevent the secrets of his private life from getting out. He brightened up visibly, thanked me and said once again that he had now told me things that could cause him great embarrassment and spell disaster for his new practice.

So our conversation ended on a relatively good note. He promised that he would be available for further questions over the next few days, should that be necessary, and wished me luck with the investigation. I made my way home, feeling a mixture of sympathy and contempt for him. But I was remarkably sure that Patricia was right, and that Danielsen's theory that Trond Ibsen was the murderer was a red herring.

# XIX

To my astonishment, I was asked to wait for a moment – a rare occurrence indeed – when I turned up at Patricia's as agreed at half past nine. When I was shown into the room three minutes later, Patricia was sitting waiting with coffee and cakes, and apologized that she had had to take an unexpected phone call.

She had fully regained her composure, and congratulated me straight away on the day's great success. But it did strike me that there was something, if not exactly unfriendly, perhaps rather slightly brusque about her this evening. She listened dutifully to my detailed account of the drama at Frogner Square, and repeated afterwards briefly that one could only hope that the patient would recover.

While waiting to hear more from the hospital, I tried to think as little as possible about Miriam Filtvedt Bentsen. So instead I congratulated Patricia on her brilliant reasoning that had foiled the attempted assassination of the leader of the Labour Party. She shrugged dismissively, and looked uncomfortable.

'I should have picked up on the time and place earlier. As soon as I knew that Bratten was going to give a speech at Frogner Square today and heard the words Heftye 66, I should have realized that it was the street and not the person. The fact that it might refer to the age of one of the parties involved was distracting, but I should have seen the connection. And I should have guessed earlier that the SP stood for Super Pater. The pieces only fell into place suddenly when I discovered the explanation for the letters in Henry Alfred Lien's diary. B fitted perfectly with bank manager, who was also the man Falko had called Super Pater, and what's more, he lived in Frogner. I have not been very focused for the past couple of days, so please excuse my outburst; it's simply frustration at myself.'

We then moved on to discuss the investigation of Marie Morgenstierne's murder.

Patricia nodded approvingly when I told her about my visit to Trond Ibsen and then swiftly took up the thread.

'Just as I thought – so the solution should be just around the corner now. We can rule out the idea that Falko Reinhardt was the father of Marie Morgenstierne's unborn child.

And Trond Ibsen's history is such that it gives us every reason to believe that he was certainly not Marie Morgenstierne's lover.'

I interrupted her and asked how she could so categorically dismiss the possibility that Falko was the father. She lit up with an almost childish grin.

'The simple fact that he was still a long way from Norway, according to the tickets found in his pocket, when some man peeled off his fiancée's panties here in Oslo. On the other hand, there is more and more to indicate that Anders Pettersen was there when that happened. Confront him with it, and with the fact that he was standing in one of the side streets when she started to run. I don't know if he saw Falko, or if Falko saw him; nor do I know if Marie Morgenstierne saw either of them. But I am almost certain that it was him standing there.'

I stared at Patricia, baffled, and asked how she could be so sure of that.

'A theory that I have had more or less from the start. As I pointed out at an early stage, Marie Morgenstierne was walking extremely slowly and apparently happily towards the station, even though she was wearing a watch and knew that she would not make the next train. She was secretly hoping to bump into someone. And that someone was Anders Pettersen, who would have had the time to cycle round, precisely because she was walking so slowly. The fact that she said no to a lift from Trond Ibsen could of course have been a decoy, if she wanted to meet him in secret. But she also had to hand over the recording first. If it was Trond Ibsen she was going to meet, there would be no need to walk so slowly. As he had a car, he would have got there long before her anyway. This all fits with the other pieces that are gradually falling into place.'

I looked at her with admiration, and thought with a silent sigh that Danielsen might have the last laugh after all. But when I asked Patricia straight out if she thought that Anders Pettersen was Marie Morgenstierne's murderer, she drew out her answer.

'That is not what I said, nor, for that matter, my conclusion. As Falko said, there are two possibilities. And he no doubt thought that both were sad or tragic. The one decidedly sad alternative is that Falko's best friend and admirer Anders Pettersen killed his fiancée, and thus also his own child. But there is still another alternative, which is no less sad or tragic . . .'

Patricia sat for a moment and stared gravely at something in the air in front of her. Then she drained her coffee cup and turned her focus back to me.

'No matter how you look at it, there are a number of family tragedies here. The Morgenstierne daughter is murdered along with her unborn child, and the father is jailed for two other murders. Falko Reinhardt leaves behind him a broken-hearted lover and two depressed parents. Henry Alfred Lien was never forgiven by his son, although he longed and deserved to be. I can only imagine what the son will think when he hears the story.'

'And, not to be forgotten, Miriam Filtvedt Bentsen is hovering between life and death. I wonder how her parents are feeling now,' I added.

Patricia nodded, and promptly carried on.

'So, let's follow Marie Morgenstierne's murder through to the end, no matter how sad the truth might prove to be. Go and see Anders Pettersen, tonight if you can, and confront him with the fact that he was Marie Morgenstierne's lover and the father of her unborn child. Ask him if he knew about the child, and if so, how he found out. And ask him who else knew about his relationship with Marie Morgenstierne, and when they found out. Come back here afterwards: then I should hopefully be able to tell you whether it was Anders Pettersen, or the other possible murderer, who shot Marie Morgenstierne. You can come no matter how late it might be.'

I looked at the clock. It was already nearly half past ten. I said that I thought it was a bit late to start a new round with Anders Pettersen now, after such a long and demanding day. It would have to be first thing tomorrow morning.

Patricia nodded and said that that was understandable, but asked me to go as early as possible.

I sent her a questioning look. She squirmed uncomfortably in her wheelchair.

'There is something else I would like to do tomorrow morning if possible, but your murder investigation is of course more important, so just come when it suits you.'

For a moment, curiosity got the better of me, and I was tempted to ask Patricia what else it was she had to do tomorrow. For a moment I wondered whether she perhaps had a boyfriend of one sort or another, and felt a stab of jealousy.

Patricia said nothing, however; and I was not in the

mood to push her to talk about it. So I thanked her for her hospitality and promised to be there as early as possible the next day.

At twenty-five to eleven, I stood alone by my car in Erling Skjalgsson's Street and admitted to myself that there was a reason I did not want to go to see Anders Pettersen this evening. I felt it was more important that I went somewhere else. And I did drive home, but I drove home via Ullevål Hospital.

# XX

I met Bernt Berg, the head surgeon, at eleven o'clock, as he was tearing across the hospital car park after his evening shift.

I said that I was glad to bump into him. To my surprise, he told me he had called me at home without getting an answer.

My heart was pounding as I asked if that meant there was good news. His answer was succinct: 'No.'

I looked at him questioningly, and said that I hoped at least that the news was not too bad.

'There has been a complication, and there is an acute danger of blood poisoning as a result. I have little hope that she will make it through the night.'

He said no more. It felt as though the earth was collapsing under my feet as I stood there, talking in a hushed voice to a middle-aged man in the darkness of the hospital car park.

I gave him a pleading look. He continued without me having to ask.

'There is still a slim chance. She is physically fit, and mentally strong. But all the same, you should be prepared for the possibility that she might die tonight.'

I vaguely registered that an odd feeling of complicity had developed between me and this chronically calm man of few words. I now got the impression that the stony face and monotonous voice were a defence mechanism, and that behind this he was a passionate man with deep empathy for each of his patients.

I thanked him for all he had done, no matter how things might end. He said that regardless of the outcome, he would try to call me as soon as possible when he was due back at the hospital at nine the next morning.

Then we silently parted and went to our separate cars in the dark.

I drove home alone through the night, which even though it was summer, felt darker than I could ever remember.

Once back at my flat in Hegdehaugen, I ate two slices of bread and sat by myself in an armchair by the window. I suddenly felt overcome by sheer exhaustion, but could not sleep all the same. So I stayed there, looking out into the dark.

I barely gave a thought to Marie Morgenstierne's murder. After my experiences today, I had more or less blind faith in Patricia's assurances that it would be solved tomorrow. My thoughts were filled instead with Miriam Filtvedt Bentsen. Images of her from our first confusing meeting outside the party office, and my last glimpse of her lying in a coma in hospital crowded my mind.

It was past midnight, and only one light shone into the dark from a flat in the neighbouring building. In a strange way, this resolute, lone light came to symbolize my hope. I therefore jumped up when it suddenly went out at a quarter to one. I have never been superstitious, but when the light went out, my anxiety surged. I was almost paralysed by the idea that Miriam's life had also gone out.

At half past one I finally managed to haul myself to bed, but was still far from being able to sleep. I initially set the alarm for half past seven, but then got up and changed it to eight, and then to ten to nine.

When I got back into bed, I realized I could not remember the last time I had cried, or why. Nor could I remember the last time I had prayed, or what for. But I cried and prayed desperately until I eventually fell asleep around half past three in the morning of Wednesday, 12 August 1970. It was the wounded Miriam for whom I cried and prayed. Three times I swore to God and to myself that I would race to her bedside with flowers, and a book, as soon as she regained consciousness – if she ever did.

With sleep, I was finally able to let go of the horrible images of Miriam lying motionless, and of her blood on the asphalt in Frogner Sqare – as well as the even more horrible feeling that it would be my fault if she died in the night.

# The triumph and the tragedy

## I

When I finally got to sleep early in the morning of Wednesday, 12 August 1970, my sleep was deep and dreamless. I was woken with a start, not by the alarm clock but by the telephone.

Instinctively I leaped out of bed when I heard it. Then I remembered what had happened the day before and dashed as fast as I could into the living room, in only my underpants. I got to the phone in time, on the fifth or sixth ring.

It occurred to me that it was strange that the alarm clock had not woken me. So I glanced over at the clock on the wall and discovered that it was twelve minutes to nine. Bernt Berg, the head surgeon, would not have started his morning shift yet. I was therefore terrified to hear his voice on the other end all the same.

'This is the head surgeon, Bernt Berg. I hope I did not wake you. I got to work a little early today.'

His voice was just as monotonous and grave as when

he had told me the evening before that Miriam Filtvedt Bentsen might not survive the night. The complicity was no longer there. My heart sank and my pulse raced.

I realized that the surgeon had gone to work early so he could call me as soon as possible – yet he said nothing, waiting for me to ask, which was even more alarming. I asked with trepidation if there was any news of the patient.

He replied swiftly and briefly: 'Yes, we managed to prevent blood poisoning and the crisis is over.'

Everything suddenly seemed surreal. For a moment I feared that I was dreaming. I banged my left arm on the edge of the table, and to my great relief, it hurt. And just then the alarm clock started to ring in the background. I was very definitely awake. And the doctor's voice was very clear on the telephone.

'I hear your alarm clock ringing,' he said, with unflappable calm.

I apologized for the alarm clock and asked what he thought the patient's chances of survival were now.

'Almost one hundred per cent. A truly miraculous improvement,' he replied.

The greatest sense of relief I had ever felt in my life swept me off my feet. I felt lighter and giddier than I had ever felt before. I put down the receiver and jumped up and punched the ceiling with joy.

Then I picked up the receiver again and said to Bernt Berg that he was an excellent doctor and one of the best people I had ever met.

Whether the surgeon found it pleasing or confusing to

be told this by a policeman or not, he did not allow himself to be affected in any noticeable way.

'There is a good chance that the patient will be able to talk to you for a few minutes if you come by sometime later on this afternoon. Have a good day in the meantime,' he said, then put down the phone.

I stayed sitting by the telephone in only my underpants, giddy with relief, for about ten minutes before I managed to pull myself together. I let the alarm clock ring, suddenly loving the sound of it. When it finally stopped, I went into the bedroom and got dressed.

I felt it might be irresponsible to drive in my semi-ecstatic mood, so I walked to the nearest bookshop to buy a six-volume work on the history of Norwegian literature. Then I walked back the other way to buy flowers. As I then walked home, I realized that I had not yet eaten breakfast or looked at the newspapers.

It was a quarter to ten by the time I got back to the flat. I quickly ate three slices of bread while I skimmed the papers. My elation was in no way diminished to see that the Mardøla protest and SALT negotiations had now very definitely been squeezed to one side in the papers, and the attempted assassination of the Labour Party leader was all over the front pages. Longer articles inside explained that it was I who had personally managed to foil the attempt at the last minute, and that the arrested assassin had also admitted to both of the Valdres murders.

The fact that a female onlooker had helped to prevent the assassination, and been badly wounded as a result, was mentioned in both *Aftenposten* and *Arbeiderbladet* without any further details or the victim being named. But both promised to print more details about her, and the case in general, the next day. And both expressed heartfelt praise for the head of investigation's efforts in connection with the Valdres murders and the attempted assassination in Oslo. They both concluded with the news that the arrested assassin was the father of the late Marie Morgenstierne, and that her murder had still not been solved.

I now felt I was in a fit state to drive a car again, but wanted if possible to have the murderer with me the next time I met Detective Inspector Danielsen. So I dialled Anders Pettersen's number from my own phone. There was no answer at a quarter to ten, or at five to ten. But at five past ten, he suddenly picked up the phone.

Anders Pettersen sounded very sleepy indeed, or just plain hung-over. I was terse and said with some authority that there was every hope that the murder of Marie Morgenstierne would soon be solved, which I believed would be of interest. He gave a slow yes to this, and then another when I asked if he could be available for further questioning in half an hour.


# II


I was interested to see whether Anders Pettersen would be at home when I rang his doorbell half an hour later. If he had done a runner, it would be as good as a confession.

Anders Pettersen was both sleepy and hung-over, but he had definitely not done a runner. The door was opened as soon as I rang the bell, and the inhabitant had managed to have a shower and put on a nearly presentable black suit in the meantime. He shook my hand and congratulated me with something akin to respect on foiling a 'Nazi plot' the day before.

I suddenly doubted whether he could be the murderer, which spawned an equal curiosity as to who else Patricia might have in mind. First of all, I had to see what kind of statement Anders Pettersen would give in his defence, given the circumstantial evidence against him.

It would be wrong to say that Anders Pettersen's flat was tidy. There was a half-finished painting on an easel in the middle of the living room, and a long row of empty beer bottles lined up higgledy-piggledy by the kitchen door. He had, however, tidied the coffee table and the chairs. Once seated, we got straight to the point.

I started by saying that I had reason to believe he had not told me the whole truth with regards to Marie Morgenstierne, but that I was now giving him another chance to do so. He nodded hastily to show he understood.

'I apologize profusely for not having told you the truth before. This was partly due to my lack of trust in the police, but more than anything, due to the shock when Falko came back.'

'You feared his reaction if he discovered that you had started a relationship with his fiancée in his absence?'

I held my breath in anticipation of a fierce denial. But instead he nodded, and shrugged with open palms to underline the point.

'I am not easily frightened. It was more shock than fear.

We had all been in Falko's shadow: he was our guiding light when he was here. Everything changed when he disappeared. Time passed. Whenever we met, we of course always expressed our hope that he would come back. But after eighteen months with no sign of life, we all thought he was gone for good. The group needed someone new to lead our fight for a fairer society – and Marie needed a new man to support her in life.'

He fell silent, then hesitated, but did eventually carry on with determination.

'If we had known that Falko was still alive and would come back, we would never have done it.'

He repeated this twice, as if to ensure that both he and I believed it. I wanted to move on, so allowed myself to be easily convinced.

'I believe you, and it is perfectly understandable that you all thought he was dead. So you started a relationship with his fiancée in the belief that he was gone forever. And you initiated it, didn't you?'

He nodded.

'She was very attractive, and her personality shone all the more when she emerged from Falko's long shadow. Slowly things developed between us. I played the role of sacrificial friend for a long time, but during the spring I began to hint that she needed to build a life without Falko. She dismissed this initially and seemed to think of me purely as a friend. She was cold towards me physically whenever I touched her. She said several times, almost as an apology, that the uncertainty about Falko's fate made it impossible for her to think of anyone else. Towards the end of April, I thought to myself that never before had I spent so much time talking to a woman and getting so little in return. Then suddenly in the middle of May, things started to move, and then they moved fast. One Tuesday she phoned me to say that she thought I was right, that Falko would not come back alive. On the Thursday she told me that now, in retrospect, she recognized some of the less positive aspects of Falko's character, and that as he had left us guessing for so long, it was perhaps no bad thing if he didn't come back. And by the Saturday, when I greeted her with a hug, she was suddenly smouldering . . .'

A smug grin slipped over his face. For a moment, his eyes became dreamy and unfocused. But then he snapped back into the present again, his face grave once more.

'So it was me who initiated things in the spring, but by the summer she was far keener than me. And I enjoyed it, believe me. She was my dream woman, in terms of her personality and politics. But the uncertainty about Falko was there all the time, and then it seemed to bother me more than her. She talked about making our relationship public and once even asked if I would move in with her. All of a sudden, it seemed she had no inhibitions. But he'd been like a big brother to me when we grew up, and still was. So I hesitated and asked if we could keep it secret until the second anniversary of his disappearance. She agreed reluctantly.'

I suddenly remembered Patricia's question, and asked who else had known about the relationship. A sneering smile played on his lips.

'We assumed that the police security service, and thus

also the CIA, knew as a matter of course. You'll have to ask them yourself when they found out. But I'm guessing it was before we did.'

I did not laugh. He was serious again.

'I reckoned that Kristine had guessed, but I never mentioned it to her and I don't think Marie did either. They had been close friends, but seemed to be drifting a bit. I did, however, mention it to Trond. He had shown obvious interest in Marie himself so I thought he had a right to know, in a way. But as I said, our psychologist has a bit of a complex when it comes to women and did not like to be reminded of his numerous failures in that area. So I was sure that he wouldn't pass it on to anyone.'

I nodded, both to him and myself. The painter's version was more idealized, but it still fitted with what Trond Ibsen had told me.

I waved him on, but he just looked at me and waited. I could not help asking, even though my pulse still raced whenever I mentioned her name.

'Miriam Filtvedt Bentsen?'

He shook his head.

'We had no contact with that class traitor and revisionist. I haven't spoken to her for over a year, and I don't think that any of the others have either. Certainly not about that. Of course, we hope that she'll survive being shot by a Nazi, but otherwise – well, no thank you.'

I pushed on.

'What about Marie's father?'

He gave a scornful laugh.

'On the subject of Nazis . . . No thank you, absolutely no

way. Neither of us wanted to talk to him, and certainly not about this. She commented that we could tell him with a wedding invitation when the time came – and that we could invite him without worrying about whether he would turn up.'

'Your parents?'

He shook his head with a faint smile.

'I've taken a few too many girlfriends home in my time. My parents told me that they didn't want to meet any more until I was engaged. Marie wanted to meet them, but I held back. But . . .'

I looked at him expectantly.

'But I do think that Falko's parents might have known about us. We were standing hand in hand on a street corner one warm summer's day in July, when suddenly we realized that the woman who had passed us was Falko's mother. We weren't sure if she had seen us and it didn't seem natural for any of us to keep in touch any more. We didn't hear anything from them. Marie took the episode as an argument for us soon to go public, but I was still reluctant.'

'Then she discovered she was pregnant. When did you find out?'

He started, then shrugged – and now, at last, he became emotional.

'Believe it or not, only when you told me yesterday. It was more of a shock than it perhaps should have been, given that she wanted us to be open about our relationship. And having played it so cool only weeks earlier, by the early summer she was dynamite – like a wild animal in bed sometimes. The neighbour below me here said with obvious envy that he hoped I would soon find myself a quieter lover.'

The smug charmer's smile slipped onto his face again. There was something ambiguous about him: sometimes I felt sympathy for him, at other times contempt.

'But she said she was taking the pill and I was more than happy with the situation, so I chose to believe her. It was a great shock to hear she was pregnant and I was just about to tell you the truth. But then I realized it would leave me in a very vulnerable position if I was suddenly to change my story at such an important juncture.'

It felt like we were getting somewhere now. I noted down that if Anders Pettersen had not known about the pregnancy, he did not really have a motive. But we still only had his word for this.

We sat in silence, both watching and waiting. It felt as if there was a sheet of ice stretching across the table between us. I was the one who finally ventured out onto it.

'Well, let us move on to the evening that your girlfriend was shot. I do not think it was you who shot her, but there is much to indicate that you have not told me the whole truth about what happened either.'

He looked at me coldly for a second. Then he stepped out onto the ice to meet me.

'Right on both counts. I was there, and I was there because she had asked me to come. She had called me a couple of hours earlier to say that there was something important she had to discuss with me, but we couldn't talk about it on the telephone. I was worried that she either wanted to split up or give me an ultimatum to make our relationship official. She suggested that we should meet at the train station after the meeting, but for some reason did not want us to go there together. So she said that she would walk slowly in the direction of the station, and that I should cycle round to meet her there.'

'Which you did. And you were standing waiting in a side road when she walked by. What did you see?'

He shrugged.

'Yes, I was standing in the side street. But I didn't see much, because it was dark. I recognized Marie from the way she walked, but the others who were further back down the road were too far away for me to see much. But then suddenly, to my great shock, I saw Falko in the road opposite.'

The memory of his reaction was clear in Anders Pettersen's face as he spoke. His eyes opened wide and his voice changed to a whisper.

'I didn't even think he was alive – let alone that he would show up. We spotted each other at the same time, and both of us were startled. We stood there staring at each other, and only looked away when Marie hurtled past at full speed. We were both totally bewildered, I guess. Neither of us followed her. Falko disappeared in the opposite direction, and I jumped onto my bike and pedalled home. Then I called her again and again throughout the evening, but there was no reply. I fell asleep fearing for my darling's life, and woke up to my greatest nightmare.'

I found Anders Pettersen more and more complex. His otherwise zealous political language every now and then slipped into almost pathetic romantic clichés. It happened again when he said that was all he had to tell me, and that he hoped that it would help me to find 'my beloved's murderer'.

Then he simply sat there, with his eyes suddenly swimming in tears.

I asked him to stay within the city boundaries and to keep himself available for further questioning, but was not sure whether he even heard me. In any case, I had no more questions for him at that moment. I left him sitting there by the coffee table like a statue, and found my own way out.

I strongly suspected that Anders Pettersen had escaped into a happy fantasy world where people were queuing up to buy his paintings, where the group was able to mobilize the masses under his leadership to revolution in Norway, and where Marie Morgenstierne was once again naked and wild in his bed. But I no longer suspected him of killing her. And I was even keener to know who had done it.

# III

It was now midday, and the table was set for lunch at Patricia's. She had not asked, and I had not told her, any more about Miriam Filtvedt Bentsen. Instead she listened in grave silence to my account of my meeting with Anders Pettersen.

'So, did I get the answers you needed to finally uncover the murderer's identity?' I eventually asked.

Patricia's face was grim as she finished her cup of coffee, but her answer was short and simple: 'Yes.'

I looked at her, taken aback, as she poured another cup of coffee.

'Eureka – I have the answer to what is almost a Greek tragedy. This case just gets worse and worse the clearer the answer becomes,' she concluded.

I had to admit that this left me none the wiser. So I asked her straight out who was responsible for Marie Morgenstierne's death.

'The person I have always most feared it to be. There were so many possible alternatives along the way, but now only one realistic one remains. And of course it had to be the most depressing one.'

Patricia sighed again, and drained another cup of coffee in one go. Then she leaned over the table towards me.

'The crucial question has always been not who killed her, but who or what did she see that so terrified her, as you yourself saw?'

Patricia's voice was starting to break. As was my patience.

'But who and what *did* she see? I have to know if we are going to close this case today.'

For a moment, Patricia pressed her serviette to her face. Then she found her voice again and pressed on.

'A few yards behind her down the street, she saw what would be a harmless sight to anyone else: an elderly man with a stick. Marie Morgenstierne had feared that this man or his wife would kill her because they wrongly suspected her of killing their only son. Despite her newfound happiness, she was constantly on edge because she had not told them that she had a new lover, but they had discovered it all the same. So that was the situation when she suddenly saw a man behind her whom she had never seen at Smestad before, but whom she knew had killed before. He had himself told her about his experiences in the fight against the enemy during the Spanish Civil War. She saw a man who was old, but she knew perfectly well that he did not need a stick. And she saw a cunning murder weapon that he had perhaps shown her himself at some point: a walking stick that housed a salon rifle. Marie did not see anyone or anything else now: just that. And it is not surprising that she then started to run for her life.'

Patricia breathed out slowly, and then continued. I sat there staring at her in fascination.

'Unfortunately, she started running a second too late to save herself. If she had started a second earlier, she and her unborn child – and the others who have been killed – might still be alive. And you would not have had to drive over to Grünerløkka now to arrest an old married couple who are no doubt devastated at having lost their only son so recently. The story might have been different and far happier if other coincidences had not happened, for example, if Mrs Reinhardt had not walked by when Anders and Marie were holding hands that summer day. Or if Mr Reinhardt had seen his missing son standing there only a few yards away on the evening he killed Marie.'

We sat and looked at each other in sombre silence. I realized that she was of course right. But I could not understand how I had failed to think of this possibility at an earlier stage myself.

I relived my painful encounter with the terrified woman on the Lijord Line seven days earlier. It struck me that the story might have been very different if I had had the sense to pull the emergency brake. It seemed highly unlikely that Patricia had not thought of this. And I was very grateful to her for not having mentioned it at all.

I said that it was a truly sad story, and that I would have to conclude it now by going to Grünerløkka.

Patricia gave a slight nod, and asked in a quiet voice if I would be needing her help any more.

I said that I realized the case had been very demanding for her, and that she no doubt wanted it to be over as soon as possible. I would, however, appreciate talking to her a little bit more once I had arrested the murderer, in order to fill in the final missing details.

She let out a heavy sigh, nodded in resignation and asked me to come back as quickly as possible. She said nothing more, but sat there in silence, waiting.

# IV

There was no great drama at Seilduk Street in Grünerløkka when I arrived there at a quarter past one. Arno Reinhardt was on his own when he opened the door this time. He said that his wife was grief-stricken, and had gone to lie down. I told him that we could talk without her for the moment.

He nodded gratefully and showed me into the living

room. In a strange way, it felt like we both knew why I was there. As we walked down the hall, I noticed an old travel bag standing there, packed and ready.

I said that we now had information that meant we sadly had to question him again about his whereabouts on the day that Marie Morgenstierne was murdered.

He indicated that he understood.

I added that four police constables were now standing on duty outside the building, as was the case.

My eyes moved to the wall of photographs, and to the last picture of Marie Morgenstierne together with Falko and his parents, here in the flat. Arno Reinhardt followed my gaze.

'I can always turn my back to that wall, but I can never get away from her. Not here, not in the other rooms, not out on the street,' he began quietly. 'I waited and waited. One day before he disappeared, Falko mentioned that he suspected that his fiancée was a mole. I couldn't prove anything, but the idea that she was, and that she had something to do with his disappearance, took root. So I sneaked out and followed her, and saw her handing something over to a man who passed her on the street after one of their meetings. And still I hesitated. It was only when . . .'

His voice broke, and I had to finish the sentence for him.

'It was only when your wife came home and told you that she had seen your son's fiancée hand in hand with another man – your son's friend, no less – that you were galvanized into action?'

He looked down, and said nothing.

I did not know what else to say. So in the end, I stated

the obvious: that he should not have taken the law into his own hands. Slowly he raised his head, showing a bitter smile.

'We communists have always had to take the law into our own hands, because the police have never done it for us. But I punished an innocent person. Even if the law grants me mercy because of my age, I will never be able to forgive myself. I could live with the fact that I had killed someone who was guilty. But then, just when I was over-joyed to see my son again, my world fell to pieces when I realized I had shot an innocent person.'

'The fact that she ran for her life made no impression on you?' I asked.

He nodded, and buried his face in his hands for a moment.

'To me it was just confirmation of her guilt. When fighting against the Falangists in the Spanish Civil War we learned that those who ran fastest were the guiltiest. I had thought of hearing what she had to say for herself. But when she started to run, I was left in no doubt. It was my doing, and mine alone. My wife didn't even know that I went out that evening,' he added, hastily.

I wanted to believe this, but did not know whether I could. Fortunately, I did not have to decide. His wife appeared at that moment, fully dressed and sombre, and sat down beside him without hestitation.

'No matter what happens, we will always stand together, for better or for worse. It's true, I did not know that my husband went out that night. But I was the first one to suspect that she had betrayed our son. I was the one who was convinced when I saw her standing there, holding hands with another man we knew nothing about. I was the one who asked my husband on the second anniversary of my son's disappearance how long he had thought of letting those who were guilty go free. And when he came back that evening, it was I who said that he had done the right thing, and promised to help him conceal it.'

I looked at him. He nodded imperceptibly. Their fingers were now firmly entwined.

There was a strange, slightly unreal atmosphere in the room. There I was having an apparently relaxed conversation with an elderly couple, in the process of closing a complex murder case, and yet was experiencing one of the worst moments of my life.

I had nothing more to ask them. This was clearly a terrible tragedy.

She was the one who broke the silence.

'Do you mind if we ask you a question? It could mean so much to us in the middle of all this . . . Is it really the case that our son might have been alive today, if we had not made such a fatal misjudgement?'

I had to think about this for a moment before I answered. I could not lie to two people who were guilty of murdering a young, pregnant woman. I could have said that their son would also still be alive had it not been for his own misjudgements, his exaggerated belief in his ability to sort things out alone and his inability to trust others, including his own parents and fiancée. But I thought that criticizing their son or his upbringing would not make things any easier. So I told them the truth: that it was sadly their fatal decision to take the law into their own hands that had resulted in the death of their son, and all that followed.

It was only then that they started to cry. And in a peculiar way, their tears made it easier. My sympathy for them waned when, seven days after killing an innocent young woman, the only thing they could cry for was the loss of their son.

I stood up and said that it was time to go.

They remained seated, holding each other tight.

He asked in a quiet voice if they could have a few minutes alone together first. And in a strange way, it felt as though we understood each other.

I thought about it for a moment or two. I definitely thought more about myself and the police than about them. Then I said that human life was sacrosanct for a country and its people where the rule of law applied, and that too many lives had been lost in this tragic case already. They gave an almost apathetic, synchronized nod, then stood up without any further protest.

On our way out, we stopped for a moment by all the photographs on the wall. None of us could bear to look at the last photographs. We stood instead looking at the first picture, the one of a little Falko with his smiling parents on their return to Oslo in 1945. They were holding hands in exactly the same way tonight. But their hands were old now, and Falko was no longer there. Arno Reinhardt picked up the old travel bag with one hand and held onto his wife's with the other as he left his home for the last time.

# V

Back at the main police station, a couple of hours were spent on congratulations, press releases and other formalities. My boss gave me flowers and endless congratulations on solving the final murder. He said that I would be on the front pages of all the national papers on Monday as a result, and that with three successful murder investigations under my belt I would soon be the country's most famous policeman. It would only be a matter of time before I was promoted, despite my young age, and several people had suggested me for the rank of detective chief inspector.

Danielsen was nowhere to be seen, but according to unconfirmed rumours had handed in a sick note for the rest of the week. I resisted the temptation to suggest that he should be sent to Mardøla on his return. My boss was all smiles, happier than I had ever seen him before, and might easily decide that sending both Danielsen and me to Mardøla was a good way to resolve our conflict.

Other colleagues were more or less queuing up to congratulate me when I left my boss's office. In short, the day at the station was almost perfect.

It was half past three before I could drive over to Patricia's, and ten past four by the time I stepped into her library. She had coffee and cake waiting on the table, but still did not look like she was in a celebratory mood. Without saying a word, she indicated impatiently that I should sit down.

I told her in brief, and without too many details, about

the arrest. She nodded but asked no questions, and seemed almost impatient to be done with the whole thing.

'Many congratulations on another success. But unlike our last case, this does not call for celebration,' she commented curtly.

She let out a deep sigh, then continued.

'Your latest triumph is framed by tragedy. The Reinhardts were broken by their son's disappearance, took the law into their own hands and killed another man's only daughter. This, paradoxically, made him pull the trigger and set in motion a chain reaction that culminated with Martin Morgenstierne taking the life of the Reinhardts' only son. The two young people are gone forever, and their three broken parents are in prison. And Henry Alfred Lien's valiant attempt to atone for his old sins by preventing the assassination of the leader of the Labour Party ended in Lien losing his own life, instead of being forgiven by his son. Even the fate of the two former Nazis could perhaps have been different if sad family histories had not left them bitter old men. This case seems to have no end of devastating stories of parents and children.'

I allowed myself to point out that we had after all cleared up all the crimes, and what is more, averted the attempted assassination of the Labour Party leader at the last moment. I hastened to add that this was largely all thanks to her brilliant conclusions, and that I would never have managed to solve the case without her.

Patricia's smile was tenuous. She thanked me for the compliment, but still seemed to be in a sombre mood. Something was clearly bothering her, and I was beginning to suspect what it might be. There was an important unanswered question between us, and I now waited with increasing irritation to see if Patricia would bring it up.

Which she did, with yet another sigh, at five past four.

'And how is the unfortunate Miriam Filtvedt Bentsen, who was caught in the firing line? Is there any news from the hospital about her chances of survival?'

I nodded happily, and was about to answer, when something totally unexpected happened.

The telephone on Patricia's desk started to ring.

Never, in all my many previous visits, had I heard her telephone ring. And I had therefore, for some reason, imagined that I was the only one who knew the number and might use it. I was rather annoyed with the telephone for having the audacity to ring at such an inconvenient moment. At the same time, my curiosity was piqued as to who it might be.

Patricia lifted the receiver on the second ring and held it to her ear. Much to my relief, it was a very brief conversation. Patricia listened to the short message given by the person at the other end. She nodded pensively. Her reply was brief and polite.

'That is just as we thought. Thank you so much for letting me know, all the same.'

There seemed to be no drama. The person at the other end continued talking, but I was not able to make out the words.

Patricia listened for a few seconds more, but then interrupted briskly: 'Thank you. Hopefully everything will be all right. I will call you back later today.'

She put down the telephone and apologized for having answered it, but gave no explanation as to who had called or what it was about.

For a short while afterwards she sat deep in thought, staring straight ahead. Then she returned to where we had left off the conversation.

'Yes, we were talking about Miriam Filtvedt Bentsen. Have you heard any more about her condition?'

I said yes, and that all was well with Miriam Filtvedt Bentsen, given the circumstances. There was a danger that she would suffer from the injuries to her neck and shoulders for a while, and that it would be some time before she could write again. But she had regained consciousness an hour ago and was now definitely out of danger after the operation. She would survive, and live a meaningful life.

'Good,' Patricia said.

She said it so perfunctorily, without the slightest bit of feeling. This only fanned my earlier irritation that she had so obviously delayed asking the question.

I also had the strong feeling that she would have preferred it if I had said that Miriam would not survive. And so, for the first time in my life, I was truly angry with Patricia.

Later, I could not remember my exact words. But I had one of my rare, furious outbursts and said exactly what I thought and felt at that moment: that Patricia had always disliked Miriam and been jealous of her. And that I thought that she had now shown an alarming lack of human empathy for a young woman who might suffer permanent injuries and had nearly lost her life, thanks to her heroic attempt to foil a political assassination. I apparently finished this rant by asking Patricia whether she had any consideration for people in the world outside this house.

Patricia heard me out, remaining unusually still for an unusually long time.

'Consideration. Yes. One of us is certainly not showing any consideration here,' she said in the end. Then she was quiet again.

My rage had passed, but my anger on the part of the wounded Miriam Filtvedt Bentsen remained. So I said that I would shortly have to show consideration to some other people, and pay someone a visit.

Whether it was my intention that Patricia would understand the context or not, I was not able to say in retrospect. But she had of course understood instantly.

'Pay someone a visit today . . . Yes, of course. At Ullevål Hospital, perhaps?'

I nodded, almost defiantly, I realized, as soon as I had done it. I was still very angry with her.

'And so everything crashes around me,' Patricia said, with a deep sigh. Her head fell forward onto her chest as she said it.

I did not understand, and she said nothing more in explanation. Instead she kept her mouth firmly shut, as if in panic.

We sat there in tense silence for a few seconds. Then I made a point of standing up.

'Please, just go if you must, if that is how you want it to be. It is important to visit, especially if it is someone you care for,' Patricia said.

Then once again she sat quite still in her wheelchair.

I left, with quicker steps than usual.

I turned around just outside the door, went back into the room and thanked her again for all her help with the investigation. But later I doubted if she had even heard me. For once she said nothing in response, but continued to sit huddled in her wheelchair. She seemed to have withdrawn entirely into her own world.

I thought I saw a tear run down her left cheek. But I might have been mistaken, and in my agitation, I did not feel the need to approach her. Her comment about everything crashing around her only seemed to confirm her egoism, as the situation now stood.

Patricia looked like the loneliest person in the world, sitting there in her library among all her books and with the remains of our coffee on the table. But when I thought of Miriam Filtvedt Bentsen lying lifeless on the asphalt in Frogner Square, and her subsequent fight for life in a hospital bed, I thought that Patricia deserved to be left with her own thoughts today. And in any case, I was certain that the maid was there and would appear as soon as I had left.

So I closed the door behind me a little more loudly than necessary, and left the house without turning back.

# VI

The atmosphere in Room 302 at Ullevål Hospital was far more pleasant and uplifting.

Miriam Filtvedt Bentsen was in better shape than I had feared. Her shoulders and arms were tightly bandaged, but she was awake and reading a book about the history of French literature when I came into the room. She had obviously learned to turn the pages with her nose. She put the book down as soon as she saw me, and lit up the room with one of her smiles. And the mood soared when I put down the flowers and the books on the table beside her.

'Oh, I don't know what to say,' Miriam Filtvedt Bentsen exclaimed, when she saw the gifts.

It may sound strange, but she looked just as in control when she said this as she always did. So I chuckled and she laughed at me laughing at her.

There was still a danger of permanent damage to her shoulder, but she would possibly be able to write again in time for the autumn exams. But whatever the case, it was simply a huge relief for her to be alive and to be able to read again. Her parents and younger brother had already been to visit. And it was a lovely surprise that I had come too, Miriam Filtvedt Bentsen said with a bold little smile from her sickbed.

I told her that she had been exceptionally astute to run to the stage and prevent Trond Bratten from going on, given that I had not even had time to tell her. She thanked me, and with another smile said that that was precisely why she had understood. I had mentioned that there might be an assassination attempt earlier, so when I just ran on straight into the building without even apologizing, she could not think of any explanation other than the planned assassination. She had simply done what she had to for society and democracy, and despite the pain, she did not regret it at all.

I assured her that when she left hospital there would be many more gifts and congratulations, from both friends and strangers. The newspapers had already made several enquiries to the police asking when she could be interviewed. Miriam raised her head with an inquisitive look in her eyes and asked if I knew which papers had rung. Her eyes opened wide when I said the local Lillehammer paper *Dagningen* and the SPP paper *Orientering* had called at least twice, and that *Aftenposten*, *Dagbladet*, *VG* and *Arbeiderbladet* had all been on the phone. When I added that the NRK radio and television had also been in touch, Miriam looked like she wanted to jump out of bed and call them all immediately.

As this was all positively received, I added with some trepidation that her efforts in saving the party leader would no doubt increase support for the SPP. And even more hesitantly, I added that my own sympathies for the party had certainly increased thanks to her efforts in recent days.

Then I hastily asked whether she might allow me to take her out to dinner as soon as she got out of hospital. And we would then have plenty of time to talk about the case, and other things, at one of the best restaurants in town.

Miriam Filtvedt Bentsen's smile widened even more. She commented with some irony that she would have to look at her timetable first, but that she should be able to find time for dinner in a restaurant once she was out. As a student, one could live for several days on a good restaurant meal, given the current rates on student loans.

We laughed a bit and ended our visit on a cheerful, happy note, despite the serious nature of the case. In the end I was chased out by an almost militant head nurse who was concerned about complications, stress and exhaustion, despite the patient's mild protests. I tried to excuse myself by saying that I had been there barely half an hour, but had to back down when both the head nurse's watch and my own proved that I had in fact been there for more than two.

'Even the police risk being hounded by the military!' Miriam joked in a whisper as I got up from the chair by her bed. Then she laughed her peculiar, almost sadistically sarcastic laugh. Both this and her joke made me laugh, and I whispered back that the police would be back for another inspection tomorrow.

My fascination and admiration for Miriam had grown in the course of these two hours at the hospital, when I saw the calm and self-control with which she accepted the fact that she had been exposed to a shock and injury that might affect her for life, through no fault of her own. And in parallel, my anger at Patricia's jealousy and lack of empathy also increased. And I was quite exercised by the time I left Ullevål Hospital at half past seven.

I waved happily from the doorway, remembering a few seconds too late that Miriam could not wave back. But she took it with good humour, and sent me a crooked smile as I shut the door.

# VII

The telephone rang just as I let myself into my flat in Hegdehaugen around eight o'clock, and carried on ringing until I answered it.

I was at first relieved when I heard my mother's voice. But to my surprise, it was not her usual cheerful voice, and she had definitely not called to congratulate me on closing the case.

'Have you heard the terrible news?' she more or less cried into the phone.

My mother was normally a woman of great composure, so I realized immediately that something was seriously wrong. My thoughts swirled around my father, my sister and her little girl. I had in no way anticipated what was to come.

'It's so sad. I have just heard that Professor Borchmann died of cancer at the University Hospital this afternoon! Is there no end to the misfortune that poor family has to suffer? We were not even aware that he was ill. How could you guess something like that?'

The words hit me like a blow to the chest – it was a knockout. I do not remember sitting down, but suddenly realized that I was.

When I found my voice again, I said that I had certainly had no idea, and could not have guessed either. Professor Director Ragnar Sverre Borchmann had always seemed so strong and solid to both me and my mother. We simply did not imagine that he could die.

I heard myself promising my mother that I would pass on the family's condolences to the young, now parentless Patricia, if and when I spoke to her again.

Then I found myself asking if she had heard when exactly Professor Borchmann had died this afternoon.

It had been around four o'clock.

As soon as my mother said that, all communication between my brain and my arm was broken. I do not remember saying goodbye. But I suddenly realized that I was sitting with the receiver in my hand, and my mother's voice was no longer there.

The receiver felt as heavy as lead in my hand. I finally put it back in the cradle. This did not help. When I picked it up again a few minutes later, it felt even heavier. My hand sank listlessly twice before I managed to dial the number correctly with a shaking finger.

# VIII

I had never before experienced the telephone on Patricia's table ringing more than three times before she answered. This time it rang for thirteen eternal rings. And when I finally did hear a voice at the other end, it was the maid, Beate, and not Patricia.

I apologized for calling so late on this of all evenings, and asked if it would be possible to pass on our condolences and to have a few words with Patricia.

Beate said that Patricia had told her I would call, and had given her a short message to read over the phone.

The message was as follows: 'Thank you for your thoughts with regards to the death of my father. I hope that you will understand that I will now have to focus on the various formal and practical things that have to be done in connection with my father's funeral and the continued operation of his companies. I would be very grateful if you and your parents would come to the funeral. Best wishes, Patricia Louise I. E. Borchmann.'

There was silence on the line for a moment. I thanked Beate, and asked if she could send a message back that I and my parents would of course come to the funeral.

Beate's voice was trembling when she promised to give Patricia the message. Then there was another moment's silence.

'There's something I would like to tell you, even though maybe I shouldn't . . .' Beate stammered.

She stopped, hesitant, until I asked her to continue. I had no idea what to expect, but did not imagine it could make things any worse.

Beate lowered her voice to little more than a whisper when she continued.

'They called Miss from the hospital yesterday just before you came. I was standing right beside her and heard what was said. The doctor started by telling her that her father was extremely ill, and that the end was now perhaps only a matter of hours away rather than days. Then the director came onto the phone. He said that she should come now if she wanted to see him again.'

I felt a lump building in my throat. I was whispering now as well when I asked what Patricia had answered.

'Miss said that she would of course come as soon as she could, but that she did not dare to leave the house and telephone until the case was closed and the murderer had been arrested. It could cost other people their lives and it was extremely important for you, she added. And she couldn't tell you the truth because she was afraid it would distract you from such an important murder investigation. The director said that he understood and just hoped that she would get there on time. Then he asked her to send you his greetings, and to wish you all the best with the rest of your life.'

The lump in my throat was now enormous and hard. I struggled with it for what seemed like a small eternity before I managed to whisper a final question. And that was whether the conversation she had just recounted to me was the last time that Patricia and her father had spoken together.

Beate replied very quietly and slowly that yes, it unfortunately was.

I thanked her in a barely audible whisper for telling me. Then we put down the telephone at the same time with great care and no noise.

I just sat there for the rest of the evening, old images of Ragnar Sverre Borchmann's dashing figure flickering through my mind, alternating with Patricia's immobile expression earlier in the day. I sat beside the phone with my memories until well past midnight, in the hope that it would ring again. But it never did.

The fact that I had successfully closed my third murder investigation brought me as little joy in those few long hours as Patricia's fortune would bring her. I thought to myself that one did not know what real loneliness was until one had sat alone in oppressive silence: alone in a room with a telephone that never rang, no matter how desperately one might want it to.

It was only many years later that I found out that in the course of my conversation with the maid, and throughout the evening that followed, Patricia had been sitting silently in her usual place by the telephone, chain-smoking. Around midnight, Beate had ventured to say that Patricia should perhaps call me. She had promptly been told that a maid who tried to make a career as a counsellor could just as easily end up without a job.

As I sat there alone in the silence, I felt like the loneliest person in the world. Finally I understood what Patricia had meant earlier in the day. There was no end to sad stories about parents and children in this investigation. And my great triumph was now overshadowed by tragedy. It really did feel as though everything had suddenly come crashing down.

# Afterword

My third thriller is also, like the first two, a historical novel. I have again tried to present a realistic picture of Norwegian history forty-two years ago, but have also allowed myself creative licence. Those readers who know the geography of Oslo will be able to find the streets, but not the house numbers. Those who know their history will recognize some of the minor characters from political circles at the time. But they will also notice that certain details do not fit: for example, the head of the police security service in this book has far more in common with the man who developed the service before retiring in 1967 than the man who held the position in 1970.

And once again, the author is more than happy to receive honest feedback from readers. This can be sent via Facebook, or by email to hansolahlum@gmail.com.

While working on the novel, I have also benefited from the advice and support of many people. My most important adviser at the publisher Cappelen Damm was, as always, my excellent editor Anne Fløtaker. Anders Heger has also been a much-valued adviser, Sverre Dalin a sensitive and focused copy editor, and the knowledgeable Nils Nordberg has acted as an expert adviser.

As for my personal advisers, my greatest thanks go to my loyal primary adviser, Mina Finstad Berge, who once again has made some invaluable comments with regards to the language and content. A legendary inventor is said to have kept the plans for his machines in his head for several weeks after seeing the drawings, and could therefore predict any weaknesses they might have. I was inspired by this story to include one of my primary advisers in the plot this time, as an experiment, and Mina deserves special thanks for agreeing to participate in this unpredictable and revealing literary experiment.

I also owe a huge thanks to my good friends Ingrid Baukhol, Jorunn Bjørgum, Tone Bratteli, Lene Li Dragland, Marit Lang-Ree Finstad, Anne Lise Fredlund, Kathrine Næss Hald, Else Marit Hatledal, Hanne Isaksen, Bjarte Leer-Salvesen, Torstein Lerhol, Espen Lie, Kristine Kopperud Timberlid, Arne Tjølsen and Magnhild K. B. Uglem, as well as my sister, Ida Lahlum. Of these, Arne and Magnhild deserve particular thanks this time. I would also like to thank the historian and writer James Godbolt for his advice on radical left-wing groups in 1970, and the historian and writer Roy Andersen for his advice regarding what is said about the police security service.

My last crime novel, *Satellite People*, was hugely inspired by the queen of classic crime, Agatha Christie, and was accordingly dedicated to her. The plot of *The Catalyst Killing* is set in 1970 and makes the leap from a locked room to a public space. Rather than Agatha Christie and other earlier British crime writers, I drew inspiration this time from one of the greatest crime writers of the decade, the American Ross Macdonald (1915–83). Tragic family stories are a major theme in Macdonald's novels, inspired both by Greek tragedies and by his own background. Following his example, I have made tragic stories of parents and children a pervasive theme of this book.

When I started writing, my intention was to dedicate *The Catalyst Killing* to Ross Macdonald. But then it dawned on me that my third novel should be dedicated to a representative from my group of advisers. It also developed into a political novel, which was never the case with Macdonald's novels; and even though the book has in a many ways a depressing ending, there is a much stronger sense of optimism about the future than in Macdonald's work.

Of all the representatives from various extremist milieux, it is Miriam Filtvedt Bentsen who represents hope. She is a young and idealistic person who is herself, without any thought of personal gain. The young Miriam clearly distances herself from dictatorship, violence and totalitarian ideologies, and in her free time works for a democratic party to fight for a fairer society. In this novel, she is a young SPP member in 1970, but she could equally have been a member of various other youth associations in 2012. And following the violent and bloody attack on our democratic and open society that we experienced in summer 2011, it is particularly important to nurture the hope for the future that she represents here in Norway today. The best possible response to the terrorism and extremism of our day is the peaceful political mobilization of new generations of socially engaged young people. And the author and other people involved in Norwegian cultural life must do their utmost to highlight this.

So I eventually came to the conclusion that this novel should be dedicated to my fictional character, Miriam Filtvedt Bentsen. Or Mina Finstad Berg, as she is called out there in the real world.

Hans Olav Lahlum
*Gjøvik, 1 January 2012*